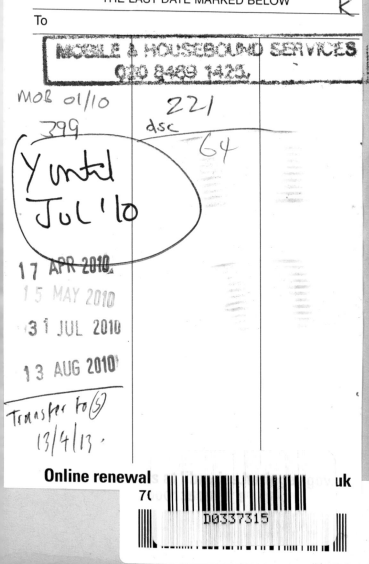

MARRIED AT NEW YEAR!

Mills & Boon® Medical™ Romance is celebrating! This New Year it's not just the fireworks adding sparkle to the festivities—there's most definitely dazzling romance in the air…

This January two devilishly handsome doctors have one New Year's resolution in common: marriage!

POSH DOC, SOCIETY WEDDING
by Joanna Neil

NEW BOSS, NEW-YEAR BRIDE
by Lucy Clark

MARRIED AT NEW YEAR!

As the clock strikes twelve it seems New-Year dreams really can come true…

POSH DOC,
SOCIETY BRIDE

BY
JOANNA NEIL

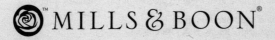

All the characters in this book have no existence outside the imagination of the author, and have no relation whatsoever to anyone bearing the same name or names. They are not even distantly inspired by any individual known or unknown to the author, and all the incidents are pure invention.

First published in Great Britain 2009
Paperback edition 2010
Harlequin Mills & Boon Limited,
Eton House, 18-24 Paradise Road, Richmond, Surrey TW9 1SR

© Joanna Neil 2009

ISBN: 978 0 263 86975 0

Harlequin Mills & Boon policy is to use papers that are natural, renewable and recyclable products and made from wood grown in sustainable forests. The logging and manufacturing process conform to the legal environmental regulations of the country of origin.

Printed and bound in Spain
by Litografia Rosés, S.A., Barcelona

When **Joanna Neil** discovered Mills & Boon®, her lifelong addiction to reading crystallised into an exciting new career writing Medical™ Romance. Her characters are probably the outcome of her varied lifestyle, which includes working as a clerk, typist, nurse and infant teacher. She enjoys dressmaking and cooking at her Leicestershire home. Her family includes a husband, son and daughter, an exuberant yellow Labrador and two slightly crazed cockatiels. She currently works with a team of tutors at her local education centre, to provide creative writing workshops for people interested in exploring their own writing ambitions.

Recent titles by the same author:

HOT-SHOT DOC, CHRISTMAS BRIDE
THE REBEL AND THE BABY DOCTOR
THE SURGEON SHE'S BEEN WAITING FOR
CHILDREN'S DOCTOR, SOCIETY BRIDE

CHAPTER ONE

THE doorbell made a cheerful jangle as Izzy walked into the village store, and the scent of freshly baked bread came to greet her, wafting on the air, teasing her nostrils and making her mouth water. Hunger pangs clutched at her stomach, causing her to frown momentarily. When had she last eaten? Could she count the couple of bites she'd taken from a sandwich several hours ago before all hell broke loose in A&E?

'You look as though you're ready to be off home, Izzy. Has it been a difficult day for you?' Mary the shopkeeper came forward from behind the counter, her all-seeing glance taking in Izzy's pale countenance, a smile softening her features.

'You could say that.' Izzy's mouth made a faint curve in response. Mary was a motherly figure, always ready to talk, the sparkle in her blue eyes belying the years hinted at in her grey hair. 'Unfortunately there was a triple-car accident on the dual carriageway earlier, and we were kept busy for most of the day dealing with all the casualties. We patched up the ones who were really badly injured, and sent them on to the hospital in Inverness.' Izzy broke off to glance around the shop, taking in the wide assortment of goods on display.

Mary nodded. 'I heard about it on the local radio. I guessed they would be taken to your A&E first of all, it being the nearest. It was a marvellous day when they gave the go-ahead to set up the unit next to the health centre, wasn't it? You and your doctor colleagues must have helped so many people there over the last few months.'

'It's true we've been in demand.' Izzy turned her gaze from shelves filled with household essentials and pushed back a swathe of chestnut coloured hair that had fallen across her cheek. 'Living here in the Highlands, people have always faced a long journey to hospital, but now the new A&E unit acts as a halfway station. Knowing it had been given the go ahead was one of the things that drew me back here…that and the fact that I can go out as an immediate care responder. It makes for variety and gives me a sense that I'm doing something worthwhile.'

Izzy's gaze wandered again. She had dropped in here planning to pick up a set of teacloths for her kitchen, but her senses were filled with the appetising aroma of hot meat pasties and oven-fresh bread.

Mary smiled. 'I guessed you would come back to us before too long…once you had completed your medical training. This place is in your blood. You were always one to love the hills and the mountains, and I remember when you were a teenager you could often be found down by the harbour, watching the boats.'

The shopkeeper contemplated that for a moment or two, but then her face straightened, her mouth pulling in a flat line. 'Unlike some I could mention. You'd think the Laird would put in an appearance at the castle from time to time, wouldn't you, instead of leaving everything for Jake Ferguson to handle? Not that Jake's done a great deal to help things along in the Laird's absence… And now it looks as though he'll be doing even less, if it's true he's thinking of moving down south to be with his daughter.'

'Is he?' Izzy raised a brow. No wonder she hadn't received a reply to her request for various repairs to be carried out on her rented property. Jake obviously had other things on his mind. Why was she the last to know what was going on in the village? Her mouth made a rueful quirk. That was what came of working all hours and trying to mind her own business.

'That's what Finn the postman reckons.' Mary was frowning. 'He's always the first to know the gossip.' She gave a small gesture of dissatisfaction at the complexities of life before gathering herself together once more. 'Anyway, what can I get for you today, Izzy?' she asked. 'Will you be wanting a loaf of bread to take home? I've just brought a batch fresh from the oven, and I know how much you like it.'

'Thanks, Mary. That would be lovely…and a couple of those pasties, too, since I'm in no mood for cooking today. I'm so hungry I could eat one here and now.'

'Then you must do that,' Mary said with a chuckle, handing her a pasty along with a serviette.

'Thanks. You're a life-saver.' Izzy took a bite, savouring the tender meat and flaky pastry before brushing crumbs from her mouth. 'Mmm…that's delicious.' She closed her eyes fleetingly, to better relish the experience. 'And will you add a bag of my father's favourite mint sweets? I'll drop them off to him on my way home. And my mother's magazine, if it's come in.'

'Aye. I can do all that. And we've a new batch of diaries in, ready for the New Year, if you're interested.

I'm very taken with them, with the gold embossed lettering and the soft feel of the leather.'

Izzy glanced over to the display rack where the diaries were set out, and paused to run a clean index finger lightly over the cover of one that stood to the front. 'You're right—and I will take one with me, before they're all snapped up. They're beautiful, aren't they?' She gave a gentle sigh. 'If only we could really start afresh with each year that comes along. We've still a few weeks to go before then, though, haven't we? It seems like an eternity. These last few months have been so difficult, in one way or another… For all of us, not just for my family. I can't say I'll be sorry to see an end to this year.'

'Me, too.' Mary put in a heartfelt acknowledgement. 'The business is limping along, but I'm not alone in that…all the villagers are having a tough time of it.'

Izzy nodded, taking a moment to finish off her pasty before wandering over to the shelves where the tea-cloths were stacked. 'The crofters haven't been doing too well, have they?' She frowned, pausing to pick up a linen cloth, holding it up to the light of the window. It was pleasingly decorated with a Highland scene, depicting a shimmering loch bordered on either side by craggy, heather-clad mountains. 'I know the harvest was poor this year, so it's probably just as well the majority have other jobs to keep them going.'

'It is,' Mary acknowledged, 'but I can't help thinking you've come off worse than any of us, with your cousin Alice being in hospital and all. Your poor mother was terribly shaken up by it, I know.'

'Yes, it hit us hard, all of us—my mother especially. Hearing about the car crash came as a dreadful blow. After all, Alice lived with us for a few years after her parents passed away, and she was more like a sister to me.' Izzy was still shocked by the thought of the accident that had kept Alice in hospital these several months. It saddened her that she was helpless to do anything to speed up her recovery, and it wrung her heart that there was so much bitterness and recrimination associated with the whole event.

Her father had never reconciled himself to the circumstances that had taken Alice away from them, some six or seven years ago, and now her return to Scotland was tinged with unhappiness.

She tried not to think about it. Instead she looked out of the window at the landscape of her birth, a sight that invariably had the power to calm her. In the distance she could see the glorious hills and mountains of the West Highlands, with white painted houses clustered along the road that wound gently through the glen, and if she looked very carefully she could just make out the curve of the bay and the small harbour where boats bobbed gently on the water.

Bringing her glance closer to home, she looked to where the side road led on to the paved forecourt of the village shop. She thought she heard the soft purr of an engine drawing closer. Moments later a gleaming four-by-four made an appearance, gliding to a halt in front of the store.

'Well, there's a vehicle that makes a grand statement, if ever there was one.' Mary came to join her by the window, and both women looked out at the majestic silver Range Rover that had come into view. 'Now, who do you think that belongs to?' the shopkeeper queried absently. 'No one from around here, that's for sure.'

Izzy didn't answer, but watched as the driver slid

down from the car and walked purposefully round to the passenger side. He pulled open the door and reached inside the vehicle, resting his arm on one of the seats as he paused to speak to someone who was sitting in the back.

Perhaps it was the casual, loose-limbed confidence in the way he moved that caught Izzy's attention, or maybe it was the taut stretch of black denim straining against his strong thighs that alerted her, or even the sweep of his broad shoulders, clad in a supple leather jacket… Either way, Izzy's senses were suddenly geared into action. A band of tension tautened her abdomen. She realised there was something intensely familiar about the rugged, long-legged man who had come out of the blue to fill her vision.

Right now he was inviting a tawny-haired child to step down from the vehicle, and when the girl hesitated he lifted his arms to grasp her with both hands and swing her effortlessly from her seat, setting her carefully down on the ground. For a second or two, as he paused to steady her, he looked towards the far hills, so that his features came momentarily into sharp relief. Izzy pulled in a brief, harsh breath of recognition.

What had Mary said about the Laird not coming home? She watched as he stood aside to encourage a young boy to jump down from the car, and beside her Mary echoed what they were both thinking.

'Well, I never. Talk of the devil. If it isn't himself, come to grace us with his presence. And aren't those children with him your Alice's bairns? I thought they were staying with their aunt, Alice's sister, down in the Lake District?' She frowned. 'I wonder what brings him to these parts after all this time? How long has it been? About six years, do you think?'

'That sounds about right.' Izzy struggled to find her voice. 'It must be all of six years since the old Laird died.'

'And hardly a sight of the new Laird since—though I suppose he must have been in touch with his estate manager on a fairly regular basis. How else would Jake have had the power to put the rents up and cut the timber hereabouts? Things could be falling apart up at the castle, for all Ross Buchanan knows. That's what comes of being an absentee landlord. Everything goes to rack and ruin.'

Izzy was still struggling to come to terms with seeing Ross back on his home ground, but now she stifled a discomfited laugh. 'You're beginning to sound an awful lot like my father,' she murmured.

Mary chuckled. 'And your father doesn't even have the excuse of being a tenant, does he? Now, there's a man with more than his fair share of common sense.'

'I think it has rather more to do with a determination never to be indebted to the Buchanans in any way,' Izzy said with a rueful smile. 'He's a fiercely proud man, my father.'

The sound of children's excited voices floated on the air, coming closer, and Izzy felt her whole body tighten as she waited for the shop door to open. How was she going to cope with coming face to face with Ross Buchanan after all this time?

'I'm thirsty,' the boy said, bursting into the store with the noisy rush of energy of a youngster who had been imprisoned inside a car for far too long. At six years old, he had no time to waste. Life was for living. 'Can I have a can of fizzy pop?' He directed the words behind him as he continued on his path. 'I'm not going to be sick again. You said I could have a drink, and I really want fizzy pop…and an ice cream with lots of sprinkles on it and a chocolate flake.' He headed towards the snacks section.

The girl followed him in a slower, more measured fashion, taking time to look around. The lingering rays of afternoon sunshine lent glimmering highlights to her hair, and Izzy saw that her green eyes were thoughtful, as though she wanted to weigh up the situation before making any decisions. She was younger than the boy, about five years old, and a pretty girl, so much like her mother, but with a shy expression. Now she put out a tentative hand to examine a packet of potato chips, only to have the item whipped out of her fingers by her brother.

'I saw it first,' he said. 'They're barbecue flavour and that's my favourite and it's the only one.'

'You snatched it from me,' the girl protested. 'Give it back.'

'You'll stop fighting this minute, both of you,' Ross said in a quiet, authoritative voice, 'or neither of you will have anything. You're on someone else's property and you will respect that.' He held out a hand for the crisp packet.

The boy's mouth clamped in a mutinous line, and he glared at his sister. She sent him back a daggers-drawn look, sparks of steel arrowing towards him, her body poised ready for action.

Ross retrieved the offending packet and glanced at Mary, who had stepped forward. 'I'm sorry about that,' he said softly, his voice a low rumble like smooth velvet trailing over a roughened surface. 'They're usually much more well behaved, but they've been cooped up in the car for a few hours. That was my fault—I wanted to get here before nightfall.'

'That's all right,' Mary answered. 'Perhaps they might like to run around out back for a while and let off a bit of steam? There's a patch of grass and some wooden benches where they could sit and eat, and there are some swings. We don't have the café operating now, since the tourist season has finished, but the facilities are available for them to use, and they can take a snack out there with them if you like.' She looked fondly at the children, who were optimistically replacing glowers with cautious, expectant glances.

'Thanks, Mary. I appreciate that. I'm sure that will be just the thing.' He studied her, a brief, all-encompassing look that took in her neat skirt and blouse and the softly styled hair that framed her face. 'It's good to see you again. You're looking well.'

'Thank you. And the same goes for you… Though we were just saying that we were surprised to see you back here after all this time. But perhaps you're here to see Alice, now that she's been brought up to Inverness?'

'We?' Ross glanced around, but Izzy had already moved forward, pausing to crouch down and say hello to the children.

'Molly, Cameron—it's so lovely to see you again.' She hugged them both, and they in turn smiled a bright-eyed welcome.

'Auntie Izzy, you came to my birthday party, do you remember?' Molly's eyes were shining with happiness. 'You bought me a dolly, and you and Mummy baked cakes for tea. And then the next day we went down to the lake for a picnic.'

'I remember it well,' Izzy said. 'We had such a lot of fun, didn't we?'

Molly nodded, her expression gleeful.

'Mum's in hospital now,' Cameron said, his gaze solemn. His hair was dark, like his father's, and his eyes were grey. 'She hurt her head and her leg and her arm, and she can't walk very well. We're going to see her tomorrow.'

'I know, sweetheart. Your mother's been very poorly, hasn't she?'

He nodded. 'We've been to see her a lot in hospital where we live, but now they've moved her.'

'But it's all right,' Molly put in, 'because she needs to learn to walk about and do things, and they have a place at the new hospital where they can help her.'

'That's good, isn't it? I'm sure the doctors will look after her very well.' Izzy stood up and waited as Mary shepherded the children towards the garden area at the back of the shop.

'Your uncle says you can have these buns to eat, and you're to share the crisps,' Mary told them as they eagerly walked with her. 'I'll bring the drinks, and maybe you can have ice creams a little later, once you're settled.'

She left the shop, and Izzy realised the moment could not be put off any longer. She straightened her shoulders and forced herself to take a good look at the man who had played havoc with her feelings over a good stretch of time. Tall, striking in appearance, with black hair dark as midnight, he was the devil incarnate, sent to try her with his powerful presence and his innate authority descending over everyone and everything.

She looked into Ross's eyes and found herself trapped, submerged in those blue-grey depths, only to falter as she had always done when he was anywhere around.

'We had no idea that you were planning on coming

here,' she murmured. 'It's been such a long time since your father's funeral that we felt sure you had decided to stay away for good.'

'And now my coming back here will well and truly set the cat among the pigeons, I dare say.' There was a glint in his eye that told how he relished that thought. 'I know there are those who would much prefer never to set eyes on me again, but sadly they're in for a disappointment. Your father will most likely be sharpening his axe at the first whisper of my return... The battle between the Buchanans and the McKinnons is set to run and run, isn't it?'

She wasn't going to let him get away with that. 'From what I've seen, you seem to thrive on any skirmishes that come your way. You've never been one to back down from a fight, have you?' Her chin lifted. 'That's why you and your own father were at loggerheads the whole time. Two stubborn men coming face to face will always clash, and it's the same with you and my father. Neither one of you will ever consider taking a different course. That would be too simple, wouldn't it? It would reek too much of losing face.'

He raised a dark brow. 'Why should I want to change my ways? I've done nothing wrong—and, more to the point, I'm the only one left to uphold the Buchanan name.' He stood before her, his long legs taut, his back ramrod-straight, as though daring her to deny it. 'That might not seem important to you, but it's something that lays heavily on me.'

'Of course it does,' she retorted, her grey eyes smoky with mocking amusement. 'That's why you left it to Jake to do what was necessary. Do you think any of us here care a jot about the Buchanan name? Whether the landlord is a Buchanan or not, he's still going to look after himself first.'

He laughed. 'You haven't lost any of your straight-talking ways, have you, Izzy? That's what I always liked about you. You could be relied on to put me right if I looked to be veering off course.' He reached out to gently cup her face in his palm. 'As I often did. But then I was young and foolhardy, and reckless was my middle name.' His voice softened to a whisper. 'It's good to see you again, sweet Isabel McKinnon.'

Izzy's skin heated where his hand lightly trailed over her cheek. The lightest touch of his fingers was enough to fire her blood, and she didn't know why he had the power to do this to her—to make her senses quicken and her heart pump faster.

It was frustrating, and above all it wasn't fair, this hold he had over her. He was the enemy, he was every-thing she should rebel against, and yet… And yet her body ignored every warning, flouted common sense and instead abandoned her to the powerful onslaught of his devil-may-care charm whenever he came near.

It wasn't to be borne, and out of desperation she decided that attack was the best form of defence. 'You might not be so pleased once you settle in at the castle and see how many complaints I've lodged with your estate manager. Or perhaps you aren't planning on staying around all that long?'

'Long enough to take the scowl from your mouth, perhaps,' he said, tucking his hand under her jaw and swooping to drop a fleeting, fierce kiss on her soft lips.

She gasped as the imprint of his mouth registered on her, leaving a tingling explosion of sensation in its wake. Her whole body responded in a surge of fizzing excite-ment. 'You…you kissed me,' she said in shocked wonder.

Heat shimmered in his gaze, laughter dancing in the blue-grey depths of his eyes. 'I couldn't resist,' he said, letting his hand fall from her. 'But I was right, wasn't I? It certainly lifted the scowl from your lips, and it only took…what…all of two seconds?'

She waited a moment or two while she battled to bring her emotions under control once more. 'I wonder if you should have more pressing things to do with your time?' she said finally, for want of any more cutting response. 'I think the children may well need your attention. Or perhaps you'd forgotten all about them?'

'I would never do that. But far be it from me to give you cause to find me wanting,' he murmured. 'I'll go right away and find out what they're up to.' He paused, though, to study her slender figure, letting his glance sweep over her from head to toe, taking in the clinging cut of her jeans and the soft cashmere of her top. 'Still as beautiful as ever, my lovely Izzy. But a sight more feisty than when last we met, I dare say, and with way more delicious curves.' His mouth curved. 'Yum.'

Her grey gaze narrowed on him. 'You should watch your step, Buchanan,' she said in a low, controlled tone. 'You're not so big you can't take a tumble.'

He put up his hands in self-defence. 'Okay, okay. You can stand down. I'm an unarmed man.' He made a mock attempt at wiping his brow with the back of his hand as she finally relaxed her shoulders. 'Phew! And I thought young Molly could shoot sparks. They're nothing compared with her aunt's artillery.'

He was chuckling as he moved away in the direction of the garden, and Izzy stared at him, firing more darts at his straight back. The man was dangerous—a hazard to all unsuspecting women who suffered under the misapprehension that he was a good-natured, easy-going kind of man. He could effortlessly take your heart and squeeze it dry.

But that was probably the least of her problems right now. How on earth was she going to break the news to her father that Ross Buchanan was back in town?

CHAPTER TWO

'WOULD you like more coffee? I just made a fresh pot.' Izzy's housemate lifted the coffee percolator, letting it hover over two brightly painted ceramic mugs in the centre of the kitchen table.

'Yes, please… Anything to warm me up. It's freezing in here.' Izzy chafed her arms with her hands in an effort to drum up some heat. 'We really need to get that central heating fixed, or at the least buy a portable heater.' She frowned, gazing around the room. 'I suppose I could make some toast—the heat from the grill will probably make us feel better.'

Lorna nodded. 'Good idea. I'll fry some bacon. I'm really in the mood for toasted bacon sandwiches to set me up for a day in A&E.' She grinned. 'Just in case we don't make it down to the cafeteria again.'

'Good idea.' Izzy took out a loaf of bread from the wooden bin. 'But I've been thinking… We could take our own food in to the hospital—sandwiches, biscuits, cereal bars…anything that we can cover with clingfilm and set out on a trolley. That way we'll have stuff on hand if things get hectic.' She smiled. 'I thought it was great when Greg brought in hot sausage rolls and pastries the other day. They gave me the will to go on.'

'Me, too.' Lorna replaced the coffeepot on its base and went to get a frying pan from the cupboard. 'As to the central heating, and all the other repairs that need doing around here, I suppose Ross will need a bit of time to settle in before he gets round to sorting things out. That's if he means to stay, of course. It could just be that he's brought the children over to be closer to Alice, and once she's up and about he'll be off.' Lorna hesitated, frying pan in hand, thinking things through.

She was a slender girl, with a mop of fair hair that had a flyaway look about it, as though it was permanently out of control—pretty much on a par with her bubbly character. Just now, though, her blue eyes were thoughtful. 'Then again,' she murmured, 'he always had a bit of a thing for Alice, didn't he? In fact, if you recall, the rumour was that she was seeing Ross long before she decided to run off with his brother. Quite the scandal at the time, I hear.'

'Yes, it was.' Izzy frowned. 'Especially where my father was concerned. He hated the thought that she had anything at all to do with any of the Buchanans.'

Lorna placed the frying pan on the hob and turned towards Izzy, throwing her an anxious look. 'Oh, I'm sorry, Izzy…I was forgetting for a minute that she's your cousin. I didn't mean to say anything out of line— it's just that everyone's talking about Ross coming back here. People are wondering what's going to happen about the crofts, and whether they can do anything to improve the general standard of living. And on top of all that they're buzzing with talk about the way your families have been at each other's throats for as far back as anyone can remember. There doesn't seem to be any getting away from it. Of course they're all siding with you and your parents and Alice.'

'It's all right, Lorna. I knew as soon as I saw Ross was back in Glenmuir that the tongues would start wagging. I don't know *what* he's going to do about the crofts. Most people hereabouts lease the land and the cottages from him, but I imagine he'll have to put his own house in order before he can find time to look into any concerns they might have about their livelihoods. I suppose he could always say that what they do with the land is up to them for the term of the lease.'

'Not his problem, you mean?' Lorna pulled a face. 'You could be right. But people seem to think Ross should do something so that they can make a decent living from the land. It's history rearing its head once again—you know how it is…people around here don't let go of the past easily. They're convinced their rights were taken from them in the Highland Clearances well over a hundred years ago. At the very least they think he should pay them compensation on behalf of his ancestors.'

Izzy switched on the grill and set bread out on the rack. 'That's fighting talk,' she said with a husky laugh. 'But, knowing how the Buchanans operate, I doubt it will get them very far. They've always known how to manoeuvre their way through the legal system and come out the winners.'

'I'm told the Buchanans have oodles of charisma when they choose to exert it, and none of it lost on the women who cross their paths…' Lorna turned the heat on under the pan and added rashers of bacon. 'That was the start of things with your families, wasn't it?' she asked. 'Your father's great-aunt being seduced by the former Laird—Ross's great-grandfather—some eighty odd years ago.'

'That's very true.' Izzy slotted the grill pan under the

heat. 'Of course it caused all kinds of anger and heart-ache and general mayhem when she died in childbirth. That really upset the McKinnons and added fuel to the fire. I think my father, when he was growing up, soaked up all the vitriol that was poured on the Buchanans, and consequently he has no time for them.

'Alice going off with Robert Buchanan was history repeating itself, and that well and truly stirred the melting pot, didn't it?'

'What happened when Robert and Alice took off?'

'My father exploded, but at least he directed most of his anger towards Robert back then. I suppose it made things worse because Alice had been seeing Ross to begin with, and at least he was the steady one, whereas Robert always had a wild streak.'

Alice and Ross… Izzy shied away from that thought. How deep had their feelings been for one another before Alice had turned to Robert? Did Ross still care for her in the same way? She pulled herself together, aware that Lorna was waiting for her to go on.

'Alice was young, and had obviously been led astray by both Buchanans,' she said, 'but for all that my father wouldn't forgive her. He's never had much to do with her children, either. My mother has always kept in touch with the family, by letter and the occasional visit, but she's very wary of what my father would have to say on the subject. She keeps things low-key and tries not to provoke him.'

She frowned. 'The only real difference, for all the scandal that it caused, was that Robert Buchanan was never going to be the new young Laird.' Izzy pondered the situation as she laid hot toast down on the plates. 'I can't help wondering if that was what lay behind all the resentment simmering between him and Ross. As the older brother, Ross was the one to take over the estate. Robert always wanted what Ross had, and unfortunately that included his girlfriends.'

'That must have been some sibling rivalry.' Lorna added tomatoes to the pan, and it wasn't long before the appetising aroma of sizzling bacon filled the air.

The kitchen was much warmer now, and Izzy began to place the plates on the table, ready for the meal. She was setting out cutlery when there was a loud knocking on the door.

'I wonder who that can be,' she said with a frown. 'It's barely seven-thirty in the morning. Who else would be up and about at this time of the day apart from farmers, doctors and the milkman?'

'I did notice the milkman giving you the eye the other day,' Lorna remarked with a hint of mischief. 'I thought at the time he was just surprised to see you open the door at that hour, but I may have been wrong about that.'

Acknowledging that with a smile, Izzy shook her head. 'You have such a lively imagination.' She went to find out who was there.

A moment later she stared down at the two children who were standing on the doorstep, her brows lifting in astonishment. 'Molly, Cameron—I wasn't expecting to see you.' She glanced around to see if anyone had come with them, but nothing stirred on the path that led down the hill except for a solitary bird that took flight from the nearby copse. 'Have you come here all by yourselves?'

'Yes,' Molly said. 'It isn't far to here from the castle, and we remembered where you lived from last time we came to visit.' She frowned. 'Uncle Ross wasn't staying with us then, though.'

'No, we came here with Mum,' Cameron put in. 'Dad stayed at home.' A momentary sadness washed over his thin face. 'He's not here any more, you know,' he said earnestly. 'Mum says he was hurt in the car accident and they couldn't make him better, but he's peaceful now.'

'I know, sweetheart.' Izzy wanted to put her arms around the children and make everything right again, but it was an impossible task. How could she begin to comfort them for the loss of their father? She contented herself instead with making them welcome, putting an arm around their shoulders and ushering them into the house. 'Come into the kitchen. It's warmer in there.'

'Mummy's not going to go away, as well, is she?' Molly asked, her voice hesitant. 'She was in the car with Daddy, and she was hurt.'

'No, Molly. Your mother is getting better every day. It will take some time before she's on her feet properly, but before too long she should be back with you.'

'In the New Year?' Cameron suggested. 'That's what Uncle Ross says…some time in the New Year.'

'That sounds about right to me,' Izzy said. Her cousin would recover well enough from the broken bones she had sustained in the car crash, but she had also suffered head injuries and internal bleeding that added substantially to her problems. The head injuries meant that she had no memory of the accident itself, though thankfully her faculties had been spared. It was hoped that in time she would make a full recovery.

She pushed open the door to the kitchen and showed them inside.

Cameron sniffed the air appreciatively. 'Are you making breakfast?' he asked in a hopeful tone, his eyes widening.

'Yes, we are.' Izzy nodded. 'Looks like we have more people to share the sandwiches,' she told Lorna. 'Do you think we can run to a couple more?'

'I think we can manage that. I'll add a bit more bacon to the pan.' Lorna smiled at the children, and then, as they stared about the room, taking everything in, she surreptitiously lifted questioning brows towards Izzy at their arrival so early in the morning.

Izzy hunched her shoulders in a bemused gesture before turning her attention back to the children. 'Sit yourselves down by the table,' she said. 'So, your Uncle Ross knows you're here, does he? Hasn't he given you anything to eat?'

'He's asleep,' Molly said, shaking her head so that her curls quivered. 'I tried to wake him, but he didn't even open his eyes… Well, just the corner of one, a tiny bit. Then he closed it again and made a sort of "hmmph" from under the duvet, and buried his head in the pillow.' She lifted her arms to show the extent of her helplessness.

Izzy's mind conjured up an image of Ross, his dark hair tousled from sleep, his limbs tangled in the folds of the duvet. It made her hot and bothered, and she quickly tried to banish the errant thought from her head.

'And I'm starving,' Cameron confirmed. 'I couldn't find the breakfast cereals in any of the cupboards, so I went to look for Maggie, but she wasn't anywhere around.'

'I imagine it's a bit too early for the housekeeper,' Lorna commented. 'From what I've heard she doesn't usually go up to the castle until after nine o'clock.'

'Well, we didn't know what to do, so we decided to come and see you,' Molly finished triumphantly. 'I remembered that you live at the bottom of the hill…and that you always have a cookie jar on the worktop. I remember it's a yellow bear with a smiley face and a Tam o' Shanter hat.'

'That's right.' Izzy pointed to the corner of the room, where the ceramic cookie jar sat next to the microwave oven. 'There he is, just as you said. Perhaps you could have a cookie after you've eaten your sandwich?'

Pleased, Molly nodded, while Cameron fidgeted in his seat and asked pertinently, 'And me, too?'

'Of course. I wouldn't dream of leaving you out, Cameron.'

He looked suitably appeased at that, and Izzy concentrated on making them both a sandwich. Pushing the plates towards them, she looked from one to the other. 'So your uncle doesn't have any idea that you've come here?'

Cameron shook his head, looking uncertain, but Molly, after taking a bite from her sandwich, said, 'I left a note for him on the kitchen table to let him know we'd come here. Mummy said we should always make sure someone knows where we are.'

'Mmm, that's good. That was the sensible thing to do,' Izzy said with a smile. 'I think I'd better give him a ring all the same, as soon as we've eaten, just to make sure he knows what's going on, or he might be worried.' She wasn't going to let her sandwich go cold on his account, though. That was supposing he was even awake by now, of course. But if he wasn't she would simply let the phone ring until he answered it. How could the man be so careless as to let the children run loose at such a young age? 'Lorna and I have to go to work soon, you see, otherwise you would be able to stay here. Perhaps we'll take you back home when we've all eaten.'

'That's okay,' Cameron said. 'I said you'd probably have to go to the hospital. I remembered from last time we were here.'

Izzy sat down to eat her toasted sandwich with Lorna and the children, chatting to them about life up at the castle. 'Are you settling in all right?' she asked.

Molly nodded. 'It's kind of exciting. There's loads of rooms and we can go in any of them.'

'And there's a winding staircase that goes up and up,' Cameron said. 'And there are lots of doors. I nearly got lost, and Uncle Ross had to come and find me. He said I was in the pantry, but it was big—like a room.'

A few minutes later Izzy left them talking to Lorna while she went into the hall to phone Ross in private. It was a while before he answered.

'Did I wake you?' she asked.

'No. I was some distance from the phone.' His voice was deep, warm and soothing, and to hear him was a little like sipping at rich, melting chocolate. 'I was checking the rooms to see where the children might be hiding. They've taken to disappearing of a morning, and usually I manage to find them in what used to be the servants' quarters. They seem to like playing in the smaller rooms. I've never known such early birds. Where on earth do they get their energy from?'

'The fountain of youth, I should imagine.' She hesitated. 'So I take it you're still looking for them? Have you tried the kitchen?'

'I'm heading there now.' He made a soft intake of breath. 'I should have taken time to dress properly— these stone floors are cold. I need to get some carpets in here…or install under-floor heating.'

She imagined him padding barefoot over the floor, but her mind skittered away from delving any further into what he might be wearing—or not wearing, as the case may be. 'You should try living in my cottage,' she said, her tone dry. 'We don't have the luxury of central heating at the moment, since your estate manager hasn't attended to our requests for repairs, whereas you at least have the comfort of a range cooker in your kitchen, if I remember correctly.' She had ventured up to the castle in search of her errant cousin one day years ago, and the memory had stayed with her ever since.

'You're welcome to come and share it with me any time, Izzy. I think I told you that once before, but you were reluctant to take me up on the offer, as I recall. I guess you were worried about what your father might think if he found you there.' She heard a door hinge creak. 'Nope, they're not in here.'

'I expect you'll find a note on the table,' she murmured.

He was silent for a moment, taking that in, before he said on a disbelieving note, 'Are you telling me you *know* where they are?'

'That's about the size of it. Molly wanted to keep you informed.' There was a rustling of paper from the other end of the line. 'Have you found it? What does it say?'

He laughed throatily. 'Well, you're perfectly right— there are some weird hieroglyphics scrawled on a scrap of paper, if that counts. I'll see if I can decipher it.' There was a pause, and she could imagine his frown. 'Here we go, it says, "U wudnt wayk up, so we is gon down the ill to get sum fink to eet. Luv, Molly nd Camron." Brilliant.' There was a smile in his voice. 'I suppose that's not bad for a five-year-old.'

'There you are, you see. What could be clearer? The children were starving, and you were off in the land of nod, so they had to fend for themselves. Fortunately for them we were able to give them breakfast and make sure that they're warm and looked after, but I daren't think what might have happened if we hadn't been here.' She used a stern tone, but Ross was still chuckling over the note, and that served to make her crosser than ever.

'I know what you're saying,' he said, amusement threading his voice, 'and you're right, it's definitely not a good state of affairs... But you have to give them full marks for initiative, don't you? I'll come over and fetch them.'

'That would be a very good idea,' she said on a pithy note. 'Lorna and I have to be at work in around half an hour, so if you're not here in the next few minutes we'll come and find *you*.'

She cut the call and went back to the kitchen, satisfied that at least now he would have to scoot around and get dressed, and begin to take on his responsibilities. What was he thinking of, lying in bed while the children were wandering about?

Molly and Cameron had finished eating by now, and were busy drawing pictures while Lorna collected up the breakfast dishes.

'I'll take over here if you want to go and get ready for work,' Izzy told her. 'Ross should be along to pick up the children in a few minutes.'

'He's going to take us to see Mummy today,' Molly said brightly. 'He promised.'

'And he said we'd buy some flowers for her from the shop,' Cameron added. 'He said we could choose the best flowers in the shop when we get to Inverness. She likes roses, so that's what I'm going to look for.'

'I'm sure she'll love them,' Izzy said, 'whatever you

decide to buy. I'm going to see her myself tomorrow, all being well.'

She washed the breakfast dishes, leaving them to drain on the wire rack. Then she rubbed cream into her hands and checked her long hair in the mirror, clipping the chestnut waves back from her face.

Ross turned up at the house much sooner than she had expected, looking immaculate in dark chinos and a crisp shirt, and oozing vibrant energy—as though he was ready to grasp the day with both hands.

She fixed him with a smoky grey gaze. How could he possibly look like that when he'd been dead to the world not half an hour earlier? It simply wasn't fair.

'They've been waiting for you,' she said, waving him into the hallway. 'But I have to say I think you should find a way of barring the doors, so they can't simply wander off as they please. There's no knowing what they could have been up to while you were out for the count.'

He sent her an oblique glance. 'You're not going to let this go, are you? Would it help if I said the door was locked and bolted? I think Cameron climbed on a chair to retrieve the keys and unlatch the bolt.'

'Then maybe you should keep the keys closer to hand,' she said calmly. 'You should count yourself lucky that no major road passes by here.'

'I'm duly chastened,' he said, making an effort to turn down his mouth but not looking a jot sincere.

She led him into the kitchen, where the children glanced up from their drawing to acknowledge him with bright smiles.

'I've done a picture of Mummy,' Molly told him, waving her paper in the air. 'She has beautiful long hair and a pretty dress. See?'

'That's…spectacular,' he murmured, gazing down at the potato-shaped squiggle, daubed generously with a splash of bright pink crayon. 'I see you've drawn her lovely fingers, too.'

It was the right thing to say. Molly beamed with pride at her creation. The hands formed a great part of the drawing, with sausage fingers on either side, and they were her latest achievement.

Cameron, on the other hand, was tired of sitting and wanted adventure. 'When are we going to Inverness? Can we go now?'

'Soon,' Ross told him. 'I have to put a few things in a holdall first of all. We're going to meet up with your Aunt Jess at the hospital. She's come up especially from the Lake District to stay in Inverness for the next day or two, and she says she'll take you shopping as soon as you've been to see your mother. We can't have you going around looking like scruffs any longer, can we?'

Cameron shrugged, obviously not much bothered either way, while Molly looked thoughtful. Izzy guessed she was already thinking about what she would like to buy.

'Would you like a cup of tea or coffee?' Lorna asked.

Ross shook his head. 'Thanks, but I have to get a move on. Things are not going quite the way I planned this morning.' He glanced around the kitchen. 'You're having trouble with the central heating, I gather? I'll make arrangements for someone to come and deal with it.'

'That would be good,' Lorna told him. 'It's freezing in here in the mornings. And as to taking a tepid shower—I really can't recommend it.'

'No, I can imagine.' He ran his gaze over Izzy, taking

in the snug fit of her jeans and the stretch material of her jersey wrap top that clung where it touched.

She had no idea what he was thinking, but Izzy's glance was frosty. 'That's not all that's wrong,' she said. 'There are roof tiles that have been missing since the high winds two or three weeks back…and part of the fence has blown down.'

He frowned. 'I didn't notice that when I drove here. Whereabouts?'

'At the side of the house.' Izzy's mouth made a crooked shape. 'I tried to fix it temporarily, with nails and a few battens, but I doubt it will hold for very long. Carpentry's not one of my skills, I'm afraid.'

Ross's gaze was thoughtful. 'I'm sure you're a woman of many talents, but obviously you shouldn't have been put in that situation. I can only say that Jake has had a lot to contend with of late, with various things happening in his family—illness and so on—or he would have seen to it.'

'I didn't realise that.' Izzy was immediately concerned. 'He didn't say.'

'No, he wouldn't. Jake's a proud man. He's probably borne the brunt of the villagers' animosity over the last few years.' He straightened, becoming brisk in his manner. 'Anyway, thanks for taking care of Molly and Cameron for me. You, too, Lorna.' His brief smile encompassed both of them. 'I'm sorry you've been troubled.'

'They've been good as gold,' Lorna told him. 'They're welcome to come and visit any time…preferably with your knowledge, of course.'

He nodded. 'I'm sure they'll want to come back fairly soon, but next time I'll make certain they call you first.'

After that Ross didn't hang around to make conversation, and Izzy wasn't sure quite how she felt about that. It wasn't really surprising that he would leave quickly. After all, she hadn't been exactly welcoming in her manner. But perhaps he also recognised that she and Lorna had to go off to work.

Anyway, after she had given each of the children a hug, he led them away and settled them in his car. He drove away without looking back.

Izzy was filled with a strange sense of unease once he had gone. She felt somehow let down, with a hollow feeling inside despite the meal, and yet, in truth, how could she have expected anything more? As things stood, she was going against the grain by even associating with him.

If her father discovered that Ross had come visiting, he'd be have been agitated in the extreme, no matter that she was perfectly entitled to run her own life the way she saw fit. That ideology hadn't stood Alice in any good stead, had it? She had been cut off from her family for several years, and was only back now because she needed specialist care and attention.

It grieved Izzy that her cousin should suffer this way. The Buchanans had a lot to answer for.

CHAPTER THREE

'ACCORDING to his wife, the man was doing a spot of sightseeing close by the falls when he slipped and fell. Luckily for him some hill walkers saw what happened and helped bring him to safety.' Greg's voice reached Izzy over the car phone. 'As far as we know he has a broken ankle and damage to his shoulder, but he's also complaining of shortness of breath. An ambulance is being sent out, but there are traffic jams on the main road causing delays, and since the tracking system shows you're nearby, with the fast response car, you may be able to reach him first.'

'Thanks, Greg.' Greg was the consultant in charge of the A&E unit where she worked, and her patient would most likely be taken into his care, unless the situation was worse than it first appeared, in which case he might have to be transferred to Inverness. 'You're right. I'm about a mile away from the gorge. I'll head straight over there.'

Izzy drove as fast as she dared, barely able to take in the wonderful scenery in this part of the Highlands. She had left Lorna back in the A&E unit. It suited Izzy to work this way—spending some of the week in the hospital setting, and the rest out and about as a first responder.

This whole area was one of outstanding natural beauty, with hills and mountains all around, thickly wooded with natural species of rowan, alder, hazel and birch. To her left, she caught glimpses of the river as it flowed downhill, disappearing every now and then as woodland obscured the view.

Before too long she came across the road junction where she had to turn off towards the falls—a place of wonder for everyone who came to visit the area. There was a narrow road leading to a car park, and from there she hoped she would be able to find the injured man without too much difficulty.

She parked the car as close as she could to the bridge, a viewpoint where people could stand and marvel at the chasm that had been carved out by glacial melt-water aeons before, and where a majestic water-fall surged downwards to the valley below. From there the water cascaded over boulders and tumbled on its course towards the sea.

The man had been carried to a small viewing platform, Izzy discovered, and as she approached she could see straight away that he was in a lot of pain and discomfort.

'Hello, Jim…and Frances,' she said, introducing herself to the patient and his wife. 'I'm Dr McKinnon.' She knelt down beside the man, who was sitting propped up against the metal guard-rail. 'The ambulance is on its way, but I'll take a look at you and see what I can do to make you more comfortable in the meantime, if I may?'

Jim nodded. He tried to speak, but he was struggling to get his breath, and Izzy could see that there was a film of sweat on his brow. He looked anxious, his features strained and desperate, as was the case with many seriously ill people that Izzy had come across.

'I can see that your ankle is swollen and your shoulder appears to be dislocated,' she said. 'Do you have pain anywhere else?'

Jim used his good arm to slope a finger towards his chest. 'Hurts to…breathe,' he said.

'The pain came on before he fell,' his wife put in. 'He started to cough, and then it seemed as though he was going to pass out. Is it his heart, do you think?'

'I'll listen to his chest and see if I can find out what's going on,' Izzy said. 'Have you had any heart problems before this, Jim?'

He shook his head and she gave her patient a reassuring smile. 'Try not to worry,' she said. 'We'll sort it all out. For now, I'm going to give you oxygen to help you to breathe, and I'll give you an injection to ease the pain.'

Izzy placed the oxygen mask over his mouth and nose and checked that the flow of oxygen was adequate. Then she listened carefully to his chest.

'Did you have any other symptoms before the chest pain?' she asked. 'Even up to a day or so before?'

Jim frowned, trying to think about that, but his pain was obviously getting the better of him, and as he started to shake his head once more his wife put in, 'He said his leg was sore. Apart from that he was fine. We've just come back from a trip to New Zealand. This was a final weekend break before we go back home and start getting ready for Christmas.'

'Hmm.' Izzy was thoughtful. 'We need to do tests to be certain what's causing your problems, Jim, but it could be that a blood clot is blocking the circulation to your lungs. I'm going to give you medication to stop any clots forming and ease the blood flow, and then we'll concentrate on getting you to hospital as soon as possible.'

Izzy set up an intravenous line so that she could give him anticoagulant and painkilling medication as necessary. Then she moved away from the couple momentarily, to use her mobile phone and call the ambulance services.

'How long is the ambulance likely to be?' she asked. 'I need to have this patient transported urgently to hospital. I think he may be suffering from a pulmonary embolism, and I don't believe we have any time to lose.'

'Okay. Leave it with us,' the controller said. 'There's a problem with the ambulance, but we'll get someone to you as soon as possible.'

Izzy turned back to her patient and contemplated his other injuries. 'I'm pretty sure your ankle is broken,' she told him, 'so I'll immobilise that in a splint. As to the shoulder, the same thing applies. I'll secure it for you in the most comfortable position, and then the hospital team will put it back in place for you while you're under anaesthetic.'

She worked quickly to do that, all the while looking out for the ambulance. Her patient was most likely suffering from a blood clot that had passed from his leg to his lung, and she was conscious that if it was not treated quickly his life could be at risk.

'How are you feeling now?' she asked him.

'It's better now that the pain has gone,' he said, but she could see that he was still struggling to breathe. She glanced around, but there was still no sign of the ambulance. Her gaze rested momentarily on the majestic scenery of the gorge. Trees and ferns sprang from clefts and fissures in the rock, and above everything was the gentle sound of rushing water. It was such a glorious, peaceful scene that it seemed incongruous that she was here trying to save someone's life.

Then came a humming sound from overhead, like the drone of insects coming ever closer, until at last the noise was all around and an air ambulance helicopter hovered, preparing to land, its rotors spinning, fanning the air like giant flapping wings.

'Is that for us?' Frances asked, and Izzy nodded. 'It looks that way.' She glanced at Jim. 'They'll take you to Inverness,' she told him. 'At least with the helicopter you should be there within minutes.'

The helicopter came to rest some distance away, on a flat stretch of ground near to the car park, and a medic jumped down, followed by a paramedic. Between them they wheeled a trolley towards Izzy and her patient, and as she watched them draw near she made a sudden, swift intake of breath.

Surely that was Ross in the medic's uniform? What was *he* doing here? Of course she knew that he had trained as a doctor, but his work had always been in the Lake District. This had to be new, this job working with the air ambulance.

As he approached she did her best to get over the shock and try to recover her professionalism. Her patient must come first. Any questions she might want to fire at him could surely be answered later?

'Hello, how are you doing?' Ross said, coming over to the group assembled on the viewing platform and checking on the patient. He glanced at Izzy. 'Hi,' he said. 'Ambulance control told me you were the doctor on call.' Then he concentrated his attention on the patient once more. 'You collapsed, I understand, and injured yourself?'

Jim nodded, unable to speak just then, and Izzy began to explain the situation. 'He has severe chest pain and difficulty breathing, as well as a broken ankle and dislocated shoulder.' She went on to outline her diagnosis and explain what medication she had given him. 'He'll need to go for an urgent angiography, and I suspect he'll require thrombolytic therapy in order to break down any clot that's formed.'

He nodded. 'I'll alert Radiology back at Inverness. They have all the facilities there. And I'll notify the cardiovascular surgeon to be on hand to perform the surgery if necessary.'

All the time they were talking, they were breaking off to reassure Jim that everything was being done that should be done, and preparing him for transfer to the trolley. 'We'll have you secure in no time,' Ross told him. 'I can see Dr McKinnon has been taking good care of you. No worries. You're in good hands.'

They worked quickly to strap their patient safely in place, covering him with a blanket to keep him warm and prevent shock. Ross glanced at Frances. 'Will you be coming along with us? We can find room for you in the 'copter if you like.'

'Thank you. I'd like that. I want to stay with him.'

'Good.' Ross and the paramedic started to walk with the trolley towards the waiting helicopter. Izzy accompanied them, keeping a check on her patient's vital signs.

She glanced towards Ross. 'I had no idea you had taken a job with the air ambulance,' she said in a low voice.

'The opportunity came up, and it seemed too good a chance to miss,' he answered. 'They needed someone to fill in for one of the doctors who was away for a couple of months, and with Alice likely to be in the hospital for the next few weeks it looked as though the job was tailor-made for me.'

'What happened to your work in the Lake District?'

'My contract came to an end. They'll hold it open for me in case I decide to go back next year on a permanent basis, but I thought with Jake leaving it was time for me to come and take up the reins of the estate for a while.'

She studied him as they lifted the trolley bed on to the aircraft. So there was still the possibility that he wasn't going to be staying around. Why didn't that come as any real surprise to her?

'I'm even more startled to see you here today, right now,' she murmured, going into the medical bay of the helicopter. 'It was only this morning that you and the children were heading off to Inverness. What happened to your plans to go and see Alice?'

He gave a brief smile. 'Oh, we did all that. Afterwards I left them with their aunt Jess, so that I could come in to work. She's going to keep them with her in Inverness for a couple of days. At the moment things are a little tricky for me because of the shift system I'm working, but I dare say it will all work out in the end.'

The paramedic made sure that the trolley bed was locked in place and that Frances was happily settled close by her husband's side. Then he came over to Izzy and Ross. He must have heard what they were saying because he commented, 'In fact, Ross and I had a difficult stint last night. We didn't get finished until after midnight. There was a boy injured and lost on the hills, and being pitch-black out there it took us a while to find him. He was okay, as it turned out—just a little shaken up and suffering from exposure and a pulled ligament in his knee.'

'Oh, I see.' That explained why Molly had found it difficult to wake Ross this morning. Izzy felt a wave of guilt wash over her. Had she been too quick to pass judgement on him?

She checked the intravenous line and made sure that Jim was comfortable. He was struggling to take in oxygen through the breathing mask, and she settled it more comfortably over his face. 'You'll be in hospital in no time at all,' she told him. 'The doctors will do a scan to see if there's a clot on your lung. If they find one, they could decide to go on treating you with medication, or they may want to remove it using a thin catheter threaded through the blood vessel. Either way, you will be well looked after.'

She said goodbye to Jim and his wife and went to the open door of the helicopter. Ross went with her, jumping down to the ground and reaching up to help her descend. His hands went around her waist, his palms lying flat on her ribcage as he lifted her down with ease, as though she was as light as a feather.

When her feet touched the ground his hands stayed on her, as though he would steady her, and she realised with a slight sense of shock that her own fingers still lay on his shoulders. Her whole body responded as though he had triggered an electric current.

Coming to her senses, she drew back her fingers, her mind skittering with uncertainty.

'So that's why you were lying in bed this morning,' she murmured. 'I have to take back all the bad things I was thinking.' She frowned. 'Only, who was watching over the children last night if you were out working?'

'You were thinking bad things?' His mouth made a flattened shape. 'I thought as much.' He straightened, letting his hands fall away from her. 'You don't trust me at all, do you?'

'Put it down to the fall out from times gone by,' she murmured.

He gave a faint smile. 'As always. Actually, I did have things all in hand. I arranged for Maggie to stay and watch over them until I returned home. She was pleased enough to do it. Of course I'll have to organise things a little better if I'm to stay for a while. Molly and Cameron need some kind of stability, and getting them enrolled in school is going to be one of the first things I must do.'

'Yes, that's probably best.' Izzy stepped away from the vehicle. 'I should let you go,' she said softly. This was neither the time nor the place to be holding a conversation about his future plans, much as her curiosity was pricked. Wind from the helicopter's rotors tousled her hair, and she lifted a hand to hold the strands away from her face. 'If you get the chance, let me know how our patient progresses, will you?'

He nodded. 'I will. You can count on it.'

She moved away, and he slid the door of the helicopter shut. Within moments the aircraft rose skywards and zoomed away.

Watching the helicopter move out of sight, Izzy was assailed by a strange notion of unfinished business. Seeing Ross at work had given her a tremendous jolt, and along with it had come the realisation that their paths might cross much more often than she had ever expected.

Today had not been a good start. Why hadn't she guarded her tongue instead of alerting him to all her doubts and criticisms? He was simply doing a job, making the best of things just as she was, and it was wrong of her to find fault with everything he did. It was in his favour that he was taking care of the children at all. Perhaps she should leave it to her father to cast aspersions on his motives.

Her father, as things turned out, was in a highly charged mood when she visited him later that day.

'You're working with Ross Buchanan?' His tone was grim. 'As if it isn't bad enough that he's back among us. Why do we have to rub shoulders with him, too?'

Izzy's mother came into the living room, setting down the tea tray on a low coffee table. She glanced at Izzy. 'Sit yourself down, love. You've had a trying day by all accounts. You should relax with a cup of tea and some cake. I had a baking session this morning—fruitcake. Help yourself.' She shook her head, making the soft brown tendrils of hair quiver as she lifted the teapot. 'You wouldn't think so many people would manage to get themselves into difficulties up in the hills, would you?'

Izzy sat down on the sofa and leaned forward to slide a wedge of cake on to a plate. 'I'm more surprised that there are so many people who still want to walk the hills in December,' she murmured. She glanced at her father. 'As to Ross, he is at least doing a worthwhile job. You have to grant him that, surely?'

'I'll not grant him anything,' her father said gruffly. 'I've heard that he's brought builders in to go on with that log cabin project his father started on the estate some six years back. I don't know how on earth he managed to get planning permission. A lot of people objected to the development, and from my point of view it'll be certain to draw away the tourists. I'm sure that's his grand plan.'

'But you'll be all right, won't you?' Izzy said. 'You have the regular people who come every year for the fishing. That's more than a lot of the villagers have.'

'That's only because I kept hold of this land and my father and his father before him fought to stay on it. There were no thanks due to the old Laird and the generations that followed him for that. Their land borders ours, and if they'd had their way they'd have long since moved the boundaries and made it their own.'

Izzy bit into her cake and tried to keep exasperation from getting the better of her. She had learnt long ago that there was no point in arguing with her father when he was in this frame of mind.

Her mother's gaze met hers across the table. 'Your father's upset because the salmon fishing went awry this year. There's something wrong with the stretch of the river that flows across our land. He reckons it's to do with some changes the Laird made higher up, at a point before the river reaches us.'

'But Ross wasn't here when all that went on, was he?' Izzy murmured. 'I don't see how he can be to blame for everything that goes wrong around here.'

Her father's brows shot up. 'So who do you think gave Jake his instructions? And that log cabin has been a sore point for a long time. Not just the cabin, but the lodges that go along with it. He said it was just for living accommodation for the family, but what does he need with that when he has the castle? Draughty it might be, and in need of repair, but they've lived there for generations without needing any cabins or lodges. It's just an excuse. He'll lure away the tourists to line his own pockets and take away any chance we have of making a living.'

'He may not be here for all that long,' Izzy said, accepting a cup of tea from her mother and taking slow sips of the hot liquid. 'He said something about his job being kept open for him back in the Lake District. I have the feeling that he's here to make sure Alice is going to be all right and to allow the children to be with her. Perhaps he's planning on taking them all home once she's well again.'

She frowned, thinking things over. Ross had always had a soft spot for Alice. If his brother hadn't swept her away from him, who knew what might have come of their relationship? Perhaps Alice was bound to turn to him now more than ever. How would Ross react to that? Would he be pleased? Why else was he staying around to look after her when she had her older sister, Jess, to care for her?

It wasn't something that she wanted to dwell on. Thinking about Ross and Alice as a couple always had the power to upset her. Her own feelings towards him were unsettling, and had caused her many a sleepless night. She put down her cup and brushed crumbs from her lap.

'Are you all right?' her mother asked. Grey eyes studied her thoughtfully.

'I'm fine.' Izzy gave her mother a reassuring smile. She didn't want to confide in her about the way her thoughts had turned, especially with her father looking on. Instead, she murmured, 'I suppose I was thinking about Alice. It must be difficult for her, coming back here after all this time and yet still being so far away from her roots. Anyway, I'm going to see her tomorrow after work, all being well. You're welcome to come along with me, if you like.'

She was aware of her father's sharp glance resting on her as she spoke, but this was one instance where she would not back down. Alice had been like a sister to her, and the children, likewise, were precious to her…to Ross, too, if the truth were known.

'I'd like that,' her mother said. She shot a look over to her husband. 'Alice is family,' she said, 'and you have to agree that she's had more than her fair share of bad luck. Are you not going to come along with us and make your peace with her?'

Izzy's father stood up abruptly. 'You know how I feel about the situation,' he said, his tone brisk. 'Alice left of her own accord. She knew full well what she was doing when she chose to go off with a Buchanan.'

'But the bairns, Stuart. Think of the bairns. Do you have no compassion?' Her mother's gaze entreated him. 'What have they ever done to deserve being outcast?'

'You go and see her and look to the bairns,' he said. 'I have things to do. I have to make repairs and get the boat ready for next season—or there'll be no trips for the sea fishing and our income will take another dive. We have to do something to counteract the actions of our neighbours.'

He walked out of the room, his back straight, his head held high, and Izzy gave a soft sigh.

'No one could say that you didn't try, Mum,' she said.

'For all the good it did me.' Her mother poured more tea. 'You know he thinks Ross had something to do with causing the accident, don't you? He's battling with himself over that. He's trying to come to terms with what happened to Alice, but he's incensed because Ross might have had something to do with it.'

'I don't understand.' Izzy sat bolt upright, a line indenting her brow. 'How could Ross have had anything to do with the car smash? I heard he was hurt and had to be hospitalised with a chest injury.'

'He was following them. Robert and Alice were

driving over to her sister's house to pick up the children, from what I heard. Ross was on the same road, and rumour has it that they'd all argued over something and feelings were running high. Folk say it was because she always cared for Ross, and Robert resented that. They think Robert lost control of the car because Ross was edging closer. Robert tried to pick up speed to outrun him, and then he took a bend too wide and it ended up as a three-car smash. It's a wonder no one else was killed.'

Izzy was stunned by that revelation. 'Perhaps it's just that—as you say, rumour. If Ross had been driving dangerously the police would have prosecuted him, wouldn't they?'

'There was no proof. It was summertime, and the roads were dry. There doesn't seem to be any other reason for the accident.'

Izzy shook her head. 'I don't believe it,' she said. 'I don't believe Ross would have done anything to jeopardise the safety of his brother or Alice.'

Her mother laid a hand on her shoulder. 'I only told you because I don't want you to be hurt,' she said. 'You try to look for the good in people, but the Buchanans have always brought trouble. Your father takes a stance that is hard to understand sometimes, but he's protective of his family, and he was hurt when Alice ran away. To him it was like a betrayal, and the Buchanans were at the centre of it.'

Izzy understood that well enough. She just had no idea where all this bad feeling would lead. Nowhere good, that was for sure.

CHAPTER FOUR

'UNCLE ROSS, Izzy says she's going to do some baking,' Molly exclaimed eagerly, tugging at Ross's trousers. 'We want to stay and help her. Can we? She said we could if you thought it was all right.'

Ross frowned. He was standing by his Range Rover, outside Izzy's cottage, preparing to open up the door to the car's loading area. 'I don't see how we can do that today,' he murmured. 'I have to go back home and talk to the men who are doing some building work for me. I'm sorry. Perhaps another time.'

Molly's face crumpled. 'Oh, but she's making gingerbread men for the Christmas sale.'

'They're going to switch on the Christmas lights in the village tomorrow,' Cameron put in. 'Maggie said so. We wanted to make something for the stalls. Lorna said she'd ask if she and Izzy could take us to look around. They have all sorts of toys on sale. We could spend our pocket money.'

'Whoa…steady on a minute.' Ross threw up his hands as though to ward off the two youngsters. 'This has jumped a bit, hasn't it, from me dropping off a couple of heaters for Izzy? Now I'm being roped in for baking sessions and an outing to the Christmas lights ceremony. I hadn't bargained for any of that.'

Cameron put on his best angelic expression. 'Mum *always* takes us to see the Christmas lights back home,' he said, emphasising his words carefully. 'She says it's *magical* and singing Christmas carols round the tree is the start of all the celebrations.'

'And she can't go this year, so we could go for her and find her a present,' Molly added, sealing the argument. 'It would cheer her up no end to have some presents if she's going to be in hospital at Christmas.'

Ross rolled his eyes heavenwards. 'If I didn't know better I'd say you had this all planned out beforehand. Have you two been making deals with Izzy and Lorna?'

'No.' Molly and Cameron both made wide, innocent eyes, and even Izzy, who *did* know better, would have been fooled—except for Molly's soft-spoken admission. 'But we were at the shop with Maggie, and Izzy's mother said it was a nice idea, and Mr McKinnon said, "That would bring him down from his ivory tower, wouldn't it?" I didn't really understand that bit.' She frowned. 'Perhaps he meant Santa would be there?' She sent her uncle a quizzical look, while his face in turn took on a faintly stunned expression, his head going back a fraction, as though she'd just poked him in the eye.

Molly's gaze was uncertain now, and Izzy groaned inwardly, pulling a face. Turning away so that the children wouldn't see, she said in a soft plea, 'Ross, you don't have to take my father's words at face value. He's not himself lately, with Alice being in hospital and his summer season going badly. He's not approaching anything with a good frame of mind.'

'Oh, I don't know about that.' Ross's mouth made a flat line. 'I think your father's pretty much living up to expectations.' He looked down at Molly and Cameron. 'So, you think Santa might be there, do you?'

Molly nodded. 'He's going to have a grotto at the back of the community hall. That's what Mary said, up at the shop. She said it would be a treat for us to go and see him.'

'Hmm.' He studied his niece and nephew thoughtfully. 'I think I'm beginning to see a conspiracy at work here. You do realise that I might have to work tomorrow evening, don't you? I'm on call, and I may not be able to stay with you, which means Maggie will be in charge.'

'She won't mind if Izzy and Lorna say they'll look after us,' Cameron put in quickly, sensing that his uncle might be weakening.

Ross's mouth twisted at that, but he glanced towards Izzy with slightly raised eyebrows. 'Are you sure about all this? Do you know what you're letting yourselves in for?'

'I'm okay with it,' Izzy said, 'and Lorna's game, too. I'll keep in touch with Maggie, if you like, to let her know what's going on. And as for the baking—well, I could bring the children back to you as soon as we're done. I'm assuming you'll be at home later this afternoon?'

He nodded. 'I'll be showing the builders round the place. There are a few things that need doing—improving the damp course and pointing up the walls. I have to somehow try to turn the place into a home. I think Molly and Cameron are finding it a bit draughty and cold, especially in their bedrooms. They've been used to all their home comforts back in the Lake District. Which led me to thinking about your problems... I thought maybe you would be able to make use of these oil-filled radiators.'

He opened up the back of his car to reveal two mobile heaters stacked in the back. 'I've asked an engineer to come and have a look at your central heating system, but he's planned on coming along on Monday. I don't know if that will be a problem for you.'

'I'll be on duty at the hospital on Monday,' Izzy said, thinking things through. 'It's my on-call day. I'm not sure whether Lorna will be here to show him around.'

'No problem,' Lorna put in. 'It's my day off.' She grinned mischievously. 'There's no chance he'll be single, as well as tall, dark and handsome, I suppose?'

Ross chuckled. 'That depends very much on your viewpoint, I imagine. He seems okay to me, but who am I to judge? As far as I know he isn't accounted for.'

'That's sorted, then. His goose is as good as cooked.' Lorna peered into the car. 'Oh, they look just the business, don't they? And each of them big enough to heat a large room. They'll retain the heat for a while, as well, being oil filled. Great.'

'I'm glad I could help.' Ross lifted out the heaters and started to carry them into the cottage. 'I've arranged for someone else to come and look at the roof, but the fence will take a little longer to put right. The carpenter has a full work-load after all the damage caused by the storm, but he'll come and sort it out as soon as possible.'

'That's okay. At least we know that repairs are in hand.' Izzy showed him where to place the heaters on the floor of the kitchen. 'Thanks for dealing with it so speedily.'

'It's the least I can do.' He made a crooked smile. 'Besides, I wouldn't want to give your father any more ammunition to fire at me. Last I heard he was calling a meeting with the villagers to hatch a protest over the building work on the estate.'

Izzy wasn't sure how to respond to that. Her father had every reason to worry about the effect Ross's plans would have on his own tourist bookings, but as far as she could tell Ross was within his rights to go ahead with the work—unless he had extended the remit of the plans.

He bent to say goodbye to the children. 'Be good, both of you…and if you get the chance save a ginger-bread man for your mother. We could take it over to her tomorrow morning.'

Molly and Cameron whooped with excitement, before going off with Lorna to wash their hands.

Izzy walked with him back to the car. 'I wish you and my father would try to call a truce,' she said. 'Could you not arrange a meeting of your own and try to iron out a few of the problems between you?'

He laid a hand on his chest, as though she had knocked him for six. 'Do you really believe there's any chance that he would agree to it?' He shook his head. 'Living in cloud cuckoo land springs to mind.'

He walked round to the driver's side of the car and pulled open the door. 'I don't blame you for trying, though, Izzy…ever the peacemaker. Only I think you underestimate the extent of the problem.'

He smiled. 'I promise for my part that I'll try to keep things on a civil footing, but I have to bring the estate into the twenty-first century, and that means taking steps that may not be popular with everyone.' Sliding into his seat, he added, 'Will you give me a ring when you're bringing the children back? That way I'll make sure I'm able to greet you at the main door.'

She nodded, watching him as he drove away. Her

thoughts were troubled as she went back to the kitchen, but the children were waiting and she put on a bright smile.

'All right, then,' she said, looking at them. 'What's the first thing we do when we're about to bake?'

'Weigh out the flour?' Molly suggested.

'That's certainly something we need to do, but not the first thing. Good try, but no.'

'Wash our hands?' Cameron said, holding his up for her to see.

'Another good answer, but not quite what I was thinking.' She went over to the cooker. 'We switch on the oven so that it can be heating up while we mix the ingredients. See?' She turned the dial. 'Right, then. Where's Lorna? I thought she was going to help us?'

'I'm here,' Lorna said, coming into the kitchen. 'I'm hungry already, just at the thought of baking. Shall we make some chocolate butterfly cakes, as well?'

An hour or so later they were all flour spattered, and a wonderful aroma of chocolate and ginger filled the kitchen. Molly and Cameron had smears of chocolate around their mouths, and Molly was putting the finishing touches to the icing on the last of the gingerbread men.

'That one's for Mummy,' she said, 'and this one's for Uncle Ross. Do you think he'll like his green icing tie?'

'He'll love it,' Lorna answered. 'He's definitely the best-looking gingerbread man in the bunch.'

A short time later the children went up to the bathroom to clean up, while Izzy and Lorna tidied the kitchen.

'They're desperately hoping that Alice will be well enough to come home in the New Year,' Lorna said. 'Do you think it will happen?'

'I'm not sure,' Izzy said with a frown. 'She's still very weak, but the physiotherapist is coming in every day to work with her, and Greg is keeping an eye on things on the days when he's based at the hospital in Inverness.' She rinsed the baking tray and placed it on the rack on the draining board. 'The one thing she has in her favour is that she's desperate to get back home to be with the children. She's worried about how they're settling. They've been through a lot of upheaval in the last few months.'

Lorna nodded. 'It must make her feel better to know that you're keeping an eye on them. Ross seems to be doing everything within his means, but you're family, too, and they probably need that extra involvement.'

Izzy washed the pastry board, thinking about the time she had spent with her cousin in hospital. 'Alice has asked me to keep track of how they're doing—I would have done it anyway, because I think the world of Molly and Cameron. She knows Ross will do his very best for them, but she's aware of how the villagers feel about the Buchanans, and she doesn't know if any of that will rub off on the children. Once they start to go to school here there might be problems, and added to that Ross is a busy man, with lots of demands on his time and energy. She worries that they might be missing out on love and cuddles.'

'There's not much chance of that,' Lorna said with a smile, drying the mixing bowl with a teatowel. 'Every time they come round you give them a big hug, and from what I hear Alice does the same at every visit.'

Molly and Cameron came into the room, arguing noisily. '*I'm* giving Mummy the chocolate cake with icing on it,' Molly said in an emphatic tone. 'You're giving her the one with the butterfly wings.'

'I want to give her one with icing,' Cameron insisted. 'I said it first.'

'You could both give her one of each *and* a gingerbread man,' Izzy said, cutting in. 'That way she'll have a treat for nearly every day of the week.'

Satisfied, the children accepted that compromise, and some time later Izzy set off with them along the path to Ross's home, taking with her a couple of rugs from the attic that might go well in the children's rooms.

The castle was a grand stone building, with a square turret and long rectangular windows. It was situated towards the end of a long, rocky promontory, almost an island in itself, where the waters of the loch lapped gently against the craggy shoreline.

From some distance away the sea washed into the loch, and depending on the tide part of the land leading to the promontory might be flooded with water. A wide stone bridge spanned this stretch of land between the mainland and the castle, and Izzy paused there for a moment to gaze at Ross's Highland home. It was beautiful, golden in the dying sunlight of the December day, a majestic edifice set against the clear blue of the sky, with a backdrop of wooded hills and distant mountain peaks and the glassy surface of the loch all around.

Ross met her at the main door, as promised, and immediately Molly bombarded him with the delights of her baking session. 'I've made you a gingerbread man,' she said, 'and Cameron's made you a chocolate cake.'

'Just what I wanted,' he said, ushering the children into the large hall and turning to relieve Izzy of the parcels she was carrying. 'Here, let me help,' he said, placing them down on an elegant side-table.

He laid a hand lightly on the small of her back. 'Come in, Izzy. It must be years since you've been up here. Will you stay awhile and have a drink with me? I can offer you tea, coffee, or something stronger… A glass of mulled wine, maybe, or perhaps you'd like to try one of our special fruit wines?'

'Well…I ought to go back and give Lorna a hand with the chores,' she said in a diffident fashion, wanting to back out, but searching for an excuse. It was one thing to watch over the children, or meet up with Ross because of their work commitments, but it was quite another to deliberately fraternise with the enemy.

She hadn't bargained on the intimacy of his touch, though. It undermined all her defences. He was only welcoming her into his home, but his greeting felt very much like a caress. Even now it was doing strange things to her nervous system, so that all her senses had erupted into a feverish flurry of excitement.

'I…um…I just wanted to drop off these wool rugs,' she told him, indicating the parcels. 'My aunt gave them to me when I moved into the cottage, but I've never had occasion to use them since my mother also gave me some. I thought they might come in handy for the children, though. They said the floors were bare in their rooms, and it might be nice for them to have them at the side of their beds. They're very colourful, and they seem to like them, so it's a shame for them to stay up in my attic. Unless you object, that is?'

'I think it's a great idea. It saves me wondering what to put down for them.' He smiled. 'The chores will wait for a while, won't they? I know you've been in to work this morning, and now you've had a busy after-noon, so I'm sure you could do with a break. Let me show you around.' He let his hand fall from her, and with that action her head began to clear a little.

'Shall I take your jacket?' he asked. 'I'll hang it up for you.'

She gave in, curiosity about the house overcoming her reluctance to linger and be lured into his silken trap. 'All right, I'll stay for just a little while.' She shrugged out of her jacket and he went to put it on a hanger in the cloakroom, then fetched the rugs from the table.

'Maggie left a ham and some cheeses out on the table in the kitchen,' he said, 'and we could share some of her fresh-baked bread if you've a mind to. I haven't eaten yet, and I could do with a snack. I expect the children could, too—unless they've filled up on cakes and cookies.'

As he spoke he led the way through the wide oak-panelled hall into the drawing room. Light flooded in here through windows that were almost floor-to-ceiling, casting a gentle late-afternoon glow over everything. Across the room there was an oak beam fireplace, where glowing coals in the grate sparked yellow flames, giving out warmth that filled the room. The furniture was luxurious, with deep-cushioned sofas and armchairs upholstered in light-coloured plush fabrics, and Izzy saw that there was a lovely Sheraton writing table to one side, along with a bookcase made of the same beautifully polished rosewood.

'That sounds tempting,' she said, 'but I think you'll find Molly and Cameron are stuffed to the gills. They tried a little of everything as we went along.'

'You didn't?'

She shook her head. 'Lorna is the one who likes cakes and buns and biscuits. She's lucky. She can eat anything and not put on an ounce of weight.'

He studied her, his gaze shimmering over the clinging lines of her cotton top and smooth denim jeans. 'I don't believe for one minute that *you* have a problem on that score.'

A flush of heat ran along her cheekbones, and to distract him from the subject, she gazed around. 'This is a beautiful room,' she murmured. 'Is it your doing? I don't remember it from when I was here last.'

He nodded. 'I organised the renovation when I was here on one of my brief visits. I aim to improve the whole building—even if I have to do it one room at a time. In fact, I could show you the rooms where the children are sleeping. Maybe you could give me some advice on how to change the decor in there. I was thinking about laying down carpets, but in the meantime the rugs you've brought will be very useful.'

'I could do that,' she said carefully. After all, Alice had asked her to keep an eye on the children, hadn't she? 'I expect it's been difficult for you, figuring out what's best for Molly and Cameron?'

'You're right. It hasn't been easy. Though of course I did have contact with them before the accident. I used to visit my brother and Alice whenever it was possible. But my work took me around and about, so it wasn't possible to see them on a regular basis.'

He looked around. 'The children seem to have disappeared. I expect they've gone to play in their rooms.' Childish voices from a short distance away seemed to confirm that, and he said, 'Shall we take the rugs up there?'

She nodded. 'That might be a good idea.'

'I know Alice worries about how the children are getting on,' he said, 'and I've tried to reassure her. But if you see how things really are, you might be able to set her mind at rest.'

'I'm sure Alice appreciates everything that you're doing for her and for the children,' Izzy said. 'She told me how marvellous you've been, helping ever since the accident.'

'I couldn't stand by and do nothing, could I? Robert was my brother, after all, and Molly and Cameron are his children. As for Alice—I've always looked out for her.'

They went back to the hall and started up the stairs. Izzy said carefully, 'Is that why you came back here— to bring Alice closer to her family? After all, you could have found a hospital nearer to where you were living, couldn't you? Up until now you've never shown any interest in coming back here to stay for any length of time.'

He sent her an oblique glance. 'That was part of it. I knew that she would want to be near to you and your mother, and it was difficult for both of you to visit as often as you would have liked while she was in the Lake District.'

'And the other part?'

He made a brief smile. 'That's a little more complicated. I was always conscious of the need to deal with the estate, and I'd been thinking about moving back here for some time. But I was always busy with my work. I enjoyed what I was doing, and I had no real reason to come back to this place while Jake was looking after things. As far as I was concerned it was being managed well enough with my input from a distance.'

He paused at the top of the stairs, looking around. 'I knew this was what my brother had always wanted.

I offered him the chance to take over, to run the estate, but Robert wouldn't consider it. He saw it as second best. If he couldn't be the true Laird, he didn't want any part of it.'

'I'm sorry. That must have been difficult for you.'

'Maybe a little. It stuck in his throat that I had the inheritance but didn't have any inclination to take it up wholeheartedly. It caused more than a few problems between us, though in the end he and Alice decided that they *would* come back home to Glenmuir. I think they were hoping that they might eventually put things right with your father, and Robert was planning to develop his business interests back here. I'd have been happy for him to live at the castle, but he wouldn't take me up on it.'

She studied him, taking in his tall, proud stance. He wouldn't bend under pressure, nor would he simply do what he felt other people expected of him, but he'd cared deeply for his brother, and surely his actions showed that he felt the same about Alice? He still hadn't properly answered her question, though, had he? Why was he *really* here now, setting up a home for his brother's children? Was it purely for love of Alice? Just how strong were his feelings for her?

Her mind skittered. Maybe deep down she didn't want to know the answer to that. Already she had a leaden feeling in her stomach, as though she was weighed down by the possibility that Alice meant everything to him.

He walked across the wide landing and pushed open a heavy wooden door. 'This is Cameron's room,' he said. 'Perhaps he'd like to have the dark blue rug in here. It would certainly blend in with the decor.'

Cameron was sitting on the wooden floor, playing

with his toy soldiers, lining them up on the battlements of a wooden fort, but he looked up as Izzy and Ross entered the room. 'Is that for me?' he said, breaking off to give a sudden sneeze, and looking pleased as Ross laid the rug down beside him.

Ross nodded, 'Izzy thought you might like it.' He looked closely at the boy. 'Are you warm enough? You sound as though you're coming down with a cold.'

Cameron nodded and sneezed again. 'It's better now that you've put the heater in here.'

'Good.' Ross glanced around. 'I thought Izzy might know how to brighten the room up a bit for you. I'm not exactly sure what you'd want in here.'

'An outer-space duvet,' Cameron said. 'Or a pirate one. And a table where I can do my drawing. That would be good.'

Izzy smiled. 'There's a boy who knows what he wants. Perhaps matching curtains, and a cushion or two with some of the colours picked out from the duvet and the rug would make it cosy?' She looked around the large square room. 'I expect a treasure chest would be just the thing for toys, and an upholstered wooden bench-type seat would fit in with the furnishing throughout the house.'

'I think we have both of those in one of the old servants' rooms,' Ross commented, a thoughtful look coming into his eyes. 'I'm not sure at the moment whether we have a suitable table, but I could find something in the antique shops, I dare say.'

'It doesn't have to be a table,' Izzy murmured. 'What about a small writing desk and a set of book-shelves? I imagine you must have those somewhere in the house?'

His mouth curved. 'You're right—we do. There's a

child-size desk in the study, and we have lots of book-cases around the place.' He sent Cameron a question-ing look. 'How does all that sound to you?'

'Pretty good,' Cameron acknowledged, losing interest and turning back to his toy soldiers. As Izzy and Ross left the room he was imitating the sound of gunfire, and several of the 'enemy' were being knocked to the ground.

'That's Cameron sorted. One more to go,' Ross murmured as they headed towards Molly's room next door. 'I wonder if she'll be as easy to please?'

'Pink,' Molly said a moment later, when Ross asked how she'd like her room to be decorated. 'Lots of pink.' She had been playing with the dolls in her dolls' house, but for now she seemed content to put them to one side.

'Ahh.' Ross tried to disguise a wince, and Izzy smiled.

'We can do pink, can't we?' she said, giving his ankle a nudge with her foot.

'Um…yes. I'm sure we'll be able to come up with something along those lines.' He looked to Izzy for support, his dark brows lifting a fraction, as though to say, *You're not serious?*

'Pink is good,' Izzy said, looking around. 'I can imagine dusky pink seating, pale rosewood furniture, and a pretty screen in the corner decorated with delicate flowers and leaves. And what about a touch of dove-grey in the curtains and bedspread? That would go really well with the rug, wouldn't it?'

Molly nodded vigorously. 'And that lovely pink-covered box seat from the big bedroom would be perfect in here.' She frowned. 'But Maggie said it was being used for blankets.'

'You mean the ottoman?' Ross queried. When Molly looked confused, he said, 'The big box at the end of the bed? In the room across the hall?'

'Yes, that's the one. It has little wooden arms either side and I love it.' Molly's eyes widened in expectation. 'Could I have it for my toys, and for a seat? The blankets could go somewhere else, couldn't they? *Please?*'

'I don't see any reason why not.' He gazed down at her. 'Anything else?'

She shook her head so that her curls quivered. 'No, thank you. I'm going to play now, if that's all right?'

Ross reached down and tousled her silky hair. 'That's fine, poppet. I'll be downstairs with Izzy if you need me.'

He led the way along the landing and down the stairs. 'Shall we go through to the kitchen?' he suggested.

'Okay.' She followed as he led the way. 'Just for a few minutes, though. As I said, I shouldn't stay too long.' It would be all too easy to get carried away, wandering through the rooms of this fascinating building. It was far different from what she remembered, and that must be on account of Ross's renovations over the years. For all that he had asked for her help, he seemed already to have a sure touch when it came to creating a luxurious, yet comfortable home.

'Of course—just as you like. I imagine you've had quite enough for one day and could do with some relaxation.' Sending her a fleeting glance, he asked, 'How is it that you came to be working this morning, anyway? I thought you had the weekends off?'

'I do, mostly. This is my weekend on call with the Mountain Rescue team, though. We had to go and help a woman who slipped and fell while she was out walking. She took a tumble down a slope and landed on rocky ground. I think she'll be all right, but she broke her leg and had to be stretchered back to the ambulance. It was lucky for her that we found her reasonably quickly. I gave her pain medication and managed to stem the bleeding before we took her back to our A&E unit.' Her mouth made a downward curve. 'I don't think she's having a very good end to this year, but maybe she'll be on the mend by the time the new one comes in.'

'Let's hope so. It's interesting that you go out with the team,' he said. 'I had a call from the Mountain Rescue chief the other day, asking if I'd like to join them. He remembered that I had some experience of rescue work. I said I'd think about it, depending on how much time I would have to put in and whether I could make arrangements for Molly and Cameron.'

By now they had reached the kitchen, and the room came as another surprise to Izzy. This, too, had been completely refurbished, with magnificent oak-fronted cabinets and deep shelving units bordered with decorative carving. As a centrepiece there was the huge range cooker that she remembered from long ago. To one side of the room were wine racks, filled with an assortment of bottles in colours ranging through green, red and brown to clear glass.

'I don't think I've seen *that* label before,' she murmured, looking more closely at the bottles. The designs were exotic, with beautiful Old English script overlaid on a watermark background of a castle in the glen, hinting at the richness of the wine within.

'They're our own label,' he told her. 'From what I'm fancifully calling the Glenmuir Winery. You should sit down at the table and try a glass or two.' He waved a hand towards the chair by an oak table to the side of the room. 'What do you fancy? We've a full-bodied elderberry, sweet and bursting with flavour, guaranteed to make you long for more, or there's oak leaf wine— dry, with a champagne flavour. We add raisins to that, and lemon juice to help bring it along. Maggie's favourite is the raspberry and bramble wine…light and fruity.'

She sent him a startled look. 'You're serious? Is this a new venture?'

He nodded. 'When I came over the other year I saw how many wild fruits we had growing on the estate and suggested that we might have a go at fermenting a batch. They turned out pretty well, so I'm looking into starting up a wine-making business. After all, we have acres of land here, just asking to be planted.'

He drew a bottle from the rack, placed it on the table, and then reached for a couple of wineglasses from an overhead cupboard. 'Of course I'm not sure how people around here will respond to it. I doubt I'll be able to rely on them as customers. I'm facing a bit of resistance in trying to win them over to my side, one way or another. Even Maggie has a fairly sceptical view of my motives, but I think she feels she needs to look out for the children."

He was right about the locals. The talk in the village was all about the new Laird—an incomer who didn't belong. 'Maybe that's because you've been away for so long,' she murmured. 'After all, you weren't even educated here. Your father sent you away to school.'

'That's true. I dare say that's helped to provoke the feeling among the community that I'm an outsider.' He shrugged. 'Whatever the reason, I'm back now, and I have to do what I can to win them round.'

He smiled. 'Try this one,' he said, uncorking a bottle. 'See what you think. If you aren't completely bowled over, I'm an impostor from the Lakes.'

She sent him a fleeting glance. Had he read her mind? She shook the thought away. It was common knowledge that he would have to prove himself around here. Why was she worrying about the outcome?

He poured the rich ruby liquid into a glass and handed it to her. She sipped slowly, savouring the wine on her tongue before swallowing. A sweet, warm sensation enveloped her and she took another sip. She blinked, and then looked up at him.

'I think you must be the genuine article,' she murmured. 'This is delicious.'

'I'm glad you like it.' He poured more wine into the glass. 'Have some cheese with it, and crackers.' He laid out a selection of food and pushed a plate towards her, coming to join her at the table, taking a seat opposite.

'I don't know how you manage to pull it all in,' she said. 'You seem to have a lot of ideas and various projects on the go, and yet you're without an estate manager. How are you going to keep everything going?'

'Now, there you have me,' he said. 'Let's just say my plans are fairly fluid at the moment. A lot will depend on Alice and the children and how much support they need.'

She drank her wine, and tasted the cheese and crackers, and found after a while that she was oddly replete. A warm and comfortable feeling was enveloping her, with a general light-headed sensation that made her believe all was well with the world.

Ross excused himself to go and check on the

children, but he was back just a short time later. 'Molly's still playing with her dolls' house, and Cameron's just launched a major offensive with his toy soldiers, so I think they'll be occupied for a while. Would you like to come and look at the grounds out back? I've been tidying up the kitchen garden whenever I've had the chance, and I've been thinking about a tree-planting scheme to break up the winds that blow across the north pasture in wintertime.'

She stood up and went with him to the kitchen door. 'Do the children know where we'll be?' she asked.

He nodded. 'I told them we might be looking out over the loch. They know to ring the bell that clangs outside if they have a problem of any kind.'

'That's a good idea.' She went with him to fetch her soft cord jacket from the cloakroom, shrugging into it as she walked out with him.

The cool air outside came as something of a surprise as she left the warmth of the kitchen behind. Her head swam a little with the after-effects of the wine, and Ross must have noticed because he put an arm around her, steadying her as he led her along the footpath towards the kitchen garden.

'I knew you'd appreciate the wine,' he said with a smile. 'It has quite a kick if you're not used to it.'

'You must have known that when you kept filling up my glass,' she accused. 'It's just as well that my on-call time finished an hour or so back, isn't it? At least I don't have to think about it again until morning.' She glanced at him, wondering how it was that the Buchanans were blessed with such strong features—the square jaw, the beautiful grey-blue eyes that looked at you and made you feel you were the only person that mattered in the whole world.

She tried to shake off that heady sensation. It was all in her mind, wasn't it? 'It looks as though you grow most of your own fruit and vegetables, here,' she murmured, gazing at long rows of planting.

'Well, we have a team of gardeners,' he said. 'It helps that they're all very good at what they do.'

They walked away from the kitchen gardens and around the side of the castle to a raised terrace, bordered by stone pediments and wrought iron balustrades, where they stood and looked out over the loch. The view was stunning. 'This is my favourite place,' Ross said softly.

'I can see why.' She gazed out at the gently rippling water, letting her glance move over green-clad hills and distant mountains shrouded in mist. 'It's so peaceful here. You can look out there and forget your troubles. It's so serene. I don't know how you can have stayed away.'

'You're right,' he said, wrapping his arm around her and drawing her close against the faint breeze. 'I often stand here and think perhaps things could have been different. It appears to be timeless here. I could have simply whiled away my days, looking out over the water and letting my thoughts drift.'

His hand stroked her arm and she laid her head on his shoulder, snuggling into the warmth of his body. Every part of her was content, loving this moment of deep quiet and calm. It seemed the most natural thing in the world to be standing here with him.

Except that it wasn't, of course. A cool wind blew across the loch, stirring the soft tendrils of her hair, and she looked up at him, blinking to bring her gaze back into sharp focus.

This was Ross Buchanan who was holding her close,

shielding her from the cold. The same Ross Buchanan who had encouraged Alice to spend time in the castle and forget that her family was his sworn enemy. What was she thinking of, letting him ply her with wine and lead her out here to this beautiful place, a spot just begging for sweethearts to pledge eternal love? This was madness, being here with him.

She eased herself away from him, her head clearing rapidly in the cool breeze. 'I should go,' she said.

His glance moved over her. 'Are you sure?'

She nodded, not trusting herself to speak.

'All right. I'll gather up the children and drive you back to the cottage.'

He didn't seem at all put out by her need to leave. Had she imagined the intimacy of his warm embrace, the way he had held her so tenderly? He'd just been keeping her warm, steadying her because the drink had gone to her head, hadn't he? Anything else was pure supposition on her part.

CHAPTER FIVE

'BYE. Thanks for the lift home.' Izzy raised a hand, waving as Ross turned the car on the drive and headed back along the road.

She walked inside the cottage, her mind busy turning over the events of the last couple of hours. At least she was able to think more clearly now that the mist in her head had begun to dissolve. That fruit wine was sheer sin masquerading under a veil of innocence.

'Did I just see Ross Buchanan drop you off outside?' Her father confronted her as she stepped into the kitchen.

She sent him a startled look. 'Oh, hello. I didn't realise that you were here. Is your car at the front of the house?' Perhaps her faculties weren't as fully restored as she had hoped. 'I didn't see it out there.'

'That's because your mother dropped me off. She's gone over to the village shop, but she should be back soon. We just came by to bring you and Lorna a hotpot that she made. You know how she worries that you might not be feeding yourself properly.'

Across the other side of the kitchen, Lorna signalled that she had put the hotpot in the fridge. 'I'm going upstairs to get ready for nightshift at the hospital,' she said. 'I'll leave you two to chat for a while.'

Izzy nodded acknowledgement, then smiled at her father. 'I love Mum's hotpots. I'm sorry that I wasn't here when you arrived. Have you been here long?'

'Only about five minutes. Lorna said you'd nipped out for a while, but we weren't planning on stopping. We're on our way to go and visit your gran—but I just wanted to make sure that your roof wasn't leaking. I thought I'd take a look to see if my temporary patch was holding up.'

'Thanks for checking. It seems to be working all right… At least, we haven't had any damp patches on the ceiling so far. I think the roofer will be coming along to fix it in a day or so. Ross said he'd asked him to make it a priority.'

Her father's expression tightened. 'I notice that you didn't answer my question about him dropping you off. That was Ross I saw leaving, wasn't it? I went to look out of the window to see if it was you or your mother returning, and there was his fuel-guzzling monster outside.'

'He says it's the best vehicle to have on these roads in the winter. He has to drive over to Inverness quite regularly, so it's best for him to have a car that will be reliable and safe in snow and ice.'

Her father made a non-committal mumble at that, and she sent him a brief, considering look. 'Yes, I've been over to the castle and he brought me back.'

'So you've gone the way of Alice, have you? Spending your time up there? I thought you would have had more sense.'

'I took the children back to him,' she said, a wave of exasperation taking hold of her. 'They spent the afternoon with us, and I promised I would return them safely.' She gave a soft sigh. 'It's pointless to imagine that our paths will never cross. He's a doctor, and I have to work with him from time to time. We're not living in the Dark Ages, after all. It's something that you just have to get used to.'

'I'll never get used to it.' His voice was sharp. 'I don't see why he had to bring the children here at all. They could have stayed with Alice's sister.' He sent her a peevish glance. 'What does he know about bringing up youngsters, anyway?'

'Not very much, probably, which is why Alice is troubled.' She studied him. 'Look, I don't want to argue with you. I know how you feel. But I promised Alice I would look out for the children, and I aim to keep my promise—even if it means that I might rub shoulders with Ross from time to time. I don't see that it can do any harm, and he might not be as bad as you think.'

His eyes narrowed on her. 'I can see he's been working on you already. You'd do well to remember that the Buchanans never do anything by chance. There's always an ulterior motive lurking somewhere in the background. Like this business of the log cabin and the lodges he's building. It was all supposed to have been laid out crisp and clear, what he was doing and how far the building would extend, but now he's changing the format. I drove along the coastal road, where one of the lodges is under construction. It seemed to me that the building was wider than shown in the original drawings.'

'Will that matter?'

'Not necessarily, in itself, but what else might he decide to change? I don't trust him. Next thing he'll be adding garage blocks and new access roads, bringing more traffic along our way.'

'I'm sorry you feel like that about it.' Izzy's gaze was

troubled. 'I hate to see you angry and upset. I understand how you feel, but surely you're reading too much into it. Perhaps we should all try to move on and put the past behind us?'

'You wouldn't feel that way if your livelihood depended on the goodwill of your neighbours. I had trouble with the old Laird, his father, and his constant attempts to stake a claim on my land with his tree planting and his new stone walls. Every now and again he would set up dams on the river to ruin the salmon fishing. He said it wasn't deliberate, but I never believed him.'

He scowled. 'His son hasn't done anything to remedy the problems along the course of the river in so much as they affect my being able to scratch a living, and now he's hatching a scheme to plant woodland that will block access to my cabins. We've always had a right of way to the old mill race, and now he thinks he can abandon it because he wants to set up a timber business. Without that footpath people will have to go the long way round to get to the holiday homes. He has a lot to answer for.' He glowered at her. 'It grieves me that my own daughter's getting involved with him.'

Izzy's mother arrived back from the shop in time to witness the tension between father and daughter. 'I knew it,' she said. 'As soon as I saw Ross's car heading up the hill away from here I knew I shouldn't have left you two together, even for five minutes.'

She gave Izzy a hug. 'Lorna put my hotpot in the fridge. Make sure you heat it through thoroughly…and I bought you a jar of coffee from Mary's shop. I noticed you were running short.'

'Thanks, Mum, you're an angel.'

'We'd best be going,' her father said, his tone abrupt. 'Your gran will be expecting us.'

Her mother went to the door. 'Perhaps we'll see you at the Christmas lights ceremony tomorrow evening?' she said. 'I'm running one of the stalls at a community centre…homemade crafts and pots of jam.'

Izzy embraced her parents and watched them drive away. It was upsetting to argue with her father. Would he ever come to see Ross Buchanan simply as a neighbour? Somehow she doubted it.

She tried not to think about the troublesome situation, and instead spent time getting on with various chores. Putting away freshly ironed laundry helped to lighten her mood.

The next day in the afternoon she was clearing away brambles from the garden when the phone rang. She hurried to answer it.

'The Mountain Rescue team has been called out.' Finn, a man in his late thirties who worked six days a week as the village postman, was also a member of the Mountain Rescue group, and now he said, 'We've had reports of a woman who has been injured on a crag by Beinn Dearg. Her companion used her mobile phone to call for help. She said she fell, and can't move without a lot of pain, so we have to get to her as soon as possible. I've already checked, and there's no way we'll be able to get a helicopter out to her, so it means we're in for a bit of a climb.'

'I'll get ready,' Izzy said.

'Good. I'll come and pick you up in five minutes.'

Finn was as good as his word, and within a very short time the whole team had assembled. 'We'll drive as close as we can to the hills before we need to start the climb,' Finn told them.

They started their trek from a forested area, heading for higher ground, keeping a tumbling stream to the left and below them. Izzy was startled to see that Ross had joined them somewhere along the route. 'You decided to give it a try, then?' she said.

'I did. I wanted to come out and see if it was something I'd like to do on a regular basis.' He looked out over the distant mountains. 'It's been quite a while since I did any climbing or hill walking. It's good to be able to help people, of course, and then there's always the aspect of keeping fit and enjoying the mountain trek.'

'What have you done with Molly and Cameron?'

'I left them with the local GP. They made friends with his children last week when I went over there to discuss a patient with him. In fact, he's going to be taking over the aftercare of the man who was injured by the waterfall.'

He walked beside her, and soon she was struggling to keep up with his long, rangy stride. Izzy studied him. 'You mean, the man with the pulmonary embolism? You know how he's doing, then?'

Ross nodded. 'His shoulder's still a bit sore, but they fixed the dislocation at the hospital and his ankle's in plaster. His breathing is much better, and he seems to be making a reasonably good recovery from his surgery, but of course his GP will have to keep an eye on him to make sure he doesn't suffer any more blood clots.'

'Yes, he will, but I'm glad that he's doing well over all.'

At one point they had to cross a stream, using flat rocks as stepping-stones, and Izzy hesitated for a moment, attempting to keep her balance. As she wavered, Ross placed a hand under her arm to steady her.

'Thanks,' she said, glancing up at him, her mouth making a rueful shape. 'I was just taking my time, that's all. The last thing I want is to spend the next few hours soaked to the skin.' She didn't want to notice his strength, or how capable he was, and how sure of foot he appeared to be, but it was true all the same. And as the heat from his hand at her elbow penetrated through the material of her jacket, it was more than enough to warm her through and through.

His eyes crinkled with amusement. 'No wine to blur your senses today,' he said. 'That's a shame. I quite liked it when you were soft and dreamy and wrapped up in my arms.'

They reached the other side of the stream and she threw him a quick glance. 'You were out of line yesterday,' she told him. He still was, if he thought he could sweet-talk her into getting close to him. She was more than wary on that score. 'You didn't tell me that your home brew packed such a punch. I thought—Fruit wine, lovely, no worries. If you do get a licence to sell your produce, at least you'll have to state the alcoholic content and people will know exactly what they're in for.'

He grinned. 'To be fair, I didn't realise it would hit you quite so hard. You probably hadn't eaten enough to soak it up.'

'Yes, well, I won't make that mistake again in a hurry.'

'That's a shame,' he said, affecting a downturned mouth. 'I couldn't help thinking how great it was to see you looking so relaxed, and you were definitely happy to snuggle up and keep warm.'

She shot him a warning glance, and he laughed.

It took more than an hour of climbing over boulder slopes before they reached the point where the woman, who looked to be in her forties, was lying injured. She was resting on a narrow plateau at the foot of a ridge, and was in a bad way.

'Thank heaven you're here.' The woman's companion looked wretched. 'Sarah fell onto her side and hit the rock. I've been trying to keep her warm, but she's in an awful lot of pain.' She frowned. 'She's very shaky, and she seems to be not quite with me some of the time.'

'We'll take care of her,' Finn said. 'Come over and sit with the rest of our team and we'll give you a hot drink. You look as though you've had a pretty bad experience yourself. The doctors will look after your friend.'

Izzy knelt down beside the woman. 'Hello, there. Sarah, is it?'

Sarah struggled to focus, but then she slowly, almost imperceptibly nodded.

Izzy said quietly, 'I'm Dr McKinnon, and here with me is Dr Buchanan. We'll have a look at you and try to make you more comfortable, and then the Mountain Rescue team will take you back down the slopes and on to hospital as quickly as possible. Can you tell me whereabouts you're hurting?'

Sarah vaguely indicated the region of her hip. Her face was pale, and etched with pain, and when Izzy carefully examined her she could see that on her injured side the leg was shorter than the other one, with the toes pointing out.

She glanced at Ross. 'I think she has a pelvic fracture,' she said softly.

He nodded. 'I agree with you.' He checked the woman's pulse and respiration as Izzy began to open up her medical bag. 'Her heart-rate is very fast, and so is her breathing,' he said in a low voice. 'I suspect she's going into shock because of internal bleeding.'

That was bad news. Untreated shock meant that the patient's condition could deteriorate very rapidly. 'Okay. We'll give her oxygen and put in an intravenous line so that we can give her fluids to replace the blood loss.' She spoke gently to her patient. 'Sarah, I believe you have a broken bone in your pelvis. I'm going to give you an injection for the pain. It should make you feel much more comfortable.'

As soon as they had completed those procedures, and Sarah's pain had retreated, Izzy worked with Ross to immobilise the injury by means of a splint. He was calm and efficient, capable in everything he did, and above all he was caring and considerate towards the woman.

Izzy turned to the other members of the rescue team. 'We need to lift her onto the stretcher,' she said, 'keeping her as still as possible.'

'No problem,' Finn said. 'Between us we can do that.'

They all worked together to transfer Sarah to the stretcher, covering her with a blanket and fastening the straps securely to prevent her from slipping and coming to any more harm. After that it was a question of carrying her back down the slope.

'I've called the emergency services and asked them to have an ambulance waiting for us,' Izzy said.

Two members of the team came forward to take hold of the stretcher, while Finn stayed with the woman's friend, keeping her company as they started back down the slope. Izzy took a moment to gaze around, looking down across the valley to the distant loch. Mist was rolling in over the mountains and the smooth silver surface of the water, signifying the close of the afternoon and a cooling temperature.

'I was really glad of your help back there,' she told Ross. 'It meant that we could treat her much more quickly and get her on her way. Time is the enemy here, isn't it?'

'It is when it's a bad injury like that one. The sooner we get her to hospital the better.'

They moved as swiftly as possible, all of them anxious to reach safe ground before nightfall. Other members of the team took over the stretcher-bearing, to give the first two a rest. Eventually they reached the forest once more, and Izzy paused to check on the status of her patient. 'It's all right, we can keep moving,' she told the rest of the team. 'She seems to be holding up well enough.'

When they finally reached the place where they had parked the rescue team's van, Izzy watched over the transfer of her patient to the ambulance and helped Sarah's friend to settle in beside her while Ross went to speak to the paramedics.

Satisfied that Sarah was comfortable, Izzy climbed down from the vehicle. Finn came to meet her. 'A job well done, I think. We've a good group of people here, and with you and Ross on call the people around here can rest easy.'

'Do you think he'll decide to join the Mountain Rescue team?' she asked. 'I gather this was something of a trial run for him.'

'I hope he will. I remember some years ago he used to do all sorts of outdoor activities—hill-walking, climbing, abseiling, to name just a few. Of course then he went off to do his medical training, and there was all that business with Alice.' Finn spoke in a low voice. 'It was a bad time all round when his brother stole her away from him. There was a breakdown of trust, if you like…not that they had ever been one hundred percent on brotherly love. Robert loved the estate, but Ross was the elder brother, and Robert tended to brood. I imagine that's why he left in the end. Though it was a bad day when he took Alice with him.'

Izzy mulled that over. How must Ross have felt when his brother betrayed his trust? Things had always been difficult between them, but that must have hurt badly. Had they still been arguing years later, as her mother had said, when the accident happened? And did that mean that Ross would now be wondering if he might get another chance with Alice? Was that the true reason he had come home? Did he want to be close to Alice?

A bleak wave of despondency washed over her—a feeling she couldn't explain, even to herself. She loved Alice as a sister, but her feelings for Ross went far deeper than that and were more complex, fraught with problems and complications.

She pushed those thoughts aside as Ross came to join them after he'd finished speaking with the paramedics. Within moments the ambulance had set off on its journey to Inverness.

'I hope she'll be all right,' Izzy said. 'We moved as quickly as we could, but these situations are difficult. The outcome isn't always what you would hope for.'

'Her age might work in her favour,' Ross said. 'She was fit and healthy before this, so we just have to keep our fingers crossed that all will go well for her. At least they're on alert at the hospital.'

Finn nodded. 'We can be on our way home now, anyway. Shall I be taking you back with me, Izzy?'

'It's out of your way, isn't it, Finn?' Ross said. 'I can take Izzy home.' He shot her a quick look. 'If that's all right with you? I have to pick up the children from Tom Slater's house on the way.'

'That's fine.' They started to walk towards the cars. 'I imagine we'll all be meeting up at the Christmas lights ceremony fairly soon, anyway. Although my offer still stands… I can take the children with me, if you would sooner opt out?'

Ross shook his head. 'I don't think that's an option—even though a majority of the villagers might prefer it if I stay away.'

Finn acknowledged that with a rueful smile. 'I'll see you both later,' he said. 'Thanks for your help today.'

Izzy was still thinking about Ross's comment. It was sad that people couldn't see beyond ancient feuds. She said goodbye to Finn and the other members of the group, and then went to stand by Ross's car.

'I don't imagine for one minute that Molly and Cameron will hear of me staying at home,' Ross said as he started the engine. 'They're hoping that I'll buy all sorts of things…Christmas decorations, for a start. Apparently those I dragged down from the attic are way too ordinary, and something far more spectacular is called for—or at least that's what they told Alice this morning.'

'Of course—you went to see her, didn't you? How is she?' Oddly, Izzy felt warmth seep all around her as she settled more comfortably in her seat. A puzzled look came over her face, and she caught Ross's quick glance.

His mouth curved. 'The seats are heated,' he said. 'It was cold up there on Beinn Dearg, so I thought you might appreciate the warmth.'

She nodded. 'Oh, I do. Just as I appreciated the hot coffee that Finn offered me. They're very well prepared for these trips, aren't they?'

'True.' He concentrated on the road as he came to a junction, and then he said lightly, 'I thought Alice was looking a little better today. It always cheers her up to see the children, and they seem to encourage her to keep on with the physiotherapy. She's beginning to walk around with help from the physios, and that's a good sign.'

'Yes, it is.' Izzy was thoughtful for a while after that. It wasn't lost on her that Alice's cheeks always burned a little brighter whenever Ross was around. He had helped her through so much these last few months, and now he was taking care of her children. That was bound to make her appreciative of him.

Ross dropped her off at the cottage a short time later, after the children had bombarded her with talk of their exploits at the GP's house. They were now very friendly with the doctor's children, it seemed, and they were looking forward to meeting up with them later on at the lights ceremony.

Izzy hurried to get ready for the evening ahead. 'I'm off now,' Lorna told her. 'But I'll see you later in the community hall.'

Izzy grabbed a bite to eat, and then went to change into a clean pair of jeans and a warm top. She ran a brush through her long hair, and added a touch of lipstick to her mouth.

A knock at the door startled her, but then she heard childish voices, and when she went to find out who was there she saw Ross with Molly and Cameron.

'We came to give you a lift,' he said. 'I wondered if you might need a bit of cosseting after today's efforts.'

'What a wonderful thought…though you worked just as hard as I did. That was some trek, there and back, wasn't it?' She smiled at the gathering on her doorstep, noting how Molly and Cameron were turning towards the car. 'I can see you're all eager to be off, so I'll fetch my bag and we're all set.'

When she came back to them, Ross slid an arm around her waist, leading her out to his vehicle and gently assisting her into the passenger seat. She tried not to read anything into that. He was just being himself. He would have done the same for Lorna or anyone else who happened to be female, probably. What was it Lorna had said? He had loads of charisma and easy charm, and without even trying he knew just how to set a woman's heart racing.

'Hop in, you two,' he said to the children. 'Buckle up.'

In the village, a crowd had congregated around the huge tree on the common, and after the local dignitary had made his speech and led the countdown for the lights to be switched on they all sang carols, their breath misting on the cold air.

Perhaps that cold had seeped into Cameron, because he started to cough. Izzy drew him close to her, wrapping an arm around him and keeping him warm. 'Are you all right?' she asked him quietly.

He nodded. 'Can we go round the fair rides, now?' he asked. 'I want to drive the train engine.'

'And I want to go on the horses that go up and down,' Molly said. She was tugging at Ross's trousers, pulling him in the direction of the small amusements section, where roundabouts and candyfloss stalls had been set out in a small side road by the tree-clad embankment.

'Okay, okay—I'm coming.' He glanced at Izzy, taking her by the hand, and they both followed the children, who were running off in the direction of the rides.

'Why is it that children are never still?' Ross said some half an hour later, as they came out of the fish and chip shop and walked back towards the community hall, biting into hot chips from overflowing cones.

Izzy fanned her mouth to take away the heat of the potato. 'Because there's always something new to be explored,' she said. 'I expect you were just the same when you were that age.'

He laughed. 'I suppose I was.' They stood and finished off their salt-and-vinegar-slathered chips at the side of a building, basking in the golden pool of light from the nearby shop.

Cameron handed Izzy his empty carton. 'I've finished,' he said. 'Can we go into the community hall now?'

'All right.' Izzy dropped all the cartons into a wastebin and wiped her hands on a tissue.

They walked into the crowded hall, and Ross took Molly to find Christmas decorations while Izzy went to see how her mother was getting on with the crafts stall.

'Everything looks lovely,' Izzy told her. 'I don't suppose you'll be left with much at the end of the evening.'

'Good. It's all for the children's charity,' her mother said. 'I want everything to go.'

'I like those boxes,' Cameron said, pointing to a small trinket box decorated with quilled scrolls and flower motifs. 'Mum would love one of those for her Christmas present.' He counted out coins from his pocket and handed them over to Izzy's mother, waiting patiently while she wrapped it up.

'I'm sure she'll be over the moon with it,' Izzy's mother said. 'It's very pretty, isn't it?'

Cameron nodded, caught out by another bout of coughing. Izzy took his purchase and watched him carefully. 'I think you might be starting a cold,' she said. She felt his forehead with the back of her hand. 'You've a bit of a temperature, too. Maybe we ought to get you home soon.'

'I don't want to go home yet.' He coughed again.

'I can't think why that boy's out and about, with a cough like that,' Izzy's father said, coming over to them from a nearby stall. 'What's Ross thinking of, bringing him here? Those children could just as easily have stayed with their aunt down in the Lake District, where they had their friends and went to school.'

Izzy pressed her lips together, biting back a reply as she saw Ross coming towards them. From his taut expression, it was clear he had heard what her father had said, and her heart sank with the knowledge that those few curt words might bring a fraught end to what had been a lovely evening.

'Are you all right, Cameron?' Ross asked.

The boy nodded. 'I want to look at the toy stall,' he said.

'Okay. Take Molly with you. I'll be there in a minute.' Ross watched the children go, and then turned to acknowledge Izzy's mother. 'You have some beautiful items here, Morag,' he said. 'I'll take one of the flower pictures for Alice. I know she likes those.' He handed over the money and looked towards Izzy's father. 'Cameron will be fine,' he said. 'He has a cold, that's all. He's a sturdy boy.'

'Let's hope so.' Her father's gaze narrowed on him. 'I still think it's strange, uprooting them from where they were happy.'

Ross looked at him steadily. 'This is their heritage,' he said. 'They have every right to be here and know the place where their father was born. I see no reason to apologise for that.'

He accepted the package from Izzy's mother and said, 'Excuse me. I must go and find the children.'

Izzy's gaze followed him, her heart squeezing a little. Had he really brought them here to know the ancient heritage that went through generation after generation? He was a proud man, steadfast in his beliefs, and she respected him for that—just as she understood why her father responded to him in his edgy, confrontational manner. She loved her father, and it saddened her to see them at loggerheads like this. All Ross had to do was unbend a little and try to meet him half way. Why could he not do that?

CHAPTER SIX

'HAVE you heard the latest?' Lorna broke the crust of her steak pie with the side of her fork and speared the tender meat.

'No, but I'm sure you're about to tell me.' Izzy tasted the crunchy roast potato on her plate, and then followed it up with a forkful of carrots. It was early evening and they were sitting in the lounge bar of the Shore Inn, close by the large fireplace where hot coals burned in the grate.

'Ross has brought a film crew to the castle,' Lorna said. 'They're all talking about it at the bar. Greg was just telling me he was held up on the road into the village the other day because of their truck with all the equipment. He wasn't best pleased. He said it made him late for work.'

'A film crew?' Izzy echoed. 'What kind of film are they making? Do we know?'

Lorna shrugged. 'I've no idea—but something swashbuckling, I bet. Apparently there was a horsebox in the line of traffic that kept Greg waiting, so I expect there'll be scenes of riders dashing across the bridge up to the castle. Sounds exciting, doesn't it?'

'It certainly does.' Izzy's eyes sparkled. 'This is the

first time we've had anything like that happening around here. I wonder what the rest of the villagers will think about it?'

'The landlord's hoping they'll be here for quite a while,' Lorna said, waving her fork lightly in the air before scooping up a mouthful of mashed potato. 'He's looking forward to having more customers, and Mary at the shop is apparently checking her stock for things they might want—like souvenirs to take home, post-cards and so on.'

Greg came to join them at their table. 'They're all full of it back there,' he said, sitting down and taking a long swig from his glass. 'I'd say it's about half and half, those in favour and those against.' He put the glass down. 'I suppose the people who keep the hotel are quite pleased, too. With all those film folk needing a place to stay, trade will be looking up.'

'I heard some of the others say that it's an odd time to be filming,' Lorna commented, 'with the threat of snow in the air. But I suppose if they're filming inside the castle that won't really matter. They could do all the outside shots first. That's the thing with filming, isn't it—you do things out of sequence?'

'I suppose that's true,' Greg answered, staring into the fire. 'Not that I get much chance to watch films these days, let alone see them being made. After working at the A&E unit all day, and travelling to Inverness two or three times a week, I'm too shattered to take much notice of anything else going on.'

He sent a glance in Izzy's direction. 'Your Alice is looking much better of late, by the way. Apparently the children have an Advent calendar to help them to count down to Christmas, but they seem to think it's also like counting off the days until she'll come home. Ross has had to explain to them that it's a bit more complicated than that.'

Izzy smiled at him. 'It's comforting to know that you see Alice on a regular basis. I've been trying to get over there as often as I can, but it isn't always easy with work getting in the way. Mostly I've been going over of an evening.'

A strange silence fell in the usually noisy lounge of the inn, and a faint breeze wafted into the room as someone opened the outer door. Izzy looked around to see why the chatter had suddenly come to a stop, and saw Ross's tall figure in the doorway.

He looked around and nodded to the various people sitting at tables or standing by the bar. The landlord gave him a cheery welcome, but Izzy could see that others were hesitant.

'What will you have?' the landlord said.

'A half of lager and a ploughman's, please.'

'Coming up. Are you on your way home, or are you planning on staying a while?' He started to pour out the lager, and then pushed a platter of baguette, cheese and salad towards Ross. 'We're all keen to know what's going on up at the castle with all your visitors. Is Maggie catering for them all? I'm not sure how that would go down with her.'

Ross shook his head. 'Maggie has enough to do already. When she's not seeing to the meals and doing the housework she's looking after Molly and Cameron for me. The people at the hotel are sending out a selection of hot food for the film crew by van every morning, but I dare say you could get in on the act if you wanted. There's bound to be someone who wants something other than what's provided.'

'I might look into that. So, they're all staying at the

hotel, are they? No hope of any leading ladies being entertained up at the castle after hours, then?' the landlord teased.

'Oh, I wouldn't go as far as to say that,' Ross said with a smile. 'They've only been here for a couple of days, but I'm getting quite used to having them around.'

'It's all right for some.' A disgruntled male voice sounded across the room. 'Some people were born with the proverbial silver spoon in the mouth.'

'Maybe it's lucky you weren't, then,' Ross came back, quick as a flash. 'With a mouth like that you might easily have choked.' A faint hum of laughter went around the room.

'With all this money rolling in from the filming, you'll be able to put the rents down hereabouts, then?' someone else said. Izzy recognised a man who worked as a carpet fitter in the nearby town.

'I seem to remember a hefty bill for the new carpets I just had laid down at the castle. Will you be charging everyone less for your services in the future?' Ross raised a dark brow. 'When that day comes, I might consider it.'

The man made a face, and after that the general conversation resumed. Ross looked around and came over to Izzy's table.

'Hello, there,' he said. 'Might I join you?'

'Of course.' Izzy waved a hand towards the empty seat next to Greg. She and Lorna had both finished eating, and they pushed their plates to one side. 'We were just talking about the film crew descending on the village. How did that come about?'

'They approached me some time ago and I agreed that they could do a shoot. I decided the fee would come in handy for the tree-planting. It's only now that they've managed to fix their schedule.'

'Are we talking documentary or entertainment?' Greg asked. 'And how about top actors and actresses? I think the girls here are hoping for swashbuckling heroes and lots of derring-do.'

Ross nodded. 'That's not too far off. A couple of top names, too. But I don't think they'll be around for long—maybe a week or two at most. They're only shooting a few scenes here. The rest will be done at studios.'

'I hope I'm to have an invitation to come and see them in action,' Lorna said, looking brazenly optimistic. 'I could always make myself useful—providing cups of tea and so on.'

'By all means,' Ross agreed with a smile. 'Consider yourself invited…you, too, Izzy—and Greg. I'll be at home mid-week in the afternoons. I'm not sure, but maybe they'll be looking for extras.'

'Whoo-hoo.' Lorna chuckled. 'Hollywood, here I come.'

'Now, see—she's getting carried away,' Izzy said, her mouth curving. She sent Ross a disparaging glance. 'Now look what you've done.'

'It isn't fair,' he said, his jaw dropping as he looked from one to the other. 'I get the blame for everything around here.'

'Always have done, always will,' Greg murmured, and they all laughed.

They talked for some time about the film crew, and their work at the hospital, and the air ambulance and mutual friends.

'I must go,' Izzy said after a while. 'It's getting late, and I have to sort out a few things before morning. I'm on call with the ambulance team from the early hours, so I need to be organised and ready.' She glanced at Lorna. 'Are you staying for a while?'

Lorna nodded. 'I have a day off tomorrow…several hours all to myself…so I plan to take it easy. I expect Greg will give me a lift home—won't you, Greg?'

'Of course.'

Izzy stood up to take her leave of them, and Ross said, 'I'll walk you to your car. I need to go home and relieve the babysitter.'

They left the pub together, and Izzy paused for a moment by her car. 'I think it's good that you came to mix with the locals for a while,' she said softly. 'It's the only way that you're going to break down the barriers.'

'Do you think I need to do that?' he asked.

'If you want to be accepted around here, yes, I do,' she said. 'You might think that you can turn your back on criticism, but I don't think that will do you any good in the long run.' For some reason she cared deeply about how he fitted in here. She wanted him to be accepted, to be part of the fabric of her home village.

'I don't see why I should have to explain myself to anyone,' he said, coming to stand beside her. 'I grew up with half these people. They should know who I am and what I believe in. If they can't accept me for who I am, then that's their problem.'

'So you don't think that their worries about rents are of any consequence? Or that any unsettled feelings they might have about leasing land they feel is already rightfully theirs has anything to do with you?'

'Why do you care about what they think of me, either way?' He said it softly, but it was a challenge all the same.

'You're right. Why should I?' Perhaps he hadn't meant it in a harsh manner, but she braced herself, standing up very straight, unwilling to show any sign of weakness. Caring about someone who was heading helter-skelter into a quagmire was always going to be a difficult business. It led to all sorts of doubts and concerns, and it undermined confidence. But the fact was she did care, very deeply, about Ross Buchanan. Try as she might to tell herself that his problems were not hers, the thought had a hollow ring. How was it that he had managed to work his way into her affections?

He reached out a hand and lightly stroked the soft silk of her hair. Heat rose in her as his fingers left behind a trail of fire. 'Much as I appreciate your concern, you don't need to worry about me,' he said. 'I promise you I can take care of myself.'

'I know that.' That was the problem, wasn't it? He was proud, some might say arrogant, but his attitude was all part and parcel of the way people around here felt about him. 'It's just that a lot of these problems are not actually truly yours. They're hand-me-downs from your father, and from the fallout from your brother leaving. No matter what people say, I think you have an affinity with this place. It's in your soul. It's part of you.'

'So you don't see me as an outsider? I know that's how others think of me.'

'I don't.' She was all too conscious of his fingers threading through her hair, of the way his thumb lightly trailed along the line of her jaw. That faint touch was enough to send her whole body into meltdown. Why was he being so gentle with her? Caressing her as though she mattered to him? Was he simply flirting with her because it came to him as naturally as breathing air?

Her parents' warnings came back to her a hundred-fold. She should stay away from him. He was trouble—a man at odds with himself and with the world in general.

'You didn't come back here after you qualified as a doctor—I think people expected that you would do that, but you stayed away. Perhaps while your brother was alive you felt you couldn't take the reins. I don't know. I don't know what was going through your mind. But I don't believe that you had no interest in coming back.'

Perhaps the simple truth was that he'd wanted to be where Alice was? Why else had he followed them, leaving his home village shortly after his brother?

'There was nothing complicated going on,' he said. 'I worked hard to become a doctor, and I enjoy the work I do. With no family to provide for, there was no need for me to come back and become Laird.' He let his hand fall to his side. 'Whatever the crofters say, the rents are fair. I've looked into it, and the charges are reasonable. Perhaps the real problem is that they don't want to be tenants at all. They want ownership, and that is quite a different thing. It's a huge responsibility and one not to be taken lightly—as I've discovered.'

She sent him a thoughtful glance. 'And that's the reason why you've allowed a film crew to invade your family home, is it? You have the responsibility of making it all work. It's the reason you're planting trees and planning to start your own winery. Perhaps you're not thinking about going away after all? And if that's the case you really need to work on getting along with the people around you.'

'What a great adviser you are,' he said, his tone lightly mocking. 'Perhaps I should persuade you to come and be my personal assistant—to guide me through the shark-infested waters.'

She lifted her brows. 'Is that another action plan— to market the castle as having a loch where sea monsters lurk?'

He made a soft chuckle. 'I can see you're a force to be reckoned with, Izzy. You don't deal in romantic fantasy, do you? Everything is cut and dried, and you can see it all so very clearly. There are no blurred lines, no greying of images or taking the option of letting things ride to see how they work out. You're certainly your father's daughter, aren't you? You see everything with a clinical eye.'

He moved in closer to her. 'Perhaps I should work on that and try to win you round to my point of view. I could show you how to be more laid-back, more lackadaisical about what people think. Perhaps I could persuade you to think of me more fondly.'

The trouble was he could probably do it, too. She was already thinking of him far more than was good for her. She eased herself away from the car, away from his circle of power. 'I must go,' she said. 'You'll do as you please— as always. I'm just sorry that you might be wasting a golden opportunity to turn this community around.'

His mouth curved in amusement. 'It isn't this community that I'm concerned about,' he murmured. 'I'm much more interested in a sweet-natured girl with chestnut coloured hair and a figure straight out of paradise. I've always wanted you, Izzy. You've always been the girl for me.'

'No—don't say that. I don't believe it. Not for a minute. Alice was the one you wanted, the one you flirted with and kept close by. It was always Alice.' How could he even say otherwise? His words stung her far more deeply than she might have expected. Was he playing with her? Teasing her? It had always been Alice that he loved. Everyone knew that.

He shook his head. 'You're wrong, Izzy. It wasn't like that.'

'I can't talk to you,' she said, pulling open the door of her car and sliding into the driver's seat. He was treating her as a would-be conquest—someone to be won over to his side. 'You're impossible.'

She started up the engine and backed out of her parking slot. Her exit was more a desperate escape than a strategically planned retreat. The last she saw of him, he was standing by the fence, watching her drive away, and she felt a sudden qualm of loss, her emotions pricking her, chiding her for not ignoring her inner warning system and staying a while longer.

Perhaps it was fortunate that her work kept her from dwelling too closely on thoughts of Ross and how he made her feel.

The next day, as she was progressing from one callout to the next, it began to snow. It started with a light dusting of flakes at around lunchtime, and by the middle of the afternoon it was coming down like a thick curtain, settling on the fields and the hedgerows, coating everything with a layer of frosty peaks.

At any other time it would have been a wondrous sight. Looking out over the snow-capped mountains and gazing in wonder at the white-spangled branches of the pine trees would have been a vision to melt the stoniest heart. Now, though, as Izzy drove along a country lane to her next call, it only made her conscious of how difficult it was going to be to return home along these icy, snow-clogged roads.

She reached her destination—an isolated farmhouse, set back among trees and bordered by a huddle of barns and outbuildings.

A harassed-looking man, with hair that appeared as though he had been raking his hands through it for the last hour or so, greeted her at the door of the house.

'Are you the doctor? I was so afraid you wouldn't get here,' he said. 'The midwife is stuck in snow, and they say the ambulance will be some half an hour or more yet. My wife, Jenny, is having the baby. It's not due for another week, but she's definitely in labour. I don't know what to do.'

'Perhaps you should take me to her,' Izzy murmured, 'and I'll see how far she is along.'

'I will—of course. Here, let me take one of your bags.'

'Thanks.' She handed him the one with the oxygen equipment, and he weighed it in his hand briefly.

'It feels as though you must have everything you need in here,' he said. 'It's pretty heavy.'

'I have most of the things I might need in the car,' she told him. 'We come supplied for emergencies.'

He led the way up the stairs to the main bedroom, where his wife, a woman of around thirty years old, was lying on the bed, pale-faced and covered in beads of sweat.

A look of relief came into her eyes as Izzy walked into the room.

'Hello, Jenny,' Izzy said, going over to greet her and check her condition. 'Let's see if we can make you more comfortable, shall we? How often are the contractions coming?'

'Every…couple…of minutes,' Jenny answered, pain contorting her features. She looked as though she was about to pass out.

Izzy checked her blood pressure and listened to her heart. Then she checked the foetus's heartbeat, listening carefully for any sign that it might be in distress.

'Your blood pressure is very low, Jenny,' she said. 'I'm going to turn you over on to your left side. That should help to relieve the pressure and make you feel a little better.'

Turning to Jenny's husband, Izzy said, 'We're going to need to clean towels and a crib for the baby. Do you have one? Otherwise, something like a laundry basket will do.'

'I…um…yes. I can see to that.' He looked as though he was glad to be given something practical to do.

In the meantime, it was clear to Izzy that the baby's arrival was imminent. She gave Jenny pain relief through a mask held over her nose and mouth. As another contraction started, Izzy examined Jenny once more.

'I can see the baby's head,' she said. 'Try to push with each contraction. That's it.'

The contraction faded, and Jenny sank back against her pillows.

The woman's husband came back into the room. 'I didn't know how many towels you might need,' he said, 'so I brought them all.' He laid them down on the end of the bed and then swivelled around, looking bemused, as though he wasn't sure what to do next.

Izzy looked at him. 'The crib?' she said.

'Oh, yes. I'll go and get it.' He hesitated, his expression blank, and then stared at his wife as though she might provide the answer.

Jenny had other things on her mind. Another contraction overwhelmed her, and she concentrated on pushing as hard as she could.

'It's coming,' Izzy said. 'You're doing really well.'

As the head appeared, Izzy worked quickly to clear secretions from the baby's nose and mouth. 'That's great, Jenny. Rest now. Wait for the next contraction.'

Her husband stood at the side of the bed, overwhelmed and uncertain.

'James, weren't you going to look for something?' Jenny reminded him wearily.

'Was I?'

'The crib?' she suggested.

'Oh, yes.' He looked confused.

'Try the baby's room,' Jenny murmured in a resigned tone.

'Of course.' He gave a sigh of relief. 'Yes, of course—that's where it is.'

Izzy began to smile, but Jenny merely looked exasperated and lay back, worn out by her exertions. 'Men,' she muttered.

More contractions followed, and within minutes the baby was born. Izzy said softly, 'It's a little boy. You have a beautiful boy, Jenny.' She wrapped the infant in a clean towel, drying it as quickly as she could. Then she gently rubbed the baby's back until he gave a soft cry.

Izzy clamped the umbilical cord in two places, and then cut between the clamps. As soon as she had checked that all was well, she wrapped the baby snugly once more and handed him to his mother.

It was a joyous, wonderful moment for the parents, but it was equally exhilarating for Izzy. To be privileged enough to help a baby into the world was always a breathtaking experience, one that she cherished.

Would she one day have a child of her own? It was something she almost dared not think about—because she had a strong feeling that the one man she would even remotely consider for its father was perhaps the one man she could not have.

A few minutes later the afterbirth was delivered, and Izzy checked that the mother was comfortable and that her blood pressure and respiration were normal.

'What's the betting that the midwife and the ambulance will both arrive now that my baby is safely here?' Jenny said. She stroked her baby's cheek and nestled against James, who had come to sit beside her.

Sure enough the doorbell rang a few minutes later, and Izzy glanced out of the window to see who was there. 'It looks as though your midwife *has* arrived,' Izzy said. 'I'll go and let her in. I expect she'll want to stay with you for a while, to make sure that all is well.'

Izzy handed her patient over to the midwife, and then tidied up all her equipment and said goodbye.

James went with her to the door. 'I'll put your bags in the car for you,' he said. 'I can't thank you enough for all that you've done. I've no idea how I would have coped if you hadn't turned up.'

'I'm sure you would have managed somehow,' Izzy said.

She started back along the road, heading for home. Her stint on call had finished now, and she was looking forward to getting back to the cottage and home comforts.

The road, though, was treacherous. She drove carefully, taking her time, and after twenty minutes or so of travelling she began to wonder when the snowplough would reach this area. There was ice everywhere and now darkness was falling, bringing an eerie quality to the surrounding area.

She was still some half an hour away from home, and there were no other cars on this stretch of country road. As she negotiated a bend, her car skidded, not responding to her attempts to straighten up, and she went headlong into a snowdrift. The engine stalled and spluttered, and then there was silence.

Izzy waited for a moment or two and then tried to start the engine once again. Nothing happened.

She sat for some time, wondering what she ought to do next, and after a while took a torch out of the glove compartment and climbed out of the car to see what the problem might be.

The car had come to rest at an angle, on the verge by an ancient tree, and just a few inches away the ground sloped towards a ditch. Judging by the angle of the car, and the way it was embedded deep in snow, she doubted she would be able to push it free. Even so, she gave it a go.

Nothing doing. She sat back in the car and tried the radio. It cut out after a few seconds. After a few more attempts she gave up trying, and used her phone to call the garage.

After that, she settled down to wait. The garage was some half an hour distant from here, and they were busy with an unprecedented amount of calls. She had no idea how long it would be before she was rescued.

She was shivering a little, and her teeth had begun to chatter, when she eventually heard the sound of a vehicle approaching. Surely this must be the garage rescue service? Would the driver see her in the darkness? Quickly, she flashed the car lights to draw the driver's attention.

It wasn't the rescue service that had come to her aid, though. It was Ross.

'Good grief, Izzy…of all the times to choose to go and drive yourself into a ditch.' He pulled open her car door and reached for her, pulling her into his arms. 'You're freezing,' he said. 'Come on into my car and let's get you warmed up.' He looked at her. 'I know you like the heated seats, but you didn't have to go this far to get yourself a ride.'

She bunched her cold fingers into a fist and feebly thumped him on the arm. 'I'm really not in the mood for jokes,' she said.

CHAPTER SEVEN

THE interior of Ross's car was comfortingly warm and inviting. Izzy huddled in the passenger seat while Ross enveloped her in a blanket and supplied her with hot coffee from a vacuum flask. She wrapped her fingers around the cup and revelled in the heat it provided.

'Is that better?' he asked, coming to sit beside her.

'Much better,' she said. 'I'm beginning to feel a little more human now. I'm sorry if I snapped at you.'

'Snapping is allowed when you're suffering from near hypothermia,' he murmured.

She made a rueful smile. 'It seemed like an eternity, sitting in that freezing car, waiting. I'd no idea how long it was going to be before anyone turned up. The garage boss told me they were overrun with callouts. It seems a lot of people have broken down or got stuck in the snow.' She frowned. 'How is it that *you're* here, anyway? I was expecting a mechanic to come along and sort out my problem eventually. I was hoping that maybe he would be able to get me back on the road.'

He nodded. 'That will still happen. They're going to send out a rescue vehicle. As it happens, I was at the garage when your call came through…my car was in for a service and I'd just arrived to pick it up. As you say, they were inundated with calls, and worried that they might not be able to get out to you anytime soon, so I offered to come and find you.'

'Oh, I see.' She sent him a grateful glance. 'Well, thank you for that.' She sipped her hot coffee, more to steady her nerves than anything else. 'It was a bit of a shock, going off the road that way, and then with it being dark and isolated it was all a bit creepy. I didn't realise trees and branches could make such malevolent shapes against the skyline. I guess my imagination was working overtime. I was really relieved when you came along.'

'I can imagine it must have been a scary experience for you,' Ross acknowledged. 'Everything looks grimmer in the dark, doesn't it?' He frowned. 'Unfortunately, I don't think there's anything we can do to get you back on the road this evening, though. I've had a look around, and there seems to be some oil spillage on the ground, so something has probably been damaged underneath the car. I've transferred most of your equipment to this vehicle, so there shouldn't be any worries on that score.'

'I suppose not. And at least I'll be able to use my own car to go into work tomorrow. I'm actually only on duty for the morning. At least I'm not meant to be out on call, and hopefully whatever's wrong with the fast response vehicle can be repaired in a fairly short time.' She fell silent, finishing off her hot drink, and then returned the cup to him. Oddly, her hand was shaking, and as she turned to face him she became aware of a dull pain in her shoulder, causing her to wince.

Perhaps she was more traumatised by her ordeal than she had realised. It was one thing to be cold and cut off from civilisation, but it was quite another to have narrowly missed being catapulted into a ditch.

He wrapped his arms around her. 'It's all right, you're safe now.' He looked at her, his expression concerned. 'Are you hurt in any way? Maybe I should take a look at you?'

'No, I'm okay,' she said hurriedly. There was no way she wanted him examining her. 'I think the seat belt must have bruised me a little because I shot forward with some force. I'm sure there's nothing broken or damaged too much—it's just a bit of muscular pain.'

'Poor you.' He didn't push the issue, but instead soothingly stroked her cheek and gently held her, coaxing her to lean into the hollow of his shoulder, cradling her head against him with his hand.

That tenderness was her undoing. She snuggled against him, loving the strength and warmth of his long body, mesmerised by the way he was lightly caressing her as though she was the most precious thing in the world to him. It made her feel safe and secure. As if everything was going to be fine now that he was here.

'Are you feeling a little warmer now?'

She nodded. 'I am—thank you. It was thoughtful of you to bring along a hot drink. You must have guessed I would need it.'

'I believe in being prepared.' He studied her features in the car's interior light. 'There's a little more colour in your cheeks now, at any rate.'

She lifted her face to him. 'I didn't expect to feel this way. I always thought I would cope fairly well in a crisis…I didn't imagine that I would crumble at the first post.'

He smiled into her eyes. 'I don't see too much crumbling—just a young woman recovering from a frightening experience. Thank heaven for mobile phones.'

She laughed, her mouth softening as she drank in his smoky grey-blue gaze. 'Thank heaven you happened to be in the right place at the right time.'

'I'd come to fetch you any time if I thought you were in trouble.' He spoke softly, the words muffled against her cheek as he bent his head towards her. 'You know I would do anything for you, don't you? You only have to call and I'll be there.'

In her heart, she knew that was true. Why else was he here now? It made her feel warm all over to know that she could rely on him, and when he leaned towards her, as though he was about to kiss her, she wanted it more than anything.

His mouth brushed hers before settling gently on her lips, testing their softness, exploring the sweet fullness with tender, exhilarating thoroughness. Her lips parted, faintly trembling, clinging to his, wanting more.

'Mmm…sugar and spice and creamy coffee,' he murmured huskily. 'You taste delicious. You make me greedy for more…and more…and more.'

He deepened the kiss, drawing her into his arms so that her body meshed with his and she could feel the steady thud of his heartbeat against her own.

Kissing him was like drinking deeply of intoxicating wine. It went to her head and made her lose all sense of time and place, made her feel as though all that mattered was being here with him at this moment.

Then his hands moved over her, thrilling her with heated sensation, and all the while his fingers trailed and teased she was aware only of a fiery need to draw ever closer to him. Her breasts were softly crushed against his chest, her fingers tangled with the hair at the nape of his neck, and her lips were under siege, tingling with the sheer ecstasy of his passionate embrace.

She didn't know what it was that made her finally realise that reality was a lonely, dark road in the middle of the Scottish Highlands. Maybe it was the faint creak of leather upholstery, or the brush of the gear lever against her leg. Either way, she came back to the present with a sense of shock.

He must have latched on to similar thoughts, because he eased away from her a fraction and gazed around with a faintly bemused look in his eyes.

'Maybe we should start for home,' Izzy said, trying to gather her thoughts together. Now that her brain was starting to function again, she was beginning to wonder if she could blame her actions on the hot coffee. 'I don't know what I was thinking. It's almost as though the coffee was laced with alcohol. It went straight to my head.'

His brows shot up. 'Not guilty,' he said, and she realised that she must have actually spoken her thoughts aloud. 'I would never do anything like that. At least, I don't think I would. I suppose in the right circumstances I might resort to devious means.' He threw her a devilish smile.

'I'm sorry,' she said, her cheeks flushing with colour. 'I must have been talking to myself. It's just that everything that's happened this evening has been very unsettling. I can't think what came over me.'

'Put it down to a basic need for human companionship and comfort?' he suggested. 'We all suffer from that condition at some time or another.'

'Do we?' She studied him. 'You always seem so confident and in control. Nothing ever seems to faze you—even disputes with your father, or your brother, or the villagers. And now you're taking on the running of the estate, as well as holding down a job and looking after Alice's children.'

A momentary bleakness crossed his features. 'Eventually you learn to take most things in your stride. You deal with your problems and move on. It's the only way—as you've probably discovered.' He frowned. 'You didn't actually say how you came to be out here on this lonely road. Had you been out on a call?'

She nodded, a momentary recollection of her visit to the farmhouse filling her mind. 'Yes, to a farmhouse miles from anywhere.' Her gaze sparked with happiness. 'Oh, it was wonderful, Ross. One of the best things ever.'

A puzzled expression flitted across his face. 'Are you sure about that, given how it's turned out?' He laid a hand on her forehead, as though to check she was quite well, and then studied her curiously. 'Perhaps we ought to have you looked over at the hospital? You're obviously not thinking too clearly.'

'No, really—it's true.' She laughed. 'I delivered a baby—a little boy. He was absolutely gorgeous and it made me feel fantastic, on top of the world. I even got to wondering what it would be like to have a baby of my own to cuddle and love, just to share some of that heavenly feeling those new parents had when they were holding their baby in their arms.'

'Oh, I see.' He looked at her thoughtfully, taking in the blissful smile on her face, and then he said slowly, 'Well, we can do that. We can sort that out. Any time you like, I'm more than happy to oblige.' His arms closed around her, drawing her ever closer to him.

Her fingers tightened in her lap as his mischievous

words washed over her, and her grey eyes shot flinty sparks in his direction. 'You are incredibly out of order, Ross Buchanan. Just because you've come out here to rescue me it doesn't mean you can start taking liberties that way. What happened just now was a mistake—because I was confused and needy. It won't happen again.'

'You don't really mean that, do you?' He gave her a look that was full of mock horror, a light dancing in his eyes that promised devilment and mayhem if ever he had the chance.

'Stop making fun of me. I'd appreciate it if you would drive me home, please.'

'Spoken like a truly well-mannered girl.' He was still laughing at her, but his hold on her relaxed. 'I will, of course—if you promise to come over to the castle after work tomorrow. The film crew are doing a run through of one of their main scenes in the Great Hall. They've agreed to let visitors view the proceedings. Lorna will be there, and one or two others. The GP, along with his wife and children, Mary from the shop, Maggie, of course, and the garage boss if he can get away. We're going to lay on some refreshments afterwards.'

The invitation brought her down to earth and gave her something to look forward to. Her eyes widened. 'How can I refuse? It sounds too good to miss. I've never seen a film in the making.'

'That's settled, then.' He made a crooked grin. 'Let's get this show on the road.' He snapped his seat belt into place and started up the car. 'You're welcome to ask your parents to come along, too, if you like. Your father might want to think of it as me extending an olive branch. I'd issue the invitation myself, but I can't be certain he would consider it.'

'Thanks,' she said, pleased that he had offered. 'That's a lovely gesture. I'll mention it, but I must say I really don't hold out too much hope. My father's a proud man, and it will take a lot for him to accept any invitation from you. You know he still hasn't been to see Alice in hospital? It's worrying me quite a bit.'

'I'm sorry about that.' He started to drive home. 'I was hoping that if Alice was released from hospital in time for Christmas he might consider inviting her to join your family for the celebrations. But that's probably not going to happen, is it?'

Izzy shook her head. 'My mother wants it, but he would never agree. She's tried coaxing him, but he just goes into stiff and starchy mode and won't even think about it.'

'It's depressing to think that he would hold a grudge for such a long time.' He grimaced. 'But it doesn't matter. If she's well enough, I'll bring her to my place to recuperate. She'll be sad, though, because what she wants more than anything is to be accepted back into the fold.'

'I know.' It made Izzy unhappy to think of her cousin being ostracised this way. 'I've been racking my brain to see if I can find a way around it, but there doesn't seem to be a solution. The Buchanans are still his sworn enemy. What went on between him and your father, and his father before him, has had repercussions throughout the decades. Even thoughts of Alice's children won't melt his heart. He's only seen them briefly in passing since they've been here.'

He sent her a brief glance. 'I suppose it can't be helped. And Molly and Cameron don't seem to be too badly affected by any of this. I suppose it all tends to go over their heads. They haven't said anything about wanting to see him, although they *are* very fond of your mother. They call her Gran, and if your father happens to come into the conversation he's Grampops. I'm not quite sure how the name originated…whether it's a derivative of grandad, or poppa, or even grumpy gramps. I don't know, but it seems to have stuck.'

Izzy smiled at that. 'I know. I've heard them say it. I think it's meant to be a term of endearment. They don't know him, but they like him since he's associated with their gran.' She was thoughtful for a second or two. 'I'm sure he cares about them deep down…Alice, too. But he's been hurt by what he thinks of as her betrayal—of him and of the family name—and it's hard for him to reconcile that. I love my father, even though he can be difficult. He's a good man, but he can be immensely stubborn.'

'Perhaps he'll come round, given time.' Ross concentrated on the road ahead.

'I hope so.' She couldn't see it happening, though. It would probably take a miracle for her father to change his way of thinking. 'My mother told me that you've enrolled Molly and Cameron at the local school,' she said, changing the subject. 'How are they getting on?'

His mouth flattened. 'Not too well, by all accounts. They've taken to the teachers, and they're quite happy with the work, but there's some friction with the other children. I suppose the animosity comes from their parents, who have a problem with me as the Laird. In turn the children take it with them to the playground. They get on well enough with Tom Slater's children, though, so I'm hoping things will settle down soon. Of course they'll be breaking up for the Christmas holidays very shortly.'

She looked at him, studying his face in the half-light. 'I think you've been great with the children. You've taken a lot on, taking care of them and Alice. I doubt other men would have been so keen to look after someone else's family.'

He turned the car onto the main road leading to the village. 'I think of them as *my* family…which they are through my brother. I feel responsible for them. It's no hardship to me to give them a home.'

Some time later he dropped her off at the cottage. He went straight home to relieve Maggie of the children, and Izzy went to soak for a while in a warm bath to ease her aching limbs. She'd taken quite a jolt when the car skidded, and she was already beginning to feel the after-effects.

'I heard about you being stranded,' Lorna said, when Izzy came down to the sitting room around an hour later, snug in a warm dressing gown and ready to sit in front of the cosy fire. 'I was going to come and find you myself, until the mechanic told me Ross had gone to help you out.' She picked up the remote control for the television. 'Did Ross tell you about the goings-on at the castle tomorrow?'

'He did. He said the producer has invited us along to watch the filming.'

Lorna nodded. 'Maggie told me that Ross asked specially if we could all come along. I think it's his way of trying to win the villagers over. It should be fun. I can't wait to see the actors doing their bit. You know one of them is Jason Trent, don't you? He was in that film about the Highland rebels last year. It broke box-office records. It makes me go hot all over, just thinking about him.'

Izzy was feeling a little feverish, too. But it wasn't

Jason Trent who was stirring *her* blood. It was the memory of a close encounter in the front seat of a silver Range Rover that was causing her heart to race. Ross Buchanan had a lot to answer for, stirring her up body and soul, and what made it all worse was he was probably well aware of it.

He wasn't at the door to welcome them when she and Lorna arrived at the castle the next day. Instead Maggie, the housekeeper—middle-aged, friendly and straight-forward in her manner—ushered them into the warm kitchen and offered them mulled wine and hors d'oeuvres.

'The place is bustling with activity,' she said. 'I've never known anything like it. So many folk under the roof at any one time. I think himself is taking on an awful lot—especially with the bairns running about the place.'

The children took over from Maggie as hosts as soon as they saw Izzy and Lorna.

'Come and see how they've set out the Great Hall,' Cameron said, racing ahead of them in his eagerness to be at the centre of things. 'They've put loads of food on the big table in there. It makes me hungry, looking at it, but the director says we have to wait a while—we can tuck in when the filming's finished, he says.'

'That's good, isn't it? None of that lovely food will go to waste.' Izzy smiled, glad to see the boy's excitement.

She was definitely impressed when she looked at the banqueting table. It had been laid with all manner of silverware, and with beautiful candelabra and masses of food—turkey and hams, and great platters piled high with fruit.

'And all the actors and actresses are dressed up in old-fashioned clothes,' Molly put in. 'The ladies are wearing long skirts and blouses with lace at the cuffs, and some of them have shawls. They look really pretty.'

'I can't wait to see them,' Lorna said. 'Let's see if we can find a good place to view all the goings-on, shall we?'

'We can watch from up on the balcony,' Cameron told her. 'But we have to stay out of the way of the cameras and we have to be very quiet, or they'll have to do the film all over again. That's what the director said.'

They followed the children up the narrow staircase to the balcony overlooking the hall. 'Where's your uncle?' Lorna asked. 'Is he going to be joining us?'

'Yes,' Cameron answered briefly, 'in a few minutes.'

'He's showing Jason the broadsword from his collection,' Molly informed them importantly. 'He saw it hanging on the wall in the library and asked if he could look at it.'

'Men and their toys,' Lorna said, raising her eyes heavenward. 'I might have known.'

They joined the rest of the crowd who had come to view the filming, chatting amicably among themselves until the director called for quiet and the actors began to take their places.

The setting was a banquet, where people were gathered around the table eating, drinking, and generally merrymaking. Lorna's heartthrob took up position at the foot of the staircase, where he was talking to the lady of the house, and all was pleasant, homely interchange. Soon, though, he swivelled around to face a Highland clansman who had erupted into the hall from a door at the far side of the room. The lady moved hurriedly out of range, alarmed by the intruder.

'You'll pay for the deed you've done this day,' the Highlander said, advancing menacingly towards Jason. 'I'm here to avenge my kinsman.'

From then on it was truly as though they were witnessing a fiery feud. It was so realistic that at one point Molly hid behind Izzy, only risking a peek at the scene through one eye. Cameron's expression was awestruck, but he, too, sidled closer to Izzy.

The intruder, whose dark hair flowed with every flourish, was dressed in full Scottish regalia: kilt, loose linen shirt and waistcoat, and an impressive woollen cloak that swung importantly with every movement. Now he rushed towards the stairs with such realistic energy that the gathered crowd instinctively moved back. They could not be seen, of course, by the camera lens, since they were way above the line of view.

As the action progressed the two actors engaged in a magnificent tussle which took them halfway up the staircase. The intruder was thrown against the balustrade, and seemed to be almost done for, but then he came back at his opponent, brandishing his sword.

'Cut!' the director called, and all action ceased. 'That was great,' he said. 'Take a break, everyone. We'll do the scene outside the walls in half an hour.'

Ross appeared from a side door and waved up at Izzy and Lorna, beckoning them to come down. 'I'll introduce you to Jason and Murray,' he said.

Izzy checked that the children were all right, and not too shaken up by their experience.

'Wow!' Cameron said, brandishing an imaginary sword. 'I can do that.' He brandished his invisible weapon and chased his sister along the balcony.

Izzy went to rescue her. 'What did you think of the acting?' she asked. 'Do you think it was a bit scary?'

Molly thought about it. 'A bit.' She gave a wide smile. 'It looked ever so real.'

'I wonder if we can go and eat some of the food now?' Cameron wanted to know.

They trooped downstairs. Jason and Lorna hit it off right away, and after a few minutes moved off together in the direction of an ante-room. Izzy glanced at Lorna, lifting a brow, and Lorna made a 'go away and don't disturb me now' gesture with her hand, making Izzy chuckle.

She turned her attention back to Ross and Murray, the actor who played the part of the intruder, and Murray explained the storyline behind the action they had just witnessed.

'I think it's going to be a great film,' Izzy told him. 'It was so powerful—and colourful, too. Of course the setting's just right.'

'Can we eat now?' Cameron said in a plaintive tone. 'I can't just keep looking at all that food. Besides, everyone else is helping themselves, and Maggie is handing out drinks.'

'You're so greedy,' Molly remonstrated with him. 'Anybody would think you haven't had anything to eat today.'

Cameron pondered that. 'That was an hour ago,' he said. 'It wasn't pastry and it doesn't count.'

Molly shook her head like a wise little old lady. 'Boys,' she said.

Ross chuckled. 'Go and have something to eat,' he said. He looked back at Murray. 'What about you? Shall we go and help ourselves?'

Murray hesitated. 'Perhaps in a while,' he murmured. 'You go ahead. I'll just stay here for a minute and think about my next scene.'

Izzy looked at him closely. 'Are you all right?' she asked. 'Only I've noticed you seem to be moving a bit stiffly since filming finished. Were you hurt during the fight scene?'

'It's just a bruise, I imagine,' he said. 'One of the hazards of the job. The action gets a bit fierce sometimes.'

'Like when you were thrown onto the balustrade?' Ross suggested. 'I thought you landed heavily. It looked too realistic to have been manufactured.'

Murray grinned crookedly. 'You're right about that.' He caught his breath. 'I think I'll just go and get some air,' he said.

He started to move away, and Izzy glanced at Ross. 'Do you think we should follow him?' she asked. 'He looks a bit winded to me. I'm not sure he's as okay as he says he is.'

Ross nodded. 'I'll suggest that we go into the library. Maybe he'll let me take a look at him there. I keep my medical bag in there, so it'll be handy if we need it.'

He went and spoke quietly to Maggie, letting her know what they were doing.

'That's all right. I'll watch the children for you,' she said. There was a faint affectionate smile in her eyes as she spoke, and Izzy could see that Maggie was warming to Ross. He was making conquests all round, it seemed. It was just a pity that her father wasn't to be counted among them.

Murray agreed to go with Izzy and Ross to the library. Izzy guessed that he wanted to be able to sit somewhere for a while, away from prying eyes. He appeared to be uncomfortable and increasingly breathless.

'Sit yourself down,' Ross said, indicating a comfortable leather-backed chair. 'How are you feeling?'

'Not so good,' Murray said. He began to cough, and clutched at his side.

'I'm wondering if you might have damaged something when you fell against the balustrade,' Ross murmured. 'Would you let me have a look at you? Izzy's a doctor, too, so maybe she could offer a second opinion if we need one?'

Murray nodded, sitting down. 'It's a sharp pain,' he said. 'I'm thinking I might have broken a rib or two.'

'I'll get my medical bag,' Ross said.

Izzy went to stand beside Murray and took his pulse. He was looking increasingly ill as the minutes went by, and his breathing was becoming rapid.

'His pulse is rapid, but weak,' she told Ross when he came back with his medical bag. 'And the veins in his neck are beginning to swell.' That wasn't a good sign. It meant that pressure was building up inside the chest cavity.

By now Murray was showing signs of anxiety and distress, and she set about soothing him while Ross took a blood pressure reading.

'Blood pressure's falling,' Ross said, 'and there are decreased breath sounds in the lung.' He started to remove equipment from his medical case while Izzy explained to Murray what was happening.

'It looks as though you're right about the broken ribs,' she told him. 'Normally you would just be given painkilling medication to help you through that, but because of your other symptoms it seems that one of the ribs has punctured the lung. That means that air has gone into your chest cavity and can't escape, so it's pressing on the lung, causing it to collapse and making you breathless.'

This was a medical emergency. Murray looked near to collapse, and if they didn't remove the trapped air and restore function to his lung he could soon start to suffer heart failure and go into cardiac arrest.

'I'm going to put a tube into your chest to remove the trapped air,' Ross said. 'As soon as that's done you should start to feel more comfortable.'

'Do you want me to anaesthetise the area while you prepare?' Izzy asked.

Ross nodded. 'Thanks. I'll set up a bottle with fluid to act as a valve to prevent the air returning.' He glanced at Murray. 'We'll put one end of the tube in your chest, and the other end in the fluid in the bottle.'

Izzy carefully infiltrated a local anaesthetic into the area, checking all the time that Murray was coping with the procedure.

'I'm doing okay,' he managed.

'Good,' Izzy said, giving him a reassuring smile.

Ross made an incision in Murray's chest and carefully inserted the tube. There was a satisfying hiss of escaping air, and he sealed the end of the tube in the bottle valve. Murray's breathing began to improve almost immediately, and Izzy gave a soft sigh of relief.

'You're out of the woods,' she said, laying a hand lightly on his shoulder.

Murray's tense expression slowly evaporated as he became more comfortable. 'That feels so much better,' he said. 'Thanks, Ross—and you, too, Izzy.' He looked into her eyes. 'You have the hands of an angel and a beautiful soothing voice. You can come and take care of me any time you like.'

Ross gave him a mock-stern look. 'Don't you be getting any ideas on that score,' he said, feigning antagonism. 'You actors have something of a reputation where women are concerned, don't you? But I'm telling you, Izzy's out of bounds.'

Murray sent him a rueful smile. 'Possessive, are you? Staking a claim? Now, there's a thing. Seems to me she's a woman worth fighting for. I'm inclined not to give up so easily—warning or no.'

'You can both stop dreaming right now and come back down to earth,' Izzy said in a blunt tone. 'This is no time to be fooling around. We have to get you to hospital, Murray, to be X-rayed and monitored. And on another point, for your information, *neither* of you is on my list of eligible bachelors.'

And it was just as well to remind herself of that. Because she was getting way too fond of Ross—and it wouldn't do, would it, given all the upheaval it would cause in her family?

CHAPTER EIGHT

'I WOULDN'T be at all surprised if we had more snowfall some time today. The wind's getting up, too.' Lorna was frowning as she looked out of the window of the cottage. 'It doesn't make for a promising outlook for your journey to Inverness, does it?'

'I suppose not. But Alice is so thrilled at the prospect of coming home at last. I wouldn't dream of disappointing her—or the children.' Izzy drew out a batch of mince pies from the oven and a satisfying aroma of spices filled the kitchen. 'Ross said we would go over to the hospital and fetch her this morning, and with any luck we'll be back before things get too bad. I just hope everyone who has to travel home for Christmas gets there safely. This is not a good time of year for things to go wrong, is it?'

'No, it isn't.' Lorna turned away from the window. 'I was planning on going over to my parents' house to spend Christmas Day with them. It would be an awful blow if we were to be snowed in and I couldn't get there, wouldn't it? I thought I might take the train, actually. It might be simpler. My mother does us proud every year…there's so much lovely food that we're stuffed for the rest of the day.' Lorna frowned. 'I don't think I could contemplate not getting there.'

'Too true. I suppose if that did happen, though, you could always come over and spend the day with my family.' Izzy laid out the pies to cool on a rack. 'Unless, of course, you get an invitation to share Christmas with Jason Trent,' she added. 'I heard you and he were planning on having a meal together at a posh restaurant this weekend. It sounds as though things are heating up for you two.'

Lorna's eyes widened. 'Word soon gets around, doesn't it? I thought we'd kept that pretty much to ourselves. We didn't want the whole neighbourhood talking about it. Next thing the press will be hanging around, taking photos.'

Izzy studied her briefly. 'Then he shouldn't have told Murray about it. A nurse overheard them chatting, and now it's the talk of the hospital.' She laughed. 'Maybe you'll have to change the venue.'

'Too right.' Lorna smiled ruefully. 'I should have known.' She took a bite out of a mince pie. 'Mmm… these are delicious—hot, though.' She grinned, savouring the pastry. 'Murray's doing all right after his nasty accident, isn't he? He said they've filmed all his major scenes, and he'll be able to get by with the ones that are left because there's nothing too strenuous involved—only some dialogue and a bit of canoodling with one of the leading ladies. Greg said he had the luck of the devil, and your Alice laughed and said she hadn't realised Greg was the jealous type. She's been teasing him ever since, apparently.'

Izzy smiled, shaking icing sugar on to the golden crust of the pies. 'It sounds as though she's pretty much back on form, doesn't it? She's still unsteady on her feet, but I'm sure that will remedy itself given time.'

'She's lucky to have done as well as she has, by all

accounts.' Lorna was looking at the mince pies, debating whether to have another one. 'The crash left her with head injuries and spinal contusions, didn't it? As well as a host of other things? She's a miracle of modern medical science.' She reached for another temptingly aromatic pie.

'You're right. I can't wait to see her properly up and about again.'

The doorbell rang, and Izzy went to answer it, expecting Ross. Instead she found her parents waiting there. She hugged each of them in turn and invited them into the house.

'We came to bring Christmas presents for Lorna to take home with her, and I wanted to make sure you knew what our arrangements were,' her mother said. 'You *are* going to come to us for Christmas dinner, aren't you? Your grandparents will be there, along with your aunt and uncle.'

'Of course,' Izzy said, showing them into the kitchen. 'I've just baked a batch of pies to bring over to you. That's if there are any left after Lorna has finished dipping into them.' She grinned, and Lorna put a hand to her mouth as though to hide her guilt.

'Oops,' she said. 'Mind you, Izzy did make quite a lot. She said she was going to take a few over to Alice.'

'I thought she might appreciate a few home comforts,' Izzy said. 'Just to get her in the mood for Christmas.'

'Of course—you're bringing her home today, aren't you?' her mother said.

Izzy nodded. 'Ross is coming to pick me up in a while.' Out of the corner of her eye she was aware of her father stiffening, and her spirits sank.

'I expect the children must be over the moon.' Her

mother took no notice of her husband's attitude but smiled, clearly thinking about the reunion.

'They are,' Izzy murmured. 'But I'm not so sure that they're going to be too keen on the journey there and back to fetch her. You know how it is with youngsters being cooped up in a car. They've made the drive several times, and they get very restless. Maggie was going to look after them, but she has to see to her own family and do some last-minute Christmas shopping, with the great day being just a short time away.'

'I would have kept them here with me,' Lorna said, 'but I have to go to work this afternoon. I think Ross was hoping that he might find a babysitter. Last I heard, he hadn't told the children that today's the day.'

Izzy's mother glanced towards her husband. 'I wouldn't mind looking after them.'

'We can't do that,' he said. 'You know we're going to visit your father. He's not been well.'

'It's only a cold, Stuart,' her mother retorted. 'You're just making excuses.'

'I don't need to make excuses,' he answered. 'You know how I feel about the situation. Every day Buchanan does something to remind me of what's gone on in the past. He's even brought more earth-moving equipment onto his land in the last few days. It was holding up the traffic again a couple of days ago. What's he planning on doing with it, do you think? He's having more foundations dug out, I'll be bound. He'll have a fight on his hands if I find he's gone against the planning regulations. Is he *determined* to take away my business?'

Izzy frowned. 'I thought the building work was pretty much finished,' she said. 'Maybe he's brought the equipment in to help with the tree-planting? I know he wanted to put in some mature trees on one part of the estate to provide a barrier against the wind. They can be pretty hefty, from what I've heard, and need large cavities for the roots. And he also mentioned shoring up the land in some parts to act as a flood barrier on one area of the estate.'

'Hmmph. There's not much likelihood of that happening on *my* part of the river, is there? I'm sure he's damming it upstream.'

She could see her father wasn't convinced by any alternative explanation she tried to give. The doorbell rang again, and Izzy contemplated how she was going to manage the situation with her father and Ross in the same room. It was difficult, being plunged into the role of peacemaker, and it was something she would much rather do without.

Molly and Cameron were full of news about their plans for the day. 'We're going to the doctor's house,' they told her. 'Mrs Slater says she'll take us shopping. She says she has to buy some food for Christmas, so we're going to help her choose it, and we can pick out some goodies for *our* celebrations.'

Izzy glanced at Ross. 'So you found a solution, then?'

He nodded. 'That's right… And I managed to find a wheelchair for Alice, too.' He glanced briefly at the children. 'Luckily I hadn't mentioned any other happenings, so there are no problems there.'

'That's good.' Their comments appeared to have gone over the top of the children's heads, but now she signalled with her eyes towards the kitchen. 'My parents are here.' It was the least she could do to warn him.

Izzy led the way into the kitchen. 'Ross has managed

to find a wheelchair for Alice, for when she comes home,' she told her parents.

'I'm glad you thought of that,' her mother said, smiling at Ross. 'I was a little worried about how she was going to manage.' She studied him thoughtfully. 'You've been very kind to her, bringing her to the hospital in Inverness and making sure that she's all right.'

Izzy's father made an exasperated sound. 'Does it not occur to you that his conscience is driving him? How is it that Alice came to be in the hospital in the first place?'

'My mummy had an accident in the car,' Molly piped up in all innocence, as though she was explaining to someone who knew nothing of what had gone on. 'Uncle Ross looked after her and he called the ambulance.'

Stuart McKinnon looked uncomfortable, a frown etching itself on his brow and his mouth turning down a fraction at the corners. He probably hadn't expected a small child to take any note of what he was saying.

'Would you children like to come and see the decorations we've put up in the living room?' Lorna suggested hurriedly, obviously sensing trouble brewing. 'We've decorated the tree with gold and silver baubles. I think it looks lovely.'

The children followed her, happily unaware of any tension in the atmosphere and eager to inspect the Christmas trimmings. As soon as they had gone, Morag McKinnon turned on her husband. 'How could you say such a thing—and in front of the bairns, too?'

His shoulders moved in an awkward gesture. 'I speak as I find. Would you have me do otherwise?' He looked directly at Ross. 'It has to be guilt that's driving you. You were there when the accident happened. It was probably you that caused it, with your constant arguments with your brother. The fact that he ran off with your girlfriend must have stuck in your craw. Perhaps that's why you were following them. Everyone knows that you were driving behind them on the day of the accident. Maybe they were trying to get away from you. You're most likely the reason that Alice is in hospital.'

Ross studied him for a long moment. 'From the way you're talking, anyone would imagine that you are concerned about what happened to Alice,' he said. 'If that's the case, why haven't you been to visit her? Why haven't you tried to reconcile your differences with her? You looked after Alice as though she was your own daughter for years, and yet the instant she went against you you abandoned her—you cast her off as though she meant nothing to you.'

He frowned. 'Since she's been injured, you haven't made any attempt to visit her, or to make arrangements for where she's to stay on her release from hospital. I don't see any vestige of love in that kind of response. So why should you care either way about my involvement with her?'

'I don't.' Izzy's father started to walk towards the door, his expression dark as a thundercloud.

Izzy felt a pang of anguish as he threw a backward glance towards her mother. Would this feud never end? Could these two men never be in the same room together without arguing?

'We should go, Morag,' he said abruptly. 'Your father will be expecting us.' He went out into the hall and out of the front door.

Izzy's mother watched him leave, and hesitated

before sending Ross an apologetic look. 'I know this isn't your fault, Ross, and I hope you will try to understand—he has great difficulty coming to terms with what happened. Alice left without a word, without giving us any indication of where she was going, and she didn't get in touch afterwards for a long, long time. We had to rely on other people to tell us what was going on. She knew how we felt about her being with your brother, and I think it really hurt Izzy's father that she didn't try to talk to him about it.'

She pulled in a deep breath. 'I know why she did what she did, of course. He can be brusque and inflexible and very hard to approach. But underneath it all he cares very deeply. I know he's torn. On the one hand he blames her for leaving with the son of his lifelong enemy, and on the other he feels that she was like a daughter to him and she let him down. I don't know how to break down that barrier. I wish I could. I hate to see him hurting, and it grieves me to see Alice suffer, too.'

'I understand, Morag.' Ross gave a brief nod of acknowledgement, his mouth making a faint downturn. 'But he has to find a way to get over his antagonism before it destroys him. It's gone on for too long through the generations, and it's even affecting Alice's children at school—with youngsters pointing the finger at them. They don't deserve any of this. I'm not going to stand by and see them vilified for what went on in the past.'

Molly and Cameron came into the room. 'There's a beautiful star at the top of the tree,' Molly told Izzy's mother. 'It sparkles, and you can see lots of different coloured lights in it.'

'I like the lanterns,' Cameron said. 'They're all shiny and bright, and they kind of float in the air. Lorna says when you open the door they start to twirl.'

'I've seen them,' Morag said. 'They're very pretty.' She gave each of the children a quick cuddle, and then said, 'I must go. We're off to see Izzy's grandad. He's been poorly.'

'I want to give Grampops our card,' Molly said. 'We made it for him for Christmas.'

'We made one for you, as well,' Cameron said, handing a homemade card to Izzy's mother. 'Maggie helped us to make them. I stuck the sparkly baubles on the tree—see? They're a bit crooked, but they look pretty, don't they?'

'I think it's a beautiful card,' Morag said, deeply touched. 'Thank you very much, both of you. I shall put it on my mantelpiece where everyone can see it.'

The children beamed happily and followed her to the door. Izzy's father stood outside, a solitary figure waiting by a tree.

Molly went over to him, looking up at him in a puzzled fashion. 'Are you cross?' she asked. 'You look cross.'

'No, Molly,' he said looking down at her. 'I'm not cross with you.'

'Good.' She gave him a wide smile. 'Sometimes you look as though you're a bit sad,' she said, 'so I've made you a card. Well, me and Cameron made it together. It's Santa Claus. He's got a big smile on his face and he makes everyone happy.' She thrust the card into his hands. 'Happy Christmas, Grampops.'

He took the card she offered, holding it in his hands as he looked down at the brightly coloured Santa, with a cotton wool beard and cherry-red cheeks. He swallowed hard, and for a moment Izzy thought his eyes misted over. He blinked, though, and straightened up, saying huskily, 'Thank you for that, both of you. That was very thoughtful of you. Thank you very much.'

He patted Cameron awkwardly on his shoulder, and would have done the same to Molly—except that she reached up and hugged him as tightly as she could, and he wavered for a moment before folding his arms around her briefly.

When she let go and stood back he gave the children an uneasy wave of his hand and went over to his car. He didn't say anything more, and it occurred to Izzy that he was overcome by the simple, generous affection of a small child who knew nothing of the troubles of the adult world.

After they had gone, Izzy turned to walk back into the house and was startled to see Ross standing at the door. He didn't say anything, but laid an arm around each of the children and led them slowly back to the kitchen.

'You should say goodbye to Lorna,' he said to them eventually. 'It's time we were setting off for the doctor's house. He'll be waiting for you.'

He looked at Izzy, his expression thoughtful, his manner somehow subdued. 'Lorna's put a few of those mince pies in a box for you to take to Alice,' he said. 'If we leave now, we might just miss the storm. They say there'll likely be a blizzard towards evening, and I want to have Alice back home safely before then.'

Izzy nodded and went to get her coat. A short time later they dropped off the children at the doctor's house and set off on their journey to Inverness.

The roads were fairly clear, although there was still snow lying around on the grass verges and over the fields, and the traffic moved at a fairly rapid pace. Izzy was glad of that, because it meant they would reach Alice all the sooner. Even so, she was a little worried about the weather conditions. The roads were slippery, and though it didn't matter, since they were driving in Ross's roadworthy vehicle, she was wary of how the conditions might affect other drivers.

Ross didn't take any chances, though. He drove steadily and carefully, and after a while she began to relax. 'I'm sorry for what my father said,' she told him. 'I know my mother has tried to reason with him over the years, but it has been difficult for her—for all of us. I suppose he remembers how his great-aunt died in childbirth, and how the family grieved and mourned her loss for so many years. They blamed the Buchanan who abandoned her as soon as he found she was pregnant, and things have gone from bad to worse ever since then.'

'I realise that we're all tarred with the same brush,' Ross said. 'I have the same problem justifying my position with the villagers. There's always a wealth gap, and resentment that my family own the land that they're living on. I'm doing what I can to run the estate in a way that will eventually be beneficial for the whole community, but I doubt anyone will appreciate that.'

'I'm sure Alice appreciates what you've done for her. She told me she's so happy to be coming home, and even happier to know that you've provided a place for her and her children.'

He sent her an oblique glance. 'I know that's what Robert would have wanted,' he said. 'He was planning on coming back here at some point to show his children where he was born. I don't think he wanted to live at the castle, but he thought the lodge might provide decent living accommodation when it was finally finished. That's why I've been trying to push on with the work—to make sure that it's ready for Alice and the children. I think for a while, though, she'll want to stay with me and Maggie, so that we can look after her until she's properly back on her feet.'

Izzy smiled at him, thankful for the way he cared, but her lips stiffened and her smile froze as they rounded a bend in the road. Ahead of them a car had spun around in a wide arc that even now was etched out on the sleet-covered road. Another car had run into it. It looked as though the first car had swerved to avoid another, after taking the bend too wide.

Someone was desperately trying to direct traffic away from the crashed vehicles, and at least the accident had happened far enough away from the bend for oncoming traffic to avoid more tragedy. Other people were trying to push the vehicles onto the verge, out of harm's way.

'We should stop and see if anyone is hurt,' Izzy said, but Ross was already slowing down and steering his vehicle onto the verge some distance beyond the crashed cars.

'I'll get my medical bag,' he said.

Izzy climbed out of the car and went over to the side of the road to see if she could help in any way.

'We've called the police and the ambulance,' a man told her. 'There are a couple of people who are badly injured—a man and a woman. Both of them are still in the car. I think it's bad. The two people from the other car managed to get out. I've made them sit back out of the way until help comes. I don't know what to do for the others.'

'My friend and I are both doctors,' Izzy said. 'We'll take a look at them and see what we can do before the ambulance gets here.'

She quickly discovered that the man still in the car was the one who needed immediate attention. 'I think he has an abdominal injury,' she told Ross, meeting up with him. 'The other injured person is a woman, Carol, with a broken leg and possible spinal injuries.'

Ross didn't speak, and she glanced at him to see if he had heard what she'd said. He was white-faced, his expression shocked, and he walked stiffly towards the vehicle were the people were trapped, almost as though it was taking everything in him to do what he had to do.

Izzy spoke to the injured man, trying to see if he was able to describe any specific damage, but he was fading in and out of consciousness the whole time. It was clear that the steering column had twisted on impact and caused at least one of his injuries.

She checked his vital signs and said quietly, 'His blood pressure is low and his heart-rate is way too high. We need to get him on oxygen and put in an intravenous line so that we can give him painkillers and fluids. I can do that while you splint Carol's leg.'

Ross didn't answer, and she glanced at him once more. There was a faint sheen of perspiration on his forehead and he looked as though he was going to be sick at any minute.

'Are you all right?' she asked. 'I can do this if you need to go and take a few minutes.'

He looked around at the wreckage, and the incline of the road where it skirted the hillside. Then he pulled in a deep breath and nodded. 'I'm fine,' he said. 'I'll put in the IV line while you start the oxygen. Then one of us should go and get some splints from my car.'

She guessed that he was suffering from a feeling of *déjà vu*. Was this how it had been when his brother and Alice had suffered their dreadful injuries?

'You'll need to put a pressure pad on the woman's

leg to control the bleeding,' he said after a while. 'Do you want to check in my bag? There should be everything we need in there.'

'I'll see to it.' She glanced at him once again. He seemed to be coping, doing what was necessary to stabilise the injured man, and she concentrated her attention on the woman.

'I'm going to put a supportive collar around your neck,' she told her. 'We won't know what damage has been done until we can get you to the hospital for X-rays and scans.'

'What about John?' the woman asked, her voice shaky. 'He's not speaking. How is he doing?'

'He's breathing, and we've given him pain medication so he won't be too uncomfortable,' Izzy said. 'It's possible that he has some internal injuries, so we need to get him to hospital as soon as possible. We'll put both of you on spinal boards, to make sure that there's no chance of further injury while we take you there.'

Ambulance sirens sounded in the distance, and Izzy left the patients with Ross while she went to confer with the paramedics. Just a minute later a fire engine arrived, and the crew started to assess how best they could remove the patients from the mangled vehicle.

By now they had done all that they could for the man and woman inside the car. The two injured people who were sitting on the verge appeared to have escaped with minor injuries, but Ross still knelt down beside them and checked them out.

'You'll be given a more thorough examination in the Accident and Emergency department at the hospital,' he told them. 'For the moment it seems as though you have some bruising and pulled ligaments. We can make you more comfortable with support bandages.' He turned to the young man, who was nursing a sore shoulder. 'It looks as though you might have broken your collarbone. I'll put a sling around your arm and that should ease things for you.'

Izzy worked with him to put dressings on cuts and apply bandages to sprains. It wasn't too long before the fire crew indicated that it was safe to remove the man and woman from their car, and both Izzy and Ross went to supervise their transfer to spinal boards and then to the first ambulance.

A few minutes later the ambulance was on its way, siren blaring, heading for Accident and Emergency. Izzy went to help the walking injured into the second vehicle, while Ross spoke with the police officer who had come to investigate.

It was some time before Izzy and Ross went back to Ross's car. Ross sat in the driving seat, his whole body stiff and very still. He didn't speak but simply stared ahead.

'Would you like me to drive?' Izzy asked. 'You don't seem to be yourself. Ever since we came upon this accident it's as though you've been knocked for six.' She was concerned about him. He had hardly spoken the whole time they were with the accident victims, except to reassure them and ask relevant questions. He was still pale, and now he was gripping the steering wheel, his fingers wrapped tightly around it so that his knuckles were white. 'Is this something to do with what happened to Robert and Alice?'

He nodded. 'Everything is so similar,' he said. 'Almost as though it might have been this same stretch of road. Of course it wasn't. But the hillside, the blind curve, and then that straight road ahead…it's exactly as it was.'

He paused, shuddering a little, and Izzy said, 'I guessed that might be the case. You've never really spoken about it. What happened? Do you want to tell me?'

He was silent for a moment or two, and then he said quietly, 'I was on my way to work, and I was following them as they were heading towards Alice's sister's house. They were going to fetch the children, and they were looking forward to telling them about their plans for the future. Summer was just beginning, and Robert was thinking of coming back home. Alice was hoping that she might persuade your father to accept her back into the family.'

He pressed his lips together in a grim line. 'And then a car came out of nowhere, trying to overtake. It smashed into them, and all their dreams dissolved in an instant.'

'You saw it all? I know you must have. You were injured, too, weren't you?' Izzy frowned, wanting to comfort him yet at the same time knowing he needed to say this in his own way, to bring it all out into the open.

'I was afraid I was going to hit them. I slammed on my brakes, and tried to swerve out of the way. It all happened so fast. I remember a jolt, and I hit a tree so hard that the side of my car crumpled and I broke some ribs. I couldn't think of anything except that I needed to get to Robert and Alice, that I had to check on the others. There were two other cars involved, and people were injured in all of them. I did what I could, but it wasn't enough to save Robert. He took the worst of the impact.'

A muscle in his jaw tightened, and she could see that he was trying to bring himself under control. She laid a hand on his arm, stroking gently, wanting desperately to take him into her arms and hold him.

He drew in a ragged breath. 'All Robert could think about was Alice. He begged me to take care of her, to make sure that she came out of it safe and sound. I told him that I would take care of her, and he said, "The children, too. They should see their heritage."'

He looked at her. 'I told him that he needn't worry about any of it, that all he had to do was stay with us, and he said, 'I'm sorry. I know they'll be in good hands.'

Izzy reached for him, her arms going around him, and he leaned towards her, sliding his arms around her waist, resting his head against her breast. 'You kept your promise to your brother,' she whispered. 'No one could have asked you to do more.'

He gave a ragged sigh, and she stroked his thick, springy hair, offering what comfort she could. Was this the first time he had played it all out in his mind? Probably not, but today's accident must have brought it back to him with shocking clarity.

'Perhaps now you can begin to come to terms with everything that happened?' she murmured. 'You have to look to the future and make sure that the Buchanan name rings with pride. Surely the best thing you can do to preserve Robert's memory is to bring the estate to its full potential and make it an emblem of all that is good for the community.'

She hesitated. 'I'm sure Alice and the children will thank you for that, and you've already made a start with your plans for the winery. That will provide work for the villagers, and maybe it will stop some of the younger ones leaving for the towns.'

'You could be right.' His breath shuddered in his

throat, his shoulders moving as he tightened his hold on her, pressing her to him. 'We have to move on and put the past behind us.'

They stayed like that, wrapped in each other's arms, for a long time, both of them quiet, thinking about what had gone before.

Then Ross straightened, drawing back from her. 'We should go and fetch Alice,' he said. 'It's time to bring her home.'

He started up the engine, setting the car in motion once more.

Izzy sank back against the upholstery of her seat and tried to let the image of that terrible accident fade from her mind. It was no easy thing to do, and for Ross, who had witnessed it and been part of it, the torment must have returned in full force.

He had borne all that had happened with a stoicism that would put others to shame. He was a good man, a strong man with deep-seated principles and a streak of pride that ran through every pore. Beneath that tough, devil-may-care exterior he cared intensely for his family, and he would never let them down.

She knew it with certainty—just as she realised with a sense of shock and wonder that he was the one man, the only man, she could ever love.

Somewhere along the way he had stolen her heart.

CHAPTER NINE

'IT's so wonderful to be going home,' Alice said, sitting in a chair at the side of her bed and looking around the ward for the last time.

Izzy gathered up the last of her belongings, putting them all together by the wheelchair Ross had brought with them. She glanced at Alice. Her tawny hair was the same shade as Molly's, with wispy curls framing her face, and her green eyes were shining with relief at the thought of leaving the hospital. It was good to see her looking so happy.

'I'll come and see you just as soon as you're settled at Ross's place,' Greg said, coming to take Alice's hand in his. 'I'd have taken you home with me, except that I'm working the late shift today. I just had to come and see you off, though.'

'I'm glad you came,' Alice told him. 'It's been great to have a friend working here all the time I've been confined to this place. Thanks so much for all you've done.'

'You're very welcome,' Greg murmured, helping her into the wheelchair. 'Make sure you take it easy once you get home. You've still some recuperating to do, so no burning the midnight oil or trying to dance the Highland Reel.'

'Oh, I'm bound to do that, aren't I?' Alice chuckled. 'The most I can manage at the moment is a bit of a totter—though maybe after I've sampled some of Ross's fruit wines, anything might be possible.'

'I can see Izzy's been telling you tales,' Ross said, smiling. 'Don't believe a word of it. The wines are mildly intoxicating. You might find walking in a straight line a bit difficult afterwards, that's all.'

'Or, then again, *reel* might be a more appropriate word,' Izzy put in. 'I believe Greg had it right the first time.'

'You're quite mad, all of you,' Alice said, laughing. 'I'm really looking forward to seeing Molly and Cameron at home, away from these antiseptic conditions, and the thought of looking out over the beautiful mountains and lochs is enough to keep me going for a long time.'

'That's good. Let's get on our way, then, shall we?' Ross took hold of the wheelchair and started to guide it out of the side ward.

Alice waved goodbye to Greg, and Izzy stayed behind to speak to him for a moment, saying, 'I'll catch you both up in a minute or two.'

'You're worried about the people who came in by ambulance, aren't you?' Greg said. 'I didn't mention anything to Alice about them. I thought it might be a bit too traumatic.'

Izzy nodded. 'I know they came to you in A&E. How are they doing? Have you managed to assess them completely, yet?'

'We have. As you expected, the woman has a broken femur, which we've put right under anaesthetic. She'll be wearing a plaster cast for some time, so Christmas is going to be a little awkward for her. As to John, he's not so lucky. There was damage to his spleen and liver, so he's undergoing surgery at the moment. It looks as though he'll be staying in hospital for a week or two— at least until the New Year.'

'That doesn't seem so far away now, does it? One and a half weeks? I still have shopping to do and preparations to make.'

'I thought you were going to your parents' house for Christmas?' He raised a questioning brow.

'I am, but there's a lot for my mother to cope with, so I thought I'd help out by making a few things... A quiche and some sausage rolls, maybe some hors d'oeuvres.'

'Alice would love it...all that home cooking. I don't suppose there's any chance your father will see sense and invite her along, is there?'

Izzy shook her head. 'I don't think so. To be honest, I half wish I could get away and join her at Ross's place, but I don't want to upset my mother...or my father, come to that. And I think Maggie will make sure there's a feast on hand—and Ross will do everything he can to make her happy.'

'She'll be thankful to be with Molly and Cameron, anyway. I might suggest to Ross that I go round and pay a visit in the afternoon on Christmas Day. I come from a large family and they won't miss me too much by teatime. Do you think Ross would mind?'

'I shouldn't think so. Best thing would be to ask him and judge by his reaction.'

She took her leave of Greg and hurried to catch up with Ross and Alice. Would Ross want to keep Alice all to himself? It was hard for her to say. How much did Ross still care for her cousin? And how much of his thoughtfulness could be put down to his sense of responsibility towards her or to the honouring of a promise made to his brother?

Was there any chance that Ross might have some deeper feeling for her, Izzy? He had hinted as much, but she could never be sure that he wasn't teasing her or playing her along. The trouble was, she wanted him to care deeply. Suddenly it was the most important thing in the world to her.

They arrived back at the castle by late afternoon. Izzy stayed with Alice and helped her to settle in, while Ross went to fetch Molly and Cameron from the doctor's house.

There was huge excitement when they ran indoors and found their mother waiting for them.

'We didn't know you were coming home,' Cameron said, his eyes wide. 'No one told us.'

'We thought it would be a great surprise for you,' Ross said. 'But we have to take good care of your mother now that she's home. So you won't be able to rush around near her because if she's not sitting in the wheelchair she'll need to be very careful how she gets about. She still has to learn how to walk properly.'

'We'll be good as good,' Molly exclaimed. She went over to her mother and gave her an enormous hug. 'I'm so glad that you're home,' she said.

Izzy left shortly after that. 'It looks as though the wind is getting up now,' she told Ross, 'and I want to be home before it sets in.'

'I'll drive you,' Ross offered, but she shook her head.

'You stay with Alice. I'll walk. It will help to clear my head. Somehow today has been a lot more intense than I expected. It must be the excitement of bringing Alice home.'

He went with her to the door, and as she would have left to go on her way he wrapped his arms around her and held her close. 'I'm glad that you were with me today,' he murmured. 'There was a point where I thought I couldn't go on, and you brought me back to face up to everything that was real and important. Thank you for that. I haven't been able to talk to anybody properly about what happened, and it was good that you were there, that you listened.'

He lowered his head and kissed her tenderly on the lips. It was a beautiful, sweet sensation, being folded in his arms that way, having him kiss her as though he really cared about her. She wanted it to go on and on for ever. Just being close to him made her heart swell with joy, and her whole body was overwhelmed by the love that rippled through her. More than anything she wanted to love and cherish him and have him be part of her life from now on.

Yet that was not going to be possible, was it? He hadn't made any mention of loving her in return, and his kiss was simply a thank-you for being there when he'd needed her. And how could she even contemplate being with him when she could see how Alice had suffered and been set apart from her family simply because of her love for Robert Buchanan?

Ross eased himself away from her and she gave him a gentle smile and walked away, hurrying along the path as the snow began to fall.

The snow was still falling next day. Everything was covered in a thick white blanket, with drifts against the doors so that Izzy and Lorna had to dig out a path in order to reach their gate at the end of the front garden. A harsh wind caused the snowflakes to swirl all about them in a frenzy, and the branches of the trees swayed violently, swooping down towards the earth until the smaller branches cracked and split.

'This is really nasty,' Lorna said. 'I'm going to book my train ticket right now. There's no way I'm going to be able to drive far in this, and I have to set out the day after tomorrow if I'm to reach my parents' house in time for Christmas Day.'

'Good idea,' Izzy murmured, putting away the shovel in the garden shed. 'How long will you be staying over there? Will you be spending New Year with them?'

Lorna shook her head. 'I have to be at work on New Year's Day,' she said. 'I'll have to come back on the thirty-first, but at least that will give me nearly a week with my family. I'll book a return ticket.'

Izzy hurried inside the house with Lorna, shaking the snow from her coat and hanging it up to dry in the cloakroom. She flicked the switch on the kettle to make a hot drink.

A few minutes later Lorna came into the kitchen. 'I thought you were making coffee?' she said.

'The electricity's off,' Izzy told her. 'I hope it's just a blip. Last time it went off the power lines were down, and it took at least twenty-four hours for the engineers to get it back on again.'

Lorna pulled a face. 'That's not great news, is it? A lot of people around here use electricity for their heating, as well as for their cooking. It's going to be really hard for them to keep warm.'

By late afternoon it was becoming clear that the situation was not going to be remedied easily.

'The phone keeps ringing,' Lorna said. 'People wanting to check if we're in the same situation as them and worried about how long this is going to go on. There are some in the village who are really feeling the cold, and they haven't had a hot meal since yesterday. I think we ought to see if there's anything we can do to help.'

The doorbell rang, and Lorna hurried to answer it. Finn the postman was standing there. 'I'm coming around to tell everyone that Ross Buchanan has set up a soup kitchen at the castle. He has his own generator up there, and he's inviting people to go and get warm in the Great Hall.'

'That sounds like a wonderful gesture,' Lorna said.

'Aye. I've already taken up a lot of the old folk from the village. He asked me to come and let you girls know that you're very welcome. He's been ringing round most people, and a lot of them have taken him up on the offer.'

He made a rueful smile. 'Not your father, though, Izzy. You can imagine his answer, I expect. He says he'll make do with his charcoal barbecue for cooking food, and he has a coal fire in the living room to keep them warm. Mind you, he has offered to heat up soup and take it round to his neighbours. Your mother is busy taking tureens from house to house, checking that everyone is all right, bless her.'

'That's what I would have expected my mother to do,' Izzy said. 'As to my father, let's hope he doesn't burn the house down with his barbecue in the kitchen.'

'Is Ross going to have enough room if everybody in trouble turns up?' Lorna asked.

Finn nodded. 'His kitchen is huge, you know, and he says he's well stocked up with provisions. He's been out and about himself, fetching people or delivering heaters to those who want to stay in their own homes, but he asked me if I would come and check up on people in this area. Would you like me to take you up there now?'

'I think that would be a great idea,' Izzy said, glancing at Lorna for confirmation.

Lorna nodded. 'I'm cold through and through, and starving, so you don't need to ask me twice.'

'I know the neighbours round here are managing fairly well,' Izzy said, 'but one or two might like to come with us.'

They hunted around in the cupboards for food and drink that they could take with them to add to Ross's supplies. They chose anything that could be heated up and passed around. Izzy couldn't help thinking that it was just the sort of gesture she would have expected Ross to make. Why couldn't her father see that he was a good man?

Perhaps this would be a good time to ring him and put that question to him, while checking that her parents were coping well enough. She left Lorna with Finn, gathering more supplies, while she went to make the call.

'Well, maybe you're right,' her father said. 'I can't deny it's a good thing that he's doing. But it doesn't take away the fact that he's caused grief in more ways than one.'

'So you've been saying,' Izzy murmured. 'But you were wrong about the log cabin. It isn't meant for tourists at all, but as a special place for Alice and her family. He didn't tell you that, and maybe there are other things he hasn't thought fit to mention. Perhaps you're wrong in a lot of your assumptions? It seems to me that the two of you should get together and start talking to one another without arguing, if that's at all possible. You're both stubborn and proud, but it's high time that you listened properly to what each other has to say.'

'I don't need a slip of a girl to tell me what to do,' her father said in a blunt, abrasive tone. 'The Buchanans have goaded me endlessly over the years, and I don't need him to offer me charity, as if I'm some needy person who hasn't the wherewithal to take proper care of his family. I don't see why you keep associating with him the way you do. It goes against everything I've ever taught you.'

Izzy pulled in a steadying breath in an effort to calm herself. 'You know I love you and respect you, but I'm a grown woman and I have to make my own choices. I think you're wrong, in this instance, and I think you were wrong to cut Alice out of your life. She's our flesh and blood and she doesn't deserve any of this. She's lost her husband, and she's been very badly injured. The least you could do is go to see her and talk to her.'

She hesitated, afraid that she might have gone too far, but after a moment she plunged on. 'As for Ross, all I'm suggesting is that you take a small step to bridge the gap and allow you to start afresh. It wouldn't hurt you to take it. You wouldn't lose face by talking things through with him.' She paused once again, thinking things through. 'In fact, people might respect you more for having the courage to meet him halfway.'

'You don't know what you're asking of me. How can you not understand the way I feel—the way my father felt, and his father before him? Are *you* going to betray me, as well?'

His words shocked her, and frustrated her at the same time. Izzy couldn't stop the faint tremor in her voice when she spoke to him again. 'I'm sorry you feel that way. You know how much I care for you and my mother. I love you both, and I don't want to be alienated from either of you. That's not what I want at all. I just want you to try to look at things from a different point of view.' She sighed heavily. 'I can see that's not going to be possible. I have to go.'

She cut the call and stood for a moment, thinking over what had been said. It was hopeless, trying to talk to her father about the Buchanans or about Alice. Her mother had been trying to change his views for years to no avail. He was like a brick wall—immovable, unyielding—and too proud for his own good.

In the Great Hall of the castle the banqueting table was laden with food, and people were helping themselves to steaming hot potatoes cooked in their jackets, with savoury fillings like cheese, curried sauces and baked beans, along with a selection of meat dishes, rice and soup.

'Has Maggie been doing all of this cooking?' Izzy asked, as Ross ladled hot soup into a mug. He handed it to her and she wrapped her fingers around it to warm herself.

'No. Maggie prepared the meat dishes, but she had to go and see to her own family. Alice and I have done a lot of the work. It's amazing what she can do from a wheelchair, and she has been trying to stand every now and again to do things. I suppose it's good therapy. The children are loving every minute of it.'

'I think it's fantastic,' Lorna said, helping herself to coffee from a percolator. 'And there are so many people here. It's like a party. You've turned what might have been a miserable time into something marvellous.'

'I suppose I've been thinking of it as something like

a welcome home party for Alice,' Ross said. 'Actually, it's really good to have everyone here. It's great to see everyone enjoying themselves. It's as though they've come together to support one another.'

'That's very true,' Izzy remarked, looking around. Alice was the centre of attention, and it was good to see her face lit up with happiness. She was well and truly back among the people of the village, and if her own family were not present in their entirety, at least she could take comfort in the fact that she was accepted by everyone else.

'Shall we escape to the library?' Ross murmured. 'It's great in here, but I've been surrounded by people for several hours and I wouldn't mind a bit of peace and quiet.'

She went with him, enjoying the sanctuary of the library, where bookshelves lined the walls and a magnificent old writing table faced the long window that overlooked the garden. There was a couch in there, with soft, luxurious upholstery, along with armchairs that faced the grand fireplace, where coals burned brightly and flames flickered orange and gold.

'I thought you might like to see the floor plans for the lodge,' he said. 'I showed them to Alice yesterday, and she was very pleased with the layout. We're still having furniture moved in there, so I haven't shown her the house itself as yet. I want her to see the finished product.' He removed a collection of papers from the desk drawer and came over to her. 'Come and sit with me?' he suggested, and Izzy went with him to the couch, sinking back against the brocade cushions.

He draped an arm around her, drawing her close. 'The main living-room window of the lodge looks out over the loch—see?' he said, showing her the papers.

'It gets the sun in the afternoon, pretty much as we do in the living room here.'

'I can see why she likes the layout,' Izzy commented, snuggling against the warmth of his chest. 'It all flows so smoothly, doesn't it? There's the living room, a huge dining-kitchen and a utility room downstairs, with the kitchen overlooking the garden…and upstairs there are *en suite* bathrooms and windows that look out over the mountains.' She smiled up at him. 'She must be longing to set foot in it.'

'I'm sure she is. It'll be a month or so before she's properly back on her feet, though, I imagine.'

Izzy was looking at some of the other papers in the bundle he had brought from the desk. Some were plans for renovations to the castle itself, but one seemed to be more relevant to the land beyond the castle. 'What's this?' she asked. 'It looks like the river at the point of one of the falls.'

'It is. We often have flooding just below that point. I think it's due to debris being swept down from higher up, blocking the natural course of the river. I've had an expert take a look at it, and he's recommended that we dredge out part of the riverbed and build up the area where the debris collects. It should make the river flow much better, with fewer problems along the course.'

'Is this why my father has trouble with the salmon run?' she asked.

He nodded. 'Probably. The riverbed silts up in certain parts and causes problems further downstream. I think my father tried to put it right over the years, but nothing ever worked satisfactorily. When the dredging is finished that should all be sorted out, and Stuart shouldn't have any more problems.'

She put the papers to one side. 'I wish you would

explain all this to my father, if you ever get the chance. I don't know how to make him listen to me, and neither does my mother. All I know is that you don't deserve any of the flak that's been coming your way.' She reached up to him and cupped his face lightly in her hands. His slightly puzzled expression gave way to surprise and then pleasure when she drew him towards her and kissed him soundly on the mouth.

He didn't need any further bidding, and within a minute or two she was lying back against the cushions being thoroughly kissed in return. His hands moved over her, thrilling her with every gentle brush of his fingers, and his lips trailed over her face, her throat, dipping down to linger on the gentle swell of her breasts.

'Did I ever tell you how much I love having you around?' he asked. He swooped to claim her lips once more, stifling any answer she might have given. Then his fingers trailed over the length of her arm, tracing a path to her hand. He lifted her palm to his lips and kissed her tenderly, planting soft kisses over each finger in turn. 'I wish you would come and stay here over Christmas,' he said. 'You don't know how much that would mean to me—and to Alice and the children.'

'I wish I could,' she whispered, sadness sweeping through her. She returned his kisses, letting her hands glide over him, savouring the feel of his strong muscles and the length of his spine.

Then she laid her hands on his shoulders and gently eased him away from her, bringing herself up to a sitting position once more.

'Have I done something to upset you?' he asked.

She shook her head. 'No, nothing—nothing at all.' She looked at him. 'I wish I could stay. I wish I could be here at Christmas with you and Alice. But I can't. Perhaps I can slip away in the morning, just for an hour or so, but I have to be with the rest of my family—with my parents and grandparents. They're expecting me to be there. They want me to be there.'

His mouth made a rueful smile. 'What you mean, and what you're not saying, is that your father would blow his top if he knew that you were spending Christmas with me.'

'I'm working on him,' she said. 'I'm trying to get him to change the way he thinks.'

Ross stood up in one fluid movement. 'How long was it that Alice was married to my brother? He didn't change in all that time.'

Her gaze was troubled. 'I don't know how else to handle this,' she said.

'You don't have to.' Ross held out his hand to help her up from the couch. 'Loyalty is a finicky concept. I dare say there are always going to be losers.' He made a grimace. 'We should go back and join the others.'

When they went back into the Great Hall the assembled crowd was mellow, replete from all the good food and warm from the fire that burned in the magnificent fireplace. Villagers were chatting, one to the other, while Molly and Cameron were playing with other youngsters in between helping themselves to cookies from the table.

A local businessman came to take Ross to one side, and Izzy noticed that Lorna was across the other side of the room, talking to Greg and Finn. Alice was in her wheelchair, but she saw Izzy standing by the door and came towards her.

'We're getting short on mulled wine,' Alice said. 'Do you want to come into the kitchen with me to make some more? I can manage most things, but I'm not so good at lifting things down from shelves.'

'Of course. Just tell me what you need and we'll make it together.'

No one had ventured into the kitchen, preferring to stay with the hub of activity in the Great Hall and the drawing room. Alice fetched a bottle of red wine from the rack and poured it into a pan on the hob, and then turned on the heat.

'I'll add some honey and sliced orange,' Alice said, going over to the fridge. 'We'll need some cinnamon sticks and ginger, too. They're on the shelf up there, if you could reach them down for me.'

Izzy obliged, adding them to the mix. 'That looks lovely,' she said. 'What a beautiful rich colour.'

Alice dipped a spoon into the liquid and tasted it. 'I think we need some cloves, and maybe a quarter cup of brandy. That should do it.'

Izzy looked around the kitchen for cloves while Alice added the brandy. 'We'll let that simmer for a few minutes,' Alice said. She glanced at Izzy. 'It's so good to be back here at last.' She was lost for a moment in a silent reverie. 'Robert was planning on coming back, you know.'

Izzy nodded. 'Ross said as much. I was a bit surprised at that, because I know Robert had some issues about being here. I wasn't sure how deep the rivalry went between them.'

Alice smiled. 'I know they were always fighting, but I think that was just the exuberance of youth…two young men growing up and battling for supremacy. It ended when they realised that they were equals. The one thing they had in common was their love of this place. They both had ideas about how it should be run, but their father would never let them do anything. He always thought he knew best.'

'Like my father,' Izzy said with a wry smile.

'Exactly like Pops.' A wistful expression flitted across Alice's face. 'I can't believe I used to call him that—it was such an endearing name. I thought the world of him. I still do.' She gazed up at Izzy. 'Only I fell in love with Robert. I knew all about the friction between the two families—how could I not?—but Robert and Ross were so kind to me after my parents died, and Robert... To me he was such a wonderful man—slightly flawed, but full of energy and rebelliousness. I couldn't help myself. I didn't want to hurt Pops, but I knew he would stop me from being with Robert and that's why I left.'

'Did you have any regrets...?' Izzy frowned. 'I mean, I know you must have, because I know you wouldn't have wanted to hurt my mother or my father, but what about Ross? Weren't you and he a couple at one time? Did you worry about what he would feel?'

Alice sent her an oblique glance. 'I know that's what everybody said, and I encouraged them to think that way. I thought maybe Pops would think it was the lesser of two evils if I was going around with Ross and not with Robert... But Ross was never in love with me. He pretended to be, to tease Robert, and he'd take me out and about on the estate, or buy me lunch in some out-of-the-way place so I could talk about my troubles, but we both knew that you were the only one he ever wanted.'

Izzy's brows shot up. 'That can't be true. Surely I would have known.' She was stunned by that revelation.

Alice shook her head. 'He used to try to talk to you whenever he met up with you by accident in the village, but you always kept the meetings short. He said you seemed to like him, but you would never look twice at him because your family was so set against the Buchanans, and he wouldn't push it because he knew you could be hurt. I think that's why he followed Robert and me to the Lake District. He knew after the furore that erupted that you would be even more determined to stay away from him. You wouldn't risk going against the family. So when Robert told him about a job that had come up at the hospital, he applied for it.'

Izzy stared at her. 'You've known this all this while? Yet you never said anything—you didn't even hint at it.'

'Ross asked me not to say anything.' Alice stirred the wine. 'I'm only talking about it now because I see the way you look at him, the way he looks at you, and I made that promise when the situation was different. You have to make the decision. Ross will never make it for you. All I can say is that I followed my heart, and though I don't regret what I did it *has* been hard to take the consequences of being cut off from the people I love. I went into it blindly, not knowing what might happen but hoping Pops would come round eventually. You, at least, will know what to expect.'

Izzy laid a hand on Alice's shoulder. 'Thank you for telling me all this. I'm sorry for the way you've had to suffer all these years, and I'm glad that Ross has brought you back here to us.'

Alice acknowledged that with a smile. 'We should pour the wine into a serving dish,' she said after a while. 'Or perhaps it would be better in one of those heat-resistant serving jugs.' She indicated a cupboard, and Izzy went to have a look.

'Okay, we'll take this back into the Great Hall, shall we?' Izzy suggested.

Her head was whirling with all that Alice had told her. Suddenly she had a completely different perspective on things. What was she to do? Could she follow her heart, let Ross know that she loved him and risk the wrath of her father, or should she put family above everything?

What was it that Ross had said about her father? *'How long was it that Alice was married to my brother? He didn't change in all that time.'*

CHAPTER TEN

'ARE you sure the roads are clear enough for you to drive over there? We're expecting more snow, and that wind's getting up again.' Izzy's mother was worried.

'I'll be fine. I'll drive carefully, I promise.' Izzy gave her a hug. 'I'll be back in time to help you with the Christmas dinner.'

She was gathering up Christmas presents from the kitchen table when her father came into the room. 'You're not actually going up there?' He was frowning heavily. 'It's Christmas morning. What on earth are you thinking of?'

'I'm thinking of Alice and the children,' Izzy said. 'I have some presents for them, and I want to wish them well.'

'But it's Buchanan's place. How can you be going up *there*?' His scowl deepened as he looked at the parcels in her arms. 'I suppose you have a present for him as well, don't you?'

'I don't have a problem with Ross Buchanan,' Izzy said calmly. 'Just the opposite, in fact. Nor do I have a problem with Alice. I *want* to see them. I'll only be gone for an hour.'

'So you'd go against everything I believe in? All my principles?'

'That's just it. They're *your* principles, not mine. I'm sorry if that upsets you, but I think you're living in the past. It's time to move on and start a new way of life.'

'Why should I do that? Why should I abandon everything that I believe in?'

'Because it hurts the people that you love and the people who love you.' Izzy gazed at her father, trying to appeal to his better nature. 'It was your attitude that made Alice leave without saying anything. She didn't want to go against you, but you left her no choice. She ran away so that you wouldn't stop her. I'm not going to do that. I will always tell you what's in my mind and what I want to do. You might not always like it, but how you deal with it is up to you.'

He returned her gaze steadily, unflinching, but she thought she saw his shoulders relax a fraction, and that gave her a pause for thought. Was that what had been bothering him most of all? Had he thought she would simply walk out of his life in the same way Alice had done?

She said slowly, 'I think you should stop concentrating on the bad side of the Buchanans and think about all the good Ross has done. He is not his father or his grandfather. He has a set of principles that are every bit as strong as yours. Those are what make him the man he is—the man who goes out day in and day out to save the lives of people who are injured, the man who looks after his brother's wife and children. If nothing else, you should respect him for that.'

She left the house then and drove to Ross's home, the beautiful castle that had withstood the test of time on its craggy promontory overlooking the loch.

'Happy Christmas.' Ross greeted her with a smile. 'I wasn't sure whether you would make it after all, but it is so good to see you. Did you have any problem coming here?'

Izzy shook her head. 'It's good to see you, too. How are things going with you and Alice and the children? Have you had a good morning so far?'

'We're having a great time.' He studied her briefly as he showed her into the Great Hall. 'I'm sure there's a lot you're not telling me, but we'll set that aside, shall we? Come and see everybody. They're still opening their presents in the drawing room.'

Izzy followed him, stopping to greet Alice and the children and hand out presents. They in turn gave her gifts that brought a smile to her face. 'An angora wool scarf and lovely perfume…exactly what I wanted.'

Alice exclaimed with delight over her gift of a cashmere sweater, and the children showed her their new toys and asked for help in undoing all the ties that held them in place in the boxes.

Izzy gave Ross a brightly wrapped parcel, and he looked startled. 'You bought me a present? I wasn't expecting that at all.'

She smiled. 'I wasn't sure what would be the best thing to get for you,' she murmured. 'But then I hit on an idea and this seemed like just the thing. I hope you like it.'

He carefully opened his present, gazing down at it in wonder. It was a bottle of wine, but the glass was specially tinted and etched with a picture of the castle against a background of mountains, and the whole was highlighted with touches of gold, to make it look as though the sun was shining down over everything.

'It's actually your own wine that's in the bottle,' she

said. 'I had to do a bit of conniving with Maggie and the man who does the bottling to make it just right.'

He was still staring at the bottle. He placed it down on the top of a cupboard, putting it out of harm's reach and in pride of place at the centre. 'That is such a great gift,' he said. 'Thank you for that.' His smile warmed her through and through. 'I wonder if we could reproduce them and make special presentation bottles for the winery.' He wound his arms around her and kissed her full on the mouth, uncaring that Alice and the children were watching their every move.

He broke off the kiss after a minute or two and turned to face the others. Molly and Cameron, after looking at them wide-eyed for a second, lost interest and went on examining their toys. Alice had a wide grin on her face.

'I'm going to take Izzy to the library,' he said. 'I have a present waiting for her in there.'

'We'll be fine,' Alice said. 'You go ahead. Just remember I've planned dinner for a couple of hours' time.'

'I have to be back home way before then.' Izzy laughed.

Ross had taken hold of her hand, though, and was leading her towards the library at a brisk pace.

'I have two presents for you,' he said. 'The first is something that I thought you would enjoy…something to make you feel cosseted at the end of a hard day. Lorna said you didn't have one—not quite like this, anyway.'

He had bought her a silk robe, beautifully hand-embroidered and exquisite in its entirety. She gasped. 'It's lovely,' she murmured. 'I wasn't expecting anything—especially not this.'

'Hmm...I have to admit I've had a few problems over this robe—I kept thinking of how you would look when you were wearing it. I just can't keep up with the cold showers.'

Her cheeks flushed hotly pink, but he had already turned away, and now drew out a small box from the bureau. 'This is the present that I really wanted to give you,' he said softly. 'The trouble is, I'm not at all sure that you will accept it.'

The breath seemed to have left her body all at once. He opened up the box and inside, nestling on a velvet cushion, was the most perfect diamond ring she had ever seen.

Tears sprang to her eyes. 'Is that what I think it is?' she asked, her voice husky.

He nodded. 'It's an engagement ring. I think you must know that I love you—that I have always loved you, Izzy. What I want more than anything is for you to say that you will be my wife. Will you marry me?'

Tears began to trickle down her face. 'I want to say yes,' she whispered. 'I really want to say yes. Because I love you, too. I've known it for some time. But I don't think we can ever be happy if my father is alienated from us. There would always be that anguish at the back of my mind. I want to be with you, Ross, but I can't.'

'Are you sure about that? We could ask him to give us his blessing, but if he won't we could marry anyway. At least you would have tried to win him round.'

She shook her head. 'I want to marry in the church in the village, with my family all around me and my father walking me down the aisle. I don't want to have to hide or to flinch or to beg forgiveness for my actions. I want my family to be happy for me. I just don't see how that is ever going to happen.'

He drew in a deep breath and closed up the box. He put it away once more in a drawer in the bureau, and then closed up the door. 'It will stay there,' he said, 'until the day you change your mind.'

Izzy's emotions threatened to overwhelm her. Had she really just turned down the man she loved? It was unbearable even to think about it.

She started the drive home just a short time later. If Alice guessed that something was wrong she said nothing, and Ross put on a bluff exterior as though all was right with the world. It was only his eyes that gave him away. There was a bleakness there when he thought no one was looking, and it cut Izzy to the quick.

Christmas dinner with her family was generally a happy time. Today her grandparents were there to share the meal with them, along with uncles and aunts and cousins, and then the neighbours, who came round to share a drink afterwards and watch the Queen's speech on the television.

If her father was more quiet than usual no one except Izzy and her mother seemed to notice, and the neighbours forgot themselves enough to mention that Ross had invited everyone over for the Hogmanay celebrations in less than a week's time.

'It was on the day when the power lines were down,' one of the neighbours said. 'He said we were all invited. He's planning on making it a tradition to hold a party up at the castle. I think it should be good. It was generous of him to have us all over there when we were cold and hungry, don't you think?'

Izzy's mother glanced at her husband. 'I thought it was a nice thing to do. He sent us an invitation for the party through the post. We weren't there that day, you see.'

'Ah…yes, that's true.' The neighbour looked uncomfortable for a moment, and then sought for a way to change the subject. 'I thought the Queen's speech was very good this year, didn't you? She was showing us how people triumph over the bad times, and how people can be uplifted even when they have been suffering.'

They all started to talk about the TV schedules and disaster was averted—for the time being at any rate. Izzy helped to clear away the crockery from the dinner table, and lost herself in thoughts of what might have been if only circumstances had been different. Her body might well be here, in her parents' kitchen, but her soul was away across the miles by the loch, with the Laird of Glenmuir.

She didn't see Ross again in the week that followed, though she heard about a helicopter rescue when he airlifted an injured man to hospital following an accident on the main road to Inverness. His patient had suffered cardiac contusions, and by all accounts it had been touch and go for a while, but Ross had managed to get him there safely, and according to the newspaper reports he was now recovering from his ordeal.

The weather became more and more treacherous as New Year's Eve dawned, with the wind rising and blowing the snowflakes this way and that, so that Izzy had to keep her head down to avoid it blowing into her eyes whenever she went to put out seeds and raisins on the bird table in her parents' garden.

'They say there are trees coming down in the highest areas,' her mother said. 'According to the news report they're worried about hazards on the roads and on the railways. There was something on the television just a little while ago about a branch coming down on the line that passes by the village. I didn't hear that they've put a halt to any of the trains, though. Isn't Lorna supposed to be coming back today?'

Izzy was suddenly on alert. 'Did they say the branch had actually come down on the line? Surely they must have stopped the trains if that's the case?'

'I didn't hear all of it,' her mother said. 'Steven from next door came to ask if your father could give him a hand with the logs for his fire. He was having trouble stacking them in the shed.'

Izzy turned on the television set and tuned to a news programme. 'There's nothing,' she said in frustration. 'Lorna *was* supposed to be coming back around about this time. She has to work tomorrow, and there's only the one train running because of the holidays. I think I'll try and reach her on her mobile to see what's happening. I need to know that she's safe.'

There was no answer from Lorna's mobile, and Izzy paced the room in frustration. Maybe she had switched it off, or perhaps she was in a poor signal area. Either way, Izzy was left feeling helpless. She sent a text message, asking Lorna to get in touch.

A few minutes later her phone rang, and she seized it eagerly. It wasn't Lorna, though. It was the ambulance service, calling her out to attend to what they were calling a 'major event'.

'We need you here as soon as you can manage it,' the controller said. 'If you can get hold of Ross, we need him, too. He's not answering his phone, so it may be that he's in an area where he can't get a good signal.'

Izzy rang the landline at the castle and Maggie answered. 'He's busy with the preparations for this evening's Hogmanay celebrations,' she said. 'He's been out and about all morning fetching supplies, and then he's been sorting things out in the cellar and what have you. I'll see if I can find him.'

Izzy hurried to get into her emergency medic uniform. 'Where are you off to?' her mother asked.

'The railway line by the embankment,' Izzy said. 'You were right about the branch coming down—except that it was more than a branch, and it came down just as the train was approaching. The driver pulled on the brakes, but he didn't quite make it in time and the first carriage of the train has derailed. We need all the help we can get. We don't know how many people were on the train. I don't even know if Lorna is one of the people who are injured.'

Her father started to put on his coat. 'I'll come with you,' he said. 'They may need help with lifting. I expect Steven from next door will come along, too.'

Her mother did some rapid thinking. 'I'll organise some vacuum flasks, for soup and the like. You go on ahead. I'll get someone to drive me there.'

Izzy drove as fast as she dared, given the road conditions. Steven and her father followed on behind in Steven's car. Izzy didn't know what to expect, but any derailment was likely to be very bad news.

Ross was there ahead of her, tending to the wounded who were being brought out on stretchers. 'So far we're dealing mainly with broken limbs and cuts from twisted metal. There's been nothing too serious up to now.'

'Lorna was supposed to be on this train,' she said. 'Has there been any news of her? I keep trying her phone, but there's no answer.'

He shook his head. 'Nothing so far. All the people who were in the carriages behind the first one have managed to get out, and they've been taken to the community hall. Lorna wasn't among them.'

He waved a hand towards the carriage. 'We've brought out everybody we could reach, but there's still a part of the carriage that we can't enter. The metal has buckled, making it difficult for anyone to get in there. And we can't go in through the windows because they are too distorted.'

'What about the fire crew?' Alice looked around. She couldn't see any heavy lifting equipment in place.

'They've brought in as many people as they can, but with the holidays they're short-handed. Some people have gone away for the New Year. The lifting equipment is on its way, but it will take some time to get it into position.' He looked concerned. 'The trouble is, I *know* that there are people trapped inside, and I'm worried in case they need urgent help. There's a lot of glass about, and if they have been cut they could be bleeding badly.'

And Lorna could be one of them. 'Is there anything we can do to get through to them? I'm quite slender, so perhaps I could squeeze into a small gap?'

'Maybe if we have a word with the fire crew and gather together some helpers we could sort something out.'

In the end it was decided that there was a small section where it might be possible for Izzy to squeeze through into the compartment. The men worked together to open up the section, using what equipment they had to widen the space. Inside the cavity they could hear somebody groaning in pain. After a while the sound stopped, and Izzy began to worry.

'I'm going in now,' she said. Her father, Ross and Steven steadied the metalwork while she struggled into the cabin. She shone a torch around. In the far corner a woman lay crumpled between the seats. It wasn't Lorna, and she couldn't see anyone else in there. There was a lot of blood, and as Izzy investigated she could see that it was coming from a large gash on the woman's arm.

'I'm going to apply a pressure pad to try to stem the bleeding,' she called back to Ross. 'And I'll put in an intravenous line.' She worked quickly, giving the woman oxygen and trying to resuscitate her. Finally the woman's eyes flickered, and Izzy breathed a faint sigh of relief. 'We'll get you to hospital as soon as we can,' she said.

Shining the torch around, she tried to discover if there was anyone else inside the carriage. 'There was a man,' the woman said. 'I think he's trapped under the seat.'

Izzy went to investigate where the woman had indicated. Her pulse quickened and her mouth went dry as she saw a hand sticking out from under the metalwork. 'I need some help in here,' she said. 'There's a man beneath the seat. I can feel a pulse, very faint, but he's definitely still alive.'

It was some five minutes before they could open up the gap wide enough for Ross to crawl through. 'Your father has his back against the metalwork, holding it up,' he told her. 'Steven is helping, and the fire crew have gone to get more cutting equipment. In the meantime, let's see if we can lever this seat off the injured man.'

He looked around and found a loose bar of metal lying around—possibly one of the handrails, or maybe a piece from the table. 'See if you can heave the seat upwards while I try to lever it out of the way.'

Between them they pushed and pulled, until they felt the metalwork start to give way. 'I think it's coming,' Ross said. 'Okay, get your breath and then let's try again.'

Finally the seat tipped backwards, freeing the man enough for them to carefully pull him away to safety. But then there was a grinding noise and a piece of the overhead luggage rack started to fall away. Ross moved quickly to cover Izzy with his body and at the same time protect their patient. The piece of rack slithered away and fell to the floor with a clatter.

'Are you all right in there?' Izzy's father queried sharply.

'We're fine,' Izzy called back as Ross's arms closed around her. 'At least I think we are. I'm not so sure about Ross.' She looked at him. 'Are you hurt?'

'We're all okay,' Ross said. 'Let's get to our patient.' He knelt down beside the man.

'I'm going to put a tube in his throat to help him breathe,' Ross told Izzy. 'He'll need fluids, and splints for his arm and leg. I can see there's definitely a fracture to the tibia, and it looks as though the arm could be broken, too.'

Both of the injured people were given painkillers. When Izzy assessed their vital signs she found that the woman's condition was stabilising, but the man's blood pressure was low and he was in a critical condition. At least he was still alive.

The fire crew opened up the gap so that the paramedics could go in with stretchers, and soon Izzy emerged from the carriage into the light of day once more. Her father looked bone weary from his exertions to keep open the escape route, as did his neighbour.

'Thank you both for your help,' Ross said, as he

came out into the open air and straightened up. 'We couldn't have done it without you.'

'You didn't do a bad job yourself,' her father said. 'You and my daughter both. I was worried for her safety, as well as for the people in there, but I knew you would look after her.'

Ross's mouth curved. 'I would always look out for your daughter's safety,' he answered. 'I love her, and I want her to be my wife. She's the only one who appears to have any doubts.'

Izzy's father appeared to be shocked by that revelation. He looked from one to the other but made no comment, and Izzy guessed that he was trying to absorb what Ross had said. 'I must go and see to our patients,' she said.

'Me, too,' Ross commented, starting to follow her. He paused, turning to look back. 'I'm not sure that I feel too much like celebrating,' he murmured, 'but I don't want to let anybody down, and the Hogmanay festivities will go on as planned. It would be good to see you and your wife there with us.'

They went over to the ambulances and supervised the transfer of the injured people to the vehicles. 'I expect the man will go straight up to Theatre after he's been properly assessed,' Izzy said. 'I still can't think what's happened to Lorna, but she definitely wasn't on the train.'

'Maybe she decided to come back by road?' Ross said. He glanced at Izzy. 'Will I see *you* tonight up at the castle?'

'Oh, yes,' she murmured. 'Like you, I don't feel much like celebrating after all that's gone on today, but I do want to see an end to this year. I'm hoping that the New Year will bring fresh hope for all of us.'

CHAPTER ELEVEN

'Wow!' Ross stared at Izzy as though he was seeing her for the first time. 'You look beautiful. I'm almost lost for words.'

'That would be a very strange thing,' Izzy said. Inside, though, she was glowing at the compliment. She had chosen the dress especially for this evening. It was made of a soft, floaty material that swirled around her calves as she walked. The shoulder straps were thin, lightly spangled strips, and the bodice fitted her to perfection. Her shoes sparkled, too, complementing the straps and the tiny clips that she wore in her hair.

'Welcome to the *ceilidh*,' he said, taking her hand and drawing her towards the Great Hall. 'There's dancing in the main reception room, and music in here, too. We thought we'd have the bagpipes later on, nearer to midnight and the welcoming in of the New Year.'

Izzy looked around at the gathering of people. They were all chatting and laughing, and generally making merry. She knew all of them, either from the village or from her work at the A&E unit, and she acknowledged those who looked her way.

Then she stared along the length of the banqueting table. 'I thought we saw a feast that day when the film crew were here, and again when you set out the food for the people who'd lost their electricity, but this—this is something else again. You've done us proud.'

'Molly and Cameron like it, anyway. Cameron's eyes were like saucers. He helped us to set it all out, but I think he had a few nibbles along the way, so his tummy's quite full at the moment.'

'You must have been so busy doing all this,' she said. 'Or did you get caterers in?'

'It was a combined effort, really, between me and Alice, the children and Maggie. Mary from the shop came along and brought some food to add to the selection, and Greg brought some wine and some friends. Alice's sister and her husband have come over from the Lake District with their children to join in the celebrations and stay with us for a few days, so Alice is very happy.' He glanced around at the assembled crowd. 'Lorna's here, too. Apparently she came home by car as far as the A&E unit, and Greg brought her in from there.'

'That's a relief. Though I rang her parents to find out if they knew anything, and they told me she'd set off with a friend rather than come back by train.' She glanced at him. 'Have you heard anything more about the casualties from this afternoon? I rang the hospital earlier, and they said the man was undergoing surgery for chest injuries. Everyone else was doing reasonably well.'

'Yes, I asked one of the senior house officers to ring me and let me know what was happening. He said that the man had come through the operation all right, and that his vital signs were improving. I guess his New Year gift is that he's alive to see it.'

She tilted her head to listen to the music that

sounded all around. 'I'm not sure where that's coming from,' she said, 'but it's beautiful—lovely Highland music.'

'Ah, that's from my hidden music system. It's meant to fill your soul with dreams of romance.' He draped an arm around her and immediately her senses tipped into chaotic activity. Warmth from his fingers spread along her waist and over her hip, pooling in her abdomen. She looked up at him. She loved this man. Why could she not tell him what he wanted to hear? That she was happy to be with him at whatever the cost?

'I take it that your father hasn't said anything about coming along this evening?' he murmured.

She shook her head. 'I haven't seen him since we left the railway line this afternoon.'

'Never mind. Let's try to enjoy ourselves anyway. Shall we go through to the reception room? It's more lively in there. We have people who can play the piano and the guitar, and there are even some who can sing. We might even have a dance together. Perhaps I can persuade you that it wouldn't be so bad to be married to me? I could make you forget everything else so that there was only you and me.'

He held her close, looking down at her, and she wanted to say there and then, *That's all I want. Let's do it. Let's forget the outside world and think only of ourselves.*

In the reception room space had been cleared for dancing, and couples moved to the rhythm of the music, all of them having a good time. Across the room Izzy saw that Alice was sitting in her wheelchair and the children were by her side. Izzy and Ross made their way towards her, and a moment later Molly and

Cameron went to join their cousins and other youngsters who had come to enjoy the festivities.

The musicians struck up a slow waltz, and Greg walked over to Alice. 'I'm your Prince Charming,' he said. 'Would you like to dance?'

Alice laughed softly. 'Well, now, I'd like to very much. But I think I might have a little bit of a problem there.'

'I can deal with problems,' he said. 'I have this magic touch, you see.' He held out his hands to her, though he was still some small distance away.

Alice carefully stood up. She straightened, took a moment to get her balance, and then she took a faltering step towards him, then another, and then another. He clasped her hands and drew her to him, and together they swayed to the music. All the people nearby watched and clapped, and a great cheer went around the room.

Ross held out his hands to Izzy. 'Shall we dance?' he asked softly. 'I'm definitely not Prince Charming, but I could do a fair representation of a lovesick Scottish laird.'

She went into his arms and danced with him. It was as though she was floating on air. He was everything she needed and wanted, and she made up her mind that for the next hour or so at least she would treasure this time with him and fill her heart with hope that one day her path would be smooth.

It was some time after eleven, when they had eaten all that they wanted for the moment and Izzy had sipped a glass or two of wine, chatting with friends and dancing with Ross, that there was a faint stirring at the other end of the room. Voices became hushed, and people turned to see that Izzy's parents had walked into the room.

'We meant to get here earlier,' her mother said, a little flustered. 'But the car wouldn't start. And there wasn't a taxi—well, there wouldn't be, would there, when Jock's at the party?'

There was a faint ripple of laughter throughout the room. 'You should have rung me,' Izzy said. 'You know I would have come and fetched you.'

Her father looked at her. 'And you full of the drink? I think not. I told your mother I would fix the car, and I did—didn't I?' He looked at her mother, his brows raised in a questioning manner.

Her mother became even more flustered. She looked around the room and said, 'Go on with your dancing, everyone. You're here to have a good time, not to look at us.'

Ross came to stand beside them. 'It's good to see you both here,' he said. 'I wasn't sure whether you would manage it.'

'Well, I've had time to do a lot of thinking,' her father said. 'I had to respect what you did this afternoon—looking after the people in the train and protecting Izzy when she might have been injured.' He frowned. 'And then I heard that you'd brought in dredging equipment to sort out the riverbed. That should certainly make a difference to my salmon fishing interests. I realise that I might have misjudged you. Maybe you're not so bad as I've been painting you.'

Ross laughed. 'I'm glad to hear it. Maybe you're not such a grouch as you make out. Anyway, I'm glad to see you here.' He glanced around. 'In fact, I was just going to tell everyone about the lighting of the torches. It was young Molly and Cameron who suggested to me that we ought to revive the tradition.'

He addressed the gathering of people. 'For anyone who wants to join in, we're going to have a procession around the castle walls. The lighting of the flame is done so that we dispense with the darkness of the past and take the knowledge and the wisdom from the old year into the new one. We forget the bad things that have happened in the previous year and carry the flame of hope and enlightenment into the New Year.'

He looked at Izzy's father. 'What do you say to that, Stuart?'

Her father nodded. 'I think Molly and Cameron have come up with a great idea. Like Izzy said to me a while ago, we should concentrate on the good in people. I've been very much taken up with the bad things that have happened in the past, and it took Molly and Cameron to show me that what makes for happiness in this world is the love of family.'

He looked across the room to where Alice was sitting beside Greg. He started towards her. 'I am sorry for all the hurt that I've caused you,' he said. 'I know that you did what you did for love, and I respect you for that. Can you forgive me?'

Alice lifted her arms to him and he bent towards her, holding her tight and whispering softly against her hair. After a while he released her, and she smiled up at him. 'Will you carry a torch for *me*, Pops?' she asked. 'I'm not really up to doing that for myself this year, but I promise you next year I shall join the procession.' Greg reached over and placed his hand on hers, emphasising that vow and silently offering support.

'I will, Alice,' Stuart said. 'I'll hold it high for the world to see.'

He turned back to face Ross, and Ross gave a wide smile and said, 'Come on, then, everyone. We have the torches ready in the kitchen, and we have to do the full circuit before midnight strikes. We want to be back here together to see this New Year in properly, don't we?'

Within minutes the procession of cheerful revellers took off around the walls of the castle, accompanied by the haunting sound of bagpipes, and Izzy looked up to see that the men stood at the top of the square tower, piping the torch bearers on their way.

The torches were set finally in a brazier on the flat roof of the tower, and fireworks were let off to shoot high into the sky. 'I think we should go inside,' Ross said after a while. 'It will soon be midnight, and we need to toast the New Year.'

The heavy chimes of the clock sounded the midnight hour in the Great Hall and everyone joined in, counting down until the last chime rang out, and then a great cheer went up. Ross drew Izzy into his arms, kissing her with a thoroughness that took her breath away. All around her people were clinking glasses, toasting the New Year with champagne, but the champagne was on Izzy's lips, placed there by the man of her dreams.

Ross kept his arm around her as he led her towards the great fireplace. 'I want to make a speech,' he said, addressing the gathering once more. 'And you needn't groan, because it's a short one. There are only three points I want to make.'

Still sipping their champagne, everyone looked towards him. Izzy's parents were just a short distance away, toasting one another, and Alice and Greg and the children were close by, with Alice's sister next to her. Lorna stood with them, and behind her all the rest of the villagers, Izzy's friends and work colleagues, stood around.

'First, I thought this might be the right time to let you know that if there is anyone among you who wants to buy out their tenancy, and become owner of their land and property, I will be glad to have my lawyers draw up the appropriate papers. I'm sure we can agree fair terms.'

A hum of conversation started up.

'Just let me know over the next week or so if you're interested,' Ross said. 'And that brings me to my second statement. I know that some of our young people have been leaving the Highlands to go and live and work in the main towns and cities. I have plans for this estate, and plans to develop a winery—and I know you'll all be happy to go along with that, because you've been partaking of the wines all evening and coming back for more…'

There was laughter from the assembly.

'And I also want to go ahead with a timber plantation. For both of these projects I will need workers to keep them going. I'm looking for an estate manager, as well.' He paused for a moment, looking around. 'That's not all. I know you heard about the film crew that came here a while back. That was just the beginning, and I know that they are looking for extras to take part in the next production that will be done here. I'm sure we have some budding actors among our crowd.'

There was more laughter, and still they looked at him expectantly. 'You said there was a third thing,' Izzy's father said.

Ross looked at Izzy, and there was a question in his eyes. 'It concerns you and me,' he said softly, so that the others could not hear. 'Shall I be able to place that diamond ring on your finger, do you think?'

'Yes,' she said, smiling at him. 'You will.'

He faced the crowd once more. 'I'm hoping that we will see all of you at another gathering very shortly— in the church. That's if Izzy gives me the answer I want.'

He turned to look at her, reaching for her hand. 'Will you marry me, Izzy? Will you be my wife?'

Happiness glowed in her smile. 'I will, Ross.'

He kissed here there and then, sealing the bargain, and then turned to face the crowd once more. 'You're all welcome at the ceremony, and at the reception afterwards. We'll look forward to seeing you there.'

A cheer went up, loud enough to reach the rafters, but Izzy was barely aware of it because Ross was kissing her again, and that was all that mattered to her right then.

Some time later, when he finally released her, she gazed around to find that people were smiling and drinking and chatting to one another.

'We'll have to design a new coat of arms,' Ross said, glancing behind him at the shield above the fireplace. 'Buchanan and McKinnon.'

'Don't you mean McKinnon and Buchanan?' Izzy's father said pointedly.

Ross raised a dark brow. 'Are you trying to start an argument with me, Stuart?' he said.

'Argument? What makes you think that?' Her father's voice was sharp edged.

'Shall we say a touch of belligerence in your tone?'

'Oh, I see. So you're saying that I'm aggressive, are you? Me? I don't have an aggressive bone in my body.' Stuart McKinnon turned to scowl at the crowd. 'And I'll fight any man here who says different.' A wide grin spread over his face.

Laughter rang out. 'Way to go, Stuart.' Greg was chuckling.

'Aye.' Izzy's father raised a glass to her and Ross. Her mother joined him, lifting her own champagne flute. 'You have our blessing, both of you,' he said. 'May all your troubles be little ones.'

Ross squeezed Izzy, holding her close as she looked up at him. 'I think I'm the happiest girl in the world,' she told him.

There was a loud rapping on the outer door, and she frowned. 'Who could that be?'

'That will be someone I'm expecting,' Ross said. 'I believe it's our first-footer, come to see in the New Year with us.'

They went together to open the door, and there stood Jason Trent, the actor, tall and dark-haired, bearing gifts.

'I've brought coal,' Jason said, 'so that your hearth will always be warm, bread so that you will not go hungry, and a silver coin so that you may be prosperous into the New Year.'

'Come in,' Ross said. 'In return we'll give you whisky and good cheer, and food to fill you up.'

'Exactly what I wanted,' Jason said. 'And Lorna, of course. I take it she's here?'

'She is. She's waiting for you in the Great Hall. You know the way, don't you?'

Jason nodded, and grinned. He knew better than to expect Ross and Izzy to follow him. They were far too busy kissing.

NEW BOSS, NEW-YEAR BRIDE

BY
LUCY CLARK

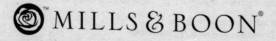
MILLS & BOON®

First published in Great Britain 2009
Paperback edition 2010
Harlequin Mills & Boon Limited,
Eton House, 18-24 Paradise Road, Richmond, Surrey TW9 1SR

© Anne and Peter Clark 2009

ISBN: 978 0 263 86975 0

Harlequin Mills & Boon policy is to use papers that are natural, renewable and recyclable products and made from wood grown in sustainable forests. The logging and manufacturing process conform to the legal environmental regulations of the country of origin.

Printed and bound in Spain
by Litografia Rosés, S.A., Barcelona

Lucy Clark is a husband-and-wife writing team. They enjoy taking holidays with their two children, during which they discuss and develop new ideas for their books using the fantastic Australian scenery. They use their daily walks to talk over characterisation and fine details of the wonderful stories they produce, and are avid movie buffs. They live on the edge of a popular wine district in South Australia, and enjoy spending family time together at weekends.

Recent titles by the same author:

BRIDE ON THE CHILDREN'S WARD
SURGEON BOSS, BACHELOR DAD
A MOTHER FOR HIS TWINS
CHILDREN'S DOCTOR, CHRISTMAS BRIDE

To Lisa & Brenton—
who inspired the pigmy blow-gun dart! Cheers!
Rom 15:1–4

CHAPTER ONE

THIS was it. Melissa Clarkson took a deep breath and looked up at the building which seemed to stand in the middle of nowhere, surrounded by rich ochre dirt.

This was it?

'What a dump,' she mumbled under her breath. How could her brother work in such a place? She frowned, then realised she wasn't here to judge him. She had come to Australia's west to meet her brother—for the first time.

Dex Crawford was the biological brother she'd been told about just over two years ago, and it had taken her quite some time to track him down. Now, today, she was finally going to meet him. He knew she was coming. He knew she was going to be working along-side him for the next twelve months as part of the Didja medical team, providing medical care to the commu-nity and the workers at the large industrial mine which was situated not too far out of town. Melissa also knew her brother hadn't been too keen at the prospect of meeting her, and she could understand that. When a complete stranger told you that you were biologically related it was bound to come as a shock.

She'd been travelling for what seemed to be for ever,

but after taking a plane from Tasmania to Melbourne, and another plane from Melbourne to Perth—with a quick three-hour stopover in Adelaide along the way— she'd made her way to the 'Outback' train station and boarded just before midnight. She hadn't slept much, whether due to the heavy rocking of the train or to apprehension at the brand-new adventure staring her in the face. Either way, when she'd arrived in Didja hope had mingled with excitement at the thought that Dex might be there to meet her.

The hope had dwindled as she'd slung her carry-on luggage across her shoulder and gathered her two suitcases, never more thankful that they were on wheels. She'd trudged out into the almost noon sun and studied a very old town map in the hope that it would show her the way to the medical clinic.

And now she stood in front of this dilapidated building, excitement at her new adventure being sucked up into the dry heat. 'This can't be it,' she murmured, not wanting to take another step further lest the building fall down right before her very eyes.

'Excuse me?'

Melissa turned at the rich deep tones and shielded her eyes as she looked up and then up some more into the face of the rather tall man who now stood next to her.

'Are you Melissa Clarkson?'

'Yes. Yes, I am.' Hope flared once more. Was this him? Was this tall, handsome stranger her brother? 'Are you Dex?'

'No, I'm Joss,' he corrected, and held out his hand. 'Josiah Lawson.'

'Ah.' Melissa tried not to show her disappointment as she shook his hand. She also tried to ignore the way her hand, which was warmly enveloped within his, felt safe and secure. Perhaps it was because she was so incredibly out of her comfort zone at the moment, and any remote sense of security would be bound to cause her to react to a simple handshake from a handsome stranger. Josiah Lawson was her new boss. The owner of the Didja clinic and the man who had offered her not only a twelve-month contract but the opportunity to take her time and really get to know her brother.

'Were you expecting Dex to pick you up?'

'I was…hoping.' And he was still holding her hand.

Unlike him, she was not wearing sunglasses—nor a hat—and when he looked into her deep brown eyes he could instantly see the family resemblance. The deep red sun-dress she wore highlighted the fairness of her skin and complemented her blonde hair, which had been swept back into a single ponytail. Joss knew she'd been travelling for well over twenty-four hours, yet somehow she'd managed to look as fresh as a daisy.

It was clear she'd been hoping her biological brother would pick her up, would show an interest in her arriving in town, but he hadn't. Dex didn't seem to care one way or the other about his new 'surprise sister'—as he called her—and it had been Joss who had needed to point out the benefits in at least meeting Melissa. Still, she didn't need to know all of that.

'Dex is in clinic, so I volunteered to come and meet your train.' He smiled politely at her. 'I apologise most profusely for being late, and then, I confess, I couldn't find you.' He gestured to the building in front of them with his free hand. 'What are you doing in this part of town?'

Melissa was a little puzzled at his words. She pointed to the building in front of them. 'Finding the clinic.'

'The clinic? You think this is the clinic?' His lips twitched into a small smile and she wished she could see his eyes, but they were hidden behind dark sunglasses and the bushman's hat planted firmly on his head.

'Isn't it? I read the town map at the train station and it said…' She shook her head and sighed. 'I am relieved, though. How anyone could practise medicine in this old…building—'

'For want of a better word,' he interjected.

'—is beyond me.'

'Well, Dr Clarkson, allow me to escort you to the real Didja clinic.' It was only now that he dropped her hand and in turn picked up both of her suitcases. 'This way, if you please.'

What on earth was he doing? He'd been holding her hand for too long—like a complete moron. She was a colleague. She was here to work and that, as far as he was concerned, was all there was to it. The fact that she was a bit of a looker meant nothing, either.

He led her down the side of the old medical centre, her suitcases proving to be no effort for him whatsoever. Melissa watched as he walked a few steps in front of her, admiring the length of his back, the broadness of his shoulders and the flexed arm muscles which were almost straining to break through his short-sleeved cotton shirt.

He wore thick socks with a pair of well-worn work boots, and a pair of long khaki shorts which provided her with the view of just enough tanned leg covered in dark curly hairs. Very nice, well muscled legs. His butt was firm from what she could see, as the cotton shirt was untucked. Combined with the hat, he looked nothing like a doctor—or at least nothing like the doctors she was used to working with in a pristine hospital setting. She had to keep reminding herself that this was, to all intents and purposes, the Outback of Australia, even though she wasn't in the Northern Territory, or Far North Queensland, where most people equated the Outback to be.

She had landed herself in the inland Western Australian Outback, and judging by the vast contrast with Tasmania's lush greenness she knew she was most definitely a very long way from home.

They'd rounded the old clinic and were walking down what Melissa realised was a small side street, although it appeared to be no more than a clearing in the never-ending dirt. Joss then turned right down an even smaller clearing. A lane, perhaps? Within another minute, Melissa found herself walking through what she belatedly realised was someone's front garden. There were plenty of green gum trees and bright flowering bottle brushes around the house, and the green of the leaves and the brown of the trunks blended in a picturesque way with the ochre ground. There was the odd patch of grass, but it wasn't a vibrant green—rather it was dull and brittle as they walked over the scattered tufts.

'Uh…' She couldn't help feeling uncomfortable. 'Joss?'

'Yes?'

'Are you sure this is the right way?'

He stopped and looked at her, his lips twitching a little. It was on the tip of his tongue to come back with a witty comment, but at the tired, confused look in her eyes he decided she'd probably had enough for the time being, and wanted nothing more than to lie down in a bed beneath a cooling ceiling fan and sleep.

'I'm sure.'

He continued on, seemingly not at all perturbed that he was walking through someone else's garden. They continued on down the side of the house and into the backyard, which boasted even more of the withered grass and native evergreen gum trees, although these trees had been decorated with bright coloured tinsel, reminding Melissa that Christmas had been just a week ago. Why did it seem like months had already passed? The New Year began tomorrow, meaning that when the clock struck midnight the beginning of the next phase of her life would really begin. Her year in Didja, working alongside the man before her and her brandnew brother, would commence.

Her stomach churned at the thought of finally meeting Dex, of coming face to face with him, of being able to touch him. Her little brother… And the moment was drawing closer and closer with each step she took.

Melissa snapped out of her reverie as Joss called a cheery greeting to a woman pegging out washing on the line.

'This is the new doctor at the clinic,' he remarked, putting her suitcases down for a moment so he could perform the introductions.

Melissa had pasted on a smile and was ready to shake hands and be polite. She was most certainly surprised when the woman dropped the pegs and wet clothes back into the basket and flung both arms around Melissa, squealing with delight as she did so.

'Oh, Doc Joss. You said you'd do it. You said you'd do it and you've done it.'

The woman was exuberant as her strong arms kept squeezing Melissa. Melissa stared with wide-eyed astonishment at her new colleague. Joss merely chuckled.

Melissa mouthed the words 'help me', but it was a good five seconds later that Joss decided to do just that.

'All right, Minerva. Put her down. Let her go.'

'You did it, Doc Joss. She's here. She's here!' Minerva was now past the point of excitement.

'I take it my arriving in town is a good thing?' Melissa straightened her clothes as she spoke.

'You could say that.' Joss dropped his tone and stepped closer, the spicy scent of whatever he was wearing winding around her with a very pleasing effect. 'I've been trying to get a female doctor to come to Didja for quite some time.'

'Hence why I've been locked into a twelve-month contract?'

'Hence,' he agreed with a smile, and dipped his sunglasses down his nose to look at her.

Melissa tried not to gasp out loud as she stared into the most gorgeous and hypnotic pair of blue eyes she'd ever seen. No wonder he shielded them. Not to protect them from the bright sunlight, but in order to make sure life continued on its merry way—because she was certain that many women could simply sit around all day staring into those gorgeous depths, sighing whilst they did so.

'Oh, Doc Joss. I'm very happy. And you, Doc Melissa. You're here. You've come. Us sheilas—we need you. Honest we do.'

Minerva's bright interjections were enough to force Melissa to look away from her new boss's face. What had she been doing? Staring at her boss? Being highly unprofessional. Minerva was heading towards her again, arms outstretched for another hug, and mentally Melissa braced herself.

'Leave her,' Joss remarked kindly, and placed both

hands on Minerva's shoulders, keeping her away from scaring off his new colleague.

'I'm gonna go call everyone. This is a happy day. Happy day,' she repeated as, without a hint of farewell, she turned and went into the house.

In another second they were alone again, and Joss picked up the suitcases, indicating they should continue on their way.

'Well, if this is the reaction you're going to get, I guess it means your clinics are going to be nice and full for quite some time.'

'I guess.' So long as she still had time to get to know her brother, she was fine with her work load. Making friends and being liked by the community were all important, but they weren't her top priority, and Melissa was the type of woman who found it easier by far to keep things in order of priority. Life seemed to work better that way, and it also led to less heartache.

At the bottom of the garden they turned right onto a concrete footpath, and there before her was the main street of the town—Didjabrindagrogalon—known affectionately to its inhabitants as Didja.

'And there's the clinic.' Joss waved his hand with a flourish and Melissa stared at the building. Now, *this* was what she had been expecting. 'We have a little ten-bed hospital out the back, and a small surgery—usually only used for emergencies.'

'And you have nursing staff?'

'Quite a few of the women in town are nurses, or retired nurses who are willing to do a few days here and there. Bub's the only nurse employed full-time. She's in charge of the hospital and rules it with a heart of gold and a rod of iron. You'll like her.'

'I have no doubt.' They headed further down the

footpath towards a pedestrian crossing. 'And you're a qualified general surgeon, correct?'

'I am.'

'And Dex is the A&E specialist.'

'He is.'

Melissa nodded, but could feel Joss watching her. 'Something wrong?' she asked.

'No. I'm just wondering whether you're going to voice the questions which I can see running around in your mind.'

'You can see into my mind?' Melissa raised her eyebrows in teasing as he stopped by the kerb. There wasn't a single moving car on the road, but still both of them stood there, waiting and looking at each other.

'I can see that you're wondering what on earth could have brought Dex and I all the way to the middle of nowhere.'

'I assure you I was wondering no such thing. Besides, I can't talk. I'm a qualified OB/GYN, and I know exactly what's brought me to the middle of nowhere, as you term it. Everyone has their own reasons for doing things, Joss. Despite whatever they may be, Didja is a fortunate town to have such highly trained doctors and a group of dedicated nurses working for it.'

Joss frowned slightly as he looked down at her, his shoulders squaring as he took a deep breath, filling his lungs. 'Wow.'

'Wow, what?'

He shook his head. 'It's been a long time since I've heard anyone talk like that.' Joss checked again for cars, but still didn't move. He was impressed with what she'd said because the few locum doctors who had previously come out to Didja had been snobbish and prejudiced against anyone who chose to live in such a place. 'I think you're going to fit in just fine here, Dr Clarkson.'

'Even though my main motive for coming here is so I can get to know my brother?'

'Even though,' he agreed with a slight nod.

Joss watched as a dog rushed by in hot pursuit of a piece of paper floating on the light breeze. He picked up her suitcases and headed across the road. Melissa followed, and the instant she stepped out onto the road, a car came around the corner. She quickened her pace, but thankfully the car was going quite slowly. The driver wound down the window and called to Joss.

'Is that her?'

'Yes,' he returned as he reached the other side of the road.

The driver waved at Melissa. 'I'll be sure to tell the missus you're in town.' With that, he drove off.

Melissa stepped onto the footpath, looking up at Joss. 'I'm beginning to feel like something of a celebrity.'

'You should be, and tonight—in your honour—the whole town will gather to celebrate your arrival.' He pointed to a group of men down the street, who were all working hard setting up a stage. 'There'll be a band, a lot of dancing, some fireworks and a whole lotta Outback fun.'

'In my honour?' she asked sceptically, not believing a word he said.

'Of course.' Joss's lips twitched.

'And not the fact that it's New Year's Eve?'

He shrugged away her words. 'Pure coincidence.' He picked up her suitcases again and headed down the street. 'Best get you out of this sun. Didn't you bring a hat?'

Melissa watched him go, amazed at the way she really liked being in his company. This man, this stranger who was her boss. This man who had founded the clinic here in Didja, who had moved to this Outback land for some reason. Whilst she'd told him she wasn't curious, that hadn't been entirely true. What made a man—a general surgeon—come to the middle of nowhere and set up first-class medical facilities? And it wasn't just Joss she was curious about but her brother as well. What had made Dex come here? Why had he stayed? Why was he so indifferent about meeting her? These were definitely top of the list in the questions department, and she hoped her time here would not only help her discover the answers but also to form some sort of relationship with Dex.

'I'm guessing you'll be wanting to find your room first and get settled in, rather than having a tour of the facilities.'

'It would be nice to shower and change.'

'No doubt.' He headed down a small driveway beside the clinic, and it was then she realised that out at the back of the clinic was another building which looked just like a small block of flats. 'It's not much,' he said, indicating the building with an incline of his head. 'But it's home. There are four apartments here— the end one is currently being used for storage, but we're hoping to have a locum come on a regular basis and that's where he or she will be accommodated.'

'With three doctors here now, do you still need a locum?'

'The mining company has just announced their expansion plans. Another two hundred workers will be in the area by the middle of next year. And we cover a huge area. Three doctors simply won't be enough. If we could get a fourth on a permanent basis that would be fantastic, and if they could specialise in paediatrics it would be even better, but a man can only hope.'

Melissa had been watching him walk again, liking the firmness of his stride. When he stopped outside a door she almost careered into him, she'd been so intent on checking him out. 'Uh…you know,' she said quickly, hoping he hadn't seen her looking so closely at his derierre, 'I might be able to suggest a friend who's a paediatrician. She's been looking for some-where different to work.'

'Really? Well, I'd certainly be interested to learn more. In the meantime…' He pointed to the door next to them. 'Here's your apartment. Number three. I'm next door in two if you need anything or have any ques-tions.' He set the suitcases down and pulled a set of keys from his pocket. He chose one and unlocked her door. 'I'll get your keys to you.'

'That would be handy—otherwise I'd have to come and find you each time I needed my door unlocked.'

He chuckled at her statement. She was funny. She was relaxed. He only hoped she'd stay for the full twelve months of her contract. He knew she'd come here to find her brother, and he'd exploited the situa-tion to his advantage by providing her with twelve long months to break through Dex's defences. He only hoped the frustration she'd feel due to Dex's indiffer-ence to the entire situation wouldn't make her want to flee.

'That wouldn't be good—for either of us. I'll also try and get you an up-to-date map of the town, so you don't end up in places where a dilapidated building could fall down around you.'

'I'd appreciate it.' She went to pick up one of her

suitcases but Joss waved her away. He pushed open her door and headed inside, his firm muscles rippling once again as he carried her bags. 'Tell me, Joss. Why do you lock the doors? I thought here in the Outback there was no need?'

'There never used to be. Of course I keep the clinic locked up tighter than Fort Knox, but as a general rule people are fairly relaxed when it comes to security. The town, though, has two full-time police officers.'

'Impressive.'

'Along with the growth of a town comes growth in crime, and unfortunately Didja isn't the sleepy little town it used to be.'

'The mining company changed all that?'

'Not the mining company *per se*, but some of the people they've employed over the years.'

'It happens.'

'It does.'

Melissa hesitated for a second. She'd been looking forward to the opportunity of showering and changing for quite some time, but now she found herself wanting to prolong Joss's little visit. He was a really nice man, and she was happy about that given that she'd be working with him for the next year. Until her arrival they'd only exchanged the odd e-mail after she'd been accepted for the position and signed the contracts, and even those e-mails had mostly been filled with instructions. Now, though, she found herself quite…intrigued by him. She'd spent the last fifteen or so minutes in his company and he'd definitely made an impact.

An impact which increased when he removed his hat and his sunglasses. His hair was dark brown, short, but slightly curling around the collar. It was as though he knew he needed a haircut but couldn't be bothered.

And those eyes. Those deep blue eyes which she'd only been given a hint of earlier on were now staring at her as though she was an enigma, a puzzle, and one he wasn't sure he wanted to figure out.

'So this is your apartment.' He turned away, needing to look somewhere else—anywhere other than at the woman who was watching him with such concentrated intent. 'Air-conditioning controls are here. Ceiling fan controls are on the wall by the bed.' He pointed, then shrugged. 'I guess that's the basics covered.'

Melissa smiled. 'You've been a great tour guide so far.'

'Tour guide?' He smiled at the words. 'I guess I have, and you're welcome. You've got some time to have a few hours' rest before the big festivities begin. Clinic—fingers crossed—should finish on time, and then it's all about the party.'

'All about the party?' she repeated.

'The community waits all year for this event. It's big.'

'Looks as though I came on the right day.'

'Looks as though you did.' He took a few steps towards the door.

'So…how do I get to these festivities? I'm presuming they're at the pub or somewhere central?'

'Exactly. Everyone will be quitting work a little earlier today, so basically all you need to do is join the throng of people heading in that direction. The pub's right in the centre of the town. That's the Aussie way of doing things. You build the pub first, and the rest of the town sort of just takes shape around it.'

'Sounds sensible—especially given how hot it is out here.'

'And it'll stay at these temperatures for the next six

months. You'll get used to it soon enough. The heat and the flies. A staple of Outback life.'

'Careful. You might make me question my decision to stay.'

'Ahh, you're contracted for a whole twelve months, Dr Clarkson, and I'll not be letting you go so easily.' There was playfulness to his words, but also a hint of underlying seriousness.

'I was just teasing. I'll not be going anywhere. You can rest assured on that point.'

'Good. That's good to hear.'

Again there was a moment of silence as they stood there looking at each other. This time Melissa didn't rush to fill the void, content just to look at him. She must have made him slightly uncomfortable, though, because he took the few remaining steps to her door and opened it, letting a bright beam of sunlight into the room. He looked good, standing there, his body half outlined by the light, all golden and shiny.

'I'll leave you to it.'

'Yes. Thanks again. Much appreciated—you know, rescuing me from old buildings and the like.'

'You're welcome, Melissa.'

'Lis,' she ventured. 'My friends call me Lis.'

'Lis.' He smiled down at her, pleased that she was opening up. This was a small and intimate community and there were no grounds for pomp and ceremony. 'Listen, just to make sure you find your way about town and don't run the risk of getting trampled by a throng of thirsty miners, why don't I meet you here at around half past five?'

The instant the words were out of his mouth he regretted them. Why had he offered to do that? She was his colleague. The town wasn't that big. She'd find her own way. Still, perhaps this was him being friendly. He raised his eyebrows at the thought. He hadn't been friendly to a stranger in…he wasn't sure how long.

She nodded, pleased she wouldn't have to take her first steps into town life by herself. 'Sounds good.'

'OK. I guess I'll see you then.' He shoved his hands into the pockets of his shorts and took a half a step backwards. 'I need to check on how many patients are left. Enjoy the break of not working, because from tomorrow, public holiday or not, you'll be seeing patients.'

'Starting me off in the manner in which you want me to continue?'

He chuckled. 'Something like that. Remember, just sing out if you need any help or have any questions. Everyone's very friendly and willing to help you settle in with as little fuss as possible.'

So she was beginning to realise—and also, she thought as she closed the door after he'd left, how great it was that her professional and personal lives had managed to interconnect so seamlessly for once. She wanted to spend time getting to know her biological brother, and the Didja clinic needed an OB/GYN. It was a win-win. At least, she hoped it was.

As Melissa shut the door after him Joss headed back to the clinic, his thoughts on his new employee. She was very pretty, and he hoped that didn't cause too much of a stir within the community. Whilst forty percent of the miners were married, sixty percent weren't, and that didn't include a lot of the other young men who lived in the town but didn't work for the mining company.

Ordinarily Dex—who had been voted bachelor of

the year for the last two years running—would have been his biggest concern, but given the family connection Joss could strike him off the list.

He nodded to himself, pleased Melissa had accepted his invitation for this evening. He was determined not only to escort her to the celebration this evening but to make sure she returned safely to her apartment—alone. It had been difficult enough trying to get a female doctor to come and live here for more than a month. He wasn't going to have one of the miners take her focus away from her work.

And there was no reason for him to be concerned about himself, because one of his main motivations for settling in Didja in the first place was to get away from women. No. His pretty colleague was just that. She was pretty and she was a colleague. Enough said.

At five-thirty Melissa was ready. More than ready, in fact. She'd had enough time to shower and refresh herself, but after that she hadn't felt at all sleepy and so had walked the short block to where the hub of Didja existed—the pub.

She hadn't felt comfortable going inside, but had instead found a store where she could purchase a sun-hat, some sun-screen and a pair of sunglasses—given that hers had broken on the train journey here. She'd also bought some groceries, adding to her pile the important insect repellent and fly swat. In Tasmania the flies only came out on hot days, and as those were few and far between she wasn't at all used to the constant need to swat in front of her face and around her body.

She'd returned to her apartment, unpacked, found a home for everything and managed to get a full hour's sleep before getting ready. She'd chosen a simple sun-dress in a pale pink colour she'd bought on impulse two days before she'd left Tasmania. She liked being on time, punctual whenever possible, which sometimes with clinics and a surgical list wasn't always possible. Still, she'd been checking the peephole through her door on a regular basis for the past ten minutes, just in case Joss had been running early. As the clock ticked towards twenty minutes to six, she realised he was actually running late.

Sighing, she decided to put the kettle on and have a soothing cup of tea. No sooner had she filled the kettle than the knock came at her door. Melissa abandoned her relaxation efforts, picked up her hat and opened the door. There he was. Her new boss. Dressed in freshly laundered shorts and cotton short-sleeve shirt, his blue eyes twinkling happily, he stood before her looking—really silly.

'What...?' A laugh bubbled up as she shook her head. 'What *are* you wearing?'

Joss flicked at a cork that swung around from the hat on his head. 'What? This old thing?' He shrugged and moved his head slightly from side to side. The little corks which were dangling down on strings from his bush hat jangled around. 'I wear it every New Year's Eve.'

'You do? What on earth for?' She came out of her apartment and shut the door behind her, placing her new hat firmly on her head. Although it was getting on for six o'clock, due to daylight saving the sun wouldn't go down for at least another three hours, and it was still rather sticky and very warm.

'To remind me not to make any New Year's resolutions.'

'You don't believe in them?' They started walking

down the street and Melissa was surprised to see so many people out and about. For a sleepy little Outback town it looked as if they were sure about to have one major humdinger of a party.

'Not really. I just don't see why people only think they can change at New Year. Anyone can change at any time in their life. You don't need to wait for a change in the calendar to make a difference to your life—especially if it's a difference that's going to make you happier.'

'Good point. But I'm still not getting the hat.'

Joss chuckled. 'The hat—due to the pure silliness of it—reminds me that New Year's resolutions are just as silly.'

'For you?'

'Yes. For me. Sorry. I guess I sound all judgemental and the like. Perhaps some people need the push of a New Year to help them to change.'

'Perhaps they do.'

Joss glanced at her through the swinging corks. 'Have you already made your resolution? Is coming here to Didja your change?'

'It is.'

'To get to know your brother?'

'Yes.'

'But you didn't wait until the New Year arrived to make the decision?'

'No.'

'With or without the changing of the calendar you still would have pursued Dex. Am I right?'

'You are.'

'So you're the same as me, then. A person of action. A person who sets themselves a goal, then figures out the best route to get there.'

'I guess.' Melissa pondered on his words for a moment. 'Although sometimes the way I choose to go doesn't always come about.'

'Sounds as though there's a story there. Bad relationship?'

'Everyone has one.' She shrugged. It was true that she liked her new boss, liked him a great deal in fact, but he was also a stranger—and telling a stranger of her broken engagement wasn't something she was about to do.

'Yes, they do. But tonight—tonight is for celebrating. To say goodbye to the old and hello to the new.'

'Yes.'

'You are going to meet so many people tonight and no doubt remember next to none of them.'

'Yes,' she repeated, with absolute gusto.

'It's going to be a great night, ending with some brilliant fireworks.'

'Fireworks? Really?'

'Well…' Joss shrugged. 'Nev and Kev are setting them up, so goodness knows what will eventuate.'

'Let's hope it's not a long night in Theatre.'

'My sentiments exactly.' Joss smiled down at her. 'Do you know something, Dr Clarkson?'

'What, Dr Lawson?'

'I think you're going to fit into Didja quite nicely.'

'It's kind of you to say so.' And she hoped he was right. The only thing was she hadn't yet met Dex, and goodness only knew how he'd take to having a big sister in town—a big sister he seemed less then keen to meet.

As the evening progressed, Melissa was indeed introduced to all and sundry. She gave up trying to remember names, except those of the nurses and other clinical staff Joss introduced her to. He played the polite host and stuck by her side the entire time, and she was grateful to be able to use him as a sort of anchor for her first night in town.

Finally, though, the moment she'd been both waiting for and silently dreading arrived, and it was once again Joss who performed the introductions.

'Melissa. This is Dex.'

Melissa smiled brightly up at the man who had almost reluctantly sauntered over to them. Her heart was pounding with excitement and trepidation. Here he was. Her brother. Standing before her. For two years she'd been searching for him and now here he was. It wasn't exactly the TV show reunion she'd been hoping for, but it didn't really matter any more. They were now in the same place at the same time. The brother she'd never had the chance to know. Tears pricked behind her eyes but she pushed them away.

'Welcome to Didja.' Dex's words were deep, his tone polite, and she realised it was just as if he was greeting a normal colleague.

Melissa looked him up and down, searching unconsciously for some sort of resemblance. It appeared that he was doing the same as they stood there, just staring at each other. He had brown hair, a bit longer than Joss's, and he had brown eyes. Brown eyes which were the exact same shade and shape as her own. His nose wasn't straight, indicating a break at some point, and his lips weren't smiling at all.

Joss watched them both, picking up on the similarities and dismissing any doubt he might have had about Melissa's claims. He could tell Dex was nervous, but it was something only he would pick up on because they'd known each other for so long. This was a big moment for his friend, and he was glad he could be there to support him.

'So you're my sister?' Dex finally broke the silence.

'Yes.' Melissa swallowed over the lump in her throat.

'My real sister?'

'Yes.'

'Fair enough.' He raised a glass bottle of light beer to his lips and took a swig. 'Enjoy the party.' He took a few steps away and then turned back. 'Oh, and Happy New Year. Hope it's a good one for ya.'

'Thanks. And for you, too.'

He shrugged, then was swallowed up by the throng of people. Melissa closed her eyes, trying to control the rising mix of emotions which were surging through her. Confusion, disappointment, anxiety, frustration, elation. They were all jumbling around together.

When she opened her eyes, she found Joss watching her very closely.

'You all right?'

'Yes.' She let go of the breath she hadn't realised she'd been holding. 'Yes, I'm fine. Thank you.' She pursed her lips and gazed out into the crowd standing around in the street, most of them with a drink in hand, the pub doing a roaring trade. 'I don't know what I was expecting, but…' She shook her head. 'That wasn't it.'

'He's a very private man.'

'He seems very…personable.' She caught a glimpse of him laughing raucously with a bunch of mates.

'He is, but the real Dex is locked up deep inside. You're a potential threat to that. Still, he admires you for having the guts to come.'

Hope flared in Melissa's eyes as she looked up at Joss. 'He said that?'

'Not in so many words, but I can read it in him.'

'How long have you known him?'

Joss thought for a moment. 'Well over a decade. We've been friends since medical school.'

'Then you're the perfect person.'

He eyed her sceptically. 'The perfect person for what?' But it was too late. He already knew what she was about to say.

'The perfect person to help me to get to know him.' With that, she finished the glass of refreshing ginger ale she'd been holding and smiled up at him. 'Now, are we going to mingle some more? I'm sure there are at least another hundred people simply dying to meet me.'

Joss found it difficult to move for a second, as the smile she'd just aimed in his direction had been a bright and trusting one which had made her brown eyes sparkle with delight. Her whole being radiated instant happiness. Something stirred deep within him—a feeling he hadn't felt for such a long time. Admiration? Attraction? Whatever it was, he didn't want it. He just wanted to do his job, to live his life, and not have to worry about the pain and consternation pretty women caused.

Still, he played the host and stayed by her side, watching the relaxed and friendly way she was with everyone they met. As he'd predicted, the men in the town most certainly appreciated the new doctor, but where he saw leering grins and ulterior motives Melissa saw only Outback hospitality and friendliness.

When the time came for the big countdown there were quite a few men standing close to her, getting ready to swoop down and kiss her as midnight arrived. She was jostled from behind, and it was purely a protective instinct which made him put his arm around her.

He steadied her and decided to let his arm stay exactly where it was, glad of the excuse to draw her a little closer to him, away from the men around them.

'Get ready everyone,' the Mayor called from the small podium which had been hastily erected in the centre of the only crossroad in town. There was an enormous crowd, and they were all packed in like sheep around the stage. 'It's time for the final countdown.'

'Ten!'

'Nine!'

'Eight!'

Melissa was pushed again from behind, and felt Joss's arm tighten around her. She couldn't help the tingles which spread through her body at his touch. Was he protecting her from the other men crowded around them? Or was he displaying an interest which was more than friendship for his new colleague? She wasn't at all sure, but decided the easiest thing she could do was to do nothing.

What she did know was that, whatever cologne Joss wore, the spicy, heady scent was driving her to distraction. The warmth of his arm against her skin almost burned through her sun-dress, and as the countdown got lower she found her mouth going dry.

'Three!'

It was getting closer. Melissa parted her lips, the pent-up air escaping. No man had kissed her since Renulf, and whilst she knew this kiss wouldn't really be real, in that it wouldn't mean anything, she was still a little over-awed at the prospect of a total stranger kissing her. It was also very exciting.

'Two!'

She licked her lips and turned to look up at him.

'One!'

His arm tightened, drawing her closer.

'Happy New Year!' everyone yelled, and Joss looked down into her upturned face. It was only then she realised that, thankfully, he'd removed the ridiculous corked hat.

'Happy New Year, Lis.'

'Happy New Year, Joss.'

And, with that, he bent his head and brushed his lips across hers.

CHAPTER TWO

SHOCK.

It was the first emotion he felt. Shock. The way the touch of his mouth against hers, even though it was the most whisperish of kisses, made his body tense with the excited need for more.

Simple.

This wasn't supposed to be a complicated moment. It was New Year and he was fulfilling the tradition to kiss the woman nearest to him as a token of celebration. The fact that he'd made sure *Melissa* was the woman nearest to him was purely for the sake of the clinic. Now, though, now that his mouth was on hers, the innocent pressure increasing to something signifying more than innocence, Joss wondered at the deeper psychology of his actions.

He edged away, allowing the smallest breath of air to flow between them. He stared at her, unsure of what had just happened.

Melissa had never in all her years been kissed with such delicacy. It was supposed to be a simple New Year's kiss, and as the countdown had fallen she'd looked at the strangers around her and been ever so grateful when Joss had slipped his arm about her waist.

Then, when she'd looked up at him, the world around her had melted away. The throng of people had become non-existent as she'd waited with mounting apprehension for his lips to be pressed to hers. Now that they had she couldn't believe the way her heart was pounding double time against her chest. Nor the way her stomach seemed to be flip-flopping with delight. Or the way her knees had turned to jelly, causing her to lean into him some more. The hard, solid muscle of his chest pressed up against her, filling her with overwhelming warmth and excitement.

They were jostled again from behind, and Melissa stared up at Joss as he stared down at her. Both of them were looking at each other with wide-eyed shock and surprise. What was meant to be a brief peck of a New Year's kiss had turned into something more… something untapped…something sensual.

Fireworks were bursting high above them, spreading their colour, sound and smell far and wide in the cloudless night sky. As the loud bang from the explosions reverberated around them she felt as though her own set of fireworks were going off inside her. Honestly, what had just happened?

'Right. Now, move over, Doc,' a bloke said from just behind Joss. 'It's my turn.'

'And then me,' another said.

'I'm next in line,' chorused yet another.

Joss broke his gaze from Melissa's to turn and look at the men in question. 'This isn't a kissing booth,' he joked as he took a step away from her, needing some distance. 'You've gotta wait for the Australia Day Fair for that to happen.' It was a throwaway line, and said in complete jest, but that wasn't the way it was taken.

'The new sheila doc's doing a kissing booth at the Fair?' one of them asked.

'Whoo-ee!' The other clapped his hands together. 'I'll be looking forward to that.'

'No. That's not what I mea—' Joss tried, but it was too late. Word was spreading like wildfire, and he looked down at Melissa and shrugged.

'There's a kissing booth at the Australia Day Fair?' she asked, a little perplexed at this town's idiosyncrasies. 'Bit outdated, isn't it?'

Joss crossed his arms over his chest. 'Outdated, eh? What would you suggest in order to bring Didja into the present century? A booth where you can dunk someone in water?'

'Well, why not? It's still fun.'

'Would you be willing to be dunked?'

'Better than a kissing booth,' she murmured, trying not to speak too loud in case she offended any of the men surrounding her. 'And by outdated I meant that in this day and age, with knowledge about communicable diseases and the like…'

'So you're telling me you've just given me a disease?'

'That's not what I meant.' Melissa sighed, feeling completely exasperated. What had happened in the last few seconds? One moment Joss had been kissing her, and now he seemed to be teasing her. She just didn't understand.

She hadn't come here to become romantically involved with anyone. In fact, it was the last thing on her mind. One failed engagement was enough for her, and when Renulf had ended the engagement she'd once more been left all alone. Scared and alone. It had seemed to be the way her life was destined to be…until Dex had agreed to meet her. Therefore romantic entanglements were way, way down on her list of priorities.

So where did that delicious kiss from Joss fit into her new world? He was her colleague, her new boss and her neighbour. He was Dex's best friend. She shook her head, unable to believe she'd allowed herself to lose her head for a moment. She would forget it had ever happened. That was what she'd do. Joss certainly seemed unaffected by it. And yet…the feel of his mouth brushing across hers was still so very real, so very new, and her heart was still racing from…

'Hello, darl. This must be the newest addition to our family.'

Melissa's attention was wrenched away from her confusing thoughts about Joss as she was enveloped in a warm hug from a woman just a little shorter than her.

'Welcome, darl. I'm Bub.'

'Oh. The nurse from the hospital.'

Bub smiled at her. 'Glad to see Josiah has covered all the important particulars. That and making sure you had someone to kiss at midnight.' Bub chuckled as she spoke.

Good Lord. Had the whole town seen their kiss? Inside Melissa was mortified—not because Joss had kissed her, but because she'd allowed him to. Two seconds in this town and she'd completely lost all her common sense.

Deciding it was best not to say anything at all, Melissa merely smiled politely and glanced at Joss. He was raking both hands through his hair, which only made him look more gorgeous with the way it spiked out at different angles. She looked back at Bub, wanting to move away from the subject of the kiss, which was still causing havoc within her body.

'I hear you rule the hospital with a heart of gold and a rod of iron?'

Bub laughed loudly. 'Sounds like something my Josiah would say. Honestly, though, between him and Dex I *have* to rule it with a rod of iron. Two boys, playing around in a big world and having fun. That's not what medicine is all about. It's serious business.' Although Bub's words were spoken sternly, Melissa could see the twinkle in her eyes as she looked up at Joss.

'Agreed.'

'It's going to be nice having another sheila around full-time.' Bub hugged Melissa close again. 'Welcome to Didja, darl, and don't you ever think of leaving.'

'Oh.' Melissa wasn't sure what to say to that. She hadn't actually thought about what she'd do once the contract was over. 'I'll…uh…'

'What am I saying?' Bub tapped her forehead absent-mindedly. 'Of course you're not going to leave—not when your brother's here.' She looked around. 'Speaking of which—where is Dex? I thought he would have been over here with you to see in the New Year. It's a new start for you two. Happy families.'

'I hope so.' Melissa's words were spoken softly. Dex hadn't minded her coming to Didja, but neither had he been enthused. His reception tonight had only confirmed that. But Melissa was a woman on a mission—a mission to get to know her brother. He was all she had left and she had a whole year to make it work.

'Dex?' Joss, who towered above both women, looked around the crowd. He needed some space between himself and Melissa, and finding Dex might be just the diversion he was looking for. 'I think I saw him go back into the pub.'

'Sounds like Dex. He likes being surrounded by people. Well…girls mainly—but still, as he's such a good-looking bloke, it seems only natural.' Bub looked at Melissa. 'You've met him, right?'

'Joss introduced us,' Melissa agreed, but it was difficult to hide the hint of disappointment she'd felt at Dex's reception.

'He'll come around.' Bub patted her arm, clearly picking up on the undertones. 'Give him time. Dex's the type of man who takes for ever and a day to process information. Having a sister he knows nothing about turn up in town—well, it's bound to shake a man and make him really take a good look at his life. Everything will work out fine. I have a good feeling about it.'

'Thank you, Bub. It's kind of you to say so.' Melissa had taken an instant liking to the woman before her, and was pleased she seemed to have at least one ally. Was Joss an ally, too? She wasn't sure at this stage.

'Good girl.' Bub looked up at Joss. 'Now, as you're still protecting Melissa from the throng of would-be sloppy kissers—which, I must say, was a very good idea on your part—why not take her into the pub and get her another drink? This is a brand-new day of a brand-new year.' Bub looked pointedly from one to the other. 'Anything can happen.'

As they entered the pub, which was chock-full of people, a chorus of 'Happy New Year!' went up and more glasses were clinked in celebration. The publicans behind the bar were working hard, but still enjoying themselves in the festivities.

'Looks as though it's going to be an interesting night,' Joss said close to her ear. She could feel him standing behind her, the warmth from his body surrounding her. 'Let's see if we can't score a couple of chairs and possibly a table.'

'Hey! Doc! Over here,' someone called, and Joss

placed his hand in the small of Melissa's back and urged her in the direction of Nev and Kev, two men in their early twenties.

'Happy New Year!' both men chorused.

'Happy New Year!' the crowd roared again.

'Happy New Year,' Joss and Melissa replied, more sedately. Joss made the introductions and Nev quickly stood to offer his chair to Melissa.

'Thank you.'

'Anything for you.' The young man looked at her as though she'd just hung the moon. It was an odd sensation to be such a superstar in a town where you didn't know anyone. 'I hear you're doing a kissing booth at the Aussie Day Fair?'

Melissa turned to glare at Joss, who merely grinned. 'Actually, I'm not,' she told Nev. 'Sorry.'

'Oh.' He looked so disappointed Melissa almost thought about feeling bad. She shook her head as though to clear it. This was a new year and she wasn't going to be a people-pleaser any more, just to keep the peace. She started chatting with Nev and Kev, asking them to tell her more about the town.

Joss listened and watched the way she interacted with them. He wasn't at all sure what was wrong with him. He sat there in a crowded pub, aware of no one else but the woman beside him. Mesmerising. That was what she was. Mesmerising Melissa. He still couldn't believe he'd kissed her. It was New Year's Eve. It was supposed to be an innocent little kiss.

She had a nice smooth voice, sweet and sultry. The desire to lean over and press another delightful kiss to those lips was almost irresistible. To think of her doing a kissing booth... To think of other men wanting to sample that perfect mouth of hers... A powerful, protective need surged through him and he was astonished by the ferocity of it.

He needed room. Air. Anything. He stood up too quickly, accidentally knocking his chair to the ground. A few people turned to look; others just cheered and called 'Happy New Year' again. Nev, Kev and Melissa were all looking up at him with surprise.

'Just going to go get a drink.' He righted his chair. 'Ahh…Melissa? What can I get for you?'

'The line-up at the bar's a mile long,' Kev told him.

'That's OK.' He needed distance between himself and his new colleague. 'I don't mind.'

'Ginger ale would be fine,' she told him, when he looked at her again. He really did have the most piercing and gorgeous blue eyes. She had the feeling she could simply look into them all day long and do nothing else but sigh. At that thought, she quickly turned her head. 'Uh…thank you,' she added.

'Right.' He took drink orders from Nev and Kev before disappearing.

'So…you're Doc Dex's sister, eh?'

'That's right.'

'The one he didn't know he had?'

'That's right,' she answered again, forcing a smile.

'We should get him over here. Best you two start to get to know each other, eh?'

Before Melissa could say a word Nev was calling Dex's name, even though no one seemed to know where Dex was.

Joss stood in line at the bar and watched Melissa closely. At least with a bit of distance between them he felt a little safer. The woman had incredible brown eyes, soft skin, silky hair and a gorgeous mouth. He closed his eyes, blocking the image of her from sight.

Who was she? She'd burst into his life a few short hours ago and ever since he'd been hard pressed to stop thinking about her. She intrigued him no end, and no woman had intrigued him this much since Christina. That in itself should be evidence enough for him to keep as far, far away from Melissa Clarkson as possible.

'Dude? You OK?'

Joss opened his eyes and looked directly at Dex. 'What are you doing here? You should go and talk to Melissa.'

Dex shrugged. 'Maybe later.'

'She's here, Dex. She's come to Didja to get to know you.'

'I thought she'd come to be our OB/GYN for a year.'

'You don't think she can do both?'

Dex shrugged again. 'I don't know.' Both of them turned to look at her. 'She looks like me. I hadn't expected that.'

'There's no real question that she is your sister. The family genes are strong,' Joss agreed.

'What's she drinking?' Dex wanted to know.

'Ginger ale. Remind you of anyone?'

Dex turned and stared at his friend. 'You're having me on?'

'Nope. She wants ginger ale. Just. Like. You.' He patted his friend on the back. 'Face it, bro. She's your sister, and I think you'll have more in common than you planned on.'

'This is too much.'

'Go talk to her. Just for a few minutes. Say more than hi. She's nice.'

'Yeah.' Dex grinned widely. 'I saw at midnight just how "nice" you thought she was.'

Joss looked down at his feet for a moment before meeting his best friend's teasing gaze. 'Hmm.'

'Yeah, *bro*. You're interested in our new doctor in more than a professional capacity.'

'Untrue.' They shuffled forward in the line. 'The clinic comes first. You know that.'

Mentally, though, he told himself he wanted to find out more about Melissa Clarkson. Did she have a hidden agenda? Did she plan on making half the men in town fall in love with her? What game was she playing? In his experience women always played games, using their wiles to get what they wanted. He'd fallen victim to it once before and he'd paid the price. Since then he'd been overly cautious, and as his new colleague was beginning to arouse feelings in him he hadn't asked for, he was right to be on guard.

Melissa glanced over at where Joss still stood in line at the bar and saw he was talking to Dex. She shifted in her chair, her feminine intuition telling her that she was no doubt top of their discussion list. She wasn't at all sure she liked it, but there really wasn't much she could do about it.

'Oi! Doc!' A man beside her spoke and leaned down on the table. 'I hear you're going to be doing a kissin' booth at the Fair.'

Melissa moaned and shook her head. Well, Joss had told her that news travelled fast in this one-pub town.

'Go away, Bluey,' Nev said.

'Leave the doc alone,' Kev championed. Thankfully, Bluey did as they suggested and left, but Melissa was starting to wonder what she'd got herself into by coming to the Outback to find her brother. Was she ready for this intimate small-town life? This close-knit community? The way Joss made her feel all gooey inside when he looked down into her eyes?

Melissa looked over to where he was at the bar and

found that he was looking back at her. She didn't turn away. She should have, but she just couldn't. It was the classic cliché. Their eyes met across the crowded room.

She stared at him, at those intense blue eyes which were solely focused on her even though there was a rowdy pub full of people between them. Everything, everyone around them, seemed to stand still, to melt into oblivion.

What on earth *was* this? Melissa's mind was far from working properly, yet the undercurrents which were passing between them were so incredibly real, and when he looked at her as he was now she had the strangest sensation that her life really was about to change. How? She had no idea, but Bub's words that it was a brand-new day and a brand-new year meant that anything could happen.

'Whaddya want, Joss?' asked Wazza, one of the bartenders, and Joss quickly snapped his head around— so fast he almost cracked his neck. Joss gave the order and glanced surreptitiously at Melissa. She was back to chatting with Nev and Kev.

'Yeah!' Dex laughed and clapped him on the back. 'You're not interested in her at all.' The tone was one of pure sarcasm, but Joss decided it was simply better to let it go—because to deny it might also be a lie.

By the time he'd returned to the table and handed out the drinks he felt more in control of his faculties.

'Great job on the fireworks, mates,' he said to Nev and Kev. 'They went off a real treat, and no casualties this year. Well done.'

Nev preened under Joss's words. 'Thanks, Doc. Yeah, me and Kev really did it—and no burns.'

'Always a bonus,' Joss agreed.

Kev held his glass up and spoke loudly. 'Happy New Year!'

'Happy New Year!' came the resounding reply yet again.

Joss picked up his glass and clinked it with Melissa's. 'To a brand-new day,' he said.

'And a brand-new year,' she agreed, clinking her glass with his. She sipped her ginger ale, ignoring the effect his nearness was having on her equilibrium.

They were joined by a few other people—all interested, it seemed, in her. She guessed that was what happened when you were the new girl in a town where everyone knew everyone else. It was a very busy night, and there were so many people in the pub—most of them standing in line at the bar. Still Melissa found herself scanning the crowds for Dex. She wanted to wish him a Happy New Year, hoping that it would be just that for both of them—that he'd develop the sudden urge not only to get to know her but also to find out about his biological parents. She had all the documentation and lots of photographs to show him, to discuss with him, but she was also a realist and knew he didn't care one way or the other about his biological link.

Joss leaned closer and pointed through the crowd. 'He's over there,' he said softly, his breath fanning her neck. 'Wowing yet another group of women.'

'Who?'

'Dex. You were looking for him, right?'

Melissa turned and looked at the man beside her, only realising belatedly just how close he was to her. If she shifted in her chair a little to the left their lips would once again meet. The thought of that was enough to distract her from her task of looking for her brother. Kissing Joss. Her gaze dropped to his mouth at the same time that her lips parted. Kissing Joss. She met his eyes again and swallowed over the sudden dryness in her throat.

This was nuts—and totally and utterly wrong. He was her boss! They were colleagues. Not to mention neighbours in a very small town. She didn't want anything like this to happen. Not now. Her brain worked overtime to remember the last thing he'd said to her. Dex. Her brother. Yes. She'd been looking for him in the throng of people celebrating the New Year.

'Yes. Thanks. I *was* looking for him.' And now that Joss had pointed him out she should turn and look the other way. But she didn't.

Joss eased back, making the decision and taking action to put some much needed distance between them.

She managed to turn her head and watch her brother, who was talking animatedly to two blondes and a redhead. 'What's he like?'

'Dex?' It was Nev who spoke. 'Sheesh. Don't you even *know*?'

'That's why she's here, remember?' Joss pointed out.

'Oh, yeah. Right. Well, Doc Dex is a real smooth talker.'

'Yeah,' Nev agreed. 'Knows how to charm the ladies.'

'Yeah.' Kev nodded. 'Wish he'd leave some for the rest of us blokes in town.'

'Besides, what's wrong with Doc Joss, eh?' Nev pointed out, and Melissa couldn't help but smile at the mortification which momentarily crossed Joss's face before he hid it.

'Hey, fellas. As much as I appreciate the gesture, I'm not in need of any fixing up in the romance department. Dr Clarkson is here to work, and as far as I'm concerned that is it. She's a valuable member of the clinic team and we don't want to do anything to scare her away.'

Kev snorted. 'Then you'd best squash that rumour that she's gonna be doing a kissing booth at the Fair, otherwise someone's gonna give her a huge smackeroo and she'll be leaving town with a miner before you know it.'

'Uh…actually…' Melissa tried to interject.

'Although if she really *wants* to do a kissing booth,' Nev said, 'we don't want you to stop her.' He smiled and waggled his eyebrows up and down.

Melissa turned worried eyes to Joss.

'I'll fix it, and I'll fix it right now.' And with that Joss stood up and called for everyone's attention. It took a few minutes, but soon everyone was quiet. 'Thank you,' Joss said loudly. 'I'd just like to say a few words. Firstly, allow me to introduce our new doctor—Melissa Clarkson—'

He got no further as a rousing round of applause broke out and someone yelled, 'Here's to the new doc!' Glasses were clinked yet again.

'Here's to kissing booths!' someone else yelled, and an even louder ruckus went up.

Melissa could only close her eyes and hope all this was a bad dream. Well…not *all* of it, but this part at least.

'I have more to say,' Joss called, and again waited for silence. 'Right. Well, I'd like to clear up a rumour that's been spreading like a bad rash. Dr Clarkson will *not*—I repeat, will *not*—be doing a kissing booth at the Australia Day Fair.'

A rousing noise went up again, but this time it was full of booing and hissing and calls of, 'What?' and 'Not fair!'

'And—' Joss called. 'And—Happy New Year.'

'Happy New Year!' went up the cheer, and good moods were instantly restored.

'Satisfied?' Joss sat down and turned to look at a blushing and perplexed Melissa. 'Problem solved.'

'Wow. So that's it? No megaphone? No need to take an ad out in the *Didja Gazette*?'

Joss couldn't help but smile at her words. 'Well…at least everyone now knows. You may still get some offers here and there, but…' He shrugged. 'It's up to you what you do with them.'

Melissa stared at him for a second, but then realised he was teasing her again. She wasn't at all sure what to do. She wasn't at all sure what she'd got herself into. There was only one thing she *could* do. She threw back her head and laughed.

'You're all completely insane,' she said between giggles.

'Welcome to the club,' Joss replied, trying desperately not to let the sound of her laughter affect him. But it was to no avail. The woman was beautiful, smart, and she shared the same sense of humour as him. A dangerous combination, and one he might need to really work on resisting.

A loud noise from the corner snapped his attention back to the other people in the room. 'Oh, no. Not tonight,' he groaned as his gaze followed a line to the disturbance.

'Problem?' Melissa asked.

'Carto and Bluey.'

'Pardon?'

Joss stood from his chair and pointed. Melissa could just make out two men on the opposite side of the pub starting to push and shove each other around. Some of their mates tried to keep them apart, but tempers were starting to flare and a few punches had already been thrown.

Joss started making his way to the bar, and Melissa decided to go with him, making sure she stayed right behind him. She searched the room for Dex and saw that he, too, was working his way over to where the two men were fighting.

'Waz,' Joss said to the bartender. 'Kit.' He need not have said anything. Wazza was already pulling a large first-aid kit from behind the bar.

'That's enough, mates. Leave it alone,' Melissa heard a man call, and looked over to see that Dex had placed himself between the two men, a firm hand on each man's chest. Carto and Bluey were still hurling insults at each other, and just as Joss and Melissa reached the area Bluey leaned forward and swung another punch at Carto. But it missed and connected with Dex's jaw instead.

'Dex!' Melissa couldn't help the rush of familial concern and rushed to his side. Bluey and Carto, now free of restraint, started laying into each other with abandon, kicking over a table, knocking down other innocent bystanders and generally causing havoc.

Melissa had to fight her way through the throng of women crowding around Dex, all of them panicking. She'd just knelt down beside him when an almighty, piercing whistle cut through the air, followed by a loud, 'Oi! That's enough!'

Melissa looked around to see Joss standing near the two men, arms akimbo, as they both looked sheepishly up at him like naughty schoolboys.

'Bluey—your lip is split. Carto—you're bleeding from your eye. Now, both of you sit down before I knock you into the middle of next week. This is the New Year. You're supposed to change. To grow. To stop fighting in the bar like you do every other week. Just as well your boss has already gone home, or you'd both find yourselves on suspension tomorrow. As it is, I'll have to file a medical report.'

'Aw, come on now, Doc,' Carto protested. 'Do ya have to?' He was hauling himself up off the floor and righting a chair before he sat down. Someone else righted the table, and people started clearing up the mess which had been made.

'We was only fighting about football.'

'You two are *always* fighting about football. It's not good enough and I've heard it all before. Add to everything, you've knocked Dex off his feet.'

Both men stared over to where Melissa was kneeling beside a dazed Dex.

'Aww, jeepers, Doc. We didn't mean to,' Bluey mumbled as he held a napkin to his lip.

'I don't want to hear it.' Joss looked at Melissa and spoke more calmly. 'How is he?'

'I'm fine.' Dex winced. 'I can't believe I didn't duck in time. So stupid.'

'Stupid was getting in the middle of them in the first place. What were you thinking?' she scolded, sounding to her own ears very much like a big sister.

'Careful there, big sis. You're starting to sound more like my mother.'

'If the shoe fits…' She shrugged and accepted the towel full of ice someone handed to her. 'Hold this.'

'Am I still in the pub?'

'Lying on the floor.'

'Everybody looking?'

'Yeah.'

'Oh, this is going to be so shaming,' he moaned, and tried to move.

She put a hand on him to stop him. 'Stay still.' She

held up her finger and got him to track it. 'Good. You seem fine.'

'Except for the totally humiliated part,' he agreed, and she smiled. 'Look—I'm fine, Melissa.' His tone was quiet, yet serious. 'I've been knocked out on many occasions before.'

'It's true,' Joss said from behind her. 'Let's get you to your feet.'

'He's up!' someone yelled, and a rousing cheer met their ears. Several girls started to crowd around Dex, all highly concerned for his wellbeing.

'Happy New Year!' someone else yelled, and once again the night's festivities continued.

'So…' Joss turned Melissa and took a coin from his pocket. 'What do you want? Tails—split lip—or heads—bleeding eye?'

'What?' She looked at him as though he'd grown another head.

'Choose,' Joss urged. 'Heads or tails?'

'Er…tails.'

Joss spun the coin into the air before neatly catching it and placing it on the top of his hand. He held the coin out for her to see. 'Tails it is.'

'All right!' Bluey punched the air. 'I get the sheila doc.'

'Is this the way you make *all* important medical decisions?' Melissa asked as she pulled on a pair of gloves from the medical kit.

Joss merely gave her one of his sexy and very disarming smiles. 'Welcome to Didja, Lis.'

CHAPTER THREE

'I'LL let you know the blood test results as soon as I have them, Mrs Dittrich.' Melissa opened the door for her patient.

'I'm just a bit worried. This is my third baby, and the pregnancy is completely different from the others.'

'You've done the right thing by coming to see me.'

Mrs Dittrich stopped at the door and placed her hand on Melissa's shoulder. 'You have no idea how great it is to have a female doctor here. It's as though a collective feminine sigh has spread through the entire district. Finally we have someone who really understands us.'

'That's nice. Thank you.'

'Uhh…not that I'm suggesting that Dr Lawson or Dr Crawford are bad doctors. I'm not. It's just that—'

'It's fine,' Melissa interrupted with a warm smile. 'I understand completely. You take care, now.'

As Mrs Dittrich walked out of the consulting room Melissa saw Joss, standing on the other side of the corridor. She smiled, and he motioned a signal for drinking. She nodded and he headed off towards the kitchen.

Quickly she returned to her desk, scribbled a few notes in Mrs Dittrich's file and wrote out the official request for the blood test. When that was done she straightened the papers on her desk so it was nice and neat before heading to have a quick cuppa with Joss. Curiosity was coursing through her at the prospect of just being in the same room as him, and she dampened it down.

She needed to be careful, because she knew if she threw herself into life here in Didja, if she became too close to Joss too quickly, then she was bound to get hurt again. It was what had happened with her fiancé. They'd met, started dating, announced their engagement and called the wedding off all within six months. Moving fast hadn't worked. Trying to fill the void in her life with people simply for the sake of it hadn't worked either.

That was when she'd realised that, no matter what, she'd needed to find Dex. She'd needed to seek him out and have *him* in her life—because he wasn't just anyone…he was her brother. So she'd written to him, asking him to reconsider meeting her. It had taken a while, but she'd received a reply telling her if she wanted to come all this way to meet him, he wasn't going to stop her. Of course it wasn't exactly the reception she'd been hoping for, but the fact that he hadn't snubbed her completely was a good sign.

It appeared that the entire town was watching them—or at least watching *her*, at any rate. They were interested in how she and Dex were getting on. They were interested in the kiss she'd shared with Joss. And a few men had almost begged her to reconsider the kissing booth idea.

'So, how are things going with you and Dex? Any progress?' Bub had asked on New Year's Day, when Melissa had gone to the hospital to check on the three inpatients.

'Not really.'

'Did you know you were adopted?'

'I did. My parents never hid it from me.'

'That would have made things easy for you. Well… easier, at any rate. Did they know you wanted to find your birth mother?'

'I didn't start searching for her until after both my adoptive parents had passed away. Although they wouldn't have stopped me if I'd tried any earlier.'

'Dex, as you may have guessed, hasn't taken the news of a new sister all that well. Josiah's been the one holding him together.'

'They're close?'

'Like brothers.' Bub grinned as she spoke. 'Closer than brothers. They've been through a lot together, and it was Josiah who convinced Dex to meet you.'

'It was?'

'Yep. Said that despite the past it wasn't *your* fault he'd been adopted, and that getting to know you would be a good thing.'

Melissa blew her fringe off her forehead. 'Well, Dex's done a great job of that so far. He's said hello and allowed me to treat him for a bump to the head. Real heart-warming stuff.'

'He needs lots of time.'

'And I've got twelve months of it to give.'

'Go to the pub at night. Dex's usually there after work. Chatting and the like. If you don't feel completely comfortable just walking into the pub like that, ask Josiah to go with you.'

'Joss usually goes to the pub at night, too?'

Bub shrugged. 'Five nights out of seven—give or take a day or two.'

'Does he have family in town or in the area?'

'Josiah? No, darl. His people are all in Perth or scattered around in the major cities.'

'I wonder why he came here in the first place?' Melissa pondered, and hadn't even realised she'd spoken the words out loud until Bub answered her.

'Why don't you ask him?'

'Huh?' Melissa's eyes widened with mortification. 'Oh. Well. It's really none of my business.'

'We're a small community, darl. All living in each other's pockets. Secrets don't usually stay secret for long. I will tell you, though, that when he moved to town he was a right little recluse. Didn't do him any good. One night, as we couldn't get him to the pub, we brought the pub to him.'

'What? Really? How did you do that?' She smiled, intrigued by the story.

'Everyone grabbed a beer and walked over to where Josiah was living at the time, which wasn't far away from the old clinic near the train station. We all went down there with our beers, and Wazza hooked up a keg, and then we sat on the ground and made him come out to chat with us.'

'And did he?'

'Too darn right he did. Ya see, he was only getting to know us as patients, not as people, and in a community like this it's important to get to know the people first. This isn't some big hospital where everyone is a number. We respond better when we know that our docs are *really* interested in us—when we can get to know them, too. To see that they're just people and we don't need to be afraid of them.'

Melissa was surprised and a little confused. 'Is someone afraid of me?'

Bub shook her head. 'Ya missing the point, darl. The

pub is like our community hall. Even though we actually do have a community hall,' Bub added as an aside, 'and we do use it—but that's not what I meant. At the pub we all gather and mix, and it's where we can all be ourselves. All equals. All needing to quench our thirst. Everyone's the same. From the lowest-paid to the highest. In the pub there's no hierarchy. There are just mates.'

Mates. Melissa had sighed over the word. It would be nice to have some more…mates.

Melissa had written up the new medication for her patients and then left Bub to care for them. She was an exceptional nurse, and also appeared to have her finger on the pulse of what was happening in the community. Taking her advice would be the right thing to do—and besides, it meant she could get to know her colleagues much better.

Her thoughts turned from Bub to Joss and the kiss they'd shared. A simple, ordinary New Year's kiss which had completely rocked her world. That had never happened to her before, and she had found it extremely difficult to stop thinking about it. The man made her tingle whenever she saw him—and now he was waiting for her in the kitchenette.

Tingles or not, he was her colleague, and hopefully her friend, and that was all there was ever going to be between them. She'd had one broken heart and she wasn't in the market for another.

Melissa took a deep breath and slowly let it out, effectively calming herself down before she rounded the corner into the kitchenette. The instant she saw him the tingles returned anew.

'Milk? Sugar?' he asked as he finished pouring her a cup of tea.

'Just milk, thanks.' She watched as he stirred the

liquid in her cup before handing it to her. 'Ahh, thank you. I need this.' She walked over to the table and sat down, sipping gratefully at the tea.

'Busy?' Joss watched as she sat. She was dressed in a pair of three-quarter-length trousers which outlined her hips and slim legs. The top she wore was pale blue and highlighted her beautiful blonde hair, which was pulled back into a sensible ponytail. The scent she wore wound around him. It wasn't too strong, yet its subtle bouquet reminded him of the flower garden his mother had used to grow when he was a boy. Nostalgia combined with sex appeal. Oh, this woman was having too much of an effect on him.

He'd seen her in the corridor outside her clinic room and she'd looked tired. When she'd seen him standing there he hadn't wanted her to think he'd been watching her—even though he had. Internally panicking, he'd mimed drinking, and the grateful look which had crossed her face had made him feel a heel. So he'd made her a cup of tea—the one she was sipping right now, her pink lips blowing delicately on the hot liquid—and now that they were in the confines of the kitchenette together he was trying to figure out how to keep his distance from her.

'Yes. Very busy,' she answered.

Joss nodded and leaned against the bench, forcing his mind to stop concentrating on watching her. 'Happens.'

Melissa smiled, feeling a little odd with his mono-syllabic conversation. 'It's just as well I'm used to a big workload.'

'Good.' For a moment Joss wondered what her life had been like back in Hobart. Had she dated anyone? Was she still involved with someone? He knew next to nothing about this woman who had been on his mind constantly since she'd arrived in Didja.

A silence fell between them. Joss sipped at his drink. Melissa did the same, trying desperately not to look at him. She glanced at the table, but there weren't even any magazines there that she could flick through.

'Is it usually this busy? Not that I'm complaining, you understand,' she added quickly.

He shrugged. 'Generally.'

Again silence. Melissa tried not to sigh with exasperation. He was the one who'd invited her in here to join him for a cuppa. What was the point if he wasn't going to talk to her? She could have made herself a drink and had it in the confines of her consulting room.

'Well, back in Hobart I worked at a few different places. I spent two days a week at the Women's and Children's Hospital, two days in Hobart at a private practice and two days a week at a King Island private practice.' She paused, realising she was only reiterating what he would have read on her résumé. 'King Island is one of the small islands between Tasmania and the mainland of Australia. Where they make the cheese.'

Melissa couldn't believe how badly she was babbling. Of course he knew where the cheese came from—and even if he didn't, why on earth would he care? Then again, he didn't seem to care about making any attempt at polite conversation. If this was the way it was going to be, it would turn out to be an exceedingly long year.

Joss nodded, which at least indicated he was listening to her rambling. Melissa looked away from him and took another sip of her drink, not caring that the liquid was scalding her throat. The sooner she finished this cuppa, the sooner she could get out of there and back to her job.

She decided to just sit there and ignore him. She'd done her bit. She'd tried to make conversation. If he wanted to stay here in silence, then that was just fine with her.

Joss watched as she sipped her tea, those lips of hers almost hypnotising him the way they were placed on the edge of the cup. His own drink was getting cold, but he didn't care. He placed it on the bench beside him and shifted his weight, wanting to talk to her, to find out more about her. It was dangerous territory, though, and he'd been stopping himself time and time again from going there. She was a colleague. That was all.

He cleared his throat. 'Do you have…? I mean—' He stopped and raked a hand through his hair. This was definitely unchartered territory, but he didn't seem to be able to stop himself from voicing the questions which had been running around in his mind for the past few days. 'Back in Tasmania, do you have… someone?'

She raised her eyebrows at that. Was this why he'd asked her in here? To probe into her private life? To find out more about her? If that was the case, he'd been doing a superbly bad job at it. And now this! 'Someone?'

'Are you seeing someone?' he finally managed to get out.

'Oh.' She grasped his meaning. 'Uh…no. I was— well, I was engaged.'

'Really?' Was she on the rebound? Suffering a broken heart? Had she decided she might as well search for her long-lost brother and get over her heartache at the same time? 'How long ago did it end?'

'Early last year.'

He frowned for a second. 'Wait. Early last year as in the year that ended three days ago, or the year before that?'

'Last year as in three days ago.' She sighed in exasperation. 'Why? Concerned that if I had someone waiting in Tasmania I might not stay for the whole twelve months? I'm contracted here, Joss. I honour my contracts, and it would take something really bad to happen for me to break this one.' She raised an eyebrow at him. 'Satisfied?'

She was angry with him. That much was evident—even though it hadn't been his intention to annoy her. The woman was incredible to look at, she was smart, she was sassy, and he couldn't help but like her. That was the reason why it was imperative that he keep as much distance between them as possible and keep their relationship purely professional. 'What about family? Where are they situated?'

'Here.'

'Here?'

'In Didja.' Melissa's voice was clear, and this time Joss detected vulnerability in her words.

'But only Dex's in—' He stopped, his mind whirring too fast. His eyes opened a bit wider. 'Wait. Do you mean to tell me the only family you have is Dex?'

'Yes.'

'Only Dex?' He wanted to be clear on this.

'Yes.' Melissa put her half-drunk tea onto the table and took a breath, deciding to get the explanation over and done with as quickly as possible. 'My adoptive parents both died four years ago, and after two years of feeling all alone and miserable I decided to do something about it. So I contacted the adoption agency and tracked down my birth mother—Eva. It was then I learned about Dex. Until that time I had no clue I even had a brother, which is a shame as I was raised an only child. Anyway, Eva died about six months ago, and when Dex finally agreed to see me I wasn't about to look a gift horse in the mouth. There. Now you have it. My sorry little story.'

'Lis.'

His voice was rich and deep, just the way she liked. She could listen to him talk all day long in those sultry smooth tones. If she'd wanted to make him feel like a heel then she'd certainly succeeded. He pushed away from the bench and took a few steps towards her. 'Thank you for telling me.'

Her words had been matter-of-fact, as though she'd gone over the story in her head time and time again, but he was sure that deep down inside there was a lot of emotion stirring and bubbling away. He felt for her so much because he couldn't imagine what it would be like to be all alone in the world. With the large family he'd been raised in it was also an impossibility, but still, his heart felt for the brave woman before him. She'd been all alone—but she'd done something about it. His admiration for her increased.

'It's fine.' She watched as he walked slowly to stand beside her. Without a word, he reached out a hand and gently touched her face.

'You're really all alone?' His words were a mere whisper.

'Yeah.' Her answer was barely audible.

'There ya both are,' Areva, the receptionist, chided. Joss instantly dropped his hand back to his side and turned, walking away from her. 'What are you doing? Drinking the bores dry? Get back to work. There's

hardly any room for the patients to sit down, there are
so many of them in the waiting room.'

'Sorry,' they mumbled contritely before Areva left.

Melissa wanted to stand, wanted to take her cup to
the sink, to rinse it out and then do as the receptionist
had suggested and get back to work. Yet at the moment
she wasn't at all sure even standing would be achiev-
able, let alone doing anything else. The way Joss had
looked at her, had touched her... Her heart was still
pounding double-time. Masses of tingles had flooded
through her body, creating more explosions than the
fireworks had done the other night.

One look. One simple caress and her bones were a
mass of jelly. At least the other night when he'd kissed
her, when he'd tantalisingly brushed his mouth over
hers, when his lips had met hers—hesitantly and
politely at first, before realisation had dawned on both
of them—at least then she'd had his arm around her for
support. If she attempted to stand now she was certain
she wouldn't be able to accomplish it and would end
up in a heap on the floor.

Why did he have to be so confusing? One second he
was monosyllabic, not seeming interested in being
anywhere near her, and then he was asking her personal
questions and caressing her cheek. She hadn't expected
him to react the way he had when she'd told him her
sad little story, and now she was more perplexed than
before.

What on earth had he been thinking? Why had he
touched her? He'd been doing really well, staying on
the other side of the room, not engaging her in conversation. And then, for some ridiculous unknown reason,
he'd gone and asked about her private life! What an
idiot he was. What he should have done was excuse

himself and take his drink back to his consulting room and get on with the work he loved so much. But, no. Instead he'd not only pried into her life but he had been so moved by what she'd said he'd been overwhelmed with compassion. He'd touched her. Touched that smooth, silky skin. And now he had that memory as well as the others to contend with. He shook his head, needing to get out of this room as soon as possible. Areva was right. They had work to do.

Dex strode into the kitchen, carrying his own cup to the sink, and it was as though he'd sliced through the intense atmosphere Melissa and Joss were trying to cope with. Interruptions were good. It was bad for herself and Joss to be alone like this. Part of her longed for it…to let go, to be free, to just throw caution to the wind and see where this attraction she felt for him might lead… But only part of her. The other part warned her against moving too fast, against believing she could have a fairytale ending to her lonely little life. She'd been there and she'd done that, and for that reason alone she had to remain indifferent to Joss. But how?

'You two got in trouble,' Dex said, with a grin on his face. 'Areva told you off.'

'You are such a larrikin, Dex. You sound like an eight-year-old,' Joss commented, but he was secretly relieved to have his friend there to break the tension. He'd touched Melissa! He'd been so enthralled by her, so focused on wanting to feel that soft smooth skin of hers, on looking into those wide brown eyes to offer her compassion and comfort. Yes—Dex being here, teasing them, was just the ticket.

'Maybe I am eight years old. Maybe I was not only adopted, but born on the twenty-ninth of February, and no one's told me that, either.'

Joss felt the way Melissa winced at her brother's words and he bristled. 'That's enough. None of this adoption thing is Melissa's fault, so don't go taking it out on her.'

'Joss.' Melissa stood, pleased her legs were now able to support her. 'It's OK.'

'No.' Dex shook his head, his expression contrite. 'Joss is right.' He looked at her, and she saw in his expression that he was truly sorry for his words. 'That was rude. I'm sorry, Melissa.'

'It's OK,' she repeated, but this time smiled at her brother. 'It's all a bit much to get your head around at times.'

As she spoke, she picked up her cup to carry it to the sink. Joss took four huge steps away from it, almost ending up in the doorway, to give her more than enough space to rinse her cup. Distance. He needed a lot of distance from her.

'Well, I'm up to date with *my* patients,' Dex commented, his tone and words striving to find some normality in all of this. 'It's you two having your little *tête-à-tête* that's putting you so far behind.'

'You just want to finish early so you can get to the pub on time,' Melissa teased. 'Don't tell me you want Bluey to give you another black eye?'

Both men chuckled at her words, and the air cleared to a happier atmosphere. Dex raised a hand to tenderly touch his eye and winced.

Melissa winced too. 'Does it still hurt? It should have started to heal by now.' Her voice was full of concern, but Dex's expression changed instantly to one of cheeky humour.

'I'm fine, but I really appreciate the concern.'

'You're most welcome. Any time you need genuine concern, come and see me.'

'Will do.' He paused and looked expectantly at Joss. 'And if I need genuine favours I'll go and see Joss.'

Joss looked at his friend. 'No.'

Dex spread his arms wide. 'You don't even know what I'm going to ask!'

'I really do, and the answer is no.'

'But…'

'No.'

'Come on, mate. You know how I hate it.'

'Hate what?' Melissa felt as if she was at a ping-pong match, looking from one to the other.

'No.' Joss beckoned for Melissa to leave. 'We have patients to see, so we'd best get back to work,' Joss continued as he urged Melissa from the room. 'Don't want to keep them waiting any longer.'

'What was all that about?' Melissa asked as they walked towards their consulting rooms. He leaned a little closer, lest Dex should hear him, his breath fanning her neck and causing goosebumps to race down her spine. Did the man have any idea the effect he was having on her?

'Dex hates house-calls.'

'He does?' Her eyes widened at this news, and in the next moment she flicked her gaze down to look at Joss's mouth. Big mistake. She shouldn't be looking at his mouth when they were this close to each other. Dangerous. Very dangerous.

'Yes, and he'll do anything to get out of going—so don't let him talk you around. Stand firm. Be strong.'

'You don't think I can resist him, do you?' The question was rhetorical, because she wasn't quite sure she would have been able to resist Dex if he'd asked her to swap with him, even though she wouldn't have had a clue what house-calls entailed out here in the Outback.

'At this stage? No. You're still in the excited stage at being so close to your brother.'

Melissa tried not to laugh at that, because she was in a bigger state of excitement simply because she was so close to *Joss*. The man obviously had no clue how his nearness was affecting her.

'You need to trust me on this. I know him a lot better than you, and you do not want to swap house-call shifts with him—because it doesn't end up being a swap; it ends up being you doing all of them.'

'Why doesn't Dex like house-calls? I thought he liked mixing with people.'

'He does. He's more than happy to see patients here, and he'll chat with people in the pub, but going to their houses?' Joss shook his head. 'He'll do it, but only under duress.'

'So you put him under duress?'

'I have to. It's part of his job description. We take turns. It keeps it fair and stops us from burning out.'

'Fair enough.' Melissa decided it was best not to argue with the boss, although she was curious as to why her brother didn't like that one aspect of the job.

'In fact,' Joss continued as an idea dawned on him, 'it might be a good opportunity for you to go with him tomorrow. That way you'll get to learn the ropes of what's expected of us as far as Outback house-calls go. You'll also get to spend some time alone with Dex.'

Melissa considered the idea for a moment, liking what Joss was suggesting. It would also give her some time away from *him*, and hopefully she'd be able to get herself better under control. Some distance was definitely what she needed, and she nodded enthusiastically. 'Sounds great. Oh, but what about my clinic?'

He waved her words away. 'We can reschedule that.

Patients have been waiting for quite some time to see you; waiting a few extra days won't hurt. Besides, I can see anyone who's urgent.'

Areva would not like him for suggesting such a plan, but if it meant he had the opportunity to put a bit of distance between himself and his new colleague then it would definitely be worth it. Melissa Clarkson was already taking up too much room in his private thoughts.

Thoughts of her had plagued him ever since he'd first laid eyes on her. Thoughts of her came into his mind, invading his otherwise organised mental patterns, at the most unusual times. Such as at three o'clock this morning. He'd been awoken by soft music and the sound of pacing. He'd listened, wondering if there was anything wrong. Was she sick? Did she require help? He'd sat up in bed, listening carefully to try and figure out what she was doing. He'd heard water go on and off in the bathroom. More pacing, more soft music, and then…soft sweet singing.

She was all right, and she had the singing voice of an angel.

He'd lain back in bed, hands behind his head, eyes closed, and just listened. Her voice had been smooth and lovely, and soon he'd found himself drifting off into a deep and relaxing slumber. He hadn't slept like that in years.

Oh, yes. He'd been thinking about Melissa Clarkson far too much, and he wasn't at all sure what to do about it. He had no idea what she'd just said, and couldn't help it when his gaze flicked from her gorgeous brown eyes to her lips—only for a second, yet it felt like for ever. Those luscious lips of hers were plump and looked delicious. The urge, the desire to lean forward and press his mouth to hers, was only intensifying with every extra moment he spent alone with her, breathing in her sweet scent.

Melissa's mind had gone completely blank with that last stare from Joss. The air between them seemed to crackle with repressed tension—and she'd do well to keep it repressed. Her heart-rate increased, her lips parted, and she couldn't have stopped looking at him if the world had come crumbling down around them.

A noise from the waiting room made them both jerk backwards.

'House-calls with Dex tomorrow sounds great,' Melissa reiterated, shifting towards her consulting room door.

'Right. I'll let him know and make arrangements for the rescheduling of your clinic.'

'Great.'

'Good.'

She couldn't believe how uncomfortable she felt, how aware she was of him, how she'd wanted him to kiss her again, right there in the middle of the corridor with a waiting room full of patients just around the corner.

Melissa pointed to her consulting room door. 'Best get back to it.'

'Yes.' Feeling ridiculous, and becoming cross with himself for yet again being unable to resist her allure, Joss turned on his heel and headed into his own consulting room, closing the door with a firm finality. 'And that is that,' he murmured.

Stalking to his desk, he sat down to go over the extra things he needed to tackle to get Melissa safely away with Dex tomorrow on the house-calls. First on the list was talking Dex into it, and he was sure his friend wasn't going to like the idea at all.

There was a knock at his door and in a moment Dex strolled in, sitting in the chair opposite his friend and putting his feet up on the desk.

'Something I can help you with now that you've made yourself comfortable?' Joss asked, glaring pointedly at Dex's shoes.

Dex didn't remove them. 'I think you should do my house-calls this week.'

'The direct approach? Interesting.' Joss sat up straighter in his chair. 'No, Dex.'

'Aww, come on. What are friends for?'

'No, Dex.'

'It was initially your turn to do them anyway.'

'That's right, but I did yours three weeks running, which means it's now your turn, Dex.'

'But I promise to do your house-calls next week.'

'No, you won't.'

'You're right. I won't. Oh, well, how about I fill in for your clinic next week on my day off? That way you'll have time to show Melissa a bit more of Didja.'

'Still no.'

'In fact,' he pressed on, as though he hadn't heard his friend, 'you doing my house-calls this week would be a great way for you to show Melissa what it's all about.'

Joss nearly choked at the suggestion. Spending all that time alone, in such close quarters with Melissa? He hadn't been able to control himself in a small kitchenette. He hadn't been able to resist touching her. How was he supposed to cope in the smaller confines of the ute as they drove around the countryside? To Dex, however, he tried to remain completely unnerved. 'Actually, I was wanting to talk to you about that.'

'About you doing the house-calls with Melissa? Great idea. I accept.'

'That's not what I meant. I was talking about *you* doing the house-calls tomorrow with your sister. Get to know her better.'

'I can't take her. No. No siree.' He shook his head.

'She's your sister, Dex. You're going to need to open up to her sooner or later.'

'I choose later.'

'Dex, I under—'

'No. You don't understand, Joss. You have parents who are definitely your parents. You weren't lied to for almost thirty years by the people you love. You didn't find out—completely out of the blue—that you have an older sister, that you were adopted!' Dex thumped the desk.

Joss watched his friend. He hadn't seen him this riled-up for a long time.

Dex took a breath and calmed himself down. 'Look, I think it's great that she's here helping out at the clinic. Scoring ourselves an OB/GYN for a year was a great stroke of genius on your part and one of the major reasons I agreed to her coming. You are also right that it would be good for me to get to know her—just in case one day I need to ask for some bone marrow or a kidney or something. But right now it's just too soon for me to even be contemplating spending a whole day with her.'

Joss felt the walls start to close in on him, and wondered if he could try another tack at convincing Dex that spending time with Melissa was a good thing. There was no way *he* could do it. Such close quarters… That wouldn't be a way for him to get his libido back under control again.

'I know you've been hurt, Dex, but as I've pointed out before, none of this is Melissa's fault. Imagine how she's feeling. She comes to town to meet you, to get to know you, and you've hardly said two words to her.'

'I've said a few more than that,' Dex felt compelled to point out.

'It's like ripping a sticking plaster off. The sooner you get it over and done with, the better.'

'Why can't you take her? You're the boss here.'

'You're an equal financial partner, Dex.'

'But you run the show. You know I'm not good at the admin thing.'

'I know, and as the "admin thing" guy, I'm telling you it's your turn to do house-calls tomorrow, and Melissa will be accompanying you. End of story.'

'Ahh, but that's where you're wrong. You see, I think secretly, deep down inside, you really *want* to do these house-calls with Melissa tagging along. I think you *want* to get to know her better. I think you *want* to see if you can find some flaws, some faults—anything to help you to stop thinking about her.'

'What? What on earth are you talking about?'

'You like her.' Dex waggled his eyebrows up and down in an insinuating manner.

Joss ignored him and tried to keep his tone strictly professional. 'Of course I like her. She's a colleague.'

'That's not what I meant and you know it. You *like* like her. I saw you both before, in the corridor, making googly eyes at each other.'

Joss closed his eyes for a moment, unable to believe Dex had witnessed those few intense moments. But it was true, and there was no use denying it to his friend because Dex knew him far too well.

'This is good, Joss. You haven't been interested in any woman since Christina.' Dex leaned forward on the desk. 'If you like her, mate, you should do something about it.'

'She's your sister. She's a colleague. She's here to work. She has a year-long contract and I don't want anything to go wrong.'

'What if everything goes right? What if she's your Ms Right? You could marry her and we could end up being real brothers! That would be cool.'

Joss shook his head, knowing his friend was only joking. 'Funny. Very amusing,' he remarked without humour.

'But seriously, this is a good time for you to let go of the past and move forward into the future.'

'Hmm.'

'You need to let Christina go, Joss. Everything that happened to you all those years ago is gone. Finished. Done. I never believed the allegations brought against you, and neither did your family. You were cleared of any charges and you moved on with your life—geographically, but not emotionally.'

'You're one to talk,' Joss commented. 'You haven't spoken to your family in how long?'

'This discussion isn't about me. It's about you. When, since you left Perth, have you ever been this interested in a woman? I'll tell you—never.'

'It's why I came to Didja in the first place. To get away from women. Besides, what if Melissa turns out to be like Christina? Ever think of that? What if she's all nice and lovely on the surface, but dig a little deeper and I might find something I don't want to know about?'

'Excuses, excuses. Believe me, I've used them all in my time. But this isn't about me; it's about you. You like her. You're attracted to her. That alone is enough of a reason to get to know her a little better. The past doesn't matter any more, and Christina wasn't any good for you anyway.'

'Apparently not.'

'You needed friends—true friends—to help build you up again, to support you.'

'And you were there.'

'That's right. And now you can be there for me by agreeing to do the house-calls this week.'

'Nice segué.' Joss shook his head and grinned at his friend. 'But my answer is still no.'

It had to be. He had to get his life back onto the nice even keel it had been in three days ago—before he'd ever laid eyes on Melissa Clarkson.

Dex's mobile phone rang and he broke off their debate in order to answer it. Joss mentally cooled his heels whilst he waited, going over the arguments in his mind. It was imperative he succeed. When Dex ended the call, he grinned very slowly at his friend.

'You look like the cat who ate the cream.'

'Oh, I have. I don't usually play dirty, but a man's gotta do what a man's gotta do.'

Joss's skin started to prickle with apprehension at his friend's words. 'Who was that on the phone?'

'The Watkinsons.'

Joss closed his eyes and buried his head in his hands, his shoulders instantly slumped in defeat. 'Oh, no.'

'Well you may cry, "Oh, no", my friend, because they're coming to Didja tomorrow. They'll be here for a whole week—and you know what that means.'

He wished Dex would keep quiet—that he'd go away. 'Can't you just gloat in private?' he asked, his words still muffled behind his hands.

'Nope. Besides, gloating is done much better in front of the person you wish to gloat about. I don't make the rules, mate, I just follow them. What a darn shame that the Watkinsons chose this particular weekend to come to Didja. What a darn shame that I need to be here to monitor their two children who have cystic fibrosis. What a darn shame I won't be able to do the house-calls tomorrow because I'll be needed here, at the hospital in town.'

'All right.' Joss sat up straight and squared his shoulders. 'All right. I'll do your house-calls tomorrow. But you are definitely going out next week and that's final. Nothing you can do will make me change my mind. Watkinsons or no Watkinsons.'

'Yes!' Dex punched the air.

'Get out.' Joss pointed to the door. 'Go on. Go gloat elsewhere. I have a lot of work to get done.'

Joss watched his friend almost dance his way out of the consulting room. When he was gone Joss shook his head, unable to believe the unlucky turn of events. Where he'd thought he'd have time away from Melissa, to control his wayward mind and body, it was now a matter of finding strategies which would see him through tomorrow.

He rubbed his jaw and exhaled slowly. Melissa was beautiful, funny and smart. Everything he'd ever wanted. Then again, Christina had been beautiful, funny and smart, and she'd ripped his heart out and crushed it. Although he was definitely attracted to Melissa, he'd also do well to be on his guard.

Women could lie. Women could be devious. Women were the reason he'd hibernated in the Outback for the past four years, keeping his distance from any sort of personal relationship. Yes, the sooner he discovered Melissa Clarkson's faults and flaws, the sooner he could move past this undeniable pull he felt towards her.

All that said, he desperately *wasn't* looking forward to tomorrow.

CHAPTER FOUR

BUB had told Melissa to pack an overnight bag whenever she went out on house-calls.

'It's just something we do out here in the Outback. You never know when the weather will turn. You could have buckets of rain coming down on you one moment and then bush fires the next. Sometimes you've gotta find shelter wherever you can, and other times you just go to the nearest farmhouse.'

'And people just let you stay?'

'Of course.' Bub had looked at her as though she was mad. 'We all support each other out here. You'll see lots of great scenery, maybe even some Aussie animals—we have quite a few emus out here. You'll meet new people, see how they all live, and be back in time to enjoy a coldie at the pub.' Bub had frowned as she'd spoken.

'Something wrong?'

'No. Not really. Just that I haven't seen Josiah down at the pub the past few nights. He's usually there. Hope he's not gonna start all that brooding stuff again.'

'He broods?'

'Oh, not for ages. But now and then, when his world is rocked from side to side, he tends to retreat back into his cave.'

'Cave?'

'A metaphor, darl. Never mind me. Off you go. Go pack your bag and get ready for tomorrow—and above all, enjoy yourself.'

Therefore Melissa had packed her overnight bag. In fact she'd packed and repacked it several times during the course of the evening. She'd been unable to sleep last night, so excited to be going out on house-calls with her brother. She would get to spend time with Dex, and even if he hardly spoke to her, just being with him, sitting beside him in the car, would be enough for her. It was happening. What she'd wanted for so long was finally coming true. She couldn't believe that her luck seemed to be changing.

With a smile on her face and a spring in her step, she made her way out of her apartment, checking she had the keys which Joss had given her. She closed the door, put her hat on her head and carried her overnight bag to the waiting ute.

'Joss!' She was surprised to see him up this early. Clinic didn't start for another two hours, so she'd presumed he'd still be sleeping. Instead, he was walking around checking the ute's fitted tarpaulin cover was securely in place.

He held out a hand. 'Your bag?'

Melissa handed over her bag. Joss didn't appear to be in a good mood at all, and she guiltily hoped she hadn't kept him awake last night with all her to-ing and fro-ing around the apartment due to her restless excitement.

Melissa looked around her. 'Where's Dex?'

'Sleeping.' Joss stowed her bag beneath the tarp before checking everything was secure once more. Then, much to Melissa's horror, he opened the driver's door and climbed in behind the wheel. Her eyes widened as she opened the passenger door.

'What are you doing?'

He looked across at her as though she were thick. 'Getting ready to drive.'

'But…but…where's Dex? Why is he sleeping? You can't… You're not doing…' She stopped, her brain working overtime to cope with this change. Joss was doing the house-calls? She took a breath and tried to get herself under control. 'I thought I was doing house-calls with Dex.'

'Something came up.'

'He's not coming!' Didn't Dex want to be with her? Spend time with her? Was this her brother's way of telling her to stay away? That she could work here but she had to keep her distance as far as trying to have a relationship with him was concerned? Pain, hurt and re-jection rose up within her.

'That's right. So if you get in we can get this day over and done with. And the sooner, the better.' He mumbled the last bit to himself, but Melissa had excellent hearing.

Melissa tried to swallow back the tears. Apparently neither of her colleagues wanted to spend time with her. Anger welled up inside. 'You don't want to do house-calls with me?' She stood outside the ute, stubbornly refusing to get in. 'Well, that's just fine. I can go out with Dex next week, and you can spare yourself from having to endure my company all day long. And if Dex doesn't want to go out with me next week, then write me a list of what I need to do and I'll figure it out on my own. Honestly, I'd heard all about Outback hospi-tality and how everyone here would make me feel welcome—well, between you and Dex I'm feeling about as welcome as a squashed bug on a windshield.'

Melissa shut the door and started walking away. Joss closed his eyes for a second, then hit the steering wheel. He climbed from the ute and hurried after her. It wasn't her fault Dex had changed the plan, and he felt like a heel. He'd let his unwanted attraction for her get in the way of his professionalism and now he'd made her feel bad. Joss knew what he had to do. He had sisters and he knew how temperamental women could be.

'Lis.' He reached out a hand to stop her, but she shrugged away his touch.

'You know, I just don't get you. One minute you're nice, and the next you're all Mr Tortured Soul and clamming up tighter than a…than a clam.' She turned to face him and pointed to the ute. 'It's a shame Dex doesn't want to do the house-calls with me, but you know what? That's OK. I can live with that. But this is part of my job and, quite frankly, I'd appreciate just a bit more professionalism on your part.'

Joss nodded. 'You're absolutely right, and I apologise for my behaviour.' He shifted his feet and shoved his hands into the pockets of his khaki shorts. 'Dex has to stay here and monitor a family who are coming to town. Two of their kids have CF and he's the expert in that field.'

'Oh.' So it wasn't just the fact that he hadn't wanted to spend time alone with her. Melissa started to feel bad about her outburst. This would have meant that Joss would have had to do some pretty fancy footwork in rearranging schedules. Still, one of them could have let her know about the change.

She could feel her anger draining and tried to hold on to it. When she was angry with Joss she didn't have to worry about fighting the attraction she felt for him.

She wasn't particularly looking forward to spending all day with him in the close confines of the ute. They could hardly cope within the close confines of the kitchenette. Still, she was a professional, and this was part of her job. Whether she liked it or not, she'd be spending the day with Joss.

He held out his hand, indicating the ute. 'Shall we?' His tone was calmer, more reasonable, and she could see the business mask he wore was back in place. 'We have a busy day to get through, so the sooner we get rolling, the sooner we'll be back and having a drink at the pub.'

Melissa nodded, and the two of them returned to the waiting vehicle and climbed in, buckling their seat-belts. 'So, boss. Where's our first port of call?'

'Interesting that you should use a sailing metaphor out here, where there is barely any water at all.' Joss was driving the ute onto the main road of the town. 'Our first "port of call", as you term it, is the mine headquarters site office. It's only fitting that you get to meet the head honchos in their official capacity, even though you've probably seen them around the town, and you also need to get a glimpse of what the mine is all about.'

'Looking forward to it.' As they drove, the buildings of the town became few and far between. It was as though there was an invisible line and houses couldn't be built beyond it, because suddenly Melissa looked around and there were only small green shrubs mixing with the red orange dirt at the side of the road.

After a while Joss turned right and headed down another seemingly endless road, and soon, as the signage depicted, they were upon the mine's security gate. After signing in, Joss parked next to a few other cars. As a way of making up for his bad behaviour earlier, Joss came around the car to open Melissa's door, but she beat him to it.

'Problem?' she asked, seeing him round her side of the car.

'Uh…no.' He felt self-conscious. 'I was just going to open your door for you.'

'Really?' Her eyebrows hit her hairline in surprise. 'Do you mean to tell me that chivalry isn't dead? Even out here in the middle of nowhere?'

'That's exactly it.' His expression was deadpan, but she thought she detected a slight twinkling of laughter in his eyes.

'In that case, then, I'll let you make it up to me by allowing you to open the door to the building.'

'Oh, thank you, Dr Clarkson. You're too kind.'

'And, should it ever rain here, make sure you have your coat handy. I loathe standing in puddles.'

He dutifully held the door open, waiting for her to precede him. 'Duly noted, Dr Clarkson,' he murmured as they headed towards the reception desk.

The area was still half-decked in tinsel and baubles as the woman behind the desk was in the process of taking them down.

'Hello, Joss,' she said over her shoulder as she came down off a stepladder. 'Happy New Year to you.' She was bright and bubbly, her yellow badge declaring her name was Veronica. She wore a floral dress, had short grey hair and had a pen pushed behind her ear. 'And to you as well…Melissa, isn't it?'

'It is.' They both returned her greeting.

'There hasn't been an emergency, has there? I haven't been notified of one.' She walked to her desk and shuffled a few pieces of paper around.

'No, Veronica. No emergency. I've brought Dr

Clarkson here to introduce her around and to help give
her a bit of a bird's eye view of the mine.'

'Good idea. Well, it's lovely to see you again,
Melissa.'

'Again?'

'We met on New Year's Eve. You probably don't
remember. It's difficult when you're the new girl in
town.' The phone on the desk started ringing. 'Go on
through. Both Jeff and Scott are in there somewhere.'
Veronica answered the phone as Joss led Melissa
through a door and down a corridor.

'Have I met Jeff and Scott? Can you remember? It's
really quite disconcerting when people know you but
you don't have a clue who *they* are.'

Joss shrugged. 'I'm not sure.' Although he was sure
she would have remembered meeting Scott. If Dex was
the charming rogue in their community, Scott was most
definitely the womaniser. If Scott had tried to sleaze
Melissa at New Year's, the woman would have remembered.

They went through into a different office, Joss not
bothering to knock as he opened the door. Two men
were sitting at a large conference table, papers strewn
before them.

'Joss.' One of them looked up.

'G'day, fellas. Just wanted to officially introduce
you to our new doctor.'

'Excellent.' The two men came over and shook her
hand warmly. Scott, however, held on to Melissa's hand
for a bit longer than was necessary.

'When Jeff told me how incredibly beautiful you
were I was immensely sorry I hadn't stayed in Didja
for New Year. I've been in Perth,' he volunteered. 'Still,
it's a real pleasure to have you join our little commu-

nity, Melissa. A real pleasure.' He shook her hand slowly as he said the last few words, and then with a great reluctance let her go.

Joss was trying not to seethe at the lecherous way Scott was looking at Melissa. If he needed to appoint himself her official protector then so be it. All for the good of the clinic, of course.

'Well…thank you.' Melissa stepped back, wanting to put a bit of distance between herself and Scott and accidentally bumped into Joss. He steadied her with a hand at her waist, letting it linger for a desperate moment before he dropped it back to his side.

As Jeff talked, telling her about the mining operation and pointing to the photographs on the wall which showed her exactly what the open cut mine looked like, Melissa was only conscious of the fact that Joss was still quite close to her.

That brief touch of his hand on her back had left a heated imprint, and the spicy scent he wore was starting to drive her to distraction. Why was she so interested in him? How did this attraction, which seemed to have come from nowhere, consume her so much?

Even when they headed out of the office so she could see the actual mine itself, she was highly conscious of every move Joss made. They went outside and walked down a set of stairs to the viewing platform, all of them standing there doing the time-honoured Australian salute of swatting flies, looking over the mining operation. Jeff and Scott pointed out the different aspects of the job, but all Melissa was conscious of was the nearness of her colleague. The platform was quite small, and therefore he couldn't really keep his distance. The heat from his torso was more prominent than the hot sun shining down on them, and it was affecting her equilibrium in ways the sun never could.

Melissa hoped to goodness that she nodded and murmured in the correct places, but knew she would probably have to research the entire mining operation on line, when Joss wasn't around to distract her.

They didn't spend too much time watching the enormous trucks—one or two of them with tinsel still wrapped around their antennae from Christmas— carting the mined rock up and down incredibly steep slopes which led in and out of the earth. Instead they headed back inside, away from the heat and the flies.

'Would you both like to stay for a drink?' Scott asked when they were back in the conference room. 'It's a bit of a scorcher out there at the moment.'

Melissa looked to Joss, unsure what their next move was. He was the boss, and today she was dancing to his tune.

'Sorry,' Joss replied a moment later, wanting to get Melissa as far away from Scott as possible. Honestly, the man had been giving Melissa such a come-on the entire time they'd been out on that platform. Joss hadn't liked it one bit. 'We need to get going. Have to get out to the Etheringtons, with quite a few stops to make along the way.'

'That's a lot of ground to cover,' Jeff remarked.

'His missus about ready to pop yet?' Scott asked.

Joss's smile was tight. 'Not yet, but that's one reason why I needed Melissa here to come along. Given that she's a qualified obstetrician, she'll be able to make sure everything is progressing well as far as mother and baby are concerned.' Joss turned to Melissa. 'Ready?'

It was strange, but even when he looked at her like that, one simple word coming from his lips, all she was aware of were his blue eyes, and the way they seemed to convey a multitude of unspoken words—especially when he lifted his eyebrows in such a cute and inquisitive manner. Talk about mixed signals and total confusion!

'Ready,' she confirmed.

They said their goodbyes and as they drove away from the open cut mine the atmosphere in the car descended into an uncomfortable silence. He wasn't at all sure what to say or do. He wanted to know if she'd been attracted to Sleazy Scott or whether she really hadn't given him a second glance. Only the last time they'd talked on personal topics he'd ended up caressing her cheek—a soft, gentle touch which still tortured him late at night. He had to come up with some sort of conversation—after all they had a good long drive to their next house-call, and that was a lot of time to fill with just silence.

It had been an age since he'd last been out with a woman, and even then it had been a double date which Dex had basically forced him to attend. It was then he'd realised it would be extremely difficult to date seriously when you were a doctor in a small community. If the relationship didn't go right, then everyone in the community had an opinion on it. Add to all of that the fact that he'd never met anyone in Didja who affected him the way Melissa did—never had he felt such an instant attraction as he did with his new female colleague.

He knew she'd come to town to get to know Dex, but Dex hadn't been as receptive as she'd hoped. Was she therefore using him as a stop-gap until she could get attention from her brother? There had to be a hidden agenda somewhere. Christina had taught him that much at least.

Joss glanced again at Melissa. There was no denying the attraction he felt for her—as unexpected as it was—but could he risk taking a chance on a relationship? How would she react when she learned about his past? Would she reject and betray him as Christina had? He shook his head, forcing the thoughts away, and reminded himself that perhaps he was misreading the signals from Melissa. When he'd touched his hand to the small of her back, purely in order to steady her, he'd felt such a strong warmth course up his arm and explode throughout his body. Why did he have to be so attracted to her?

He decided some conversation had to be better than the present path his thoughts were taking.

'So…'

Melissa broke the silence before he could get a chance. Darn it. Was this yet more evidence that they were on the same wavelength? Joss had just decided to start a conversation about the weather, because the weather was definitely a safe topic.

'Tell me,' Melissa continued. 'What are your future plans for the clinic?'

'The clinic?' That was a safe topic too. He could do that one.

'You know? The place we work at? The one you've built from scratch?'

'Oh. *That* clinic.' Yes, talking about work was a very safe topic indeed. 'Plans. Hmm… Well, we have three doctors here now. That's a start. I do the odd surgical case—just small things. Dex does the anaesthetics, and now that you're here you'll be taking over the delivery of babies.'

'All you need is a paediatrician and you'll have a full house. That should round the team off nicely.'

'Do you honestly think we could get a paediatrician

to come all the way out here? On a permanent basis?'
He spoke as though she'd asked him to capture the
moon. 'It was difficult enough trying to coax a female
doctor out. We'd advertised for well over a year before
we received your application.'

'Oh, great,' she joked. 'You're telling me I only got
the job because I was the only applicant?'

'That's not what I'm saying,' Joss remarked. 'If your
credentials hadn't been up to scratch the clinic wouldn't
have employed you.'

'I see.'

'Honestly, Lis.' He looked across at her. 'You were
hired strictly on your merits, I assure you. The fact that
you wanted to come to town anyway to get to know Dex
was simply a bonus.'

'And you knew I wanted to spend longer than three
to six months in Didja because of Dex?'

'I did. You can't blame a guy for using it to his own
advantage.'

'And I don't.'

She watched him surreptitiously as he drove,
admiring his strong profile. He was so different from
Renulf, especially in looks. Renulf was fair, yet Joss
was dark. Renulf hadn't been able to make her knees
turn to mush with just one look, yet Joss could. Renulf
had never made her swoon with the merest brush of his
lips across hers, and Joss had.

She knew it wasn't right to compare them but she
couldn't help it. The man sitting next to her was well-
liked and respected in the community, and he was most
certainly good with the patients. Joss was so vibrant,
so powerful and so incredibly handsome. She couldn't
help the way he made her feel, but she *could* control
her own reaction. Couldn't she?

'We're all motivated in different ways, and sometimes circumstances are the biggest dictators in our lives.'

He glanced at her. 'A deep comment.'

'You'd expect it from a woman who's watched everyone she ever really loved die.' Melissa swallowed over the lump which had immediately appeared in her throat.

'It must have been really difficult for you.'

'It was. Still is in a lot of ways.' She shook her head quietly. 'It's not easy being alone.'

'Why didn't it work out with your fiancé?' The instant the question was out of his mouth he wondered if he'd pushed a little too far, too fast. But if he wanted to get to know her faults and flaws it meant he had to dig a little deeper beneath the surface, and surely that meant getting a little bit more personal.

'Many reasons. I think it all boiled down to the fact that we didn't really have a strong foundation. Everything sort of happened rather quickly.' She took a deep breath, glad she had herself more under control now. 'How about you? There must have been something big happen in your life to make you settle in Didja.'

'I thought you weren't all that interested? At least, that's what you told me on your first day in town.'

'I'm interested, all right. I just wasn't as curious then as I am now."

'So you haven't heard the gossip, then?'

'There's gossip about you? No. I guess I must have missed it—although Bub did mention that you were quite reserved when you first came to town. How when you wouldn't go to the pub to have a drink with them, they brought the pub to you.'

The smile which crossed his lips was a slow one, and he nodded as memories returned. 'They did at that. I'd forgotten. It was a defining moment for me. One when I knew I needed to start letting go of the past if I was going to have any sort of decent future.'

'You're a man, all alone, working from dawn to dusk, and people only throw themselves into their work when everything else has gone to the dogs.'

'Gone to the dogs?'

'Or down the toilet. Choose the expression you like best.'

'How about up in flames?' Joss was sort of joking, but she heard the hint of pain behind his words. His hands gripped the steering-wheel tighter, his knuckles going white.

'It was that bad?' Melissa's tone was one of instant concern and compassion, and she couldn't help but reach over and give his hand a little stroke.

Joss was startled by her touch, but he didn't ignore it either. He glanced over at her, a multitude of pain reflected in those gorgeous blue depths, and she felt for him. 'It was.'

'Joss. I'm sorry.'

'For what? You didn't do anything.' He focused his eyes back on the very long, very straight road, not a house in sight, and pushed his foot down on the accelerator. The sooner they got to the next house, the better—because being confined with her like this, with her scent driving him crazy, with her gentle and soothing words affecting him, with her touch breaking through his reserve, was simply dangerous.

'I'm sorry for the pain you felt. Pain is never easy to go through—both physically and psychologically. After my adoptive parents died I was forced to do a lot of growing up. I learned the hard way about regrets, about life in general. We only have one life. One life which can end so quickly. Is the angst and frustration of fighting with the past really going to help with the future, or is it simply easier just to let it go and move on?' Melissa spoke as though talking to herself, perhaps trying to convince herself to let go of her own past.

They were quiet for a while, both seemingly lost in their own thoughts. Once more Melissa broke the silence. 'I thought we'd see a lot more kangaroos out here.'

Joss relaxed a little at the general topic of conversation, his hands loosening on the wheel, holding it more comfortably now. 'You'll see plenty of roos while you're out here, and emus. They love to race along with the car.'

'Sounds scary and fun at the same time. Don't they ever run into the car?'

'It has happened, but only on the odd occasion. Generally, I think they just want a race. Show-offs.'

Melissa smiled at his remark. The atmosphere in the car had returned to a more normal level of tension. They were able to chat more freely and relax a bit more. She asked him about the town and the patients they were going to see, the car eating up the kilometres as they talked, and it was nice and friendly, with neither wanting to spoil the sort of truce they'd found.

When Joss's cellphone rang it startled them both, but he quickly connected the call by tapping the earpiece connection around his ear. 'Joss here.' He listened intently, then checked the clock on the dashboard.

'We're about five minutes away from you.' A pause. 'Right. If you think it's that bad, then call Dex at the clinic and get him to liaise with the Royal Flying

Doctor Service. Put them on stand-by for now, until I can take a look at the situation.' He disconnected the call and put his foot down on the accelerator. There were no speed limits out here—just long straight roads which seemed to stretch on for miles.

'Problem?'

'Murphy's Farm. One of the bulls has broken free from its pen and is on the rampage.'

Melissa's eyes widened. 'Bull? Rampage?' What was she doing out here? What if she'd been alone doing these house-calls? She didn't have experience with rampaging-bull wounds! 'Is it safe? Should we be driving around here? This fast?'

Her feelings must have been apparent because Joss quickly reassured her. 'Relax. You won't need to do any bull-wrangling today. Maybe next time, but not today.'

'Any casualties?'

'Yes. Two of the station hands have been injured. Rich thinks their wounds will require surgery, but we can assess that when we get there.'

She nodded. 'Sometimes there's more blood than injury.'

'Exactly.' Joss started to slow the ute, before turning onto what looked like a dirt paddock with a few tyre tracks on it. 'You all right with this?'

'What? The new road you're intent on making, or the rampaging bull we might literally run into?'

He chuckled again. 'I meant the injuries we're going to assess. Your résumé said you'd worked in A&E, so you should be experienced in emergency situations, right?'

'I'm highly proficient—although I will say that I've never treated a patient with rampaging-bull wounds.' She put out one hand to the dashboard and one to the ceiling as they bounced around; the ground was highly uneven.

'Aren't you glad I brought the ute with the good suspension?' Joss was clearly enjoying himself.

'I am. Where are we going?'

'Short cut. This way you'll only need to jump out and open two gates instead of five.'

'Out? Gates? Do I need to remind you there is a rampaging bull out there?' She went to point, to indicate the area they were driving through, but needed to hold on instead.

'He's heading in the other direction, if that makes you feel any better.'

'How do you know where the bull is?'

'Because Rich has a chopper in the air, tracking the animal. That bull is worth an awful lot of money, Lis, and whether it's angry or not Rich isn't going to let it out of his sight. So, unless you see a chopper in the sky, we'll be as right as rain.' Joss glanced up at the sky. 'And, speaking of rain, it looks as though we might actually get a few drops here and there.'

Melissa also peered up at the sky, and saw that there was quite a lot of cloud coverage out here—and they weren't the nice white fluffy ones. 'Is that what they mean by scattered showers?'

Joss chuckled. 'I just hope Dex hasn't been doing his rain dance.'

'His what?' She was clearly intrigued and surprised.

'Rain dance. Once he went outside first thing in the morning and did an official rain dance along with Nev and Kev, in the hopes that the roads would be so impassable that he wouldn't have to do his house-calls.'

'Did it work?'

'Amazingly, it did. That afternoon, when he was

supposed to leave, Didja had its first rains in about five months. It rained for three days straight. Roads were impassable everywhere.'

Melissa giggled in disbelief at the antics of her brother. 'That's astounding. You could hire him out to those remote areas of the country which are most affected by the drought.'

Joss grinned at her, and she almost melted at the sight. 'I'd never thought of it that way before.'

'Well, here's hoping he hasn't been doing his rain dance. The last thing we need today is a bucketing downpour.'

Because if that happened, it could mean that the roads would become impassable, and if that happened it could mean that she and Joss would have to alter their plans for the day, and if that happened they might find themselves alone and in a highly secluded situation. And if that happened there was no telling exactly *what* might happen!

CHAPTER FIVE

WHEN they finally pulled up in front of the homestead, Joss was out of the ute like a shot. He grabbed the medical kit from the back of the tray as Melissa came around to stand beside him. 'We'll examine the station hands, and if necessary we'll get the RFDS out here. Chances are those men will need a transfer to the clinic's hospital.'

'Bub will have two new patients to fuss over.'

Joss smiled at her words, pleased she was getting to know the staff at the clinic. 'Yes, she will.' He was heading up the front steps of the homestead as they talked.

'OK. So where do we find our patients?' Melissa asked.

'No doubt around the back. We can take a short cut through the house.' He opened the front door and just walked right in, leaving a more hesitant Melissa to follow. She glanced up at the sky, noting the still gathering clouds as well as a sort of far-off buzzing noise. It was as though there was a giant mosquito around, yet she couldn't see it.

'The chopper,' she realised aloud as she went through the front door of a stranger's house. She wasn't sure where Joss had gone, so made her way tentatively through the comfortably furnished rooms.

'Oh, there you are, Melissa. Come this way. Joss told me to keep an eye out for you.' She was bustled through the house by a petite pregnant woman with lovely blonde hair and smiling green eyes. 'I'm Amanda, but everyone calls me Mindy. Come through. They're out the back.' As they went through the house, Melissa heard the chopper getting closer. 'I hope they find that bull, because I want to give it a piece of my mind.'

'Really? You want to tell a bull off?'

'Oh, he's really not that bad—and we do need him. He's a good source of income—breeding-wise,' she finished as they walked through the kitchen towards the back door. 'I could tell he was going to fly off the handle. Rich thought I was mad—kept telling me that I couldn't read a bull's mind.'

'And can you?' Melissa was intrigued by this woman as they headed outside to the rear of the homestead. She shielded her eyes from the glare of the sun as she looked around, searching for Joss. Mindy kept on walking so she kept on following.

'I have this intuition thing where animals are concerned.' She turned and grinned brightly at Melissa. 'Rich says that's why I married him. He's such an animal. Anyway, it's just a thing. I can tell when the animals are jittery or a bit off.' She shrugged. 'I've always had it, and my dad came to rely on it. Rich still has a lot to learn. We've only been married for three years, but he'll get there.'

'Perhaps after today he'll listen more carefully and we won't have more casualties.'

'True.' Mindy was serious again. 'I hope the boys are all right.'

'Boys?' Had some children also been hurt?

'The two guys who just weren't fast enough when the bull decided to have a temper tantrum. You'd think they'd be a little bit quicker on the uptake.' They rounded a corner near the back shed and there were the 'boys'. Joss was kneeling down next to one of them; the other man was propped up against the side of the shed in the shade, a bandage around his upper arm and shoulder.

'Do you think we'll need the RFDS?' she asked as she knelt down on the other side of the patient.

'Yes. I'd like the patients in at least overnight for observation.' He gestured to the medical kit. 'I need Vicryl sutures, double zero and zero.' He'd pulled on gloves and was just finishing injecting a local anaesthetic near the wound site. 'James here has been very lucky indeed. That bull only gave him a bit of a love nick.' Joss indicated the gash in the station hand's abdomen. 'A little to the right and you might have lost a kidney, mate.'

'So long as he wasn't initiating a mating ritual, I'll be right,' James added with a laugh, then winced in pain.

'Take it easy,' Melissa soothed. 'What analgesics have they been given?'

'I've just given them both morphine,' Joss answered. 'James here is worse than Andy, and Mindy's had a good look at Andy and applied bandages.'

Melissa went and took a closer look at Andy, checking his pupils and reflexes, listening to his heartbeat, taking his blood pressure and counting the beats of his pulse. 'You're doing just fine, Andy,' she reassured him when she was finished, then stood and looked at Mindy. 'Good work,' she praised. 'Nice pristine bandaging.'

Mindy shrugged. 'I've had experience.' At Melissa's raised eyebrows, Mindy elaborated. 'This is my farm. It's where I grew up. Rich was the foreman for years— that's how we met—and when my dad passed away last year Rich just took over. Growing up on a farm like this, out in the middle of nowhere, means you have to be prepared for anything. So I've done first aid courses and cooking courses and bookkeeping courses and several other courses to make sure I can handle anything that's thrown at me.'

'Impressive.'

Mindy wrinkled her nose and rubbed her stomach. 'I just wish they offered parenting courses on line, too.'

Joss looked up from where he was getting ready to debride James's wound. 'Given the way you keep all these blokes in line, I don't think you're going to have any trouble being a parent, Mindy.'

'That's what Rich says.'

'Then you should listen to him. I'm almost ready, Lis.'

'OK. So how do I contact the RFDS? Do I just call Dex and get him to organise it all?'

'Yes. Murphy's Farm. Two patients requiring transfer. Give him the particulars of the injuries and he can organise Phemie and her crew.'

Melissa nodded and made the phone call, giving Dex the particulars, all the while quite excited about her first contact with the Royal Flying Doctor Service. She'd heard so much about the people who ran it— most of the Didja locals heralded them as true Outback heroes—and now she was delighted at the opportunity to meet them. Although she most certainly wished the circumstances were different.

'Right.' Joss turned his attention to Melissa. 'Ready when you are, Lis.'

Melissa came over and knelt down on the opposite side of James, pulling on a pair of gloves. 'Ready, boss.'

She wanted to ask why they couldn't move James to a more sterile location. She wanted to know how they were supposed to keep the multitude of buzzing flies away from the patient, the wound and themselves as they treated him. However, Joss was ready to do what he did best, and as he had obviously done it quite a few times before, she wasn't about to question him. She'd come to an Outback clinic, and all of this was about learning how to do things the Outback way. If it meant improvising then they would improvise, and she would learn how.

'OK. If you can start by putting an IV line in. Saline is in the medical kit. Mindy, we're going to need something to hang a drip bag on.'

'I can hold it,' Mindy offered.

'No.' Melissa and Joss spoke in unison.

'You need to be in the shade if you're outside, and preferably off your feet. Get me a chair or, better yet, stick a pitchfork in the ground. Anything we can use to hook the bag over but keep it elevated.'

'I'm on it,' she called as she waddled off to the shed. By the time she returned Melissa had the needles and tubes in and was ready to connect it all.

'How are you holding up, James?' she asked.

'All the better for looking up at you,' he murmured, with a silly grin on his face.

Melissa raised her gaze and looked at Joss, who smiled back. 'I'd say the analgesics are working just fine,' Joss said.

'Why? Because he'd have to be out of it to find me attractive?' She pretended to bristle.

'No.' Mortification laced his words, but then he relaxed as he realised she was teasing. 'I only meant that usually James isn't one to speak like that—especially to a woman he's only just met.'

'He's right,' Mindy clarified. She shooed some flies away as she sat down on the ground near James's head. 'Mind if I watch?'

'Not at all,' Joss replied, and, now satisfied that the local anaesthetic had taken effect and that James was not in any pain, he began the procedure of tidying things up and stitching them closed.

Melissa noted that even with the less than ideal circumstances Joss was being quite thorough. His careful thoroughness suggested that he was an excellent surgeon, and she wondered how many times he'd had to treat patients in such remote circumstances like this. As she took a quick second to glance around, it struck her just how far away from 'civilisation' they really were. It was one thing to come all the way to a small Outback practice to try and get to know her brother, but now that she was here there was a small niggling doubt that perhaps she'd bitten off more than she could chew. Would she be able to last twelve months as an Outback doctor? And what would happen after that?

'That will do him for now. I'll take a closer look later, once he's settled at the hospital.' Joss looked down at their patient. 'How are you doing, James?'

'Sleepy.'

'Any pain?'

'Nope.' They all smiled at the way he said the word.

'OK. I'll check Andy again, if you wouldn't mind doing obs on James.' Joss changed his gloves and crouched down near Andy.

'How are *you* doing?'

'Fine.'

'No pain?'

'I'm cool. Just a nice gentle buzz.'

'No. That's the flies, mate.' Joss grinned at his patient, then looked at Mindy. 'Mindy, I'm loath to undo your clean bandaging, so if you could tell me what the wound looked like, that would be great.'

'The gash to his arm was fine once I cleaned it with a bit of saline. I had some special bandage stuff which is supposed to be good for things that might only need one or two stitches.'

'Steri-strips?' Joss asked, and she nodded.

'That's what I put on his arm, and then the bandage. His head was a similar story, but the gash wasn't as deep. James took the major brunt as far as gouging goes, but Andy whacked his head pretty badly.'

'You saw the whole thing?' Melissa raised her eyebrows as she finished James's observations.

'I did. I was at the kitchen window and I can see out as far as the paddock. They were bringing the bull in and he was just in a bad mood. You know—we all have bad days. I told Rich this morning that I'd come and help, but he forbade me to go anywhere near the bull—because of the baby.'

'A wise decision—especially given the circumstances.'

'Chest is clear.' Joss held up his finger and got Andy to track it. 'Perfect.' Joss looked over at Mindy. 'What happened next?'

'I grabbed the medical kit—I always keep it fully stocked by the back door—and went out to help. The bull was still pounding around, with everyone running clear so they didn't get trampled. Then the bull turned and ran the other way, barging through the corral fence. It just took off.'

Thunder started to rumble in the distance.

'Do you think it might have been the approaching storm?' Melissa asked. 'Some animals do have a real sixth sense where the weather is concerned.'

'You could be right. It wouldn't surprise me,' Mindy responded. 'I hope they find him.' She looked out into the distance, wanting to see her husband returning, bull securely roped and chastised for his behaviour.

'Right. Andy, I want you in Didja as well. I want head X-rays, and then we'll take a better look at those gashes tomorrow.'

'Is it necessary?' Andy asked quietly. 'I mean, poor Rich is going to be without James as it is.'

'Let's just say you need to be in hospital. You can leave this time tomorrow, but only if everything checks out. Head injuries are funny things. Symptoms can be masked for quite a while. You tell either one of us—' he indicated Melissa and himself '—if you feel queasy, or as if you're going to be sick. Any pounding headaches, you let us know. Understand?'

'Yes, Joss.'

'Good. If you feel sick on the plane, you tell Phemie. And if you feel sick when you're at the hospital you tell Bub or Dex.'

'Yeah. I get it,' Andy remarked.

'You'd better. Head injuries are serious business. Don't you dare go all macho and put up with the pain.' He looked down at their patient for another moment before nodding, hoping the message had really got through to the jackaroo. He stood and pulled off his gloves, folding them together. He gathered up their garbage, accepting Melissa's gloves from her, and put everything into the bin. 'Now, Lis, why don't you and Mindy go inside and get her check-up done. I'll call Dex again to check on the arrangements and give him an update. We still have a few more places to visit before the day is over.' He glanced up at the sky. 'And the sooner we can get under way, the better.'

Melissa did as she was told, gathering her own medical bag of tricks and going inside, relieved to be out of the heat. Mindy led the way into the bedroom, where she sat on the bed and rolled up her sleeve so Melissa could take her blood pressure.

She took out the portable sphygmomanometer and wound the cuff around Mindy's arm. 'How has everything been progressing with your pregnancy?'

'Good. No swelling of the ankles, hands or feet.'

'Good.'

'I have my own blood pressure monitor here, and the readings have been within normal limits.'

'Excellent.' Melissa waited for her own reading and indeed found that Mindy's blood pressure was just fine. 'No other problems? Indigestion? Insomnia?'

'Mild to fair. Nothing out of the ordinary.' Mindy paused for a second and looked at Melissa. 'I'm just so glad you've come to town. I'd much rather go to Didja to have my baby than to Perth.'

'Is that where you would have gone?'

'Oh, yes. Most women when they reach about thirty or thirty-five weeks pack their bags and head off to Perth. They have to stay with friends or family, and apart from going to doctor's appointments they just sit around in a strange place and wait for their baby to arrive. If things are bad they have to stay in hospital— sometimes from the end of the first trimester.'

'A lot can go wrong with pregnancies,' Melissa

murmured, but her mind was whirring. She hadn't really thought about it before. All those women having to leave their loved ones at a time when they needed their support more than ever. She was here now to provide obstetric assistance to the women of the community, but what would happen after her contract ended? Would Joss be able to get another obstetrician out here, or would the women have to go back to leaving their families at such a crucial time? It was definitely something to ponder.

'Some women,' Mindy continued, 'opt to have their babies at home, with just other women helping out with the delivery—mainly Rajene; she's like an unofficial midwife. But…' Mindy screwed up her nose at the idea. 'So much can go wrong, as you've said. However, Gemma Etherington seems to like it. She's had her last four at home and nothing went wrong— but she does have six children, so it's not as though she doesn't know what she's doing.'

Melissa listened, intrigued by the plight of these tough Outback women. 'We're headed to their place this afternoon.'

'Gemma's pregnant with number seven.' Mindy smiled. 'You'll find a lot of big families out here in the back of beyond. I guess people think we have nothing better to do with our time than to farm and have kids.'

'Do *you* want a healthy brood?'

'At the moment I just want this one to be healthy, but I think I'd settle for two or three. I really miss helping Rich on the farm, and he's had me on light duties since he found out I was pregnant.'

'It's fair enough.'

'Sometimes I feel so left out. I'm the "little woman" and so I can't go and round up the cattle any more, or drive the tractor, or lug hay bales. Growing a baby is really not that exciting.'

Joss had walked up the corridor to see how they were doing and heard the end of Mindy's snippet. If she was really feeling that way then she would be pleased to have helped out today with bandaging and looking after James and Andy.

'Ahh, the exciting part is still to come,' Melissa said. 'And, remember, it's the stronger sex who get to have the babies. Men just couldn't handle it.'

Joss's lips twitched at Melissa's words, and he figured that although he knew she was probably trying to make Mindy feel better she also had a valid point.

'Lugging hay bales and driving the tractor are easy things. Being a mother—that's a tough job,' Melissa continued.

'Do you have children?'

'No. I haven't had that pleasure yet.'

'Do you want them?'

Melissa sighed. 'More than anything. I would love to be a mother. To care for a family of my own. To nurture them, to provide for them, to be strong for them.' She smiled as she said the last words.

'Well, then, we're going to have to find you a fella. There isn't a shortage in the Outback, so you'll have plenty to choose from—especially in Didja. Heaps of the miners are single. What's your type?'

'My type?' Melissa wasn't really sure about this turn of events.

'What do you like in a guy?'

'Oh.' Melissa thought for a moment, a picture of Joss instantly coming to mind. 'Uh…I'm not really sure. I don't think I've ever consciously sat down and thought about it before.' She thought about Renulf.

Initially she'd thought he was her perfect man, but when he'd called off their engagement because he couldn't handle the dedication Melissa had to her work, even though it was that dedication which had brought them together in the first place, she'd realised Renulf really hadn't been. Her perfect man would not only understand her dedication to medicine, but would also understand when she was called out in the middle of the night to deliver a baby. She'd often told Renulf that babies didn't keep office hours, but he still hadn't been able to deal with it.

It had been a lesson for Melissa never to try and date someone outside the medical profession—not unless they were very understanding about the self-sacrifices doctors often had to make. Joss certainly understood that concept. The man had left his family, his life in Perth, and had come to Didja to set up a brilliant medical facility. He would have poured his heart, his soul and a massive chunk of his own time into it. Oh, yes, self-sacrifice was something she in-stinctively knew Joss Lawson understood one hundred percent.

She pictured him now as she spoke quietly to Mindy. 'I guess I want a man who understands my work—my dedication to it, my need to continue with it. Also, I guess, ultimately I'm looking for a man who'll love me for *me*. For who I am. Faults and all.' As Renulf hadn't been able to do.

'That's what we all want.' Mindy nodded. 'Come on. Be more specific. Just between you and me. What do you like in a man? I like nice hairy legs and big shoulder muscles.'

Melissa smiled. 'Hairy legs, eh?'

'Yep. Rich has a very nice pair. I love running my

hands up and down his legs. It makes my hands go all tingly. So, come on. What's your favourite part?'

Melissa thought for a second, remembering how she hadn't been able to stop looking at Joss's legs the first day she'd arrived in Didja. He definitely had a very nice pair of hairy legs too. And then she'd seen his eyes. 'Eyes.' She nodded as she spoke. She remembered the way Joss had looked at her just before he'd kissed her and sighed. 'Nice blue eyes. Deep in colour and very expressive.'

'Blue eyes? Mmm-hmm, what else?'

'Well, all the basics, I guess. Courteous, kind, giving. Not a party animal, but someone who knows how to have a good time—without starting a riot.'

'Oh, goodness. That strikes out half the men in Didja.'

Melissa laughed. 'He needs to have nice hands— clever hands. Healing hands.' She said the last softly.

'Oh, my gosh.' Mindy sat up straighter. 'I know the perfect man for you. It's so simple.'

'A match already? Gee, you're faster than a computer.'

'Joss.' Mindy shrugged, as though it was just so simple. 'Joss would be perfect for you.'

Joss's eyes widened as he listened to what had just transpired. He'd been waiting for a good opportunity to announce his presence but it simply hadn't come, and he hadn't wanted to break up the female bonding session. Mindy thought *he* was ideal for Lis? He swallowed over a sudden lump in his throat.

It might be true that there was an incredible awareness between himself and his new female colleague, but that didn't mean they were going to jump right into a relationship. Physical attraction and need weren't everything in life, and the thought of anything serious, anything permanent, made him break out in a cold sweat.

'Joss?' Melissa closed her eyes for a split second, realising that she had indeed just described Joss when she'd been thinking about what she looked for in a man. What she hadn't expected was for Mindy to pick up on it. She should have been more careful.

'You'd be so perfect for each other. You both have medicine in common as well, which is always a good start. Rich and I had the farm in common. It was what brought us together—that and the confines of the area. Oh, I know.' She clapped her hands, her face lit with excitement. 'You should ask Joss out to dinner.'

'What?'

'Girls can do that nowadays. Equal opportunities and all that. And, secretly, I think the guys love it.'

'They do?'

Mindy giggled. 'Of course. But if you feel uncomfortable making it an actual date, then just ask him to show you around the town, and then you could end up having dinner somewhere.'

She couldn't believe what Mindy was saying, and knew she just wasn't ready for any of this. To date? To ask Joss out to dinner? Sure, she'd enjoyed that kiss. Sure, she was physically attracted to him. But dinner? Just the two of them? That might be moving a little fast, and she was more determined to get to know the people of the town first. Then again, wasn't Joss part of that town?

'We're…uh…both a little busy back in Didja. We have clinics and house-calls and paperwork and you know…general doctoring stuff.'

Joss knew he should move. Knew he was eavesdropping. But he was glued to the spot, unable to believe the conversation going on between the two women. Was this an indication as to whether or not Melissa was really interested in him?

'But that's what makes it so good. He certainly understands the doctoring part, and you do like him, don't you?'

'He's a nice man. Clever, too. But he's my boss.'

Mindy waved away her last words. 'He's also giving and courteous and all of those other things you listed. Oh, you should totally do this. Go out with Joss. It would be good for him too.'

'What do you mean?'

'Joss has barely dated since he moved to Didja. He's a workaholic and he uses the clinic as an excuse all the time.'

'Perhaps he has his reasons for not dating.'

'Or perhaps he's running away from his problems. Lots of people come to the Outback to do that. I don't really know what happened to him in Perth before he came here. Bub might, she knows everything about everyone, but what I can tell you is that Joss certainly isn't the dating type. You could change all that.'

Melissa emphatically shook her head. 'I don't think so. I may not have come to Didja to run away from my problems, but I have no intention of becoming involved with any man—much less Joss Lawson.' She thought back to the way he'd treated her after that New Year kiss. 'Besides, he's made it crystal-clear that he's not interested in me that way. I've only known him for a short time and he runs hot and cold. He's like a yo-yo so as far as I'm concerned, he's my boss and my colleague and that's it. End of story.'

Mindy sighed and shrugged. 'Well, it was worth a shot.'

Melissa chuckled. 'Come on—we need to finish your check-up. Joss will want to go soon, and I don't want to keep him waiting.

Joss knew she was right. It was the reason he'd come up the corridor in the first place, the carpeted floor-boards masking the sound of his footsteps. They needed to get moving. Yet now he seemed unable even to shift his own feet. Had Melissa said what she'd said in order to get Mindy to drop the subject or did she really mean it?

'See? You're already in tune with him. You're thinking like he would think. You have so much in common.' Mindy clapped her hands again as she sat back amongst the pillows so Melissa could measure her stomach.

Melissa sighed. 'Leave it, Mindy.' As she listened to Mindy's heartbeat through the stethoscope, she mentally strengthened her own resolve. She hadn't come to Didja to continue being a people-pleaser. This was her chance at a new start—a new life which she wanted to build with Dex. She wasn't here to continue making the same mistakes as always. She had to be strong, to really put herself first for once. She was in Didja for family—the only remaining family she had.

Melissa put her special baby heart monitor machine onto Mindy's swollen belly and they both listened to the baby's heartbeat.

'Strong and healthy.' Mindy sighed with relief. 'I love hearing that sound.'

Melissa smiled. 'Everything's looking just fine. Keep on doing whatever it is you're doing.'

'Good. I will—and thanks for talking to me. It's so rare that I get real girly-talk time.'

'I've enjoyed it too. Call me any time.' Melissa gave Mindy her mobile number. 'Do mobile phones work out here?'

'Generally they're pretty good.'

As they continued discussing the reception of different mobile network carriers, Joss realised that if he didn't move soon he'd be discovered, and then Lis would know he'd overheard her conversation. Making his feet move, he headed silently back down the corridor.

A minute or two later, the women appeared.

'Ahh, Joss, there you are.'

Did Mindy's tone sound overly bright and cheerful? He decided to ignore it and glanced surreptitiously at Lis. She didn't seem agitated or concerned, and that helped him to relax a little.

'Here I am.' He held his medical kit in his hand and raised an eyebrow at Melissa. 'All done?' Did his tone sound husky? As though he had a secret? Could she see in his face that he'd overheard?

'All done. Are you ready to go?'

'Yes. Andy and James are being driven out to the airstrip. The RFDS should be here in about ten minutes and will complete the transfer. We can check on them once we get back to town later tonight, to review their progress.'

'We don't need to be here to hand over to the RFDS?'

'Not this time. It's all quite straightforward.' He looked at her for a moment and realised she'd been quite looking forward to the transfer part. 'You'll have ample opportunity to meet those crazy flying doctors, but unfortunately today we're on a very tight schedule.'

'Oh, sure. It's no problem.'

'Everything all right with Mindy and the baby?'

'Right as rain,' Melissa replied.

'Well, speaking of rain, that's the reason we need to get moving. There's been a bit of lightning sighted on the horizon.'

Melissa raised her eyebrows. 'Is that bad?'

'It means we don't want to be on a dirt road when the clouds open.' And neither did they want to get trapped in that ute. Together. Just the two of them. No.

'Aww, come on,' Mindy piped up. 'That's when you get a really good mudslide going.'

'And end up wrapped around a tree.'

'Yeah, but only if the tree doesn't move fast enough,' Mindy joked.

Joss grinned. 'Good point.' He nodded to Melissa. 'Let's go.' As they walked out to the front of the property they heard the buzzing sound of the chopper.

'That's Rich.' Mindy clapped her hands. 'Goody. I have so much to tell him.' Her eyes twinkled with delight as she looked from Melissa to Joss and then back again.

'Well, it was a pleasure to meet you,' Melissa rushed in, surprised when the young pregnant woman gave her a hug. It appeared she should get used to being hugged in this town, because the people were most definitely friendly and not backwards in showing their affection.

'It was great. I have a feeling that everything will work out just fine.'

As Mindy waved them off, Joss looked across at Melissa.

'What was that all about? She seemed quite jovial.'

'Oh? Isn't she always like that? You know her better than I do.'

'Not that well. Until Mindy required prenatal care,

she was as fit as a fiddle and always had been. Rarely a sick day in her life—well, at least as long as I've known her.'

'I guess she's just relieved that James and Andy are OK, that things weren't worse. Hopefully her husband is returning home with one captured and sedated bull.'

They visited the next few homesteads, trying to get through the necessary check-ups as fast as possible but also not wanting to rush their patients. The emergency with James and Andy had sucked up a lot of time.

The rain started about ten minutes after they left the second to last homestead, intent on making their way to the Etheringtons—their last port of call for the day. The problem with Outback rain was that when it started it really *started*. Melissa peered out of the windscreen, trying to see something…anything. The wipers were swishing so hard and fast she thought they might wipe themselves right off the car.

'This is bad,' Joss declared a moment later.

Melissa gave him a sidelong glance. Was he talking about the weather, or the tension which existed between them?

'I can't see a thing.'

They were now driving almost at a snail's pace, and she had to agree that visibility was extremely poor. Joss shook his head and steered the car off to the side of the road.

'Won't we get bogged? I mean, it's raining so hard the ground will turn into that mudslide Mindy mentioned.'

'We're in a hard shoulder truck rest-stop. It's usually used for truckers to pull over and catch a few hours' sleep before setting off on the next big drive.'

'What? Even out here in the middle of nowhere?'

'Trucks regularly drive along these roads. Remember—without trucks, Australia stops.'

Melissa couldn't help grinning. 'You sound like an advertising campaign.'

He frowned for a moment. 'I do, don't I?' What had got into him? Why was he trying to make her laugh? Was he trying to impress her in some way? Perhaps it was that overheard conversation which was getting to him. He hadn't liked it at all when she'd described him as a yo-yo, and it was as though he now needed to prove to her that she was wrong.

She'd sounded mortified at Mindy's suggestion of having dinner with him, of going out on a date, and whilst he knew there was a physical attraction on his part—one he wasn't doing too well at controlling right at this moment, given the confines of the ute—he could have sworn, after their shared New Year kiss, that she'd felt that attraction too.

And now he was stuck with the most incredibly beautiful woman he'd ever seen, and when she smiled at him, as she was now, he almost forgot his own name. The woman was driving him to distraction, and he wasn't at all happy about their immediate turn of events.

He flicked on the radio, trying to find something to distract them, but the rain was interfering with the reception and all they managed to pick up was white noise. He turned it off with a final click, plunging them into silence. The engine was off, the radio was off, and all that could be heard was the rain outside. That…and Melissa's breathing.

He tried not to listen, tried not to be aware of the way she breathed in and out. The way her body rose and fell with each breath. He tried not to be aware of the way her sweet, fresh scent was winding itself around him. He tried not to be aware of how stunning she was and how just sitting beside her, the windows fogging up due to their breathing, could make his body overheat. The one situation he'd been trying to avoid all day long had happened, and now he had to deal with it.

'So…' Melissa clicked her fingers. 'What shall we talk about?'

'Uh…' Joss tried not to let the sultry sound of her voice affect him. His mind, which he prided himself on keeping as sharp as a tack, was now completely blank of any suggestions. How was it that this woman could have such an effect on him? A woman who had turned his world upside down and wrenched it inside out even though she didn't know it.

'Usually the weather is the first topic of discussion when making small talk,' she ventured. 'However, I think the weather is the one topic neither of us would like to discuss, given that it has us trapped and sitting in a car.'

'In the middle of nowhere,' he added.

'Yes. So, any ideas? Hobbies? What sort of hobbies do you have?'

'Hobbies?' He pondered the thought for a moment.

'Oh, come on, Joss. Surely you have a hobby—and drinking beer at the pub with your friends doesn't qualify.'

He couldn't help but smile at that. 'Party-pooper.' He thought for another moment, then sadly shook his head. 'The clinic.' He shrugged. 'I guess the clinic is my hobby. It's where I spend most of my free time.'

'That's sad, Josiah.'

'I know. How about you? What are your hobbies?'

'Searching for my brother.'

'But you've found him.'

'Hmm.'

'That's sad, Melissa.'

She looked at him and laughed. It was a mistake. A big mistake. Because in that one second their eyes locked and held.

'You look radiant when you laugh like that.' His words were soft and he shook his head slowly, as though he wished he hadn't said what he had.

'What's going on, Joss?'

He didn't pretend not to understand. 'I don't know.'

'One minute you're nice to me, the next you're—'

'Not so nice,' he finished for her. 'I know.' He reached out and tucked a lock of hair which had come loose from her ponytail back behind her ear. 'I doubt it would help if I said I was confused.'

'I gathered that much.'

Her soft sweet tones only made the fog in his mind more dense. All he could do right now was watch the way her lips moved as she spoke. Those pink, luscious lips which had plagued his dreams. The taste of them, the pressure of them, the need to have them against his own once more. His pride at wanting to show her he wasn't a yo-yo rose to the fore. He was a good man. A catch. One of the most eligible bachelors in town. She should be delighted to have dinner with him. He knew she felt the attraction which existed between them—that strong physical pull which had left them both stunned quite a few times since she'd arrived in town.

She swallowed, noting the intense way he was staring at her. It was as though he knew he was confused but right at the moment didn't care at all. Confusion, right and wrong, the fact that they were colleagues—nothing seemed to matter right at that moment. Nothing except the way he was looking at her.

She told herself she didn't want this—didn't want these feelings she had for him. This wasn't why she'd come to Didja. Then again she reminded herself that she'd vowed to live her life for herself, to put herself first for a while, and right now what she wanted most in the world was to feel Joss's mouth on hers again. To really kiss him this time and not just be teased with the faint, feathering brush of his lips on hers.

'Lis.' He tucked her hair behind her ear again, this time allowing his hand to linger longer, to caress her cheek.

With her heart pounding wildly against her chest as she saw the look of desire in his eyes, as she watched the movement of his lips as he spoke her name, her lips parted, allowing the pent-up air to escape. She rested her hand on his arm, not sure whether to push him away or to draw him closer.

Indecision warred within each of them, both knowing what they wanted to do but unsure whether they should follow through. That was until she whispered his name and he could resist no longer.

Like lightning, he moved. His hand was at her neck, urging her closer as he leaned towards her. His mouth was crushing down on hers, and both of them were gasping with repressed delight.

CHAPTER SIX

THIS was no soft peck. This was no featherlight brush of his lips on hers. No, this was an intense, fiery and passionate kiss between two people who had been controlling themselves for what seemed like an age rather than just a few days.

It was bizzare to be lip-locked with a man she hardly knew, yet somehow, deep down in her soul, she couldn't deny the feelings he evoked. The heat, the animalistic pleasure, the heady combination of their pheromones mixing together and surging into something so wild and out of control she wondered whether they'd ever be able to tame it.

A guttural moan escaped from him as he tried to bring her as close to him as possible—which was a little difficult with the gearstick in the way. He needed her body pressed hard against his, to feel her soft flesh next to his, needed to feel everything she had to give. Her mouth was so sweet, so flavoursome, so perfect for his own. He focused on eliciting more of a response from her, needing her to be as out of control as he felt.

This was a passion which had been difficult to ignore, and whilst he'd done his best—whilst he'd kept his desire for her repressed, whilst he'd woken the past few mornings from dreams of her—this moment in time was definitely worth it. It was worth it because she made him *feel*.

It had been so long since he'd allowed himself to take such a powerful emotion from someone else, and she was definitely giving him all she had. There was no denying the attraction now. Both of them matched with startling equality the level of passion which flowed freely between them.

It was pleasure and pain. They both knew it was wrong, both knew they shouldn't be doing what they were doing, but the desire had been too strong to ignore, and the look in her eyes and the way her lips had parted…as though they were making themselves ready for him…had all been too much and he'd snapped.

He'd had to have her, and now that he had, now that he knew how incredible it felt to have her mouth against his own, to feel her body against his, he wasn't sure what was supposed to happen next. It had been so incredibly long since he'd held a woman like this, had kissed a woman in such a way, and she was kissing him right back with such abandon it was touching.

Joss loosened his hold on her, but only for a moment. Still it was enough time for her to shift her hands, so she could slide them up his strong firm arm, to feel the muscles beneath the softness of her fingertips. His shoulders were broad, and whilst she moved her mouth against his she traced those sculptured contours, loving the feel of him. When her fingers finally plunged into his hair, ensuring that his head stayed in place, ensuring that his mouth continued to create utter havoc with all of her senses, she moaned with pleasure.

Did he have any idea just how incredible he felt? Did

he have any idea just how dynamic it was to have a man appreciate her in such a way? She knew it was only physical, but to be held in such a way, to be kissed in such a way… All of the fantasies she'd had about him honestly hadn't done him justice.

Everything around them seemed to disappear into oblivion. It was the same as their New Year kiss, when the crowds had all but vanished into thin air, the focus on the two of them intense and mutual. There was no rain. There were no cracks of lightning brightening the sky for a split second. Nothing existed except the two of them, locked together in an embrace so desperate they both wondered if it would ever end.

Both had been hurt in the past. Both found it difficult to trust, to open themselves up again to the possibility of actually having a relationship. None of that mattered here and now, because the temporary emotions of need, of want, of taking, of receiving, of just *feeling* again were all that mattered.

Where she thought the intensity, the passion and the hunger would start to dissipate, after those electrifying first few moments, she found she was mistaken—for his mouth on hers was still demanding a powerful, no-holds-barred response, and she was more than eager to give it.

She was giving it her all, she was one hundred percent involved, and he had to confess he hadn't expected such eagerness from his gorgeous new colleague—not that he was complaining. How could a man possibly complain when he was kissing such a full and sumptuous mouth? When she was driving him crazy with her hands in his hair, holding his head in place, letting him know she didn't want this to end?

Still he needed more. More of her. More feeling. More…Melissa. He was utterly mesmerised by her, and whilst he didn't want to be, at the moment he honestly didn't think he had a choice. His need for her was far too great. Sliding his hand down from her neck, over her shoulder and down, down, to cup the soft underside of her breast, he wondered if he was pushing things just a little too far, too soon. His answer came a nanosecond later, when she moaned with delight and pushed herself further into his touch.

Oh, she was heaven. He hadn't expected any of this, and he was overwhelmed with how she was making him feel. The woman was hypnotic, and he was definitely eager for so much more.

She broke from his mouth, moaning once more with delight, her breathing harsh and uneven. 'Joss.' She whispered his name with such a deep huskiness he was sure she had no idea just how powerful it sounded.

He looked down at her. What little light they had, due to the black clouds that were blocking the early afternoon sun, was shining onto her face. Her eyes were closed, her lips parted in anticipation of his return, her face turned up to him in wanton rapture.

She was beautiful.

At that thought his eyes widened, and he swallowed. What had he done? He jerked his hand back from where he'd been caressing her breast and put it behind his back. What had he *done*? Her eyelids slowly fluttered open and she looked up at him, her pupils large, her irises deep with delighted emotion. He straightened, pulling away from her.

What had he done?

With his next breath he'd opened the door and stepped from the vehicle into the pouring rain, leaving a shell-shocked, blinking Melissa stupefied.

What had just happened?

She sat staring out at the rain, unsure what had happened and what she was supposed to do about it. He'd just left her, preferring to be out in the rain getting soaked to the skin to being anywhere near her. One second she'd been in his arms, his hands on hers, his mouth on her, both of them caught up in the passion of the moment and the next—nothing.

Melissa crossed her arms over her chest, feeling cold and bereft. Feeling stupid and regretful. Feeling completely insecure. Why had he left? Why had he stopped? Didn't he want her? She shook her head and buried her face in her hands, humiliation washing over her as she recalled the wanton way she'd urged him on.

What was wrong with her? He obviously didn't find her as attractive as she'd initially thought, and once again she was racked with confusion. She'd thought the pull between them had been pretty intense over the past few days, but now she wasn't so sure. In reality, she had to keep reminding herself she knew next to nothing about Joss. He might behave this way with any woman who responded to him.

Then again she recalled Mindy, telling her that Joss didn't date—in which case it could possibly mean that he was attracted to her but didn't want to be. Her mind whirled as she tried to make some sort of sense out of the mess in which she presently found herself.

What the man said and what the man did were two completely different things, and that just made matters worse. She shook her head and pushed her hands through her hair, breathing deeply to stop herself from crying. She was too emotional. She'd become too close to him too quickly, and this was exactly what had happened in her last relationship. She'd misread the signals then and she was doing it again now.

Why had she let herself give in to him? Why hadn't she been more cautious, more careful, more self-controlled?

She jumped fair out of her skin as the driver's door was wrenched open and a dripping wet Joss climbed back into the car. He buckled his seat-belt and started the engine, the whirr of the windscreen wipers starting immediately.

'It's starting to settle down. Isn't raining as hard as before.' He didn't look at her but instead fiddled with the ute's controls, ensuring the windows were demisted. 'Put your seat-belt on.'

Melissa did as he said, not sure whether she should question his decision to get them back on the road again or not. What about impassable roads? What about mudslides that ended up with the car smashing into a tree? What about keeping them safe?

She glanced over at him and saw that his jaw was firmly set. He was intent on driving them, and nothing she said or did was going to dissuade him. He was obviously a man with a mission to get them out of the middle of nowhere, to get them out of their secluded little environment to somewhere he didn't need to be so close to her. That had to be it. Yo-yo Joss was back with a vengeance, and right now, given her lack of self-control where he was concerned, she was glad he was making the decisions.

Neither of them spoke as he continued to drive the car carefully along the road. Melissa wasn't sure she agreed with him about the amount of rain currently being dumped upon them. It was really as though someone had turned on a tap and—whoosh—the rain came down. It also rammed home the point of how very different things were here in the Outback. Whilst

Hobart saw its fair share of rain, being the coldest state in all of Australia, it was nothing compared to this. Out here it was either hot or not. Raining or not. Muggy or not. The four seasons didn't seem to apply at all, and she was amazed that even though it was the same country she'd lived in for all of her life it was completely different from what she was used to.

Finally Joss pulled off the road into a graded gravel driveway which was flooded in certain parts. Again, Melissa was glad of the ute and its four-wheel-drive capabilities. When he brought the ute to a halt, he cut the engine, released his seat-belt and was once more out of the car like a shot.

Melissa shook her head, totally unsure of just how her life had become so complicated so quickly. She stepped out into the cooling rain and headed up the front steps of the large brick homestead before her.

'There you are,' Gemma Etherington said in greeting as she walked towards Melissa.

There were children of various ages around the place, and a moment later, one of the older girls handed her a towel. Melissa looked over to where Joss was just coming in the door, medical bags in tow.

'Hi!' he greeted Gemma warmly, gladly accepting a towel and quickly drying himself off.

'Just leave your wet shoes by the door and come on in,' Gemma called. 'They won't take long to dry. Nothing does in this heat. It may be wet, but it's still hot.' She laughed. 'We were expecting you quite a while ago.'

'Uh…' Joss snuck a sideways glance at Melissa before answering. 'There was an emergency at Murphy's Farm.'

'Oh, we know about that. Mindy called through

before the rains hit and told us. I guess you two must have got stuck out there. Are the roads very bad?'

Joss shrugged, making a point not to look at Melissa. He still couldn't believe he'd allowed himself to lose control like that. 'Fair.'

'Ron's over at the neighbours'. I just hope he's going to be able to get home through the dirt roads, otherwise it'll take him a good hour to go around the perimeters on the main roads.'

'He should be fine,' Joss soothed.

Gemma rubbed a possessive hand over her baby bump. 'I hope so. Anyway, come and have something to eat. You both must be starving. Peter,' she said to her son, 'set another two places at the table, please.'

'Righto, Mum.' Peter headed into the kitchen to do as he was asked.

'I'm sorry we're so late,' Joss remarked as he picked up the young three-year-old and started tickling the child's tummy. 'I hope you didn't delay lunch on our account.'

'Not at all. I've been trying to get lunch organised for the past hour and a half, but things do tend to happen, and I learned long ago not to stress about it. We eat when we eat and that's all there is to it.'

Joss smiled. 'You sound like my mum.'

'Well, she would know—having had a large brood of her own. Anyway, I've already had Yolanda make up the guest room, because I don't think this rain is going to abate. We were expecting just Dex, but it's fantastic to get to meet the new doctor.' Gemma smiled widely at Melissa and took one of her hands in hers. 'I didn't think I'd get to meet you until this little one was due to arrive.' She continued to rub her pregnant belly.

'I'm delighted to be here—you have such a wonderful home.' Melissa could really feel the warmth and welcome radiating from this harried mother.

'It's messy, dusty and noisy, but filled with love.' Gemma let go of her hand as some of the other children started to bring mounds of sandwiches to the dining table. 'All right!' she hollered, clapping her hands to get the attention of her family. 'Go and wash your hands and faces.'

Joss released the squirming three-year-old and held out a chair for Gemma. She sat down, breathing a sigh of relief at being off her feet. Melissa watched her carefully, noting the laboured breathing which took longer than normal to settle.

They were both enveloped into the Etherington household, glad to be able to focus on something other than fighting or ignoring what had happened back in the ute. She noted that Joss seemed relaxed, more so than she'd seen him in Didja, and the way he related to the entire family was quite interesting to see. It was as though this was the real him—the one he only let out on special occasions or in certain circumstances. That definitely intrigued her.

Melissa watched the noisy, happy Etheringtons with delight. All of them were welcoming, and she found no falseness—just genuine friendliness. It hammered home the realisation that this was what she'd been missing throughout her own childhood, this sort of hullabaloo, and it was…enchanting. Whilst she hadn't been lonely as a child, the older she'd grown, the more she'd had the sense that something was missing in her life.

When her parents had died, her heart had been pierced with a grief she hadn't known existed, and with it had come loneliness. It was what had prompted her to search for her birth mother in the first place, and it was also what had prompted her to find Dex.

Yet this…this joyous family simply radiated life. She'd always wanted to have children, but had never thought about how many. First, though, she had to find the right man. Mindy's words, which were still fresh in her mind, made her glance over at Joss. He was laughing with Peter, who appeared to be the eldest of the Etherington children, the two of them joking around with ease and friendliness.

No, Joss Lawson was most definitely not the right man for her. He was too hot and cold for her liking, and whilst he no doubt had his reasons for being that way, unless he decided to face them, to deal with them, there would never be anything between them—despite the physical attraction they obviously felt for each other.

She'd thought she'd found love before with Renulf, but she'd been wrong. Companionship—yes. Deep abiding friendship and a fondness for each other—yes. But not love. Even though they'd met when she'd treated him during one of her rare stints in A&E, he hadn't fully grasped what it would be like to date a doctor. She'd presumed, when he'd proposed to her, that he'd understood, but then—as she'd discovered later—he'd expected her to give up working full-time once they were married. She'd been wrong before, and that meant she could be wrong again.

When they were all sitting around the large dining room table the noise level didn't decrease. Melissa enjoyed the meal very much, but it wasn't the food which had put the smile on her face but the loud rowdiness of the entire clan. They all talked over each other as different topics were discussed. Manners were minded, yet it was one incredibly happy time. This was a real family and the yearning inside her to have this for her very own only intensified.

By the time they'd finished eating it was after three o'clock and the rain was still pouring down. Gemma went to have a rest while the older kids looked after the younger ones. Joss and Peter brought in their overnight bags from the ute.

'We're staying the night?' she asked Joss. They were standing out on the verandah, which ringed its way around the entire house. He nodded and brushed rain off himself.

'Yes.'

'We're stranded?' She wasn't alarmed, but neither was she pleased. At least, she rationalised, they didn't need to spend the night on the side of the road in the ute. That would have been... She closed her eyes for a second, not even able to contemplate what might have happened if that had been the case.

Peter heard her comment. 'And what a great family to be stranded with.' He grinned at her, his smile highlighted by the braces on his teeth.

'Oh, I'm not complaining,' she quickly explained. 'Just adapting to the Outback way of doing things.'

Peter carried their bags inside the house, leaving the two of them on the verandah. Melissa put her hands on the railing and looked out at the rain. She heard the door to the house open and close and figured Joss had gone inside, not wanting to be anywhere near her.

She hung her head and shook it. 'Stop thinking about him,' she muttered quietly to herself.

'Probably a good idea.'

Melissa spun around to see Joss standing by the door, hands in the pockets of his almost dry shorts.

'I thought you'd gone inside.' She wasn't going to

say anything. She wasn't going to be the one to promote conversation between them—because as far as she was concerned she'd done her fair share of that. He could either talk, be silent, or he could just go. She was through trying to please her colleague, trying to be overly nice and to make sure that he was coping just fine with whatever it was that existed between them. If he didn't want to know, neither did she. If he wanted to forget that dynamic, heart-melting kiss had ever happened, then so would she. If he wanted to be mono-syllabic, then so would she.

'I should.'

When he didn't move, she merely shrugged and turned to look at the rain again, effectively dismissing him. He should take the hint. He should leave her in peace. But for some reason he felt compelled to make sure she was all right.

He was still horrified at his weakness earlier, quite unable to believe the powerful hold she had over him. The sight of her parted lips, her eyes filled with desire, her body sending out those 'come hither' signals, and he'd been unable to resist.

And that kiss!

Joss closed his eyes for a moment, still able to taste her, able to breathe in deeply and have her sweet scent envelop him. It was wrong. She was his colleague and he didn't date colleagues. She was business, not pleasure, and he needed to remember that—to keep his distance. He wasn't the type of man to give his trust easily. He wasn't the type of man who could offer a woman like Melissa a bright and happy future. He'd heard her. She wanted a family, lots of children. He wasn't that man. He'd been burned so badly before that he'd learnt his lesson the hard way. Intimacy, giving his heart and his soul to a woman, had ended in such incredible heartache and betrayal that he wasn't fool enough to go there again.

And now they stood—him by the door, her at the railing with her back firmly to him. He wondered what she was thinking, but knew he'd never ask. He wanted to know if she'd been as affected by the kiss as he'd been, but knew he'd never ask. He hoped she'd be willing to help him grow, to help him trust again, but he knew that was definitely one thing he wouldn't ask, no matter how perfect she'd felt in his arms.

She was the only woman since Christina who had made him feel this way, and he was certain that the emotions he felt towards Melissa were growing stronger by the minute, surpassing the ones he'd initially had for his betraying ex-fiancée. If that wasn't warning enough, he didn't know what was.

'Yeah. I should go,' he murmured, and opened the door, going inside to get control over his wayward emotions.

After a moment Melissa turned to make sure he was really gone, before turning her attention back to the rain. 'Hot and cold.' She closed her eyes and tried to forget what had happened back in the ute. The sooner she did that, the better. The sooner she could see Joss Lawson as simply a colleague, the better.

Emotion welled in her throat and a few silent tears rolled down her cheeks. The sooner she realised she was destined to be alone for ever, the better.

CHAPTER SEVEN

THE Etherington family were quite involving, and as the afternoon turned into evening Melissa and Joss found themselves playing all sorts of games with the children. It gave them the space they needed to mentally process what had happened between them, some room to reflect and hopefully to figure out what on earth happened next.

'Dr Jossy!' Bridget, who was five, called to him, demanding his attention for a game of pairs. 'I've laid all the cards out in nice straight lines.' She pointed to her handiwork.

'So I see.'

Melissa watched as Joss crouched down onto the floor, stretching himself out and giving the little girl his undivided attention.

'She's very bossy,' Gemma told Melissa. 'I just hope Joss can handle himself.' The two women smiled.

'I think he has a fair enough chance,' Melissa replied. 'Anyway, whilst everyone's busy, why don't we get your check-up done?'

'Good idea,' Gemma agreed, and after Melissa had collected her medical bag the two women headed into Gemma's bedroom.

'Ron, my husband, says I'm on my feet too much, and he's right—but we have six kids and a farm to run. It's hard *not* to be on your feet all the time.'

'Any problems with the other pregnancies?'

'None. No pre-eclampsia, no gestational diabetes. Nothing.'

Melissa finished taking Gemma's blood pressure, a little concerned at the elevated reading. 'So how does this pregnancy compare?'

'It's different. I can be honest about that. And I have had my own niggling concerns, but that's to be expected, right?'

'That depends on what the niggling concerns are.'

'I've had one or two small bleeds. Sometimes during the night.'

'How long do they last?'

'Less than a minute.'

'Most nights? How many times a week? More than one bleed per night?'

'About three or four times a week, and usually it's two bleeds. They don't come together. They're usually hours apart.'

'Any stabbing pains?'

'Sort of. Sometimes they're more like cramps. Sometimes it's a constant pain which lasts for quite a while.'

'Like Braxton-Hicks?'

Gemma thought for a moment before shaking her head. 'No. Not that bad.'

'Have you been feeling more tired? Any nausea?'

'Mild nausea, but with my girls I had morning sickness the entire pregnancy, so I didn't think that was anything unusual. I'm tired, but I do have a lot going on.'

Melissa listened to Gemma's heart-rate and then the baby's heart-rate. Both were slightly elevated but nothing to cause great concern. 'I'd like you to come to Didja for a few days.'

'What?' Gemma was instantly horrified.

'I need to do some more tests, and I'd like to monitor the baby a little closer. Have you had a scan?'

'No. I only had scans with the first two. Is there really something wrong with my baby?'

'As you said, you have niggling concerns. I share those concerns. I'd like to put both of our niggles to rest.'

Gemma sat up as Melissa packed away her equipment. 'What about Joss? Should we ask his opinion?'

'If you'd like. I realise I'm the new kid in town, and therefore you may think I'm acting a little too cautiously. If you'd prefer Joss to give you a second opinion, we can go and ask him now.'

'You don't mind? You're not offended?'

Melissa smiled and waved Gemma's words away. 'Not at all. You need to be comfortable with your treating doctor and, whilst I may have more experience with these issues, Joss is the doctor you know better.' She left her bag on the floor. 'I'll go get him. Stay here and keep your feet up.'

She found Joss sitting on the lounge, completely at ease, the three youngest children sitting next to him as he held them enraptured with the story he was reading. She watched him for a moment, amazed at how wonderful he was with the children. When he looked up and saw her standing there, he quirked an eyebrow. 'Problem?'

He looked gorgeous, carefree and downright sexy. It took her a moment to make her mind work, as seeing him like this had completely wiped all rational and coherent thought from her.

'Uh… I need you to…' She jerked her thumb over her shoulder. 'Uh…' Come on, Melissa. Concentrate. She closed her eyes, blocking out the sight of him. 'I need you to come and check Gemma.'

His expression instantly changed to one of concern. Not wanting to alarm the children, he shifted them slowly, calling over Yolanda, the oldest girl, to finish reading to them.

'What's wrong?' he asked quietly as they headed towards Gemma's bedroom.

Joss stopped off in the bathroom to wash his hands, all the while listening to what Melissa had to say. 'Care to guess a diagnosis?'

She shook her head. 'I need to do tests. Bloods. Amniocentesis and ultrasound to begin with.'

'OK. No hunches?'

'Ante-partum haemorrhage?' She shrugged. 'She told me she's had a few small bleeds, and with the pains…' She shook her head. 'Or I could be wrong. I need to do tests. Too many possibilities.'

'How elevated is the baby's heart-rate?'

'It's up, but not on the dangerous scale.'

'Not yet. Right.' He walked purposefully into Gemma's room and proceeded with a thorough check-up. When he was finished, he looked his patient carefully in the eyes. 'I have to say that I agree with Lis on this one, Gem. Your other pregnancies weren't like this, and as you've had quite a few to compare it to that's the biggest factor to indicate there may be something wrong.'

Gemma rubbed her stomach lovingly. She was only twenty weeks, but was well and truly showing.

'We'll contact the Royal Flying Doctor Service and get you airlifted to Didja tomorrow morning.'

'That soon?' Gemma was shocked. 'But the kids and—'

'I'll get Peter to find Ron,' Joss said. 'He should be here.'

'He'll be on his way home now,' Gemma told him, then shook her head. 'Tomorrow morning?'

'The sooner we find out what's going on, the better,' Melissa encouraged. 'Your health and the baby's health are paramount.'

'But what about the rest of my kids? My family?' Her voice broke on the word and Melissa felt her pain. To have all this—such love and happiness—and to leave it even for a short time would be painful.

Tears sprang to the woman's eyes as a moment later her husband walked into the room.

'Perfect timing. I was just about to go and contact you,' Joss said as Ron rushed to his wife's side.

'What's wrong? What's going on?'

Joss and Melissa explained the situation as Ron held his wife, comforting her in such a loving way.

'Tomorrow? So soon?'

'The sooner we start on the tests, the sooner we'll—' Melissa began but he waved her words away.

'You're right. You're right. It's fine. It'll be OK. Everything will be OK. You'll see. We'll cope,' Ron quickly assured Gemma. 'We've raised all of our children to be self-sufficient, and Peter's almost seventeen now. He's the oldest, and he's more than capable of taking control of things.'

Joss looked over at Melissa and saw such empathy in her face that he couldn't help but be moved by it. She genuinely cared about her patients, she was really empathising with them, and it showed him what a good doctor she truly was. It also showed him a lot about the person she really was. He doubted Christina would ever have given people in distress another thought other than how their own distress might affect her.

He was about to look away when she turned and met his gaze. They stared at each other for a long moment, and he could see her pain at splitting up this family, but the fact remained that Gemma needed to go to Didja for tests. Joss inclined his head towards the doorway, indicating they should give Ron and Gemma some privacy.

She nodded, and together they headed out and down the corridor. Once there, she expected Joss to go in a different direction, to leave her to her own devices, but instead he held the front door open and waited for her to go out before him.

'Best to make ourselves scarce for a few minutes. Ron and Gemma will want to talk to the kids.'

She nodded, surprised at his forethought. 'They're a very open and loving family.'

'They are.'

'You were brilliant with those children. All of them were so enraptured by what you were reading.' Melissa stood at the verandah railing, looking out at the never-ceasing rain. Joss perched himself against the far railing, ensuring there was quite a bit of distance between them. 'And you're completely natural with the older children as well,' she praised.

He shrugged. 'I have siblings. Five of them, to be precise.'

'Really? I didn't know that. But then, there's a lot about you I don't know.' It explained why he was being so chatty all of a sudden. Being here with the

Etheringtons reminded him of being with his own family, and that had to inspire a certain sort of comfort in him.

He shrugged those broad, firm shoulders of his and crossed his arms over his chest. 'I guess I'm used to dealing with children, family situations and the like. You know—taking responsibility, helping out, reading stories, giving orders. Coming here to the Etheringtons' is like walking into my own home. In fact, the last time I was here I offered to help Peter do the dishes and we sort of ended up having a soapsud fight in the kitchen. Gemma got cross with both of us.'

Melissa couldn't help but laugh. 'I can imagine.' It appeared Joss was having one of his 'hot' phases, and she liked it. Of course as he was now running hot it would mean that a cold snap would no doubt come later, but she decided that for now she'd go with it. What could it hurt? He obviously had good reasons for being the way he was. Maybe, just maybe, there was something she could do to help him.

'But we cleaned the place up. Even mopped the floor.'

'I should think so—I'm sure you made your mother proud.'

His grin was wide, his face relaxed as he spoke again. It made him look more handsome than usual. 'I used to have soapsud fights with my brothers all the time. In fact on one occasion the kitchen floor was so wet that when my brother Tony lunged for me, I slipped, fell and cracked my head on the corner of the kitchen cupboards as I came crashing down.' He pointed to the side of his head. 'Four stitches.'

Melissa laughed. 'I'll bet your mother was impressed! How old were you?'

'About Peter's age.'

'So, you're the oldest?'

'I am.'

'Must have been fun?'

He shrugged. 'I guess. I don't know any different, so I can't really comment. We had noisy dinners, talked over each other.'

'Sounds amazing.'

'But there was always some job or other that needed doing. Always.'

'Especially as you were the oldest, eh?'

'Exactly.'

'Well, if it helps any, there were always jobs that needed doing at *my* house, and I was the only one there to do them.'

'I guess it doesn't matter whether you're in a brood or an only child—there will always be jobs to do.'

She smiled. 'And when you become an adult those jobs are endless.' Melissa sighed and looked out into the rain, rather than looking at him. He was so very nice when he was like this, all relaxed and talkative. She liked this Joss much better than the broody one—the only problem being that this one was harder to resist. However, resist she would. She didn't want to risk mis-reading the signals again. 'Do you have any idea just how lucky you are to have such a big family?'

'I do. I didn't for quite a while, but when I decided to move to Didja they were one hundred percent behind me. All of them.'

'You're close?'

'Yes. We usually try and get together once or twice a year.'

'That's nice. Family's important.'

It was darker now, the sun having been pushed out

by the clouds, yet still she could see the outline of his silhouette as he half-leaned, half-sat against the railing, his arms still crossed firmly over his chest. They were both silent for a while, just absorbing and listening to the sounds of the Outback, but for the first time their silence wasn't the uncomfortable kind.

'I guess it must be hard for you. Being alone, I mean.'

'That's why I like to surround myself with interesting people.'

'What were your parents like?' Joss asked, liking the fact that they seemed to be having a normal and casual conversation. She was a colleague. This was business. He was finding out a bit more about his employee.

She instantly smiled, and his gut clenched as she looked his way. She had the most amazing smile. He firmed his jaw, fighting back the attraction.

'They were sweet. Loving. Kind. Caring. The things parents usually are. They were both only children, and though they wanted a large brood of their own it simply never happened. They were in their late forties when they adopted me, and even then they only got me because I was so much older than the babies who were being put up for adoption. They didn't care, though. They just wanted someone of their own to love.'

'And your biological mother? No family on her side?'

'Eva? Not that she knew of. Her parents had both died, as had her older brother.'

'I guess I can understand why getting to know Dex is so important to you. He's a good guy.'

'Who does rain dances.'

Joss chuckled and swept a hand out at the rain surrounding them. 'And they work.' He slowly shook his head. 'Typical Dex.'

'I did read that people in the Outback can go quite insane when a drought breaks. Perhaps Dex goes insane before that?'

He shook his head. 'But the drought isn't broken yet. This is just good drenching rain.'

'Oh. So we can only blame Dex for good drenching rain?'

His eyes lit with laughter. 'Afraid so.'

'Dex sounds like fun.' Her words were quiet, intense.

'He's a good mate,' Joss agreed. 'A little insane at times, but good fun nevertheless.'

'Insane. I like that. The insanity plea always works well in court—not that I'm suggesting we take him to court for being a little insane. I'm just…well…I'm babbling.' Melissa looked at Joss a little closer. 'Are you all right? You're looking a little pale.' Was she about to get the return of the Ice Man?

The humour had drained from his face, because he knew all about court cases—especially on a personal level—and he knew just how 'insane' they could get. 'I'm fine.'

'Sorry, Joss. I was only joking about Dex. I don't really think he's insane.'

'Sure.' He tipped his head back and closed his eyes.

'Want to talk about it?' she ventured, unsure of what sort of response she'd get. Would it be hot or cold?

'What?'

He looked at her, a scowl on his face. Melissa swallowed, and then took a deep breath before plunging ahead. 'Do you want to talk about whatever it is that's bothering you?'

'Nothing's bothering me.'

She held up her hands in surrender. 'Good. Fine.

Sorry. I must have grasped the wrong end of the stick.'
The Ice Man had returned. Well, it had been nice while
it lasted, and she'd certainly discovered a bit more
about the man she hadn't been able to stop thinking
about. 'I guess I'll head in. I can hibernate in the spare
room if Gemma and Ron are still talking to their
children.'

She took a few steps towards the door, the auto-
matic sensor light coming on, blinding her for a
moment. Joss called her name and she turned to look
at him. He was so gorgeous, leaning against the railing,
arms still crossed, the rain behind him framing him to
perfection.

'Don't go on my account. You stay here. I'll go.'

'What? You're going to storm out into the rain again
just to get away from me?'

Joss raked a hand through his hair at her words,
deciding that he probably deserved them. 'You know,
Lis, you're not at all what I expected.'

'What did you expect?'

'I don't know, but not this.'

'Do you often find being around women difficult?'

'Yes. Er…no. That's not what I meant.'

'Then what *did* you mean, Joss?' She wasn't angry
with him, but she was becoming increasingly frustrated. 'I've been trying for days to figure you out, and
all I keep doing is going around in circles.'

'Why do you need to figure me out?'

'So I can cope working alongside you. So I can
work harder at ignoring this pull I feel towards you. So
I can get on with my life, which isn't supposed to be
this complicated.'

'Look—' he ground out, taking a few angry steps
forward but stopping before he got too close to her.

Being close to Melissa wasn't a good thing, especially when she had the appearance of an angel, framed beneath the artificial light. 'I don't do dating. I don't do relationships. It's just the way it is. I was betrayed four years ago by the woman I was going to marry and I vowed then never to trust another. Something happened—something which wasn't my fault. The press had a field day with it. Dex, my closest friends, and of course my family stood by—me but Christina…' He shook his head, bitterness in his tone. 'She not only believed the lie, she helped to fuel it. Right when I needed her most.'

Melissa could feel the pain and betrayal radiating from him and her heart empathised, but she was sure he didn't want it. 'I understand about not being able to trust. I understand about feeling betrayed. For years I wondered why my mother had given me up for adoption. Why didn't she want me? I guess it's the sort of question all adopted children ask themselves. And then, when I finally got my answer, I was actually grateful that she'd given me up. You see, she hadn't trusted herself with Dex or myself, fearing she might actually harm us. It was a brave decision to make, given she was so manically depressed.'

'So you forgave her?'

'Of course. If I hadn't, I might still be walking around bitter and empty, trying to fill that void with numerous relationships, not being able to come out on house-calls for fear of seeing happy families living in harmony together. I think that's why Dex probably hates doing house-calls.'

Joss pondered her words for a moment, his anger dissipating a little. 'That's quite an insight. Quite spot-on, too. I actually hadn't thought of it like that before—

why he is the way he is.' He was quiet for a moment, then asked, 'Do you still have a void?'

'I'm here, aren't I? I've tried to fill it—oh, in so many different ways. I've looked for love and acceptance in many places, but after my engagement ended—after yet another setback and someone else not wanting me—I realised I was looking in all the wrong places.'

'Hence why you're here?'

'Well, yes—but also no. You see, I needed to find that acceptance within myself first. I needed to accept that Renulf didn't want to marry me because I simply wasn't what he needed—not any more. It was different when we first met—it always is different in the beginning—and then, as time went on…' She shrugged as she trailed off. 'The point is, I'm still trying to like *me*. I'm a work in progress.'

'So you don't have time for relationships and things like that either?'

'No.'

'Hmm.'

They were silent again, and whilst she willed him to say more, he didn't, and she started to feel completely stupid standing in the middle of the verandah beneath the light. Without another word, she turned on her heel and left—and this time he didn't try to stop her.

CHAPTER EIGHT

AFTER dinner, things settled down quickly. The younger ones were bathed by Yolanda, and Peter checked their teeth. Ron, their father, read them bedtime stories before tucking them in. The older children stayed up talking quietly for a while, before heading off to their rooms. Melissa and Joss kept their distance from each other the entire time, neither quite sure what to do or say next.

'Do you know where you're sleeping?' Joss asked.

Melissa shook her head. 'Where are you sleeping?'

'Out here on the sofabed.'

'Oh.'

'Here. I'll show you where to go. I think Peter's already put your overnight bag into the guest room.'

'I was wondering where it was.'

Melissa noticed both she and Joss were being extra polite with each other, careful and particular, and trying desperately not to say anything personal.

They bumped into Peter in the hallway.

'How are you holding up with the news about your mum? Everything all right?' Joss asked the boy.

Peter shrugged in the nonchalant way teenagers did when they tried to pretend nothing was really bothering them. 'Mum has to go to hospital. It happens. It means more chores for everyone, which none of us like—especially me, as most of them will become my responsibility.'

Joss chuckled. 'Spoken like a true eldest child.' He clapped the boy on the back. 'You'll do fine. I was just showing Melissa to her room.'

He nodded. 'Bathroom's directly opposite your room—the girls' bathroom. Toby, Lee and I share the lower bathroom. Yolanda, Selena and Bridget share that one.' He pointed up the hallway. 'Mum and Dad get their own *en suite*.' He sounded as though that wasn't fair at all.

'Hey. When I was at home, all eight of us had to share one bathroom. At least you have three in this house.'

Peter rolled his eyes. 'I don't even want to go there. Eight people? One bathroom?' He shuddered. 'Total torture. Anyway—night.' He shuffled off down the hallway, and within the next instant they were left alone…again. Awkwardness filled the space between them as they both tried not to be so aware of each other.

Melissa jerked a thumb at the door behind her. 'This is where I'm sleeping?'

'Yes. Yes. That's the spare room.' Joss shoved his hands into his pockets, hoping at least this way he'd keep from hauling her into his arms and kissing her goodnight—which was exactly what he wanted to do.

'And you'll be on the sofabed?' She edged back and reached for the door handle.

'Yes. I've slept on it before. It's quite comfortable.'

'Good. Good.'

Silence.

Melissa racked her brain for something to say, but

the more she searched the less she found. It was his nearness combined with his spicy scent which was turning her mind to mush. They were close, but not too close. Far, but not too far.

Indecision. Confusion. Stress. They were all making an appearance. Heat. Need. Desire. Combine everything together and it was no wonder the tension between them could have been sliced with a scalpel.

'Well...' Joss eased back, taking a step down the hallway—because it would be all too easy to simply step forward and press his lips to hers. 'I guess I'll go check on Gemma before I turn in.'

'Oh, that's OK. I can do it,' Melissa offered quickly, eager for him to be down at the other end of the house before she tried to make sense of the emotions she was experiencing. 'I'm closer—geographically speaking.' She pointed to Gemma and Ron's room, just up from her own. 'You go get your bed set up.'

Joss shrugged. It was an out and he'd take it. 'OK, then.' Another step away. 'I guess I'll see you in the morning, then.'

'I guess you will.' Her eyes held his. Neither of them looked away. Both of them seemed to be speaking volumes, but nothing was actually said. It wouldn't take much to step forward and press her lips to his once more, and when his gaze momentarily dipped to look at her own mouth she almost faltered. Leaning back, she flattened herself against the door, wanting him to go before she really lost control.

'All right. Sleep well.'

'You too.'

Sighing, she watched him turn and walk down the hallway, back towards the living room. He had such a nice back, such a nice walk…such a nice butt. After another soulful sigh, she went into the spare room.

Her medical kit was on the bed beside her overnight bag, but she ignored it for a moment. She sat down, her whole body shaking slightly. The man was going to drive her to distraction if she wasn't careful, so careful she must be. Focusing on work would most definitely help, and after she'd taken a few deep breaths, relaxing her tense muscles, Melissa gathered the items she would need for Gemma's check-up and made her way back out to the hallway.

She knocked on the master bedroom door and heard Gemma call, 'Come in.'

Melissa went in and was pleased to find Gemma in bed, lying on her side, surrounded by pillows.

'It's already taking me ages to find a comfortable position and I'm only in the middle of the pregnancy!' Gemma complained, but not in a bad way.

Melissa smiled and knelt down beside her patient. 'I just need to check you over once more, and then I'll leave you in peace to get some sleep.' Melissa wound the blood pressure cuff around Gemma's arm and was pleased with the result. 'It's lower than before, so the rest is definitely doing the two of you good.'

Ron came into the bedroom from the *en suite* bathroom. 'How's my girl doing?'

'Better than before.' She listened to both Gemma's heart and then the baby's. Ron and Gemma shared a special moment as they too listened to the baby's heart-beat.

'It sounds so healthy.'

'It's good, but it's still a little fast.' Melissa knelt on the floor and started packing up her equipment as she spoke. 'After we've run some tests it may turn out that what you need to do is rest for the remainder of your pregnancy. Now, I know that will be difficult—but it's a must. It would be ideal for you to remain here, rather than being hospitalised—which is what we want to avoid. Separating you from your family for any extended period of time won't be good for you, but if that's what has to happen in the end, then—'

'That's what has to happen,' Gemma finished, and nodded. 'It's the first pregnancy I haven't been able to carry on through. I've even had four of them delivered right here at home, and everything has always been fine. I just don't understand what's happening.'

'And that's why we need you to go to Didja tomorrow. The sooner we find out what's really going on, the better.'

Gemma nodded. 'I know. It's all just come as a bit of a shock.'

Melissa stood, bag in hand. 'I'll leave you both to get some sleep, but if anything goes wrong tonight, if you have a bleed or any pain, you send Ron to get either myself or Joss or both. Understand? We *want* you to wake us up. Don't be considerate and let us sleep. OK?'

'Right. Be inconsiderate to the house-guests. Got it.' Gemma smiled. Melissa turned and headed for the door before Gemma called her name. 'Oh, and thanks.'

Melissa smiled warmly. 'My pleasure. Goodnight and sleep soundly.'

Joss heard her call goodnight to Gemma and Ron and then head back into her room. He lay down on the sofabed, hands behind his head, and stared up at the ceiling fan whirring softly around. The rain hadn't necessarily cooled everything down. In fact, it had made this room more humid than before. Or perhaps that was just him—sweating under the realisation that it had been so incredibly difficult not to kiss Melissa good-night.

Had she been waiting for him to do it? Had she wanted him to do it? Was she upset that he hadn't? He closed his eyes for a moment. He had no idea where he stood, and he wasn't a man who liked to be unsure of his footing.

A female doctor. That was all he'd wanted for the clinic. It had been top of his priority list. A female doctor for the female population of Didja and its surrounding communities. When he'd learned that Dex's sister had wanted to get to know her brother and that she was a qualified OB/GYN he hadn't been about to look a gift horse in the mouth. What he simply hadn't counted on was the way he'd feel so protective towards her.

Of course he'd told himself it was because he wanted to make sure she concentrated on her job here, that she didn't get side-tracked with thoughts of romance and marriage. She was here for twelve months to do a job and to get to know her brother. That was all. So why had he been so incredibly possessive of her—especially when they'd gone to the mining headquarters and Scott the Sleaze had tried to put his moves on her? It was all quite puzzling, as Joss had never been the possessive type in the past.

Still, here he was, not only feeling possessive towards his colleague but wanting to kiss her again and again. It wasn't right. It wasn't professional. Slowly he acknowledged the truth of the matter—he didn't want anyone else to have her because he wanted her all for himself.

It was wrong. So wrong. And yet when they were close, when he held her, it was so incredibly right.

When he'd initially come to Didja he'd been hurting,

trying to get his life back on track. The community had rallied around their new doctor and had certainly made him feel welcome, but there was one thing he'd realised: when it came to having personal relationships in small towns everyone knew everything and everyone. If he'd dated at all, he would have been under close scrutiny—and he'd already had his fair share of that back in Perth.

To be accused of medical negligence at a big city hospital, to have it plastered all over the media and then to be privately told that he was being offered as a sacrificial lamb by the head of the hospital had been tough. He'd lost his faith in the system—not only the hospital hierarchy but also the political leaders. At least here in Didja *he* was the boss. He ran the clinic the way a clinic should be run, with truth, honesty and integrity, and he wouldn't be made the scapegoat for any political games. Not ever again.

When the whole state, from your patients to the hospital board to the members of parliament, all thought you were some sort of 'Doctor Death'; when your fiancée—the woman who was supposed to love you—went to the press telling lies about your personal relationship and painting you to be some sort of monster; when you went from being an upstanding member of society to being threatened with jail time, the last thing you wanted was to move to a new place for a fresh start and be once more under close scrutiny. That was how Joss had felt.

That was why he'd tried to keep to himself in the beginning—until the good people of Didja had decided to bring the pub to his house and *really* welcome him to town. Still, as far as romantic relationships went it would be impossible for the whole town *not* to become involved. But he'd been hurt on so many levels before, and for four years he'd managed to keep that part of his heart locked securely away.

Until Melissa.

He wasn't the type of man who could just hand over his heart, give over his trust, open up all aspects of his being and love a woman unconditionally. Was he?

He thought about Christina, and the emotional trauma she'd put him through when he'd needed it the least. He couldn't put his heart out there again and risk it getting cut into tiny little pieces before being pulverised, then liquefied, and then tipped into the sewer.

He knew Melissa wasn't Christina, and that so far, in the short time he'd known her, she'd displayed qualities such as loyalty, generosity and integrity, but he'd been duped before and he wasn't about to be duped again.

People could change. Could *he* change? Could he open his heart to the beautiful blonde woman who was just up the corridor from him? The woman who felt so right in his arms, who kissed like an absolute dream, who listened and really seemed to be interested in him? Was he strong enough to take the chance?

Joss closed his eyes, pain and indecision piercing his chest. What if she hurt him? What if she didn't? What if what they felt for each other was not only more than an initial attraction but the real deal? What if he was being given a second chance at happiness, at friendship, at love? He'd always wanted to get married, to have children of his own, but after Christina's betrayal he'd figured that would never happen—that he'd never love another woman as much, nor would he ever trust another again.

Was Melissa his second chance? Was she worth the risk?

* * *

Melissa quickly got ready for bed, padding across to the bathroom to do her teeth before quietly settling down beneath the ceiling fan, a cotton sheet draped over her. The rain was still pattering, lightly now, outside the open window. Here she was, in the middle of the Outback, in the middle of nowhere, in a complete stranger's house and she'd never felt safer.

She knew it wasn't just because the Etheringtons had been so caring and welcoming. She knew it wasn't because the Outback was a place of untamed beauty with not one scrap of artifice. No, she felt completely safe due to the man who now slept on the fold-out sofabed in the front living room of this old homestead.

Her life had certainly changed quite a bit since arriving in Didja. The question was, was it all for the better? Was getting involved with Joss enhancing her life? All she knew was that it was definitely confusing it.

All she wanted was a man who would hold her, kiss her, want to be near her. She wanted her life to be like the Etheringtons'—to have a home, a husband, children of her own. Uncles and aunts to come and visit, bringing their own children along so the house dissolved into a mass of noise, laughter and love.

Over the years she'd invested so much of herself in relationships with others, whether it was as a loving daughter or in a more romantic way, such as the relationship she'd shared with Renulf. And yet time after time things had gone wrong. Something had always happened to change those relationships and she'd be left all alone. Again.

If it wasn't one thing it was another, and this time around she wondered whether she was getting ready to tread on that pond of thin ice again. Letting herself stay too long in a fairytale world where everything turned out right would only end up with her getting hurt— possibly hurting both of them—and that was the last thing either of them needed.

Melissa awoke the next morning to the faint buzzing of an aeroplane. She opened her eyes, unsure for a moment where she was. Then she heard high-pitched giggling and the patter of little feet down the hallway, followed by big thumping footsteps as a deeper voice growled.

She sat up in bed, remembering where she was and why she was there. The plane was sounding closer— the RFDS plane—and she glared at the clock.

'Eight-thirty!' Flicking back the cool cotton sheet, she quickly pulled a change of clothes from her bag and dressed, mortified that she'd slept so late. She had no doubt it was because she'd tossed and turned for half the night, her mind filled with indecision about what she needed to do.

She tidied the room and gathered her bags together before opening the door, then quickly stepped back as she narrowly missed being run down by a three-year-old and a five-year-old, running past her door squealing.

What surprised her even more was Joss, who was growling as he chased after them. He stopped when he saw her, straightening from his hunched-over position, and smiled in that adorable way which simply melted her heart.

'Morning.'

'Hi. I see you're…uh…busy.'

'Yep. The RFDS plane is just arriving, and Ron's driven out to greet them. Looks as though you'll get to meet the crew today.'

'Good. Right.' Work. Talking about work was a neutral way to start the day. 'I'll go check on Gemma.'

'She's resting out on the verandah,' he supplied, trying not to visually caress the woman before him. Melissa looked delectable first thing in the morning, her hair loose and gorgeous as it floated around her shoulders. It was an image he knew would stay with him for ever.

'Good. It seems she made it through the night with no complications. That's another good sign.'

'Actually, she did have a pain.'

'What?'

'About an hour ago. But as you were sleeping and I was already awake Ron came and got me to check on her. Everything was fine,' he rushed on, seeing the concern on Melissa's face. 'The baby's heart-rate; Gemma's blood pressure. No swelling. No bleeding. Everything's fine,' he reiterated.

'Right. Good. Thanks.' She paused for a moment and pushed a hand through her hair, wishing she'd been able to find her hairband so she could put it back. 'You could have woken me, you know.'

Joss had been so mesmerised by her actions, by the gorgeous blonde strands glinting in the sunlight, that he'd momentarily tuned out from what she'd been saying. 'Oh. Yeah.' He waved her words away. 'It's OK. It was no big deal. To let you sleep, I mean. It's going to be a long day.'

'It is?' Melissa put her overnight bag down and pushed her hands into the pockets of the three-quarter-length jeans she'd packed, her cotton shirt falling over the waistband. 'Listen, I've been thinking.'

'Always a good start to the day,' he replied, and she couldn't help but smile. Joss stared. Why had she done that? Why had he provoked such a smile? She was beautiful. Completely and utterly breathtakingly beautiful first thing in the morning. Her lips were redder, her eyes were richer, and her hair was so glorious he was hard pressed not to reach out and sift his fingers through the silken strands.

'Uh…I think it might be better if I go back on the plane with Gemma. That way she has immediate and constant care. I'm not suggesting,' she quickly rushed on, 'that the RFDS aren't capable of providing such care. It's just that—'

'It's a good idea.' Joss nodded. 'I was thinking along the same lines.' Mostly because of Gemma's health, but also because he wasn't sure he could handle a three-hour drive back to town with Melissa sitting so close beside him and be able to keep his hands to himself.

'You were?' Did he want to get rid of her? Was it for Gemma's sake he wanted her out of his ute for the drive back to Didja, or was it because of the repressed sexual tension which was palpable between them? 'I mean. Good. That's good. Good we're both on the same page.'

'Patient's health comes first,' he agreed. 'Plus, it's also a good way for you to get to know Phemie. She's one of the main RFDS doctors employed in this district.'

'Phemie?'

'Short for Euphemia.'

Melissa smiled again, but this time it was more relaxed. 'Great name.'

'Great woman.' He stood there, staring at her, watching her every move, wanting to plant his mouth over hers more with each passing second. Did she have any idea how beau—? No. He cut the thought off. He couldn't think like that. He needed to find a way to put some distance between them, and also find a way to stop wanting a repeat of yesterday afternoon, when she'd let him kiss her.

Joss felt a tugging at his shorts and looked down at Bridget. 'Hello.'

'Come on, Dr Jossy,' said the five-year-old. 'You're the growly ogre chasing the princess and the prince through the forest.'

'Yeah. Come on,' three-year-old Lee chimed in.

'Best get to it, then.' Melissa picked up her bag again.

Joss's answer to his little friends was to assume his hunched-over 'growly ogre' position, and the two children ran away squealing with delight. Joss instantly straightened again. 'That should hold them for a moment.'

'I'd best go check on Gemma. Make sure she's ready for this transfer.' Melissa took a step away, but was stopped when Joss placed a hand on her arm.

'Wait a second.' He dropped his hand, as though the touch had burnt him. The itch to touch her hair was becoming overwhelming. 'Lis?'

'Yeah?' Her heart-rate had started to increase at the way he was looking at her.

'I'm…um…' He stopped and breathed out, staring at her loose blonde hair. He couldn't resist her any longer and reached out to touch the silken locks. 'Glorious,' he whispered. 'The colour, the feel of it. So soft and silky.'

Melissa parted her lips at his touch, unable to believe how incredibly intimate it was to feel his fingers in her hair. 'Joss?' His name was a breathless whisper.

'Hmm?' He swallowed, and then, as though realising what he was doing, he instantly dropped his hand and moved back. 'Oh, gosh, Lis. I'm sorry.' He closed his eyes for a second before looking at her once more.

'I need to tell you that I'm not sorry about yesterday, but that doesn't mean it can happen again…and again,' he rushed on. 'Even though we might want it to.'

She dragged a breath in and slowly let it out, desperate to control her mounting heart-rate. 'Agreed. Yes. You're right. We're colleagues.'

'Yes, we are.'

'We both have plans. Things to achieve.'

'Yes,' he agreed again.

'I didn't come to town looking for…' She put her bag down again and indicated the space between them. 'For this.' Or to feel how amazing it was to have him touch her hair, or her shoulder, or to hold her hand, or to gather her firmly to his body. She hadn't come here looking for any of that.

'You came to get to know your brother.'

'Exactly. That's what I need to focus on. That and getting to know the people of this community.'

'Yes.' Part of him wanted to point out that *he* was part of the community, and that *he* wouldn't be averse to getting to know her a lot better. Thankfully, he was able to refrain. He had to keep his distance for both their sakes.

'Dex. I need to focus on getting to know Dex. He's important to me.'

'And so he should be. I do understand where you're coming from, Lis.'

'Good.' She breathed a sigh of relief. 'That's good.'

'Yes, it is. It's very good,' he agreed, knowing they both not only sounded like fools but were probably lying to themselves. But taking a step back, a very big step away from the turbulent emotions of yesterday, from the way she'd felt so perfect in his arms, was most definitely the right thing to do.

'I'm glad we had this chat.'

'So am I.'

They were both running, both hiding beneath the nearest table, locking their hearts up tight, unable to take the risk. At least not just yet.

'Good. Well…you drive safe now. You hear?'

'I will.'

'I'd best go find Gemma.'

'Yes.'

And with that she turned and walked away from him.

CHAPTER NINE

Two days after she was admitted to the Didja hospital Gemma was airlifted back home by the RFDS. Melissa had performed the tests, done the scans and come to the conclusion that it was an ante-partum haemorrhage—as she'd first suspected.

'One of the blood vessels which takes food to the baby isn't working too well. What we can do, however, is give you daily injections and monitor you. That way the baby will receive what it needs to grow, and also you'll be able to stay home. Complete bed-rest, though.' Melissa had been stern.

Thankfully, Rajene, the woman who had helped deliver Gemma's last four children, had come to the hospital to visit Gemma, and Melissa had discovered that Rajene, who was almost seventy-five years old, had trained as a midwife in an island country called Tarparnii. Whilst she held no official qualifications in Australia, she was more than capable—and close enough in distance—of giving Gemma the daily care required. Joss had confirmed that he trusted Rajene, and that she was indeed a very good midwife, so Melissa's initial fears were calmed.

'I will make sure she does not do too much. I will

help her. You shall see. This babe will be as strong as the others,' Rajene promised.

'I have no doubt.'

During the following week Rajene called Melissa on a daily basis to report on Gemma's condition.

'She is behaving well and very much resting. We are all so proud. Peter and Yolanda are doing marvellous with the helping. Gemma stays in her bed or on the sofabed. Blood pressure has improved to normal levels, the babe's signs are good, and there has been no more bleeding.'

It was much the same as Rajene had reported the day before, but this was the type of good news Melissa didn't mind hearing again and again. 'Good to hear. Thank you, Rajene.'

As she put the phone down, she reflected on her first full week in Didja. It had been mostly good, with the people of the community still continuing to welcome her. She'd visited the pub a few nights, but on others had preferred simply to unwind in her apartment.

On those nights she would lie on her bed beneath the ceiling fan, trying to get cool and pretending to read a book, whilst all the time she'd listen for noises coming from Joss's apartment next door. She'd learned that his apartment was a mirror image of her own, which meant that their bedroom walls were a shared wall. It was strange to think that when she put her hand up to the wall he was on the other side. Sleeping. In his bed. Probably wearing next to nothing.

She closed her eyes, trying to school her thoughts. She was in the middle of a clinic and she was once more thinking about her boss. This wasn't professional behaviour at all, and she knew she needed to conquer the emotions Joss continually evoked within her.

Melissa had been as jittery as a cat on a hot tin roof

until Joss had arrived safely back in Didja after their
house-calls. He'd come instantly to the hospital to
check on Gemma, where Melissa had taken great
pleasure in announcing the results of their patient's
tests. Afterwards he'd disappeared into his apartment,
and she hadn't seen him until the next day.

Neither had mentioned the kiss, even though the attraction they were working hard at ignoring was still
definitely palpable between them. But they both had
things to do and concentrate on, and that was exactly
what they were doing.

Even yesterday, when Joss had given Melissa her
medical check-up, he'd been the consummate professional. Bub had been present as he'd checked her blood
pressure, listened to her chest, checked her eyes and
taken a blood sample.

'It's all just for insurance purposes,' he'd explained,
before beginning.

'I completely understand. Standard procedure
when starting a new job in a medical environment,'
she'd replied, very aware that Bub was watching
them very closely, no doubt picking up on the undercurrents which both doctors were working overtime
at ignoring.

On the Friday two weeks after she'd been out on the
house-calls with Joss—two weeks since he'd held her
in his arms and kissed her so passionately—Melissa
finished off her clinic and headed to her apartment.

She didn't feel like going to the pub this evening. She
knew Dex was going, but during her time here he'd been
merely polite and professional, treating her like just
another colleague and nothing more. She knew she
shouldn't feel hurt, but she did, and she couldn't face

going to the pub and having her brother ignore her yet again.

But that's not the real reason, she told herself as she quickly did her dinner dishes and poured herself a relaxing glass of wine. She closed her eyes and gripped the kitchen counter with both hands as she admitted the real reason she didn't feel like company tonight—because Joss had been out all day on house-calls and he still wasn't back yet.

Of course Dex had initially been meant to go, and when she'd learned that Joss was doing them again she wondered whether he'd volunteered this time around. Perhaps it was simply easier for him to leave the clinic for a day and therefore not have to worry about running into her.

When she'd paid a quick visit to the hospital before leaving for the day, Bub had tut-tutted about 'poor Joss'.

'He's not what he used to be. There's something wrong with him. I can feel it.'

'Do you think he's sick?' Melissa asked.

'Not sick, but—oh, I don't know. Out of sorts, I guess is the best way to describe him. He snapped at Areva last Monday, and he's only been going to the pub on occasional nights. Incidentally,' she said, eyeing Melissa closely, 'he's been going on the nights that you *don't*. What is this? Tag team socialising? Only one of you can go at a time?'

'I think you'll find that Dex is usually there, so if Carto and Bluey decide to have another scrap there's at least one doctor on hand.'

'That's not what I'm talking about and you know it.' Bub sighed and lowered her tone. 'There's something going on between you and Joss.'

'No, there isn't.'

'OK. Let me rephrase that. There *should* be something going on between you and Joss. Even a blind man can see that you're both—'

'Don't say it.' Melissa held up her hand. 'He's a colleague. Nothing more. Dex is my brother. Nothing more.' She tried not to choke on the words as she said them. 'I'm learning to deal with those two facts, and right now I don't particularly want to talk about it, if you don't mind.'

Bub could see the strain on Melissa's face and smiled in acquiescence. 'Of course, darl. Go. Rest. Things will settle down eventually. You'll see.'

'I hope so, Bub.' And so she'd left, and decided that for tonight relaxing in her apartment was a definite must. There was a nice cool breeze, and Melissa decided to sit outside to try and unwind. At the rear of their apartments was a communal courtyard, and she carried her wine glass out through the back door towards the outdoor setting. It was quiet and peaceful, and she placed her glass on the table and sat, sighing heavily as she looked up at the stars.

'They're much brighter in the Outback, don't you think?' Joss spoke from just behind her, and Melissa jumped at the sound of his voice. 'Sorry. Didn't mean to scare you.' He walked over and sat in the chair opposite her.

'You're back!'

'No. Actually, this is a holographic image I had made up weeks ago, designed to keep people away from my relaxing courtyard.'

'*Your* relaxing courtyard?'

'Dex rarely comes out here.'

'So you've had it all to yourself for quite some time, then?'

'I have, but...' he pondered for a moment '... I guess I can share.'

'Does that mean the holographic projection is about to end?'

Joss grinned at her, loving that they were on the same wavelength. She understood him. It was just one more thing that helped fuel the attraction he felt for her. They might not have spoken much in the past two weeks, they might have been playing a slight avoidance game with each other, but it hadn't helped to change the way he thought about her—which was constantly.

He felt as though he was going around in circles and living in a perpetual state of confusion. Melissa was his colleague. She'd be here for quite some time. Tonight, instead of keeping his distance from her, he'd decided to seek her out and to hopefully try and come to a better arrangement than the avoidance one they were currently operating under. He had no idea what that arrangement might be, but it had to be better than where they both were at present.

'Hopefully not,' he replied.

'So...how were house-calls?'

'Good. Fine. Quite boring compared to the week we went out, actually. No emergencies. No pregnant women. No rampaging bulls.'

'Do you mean to tell me that isn't the usual way things run?'

He chuckled, and she allowed the sound to wash over her. He was definitely in a good mood and she wasn't about to ignore that fact.

'Today was lots of immunisations. Check-ups. That sort of thing.'

'The usual?'

'Basically, yes. How about you? Anything exciting happen in today's clinic?'

Melissa thought for a second, mainly because she couldn't get over how jittery she felt having him there, talking to her. She'd missed him, she realised. Missed just sitting and talking as they had out on Gemma's verandah. But, whilst she was delighted he'd sought her out, she was still a little wary at why he had. Did he have something drastic he needed to impart? Was he simply trying to be nice? She'd just have to go along for the ride and see where it ended up.

'Andy and James came in for their check-ups.'

'Good to hear. Rich is a stickler for follow-up appointments. A lot of bosses don't let their jackaroos have time off for follow-ups.'

'Well, they were both here and are generally doing fine. James had popped a few stitches. Thankfully Mindy had come to the rescue with her expert bandaging, so there was no infection. I've sorted him out now.'

'How did he pop his sutures?'

'He was horse riding.'

Joss shook his head. 'He would have been in trouble for that.'

'Yes. He said that Rich tore strips off him.'

'He's a good boss. Firm. Has his head screwed on, does Rich.'

'So you've said.'

'Sorry. Didn't mean to sound like a broken record.'

'You don't.'

'And how have things been going with Dex?'

Melissa shrugged. 'He's polite and all, but that's about it.'

'He's very slow. Takes a lot of time to process things.'

'You've said that before as well. I'm starting to wonder whether it wasn't a mistake, coming here.'

Joss felt as though she'd slapped him. He'd sought her out tonight in order to try and figure out a different way to deal with the attraction they felt. He'd hoped she was on the same page as him, wanting to move forward rather than to go around and around in circles, and now she was talking about leaving? He was stunned. 'You want to leave?'

'I don't know.' She shook her head and looked up at the stars. 'I don't know what I want any more. I'm confused.'

'Well, you can't leave,' he bristled, still a little shocked to have heard her speak that way. Just as well he hadn't come right out and confessed how she made him feel, because that would have been sacrificing himself yet again. 'Aren't you happy here?'

Melissa laughed without humour. 'Joss, since I arrived my sedate, calm little life has been turned upside down and inside out.'

'Dex will come around.'

'I'm sure he will—but the question remains, do I need to be *here* when he does? I mean, I could leave, go work in Perth, write e-mails to him. When he's finished processing, when he's finished figuring things out, he could call me and then we could catch up. We wouldn't be living in each other's pockets.'

'But you have a contract,' he felt compelled to point out. He needed to stop all this talk of her leaving. She wasn't leaving. She *couldn't* leave. He needed her. Both for the clinic and for himself. However, there was no way he could tell her that. Not now.

'I know, Joss. Relax. I'm just thinking out loud.'

'So you're not happy here? Is that what you're saying?'

'Remember when I told you I was trying to like myself, to figure out who I really am? Well, I'm still trying to do that—but between you and Dex the confusion side of things reigns quite high.'

He sat up a little straighter in his seat. 'You're confused about me?'

Melissa laughed again and shook her head. 'What rock have you been living under?'

'Oh.' A dawning realisation crossed his face. '*That* type of confusion. Yeah, well, I'm right there alongside you when it comes to *that* type of confusion. We've both come from prior relationships that didn't work out, and in my case things not only didn't work out, I was completely betrayed. It's difficult to recover from something like that.' He took a deep breath. Maybe this was a good time to open up to her a little. He knew he needed to do it, and now was the perfect moment. 'When we were with the Etheringtons I found it really easy to talk to you.'

'Really?'

'Yes. Some of the things you said—such as liking yourself and being able to forgive your birth mother— really hit home. So I guess it might be time for me to open up a little, to tell you more about myself. But this isn't an easy thing for me to do.'

'Are you sure you *want* to do it?'

If there was ever going to be anything real between them then Joss needed to tell Melissa about his past. About *all* of it. It would also be a test to see how exactly she would react to what he was about to say.

'I am.'

'OK. I'm all yours…er…I mean I'm ready to listen, Joss.'

'Right.' He took a few deep breaths before plunging

in. 'My fiancée, Christina, literally changed overnight, and I found myself facing a total stranger. I had no idea she was so deceptive, so dishonest, but apparently when things didn't turn out the way she planned she decided jumping ship was a far easier option than trying to understand.'

'Joss.' She could feel how painful this was for him. 'What on earth happened to make her not understand?'

'I was accused of medical negligence.'

Melissa gasped in horror. 'What?'

'It went to trial.'

'Oh, Joss.' She clutched her hands together to try and quell her anxiety.

'The patient who died was a man pretty high up in political circles so it was big news. The hospital offered me up as their sacrificial lamb.'

He had himself under control now and the matter-of-fact way he spoke made her wonder just how often he'd gone over this story in his head to make it sound so emotionless. Surely he had to be hurting, had to have some feeling towards it?

'What a disgusting thing to do—although if it helps, I too have worked in hospitals that have corrupt administrators. They do exist.'

Joss nodded. 'I lost all faith. I wanted to quit medicine completely.'

'What stopped you?'

'Dex. My family. They stood by me. Supported me.'

'And Christina?'

He shook his head sadly. 'She joined the slander campaign, went to the media and painted me as some sort of monster. I was called "Doctor Death". Catchy, eh?'

Melissa's heart was bleeding for him and she wanted

him to stop. To stop talking. To stop remembering. To stop torturing himself.

She cared. Where Christina hadn't, Melissa did. She'd passed his silly test with flying colours, and his heart had started to open up once more. It was just the two of them, the moon and the stars, and he could see the glistening stream made from a lone tear which had slid silently down her cheek.

'Tears?'

'I can't believe what they did to you.' Emotion choked her words.

Joss leaned over and tenderly brushed the tear away with his thumb.

'You're a remarkable woman, Lis,' he whispered. 'Thank you.'

'For?'

'Listening. Believing. Caring. You are so incredibly beautiful. Do you know that? Do you have any idea just how much you affect me?' His words were soft as he came around the table to sit next to her. 'I can't help but watch you when you walk by. I find it difficult to concentrate when we're in business meetings simply because the scent of your perfume is driving me wild. I've hardly slept because I'm too busy lying awake, thinking of you on the other side of that wall. Imagining what you look like in your bed, lying beneath the whirring of the ceiling fan.'

She gasped at his words, unable to believe how closely his thoughts of her mirrored the ones she'd been having of him. 'Joss.' His name was a breathless whisper on her lips.

He swallowed. 'I like it when you wear your hair down, or just clipped back at the side as it is now. I like the way you relate to the patients. I like the way you listen so intently when someone is talking to you, focusing on them, making sure you don't miss a single syllable of what they're saying…just as you're doing now.'

Her breathing was shallow, her heart was pounding wildly beneath her chest and her body was alive with heat and wonder simply because of what he was saying. His words were like an aphrodisiac, and it was definitely working on her.

'I've missed you—and I'm not just talking about these past two weeks.' He shook his head as though to clear his thoughts. 'You've burst into my life. Until you came, I had no idea there *was* anything missing. You won't believe how many times I've wanted to just hold you, to drop a kiss to your lips, to see happiness light your eyes.'

Melissa could hardly breathe, but breathe she did as she met his gaze and urged him a little closer. 'Kiss me, Joss.'

The words were a whispered command and one he seemed more than ready to follow as he brought his mouth to meet hers for the first time in weeks.

She sighed as the touch, the taste and the hope she'd been dreaming about flowed freely through her body. It was a strange feeling to have a sense of belonging, but that was exactly how she felt every time Joss kissed her.

She loved the way his mouth seemed to fit perfectly to her own and her heart soared. He was remarkable as a man. He'd been through so much and yet he'd continued on with his life. He'd opened himself up to her, had shared a deep and intimate part of his past and trusted her with it. That spoke volumes.

'I feel so…alive,' she whispered against his mouth, her breathing erratic.

At her words, the heat between them intensified. Where he'd been a little concerned that he might scare her off, she matched him—moment for moment, sensation for sensation. The sweet sunshine of her scent became absorbed by his senses, fusing itself into his soul. Her soft moan of delighted pleasure became lodged in his memory, and he had a sense of deep satisfaction knowing that *he* was the person who had brought forth that sound from within her. He affected her just as much as she affected him. The taste of her mouth beneath his, the feel of her lips opening to his, accepting his need, became something he knew he'd crave for the rest of eternity.

'What do we do?' he choked out as he put his hands on her shoulders and drew them both apart. They stared at each other as rational thought slowly began to return.

'What do we do about… this?' she clarified, and he nodded.

'Yes. I mean, do we do anything about it at all? Do we go back to ignoring it?' Now that he'd told her about Christina, now that she'd passed his test and he'd seen just how sympathetic and understanding she really was, Joss wanted to know more about her. He wanted to spend more time with her. It was as though she'd managed to unlock a part of him he'd kept locked up for too long, and it made him wonder whether he really did have the strength to take that step and move forward with his life…take a step towards Melissa.

'Where will ignoring it get us?'

He thought for a moment. 'Back here, I guess. Fighting the attraction and then giving in to it.'

'Doesn't sound healthy.'

He eased back and raked a hand through his hair. 'This is so confusing.'

'Tell me about it.' Both of them thought for a moment. 'What about…going out on a date?' she suggested, not at all sure how he would respond.

'Dating?'

'Dinner, perhaps?' When he didn't say anything, she continued, 'Or not. I understand if you're reluctant.'

'It's not that. I'm more concerned about the fishbowl syndrome.'

'The community?' She raised her eyebrows. 'I guess I hadn't thought about it from that angle.'

'We're such a small, close-knit community. Everyone's bound to talk. We'll be the main discussion topic at every shop counter, at the bar in the pub, at the traffic lights in the street.'

'We can try keeping it quiet if you prefer, though I'm not sure how easy that will be. Joss, you've been the centre of attention in the past. Are you sure this is what you want?'

He shook his head. 'What I want is honesty, Lis. If we're going to go out to dinner, then it needs to be done the right way. People will talk, but I guess…we'll get used to it.'

'So, dinner?'

'Yes.'

'When?'

He thought for a moment. 'How about tomorrow night? Saturday night is still date night, even out here in the middle of nowhere.'

She gulped. 'That soon? Boy, when you decide to move, you move!'

Joss grinned. 'I guess I do.'

'And do you have any thoughts on where we'll be having this date?' She hoped he didn't just take her to the pub, because that wouldn't feel like a date at all.

'Relax. I know just the place. Leave it to me.'

Later that night—after Joss had joined her in a glass of wine, after he'd walked her to her door and raised her hand to his lips in a gallant goodnight kiss—Melissa stared up at the ceiling fan whirring above her bed, trying not to think of him on the other side of the wall.

Joss. The man she was sure she was falling in love with. The more he opened up to her, the more she liked him. Still she was racked with indecision, trying to figure out if she was really doing the right thing. Yes, she was almost positive she loved this man. Yes, she wanted to date him, to get to know him, to make this relationship work. But she'd had little success with relationships in the past because she'd been trying to use them to fill the empty void in her heart.

'But Joss is different,' she whispered. He made her feel one hundred percent alive whenever he listened to her, whenever he held her, whenever he kissed her. She was also concerned about Dex and his reaction to this turn of events.

Would this wreck her chances with Dex? Would this put even more distance between them? They were already estranged, and she didn't want that chasm to become any wider that it already was. Dex meant everything to her and the last thing she wanted to do was to hurt him.

Was going out with Joss—in front of the whole town—the right thing to do? She honestly had no idea.

CHAPTER TEN

As THEY walked side by side to the only really decent restaurant in town, Melissa was acutely aware of people looking at them. Everyone they passed called a greeting—'Hi, Docs.' Or, 'Nice night.' Or the typically Aussie greeting of 'How's it going?'

'I feel like everyone is looking at us,' she murmured as they continued along the footpath.

'That's because they are.' He'd known this would happen. He'd known going out on a date with Melissa would mean extra attention from the community. However, he was the one who'd insisted they keep whatever was happening between them as open and as honest as possible, so he'd just have to put up with the choking feeling which was telling him to run and hide.

'But we've walked down here together a few times and no one's paid us the slightest bit of attention,' she protested. 'We're not dressed any differently.' She motioned to their casual attire.

Joss looked at her and noted that she did look especially beautiful tonight. She was wearing a pair of three-quarter-length denims, a pale pink top and a simple gold chain. Her hair was loose, the way he liked it, and he shoved his hands into the pockets of his jeans to stop himself from sifting his fingers through her glorious locks.

When someone else called a friendly greeting to both of them, she felt as though a sign was pinned to her back. 'We're not even touching,' she pointed out.

'Yet I still feel as though everyone knows we're out on a date,' Joss confirmed as they walked past the pub.

'Hey, Joss!'

They both turned to see Carto and Bluey, waving at them with silly grins on their faces. 'How'd you get to be the lucky one taking the sheila doc out?' Bluey called.

Melissa closed her eyes for a split second, unable to believe this was happening. She didn't like being the centre of attention, but it appeared if she was going to date the gorgeous bachelor doctor, then she'd best get used to it. She smiled at the two larrikins.

'Probably because I shower regularly and wear deodorant,' Joss answered back, and with that he reached out and took Melissa's hand in his and continued up the street towards Stiggies. 'We may as well flaunt it,' he told her. 'Everyone already appears to know we're on a date.'

'I guess.' Melissa tried to cope with the mass of tingles which flooded her body at his touch. Joss was holding her hand—willingly holding her hand—in public! This man was such an enigma, and she was starting to wonder whether she shouldn't bother trying to figure him out but just go with whatever happened. He'd gone from swinging between hot and cold to being hot, hot, *hot*. Not that she was complaining, but after he'd told her about his past it had been as though he was a different person.

Perhaps telling her had removed a huge weight from

him and given him the impetus he needed to move forward into the future? Or perhaps her reaction to the news had been some sort of test…one she'd obviously passed. He was very relaxed, very open, and he was holding her hand as they walked down the main street of Didja!

Melissa felt so self-conscious, still trying to figure out how everyone seemed to know they were on a date. As they walked into Stiggies, the owner himself came up to them. Stig was a short Italian man who had lived in Didja for most of his life yet still spoke with a strong Italian accent.

'Good evening, you two lovebirds. And how are you both this evening?'

Melissa and Joss looked at each other, then back to Stig. 'We're fine,' they replied in unison.

'Ahh…cute. I have your reserved table ready. Right this way.' Melissa let go of Joss's hand as Stig led them over to a candle-lit table in the most secluded corner of his establishment. The other patrons all called out greetings as they passed, everyone wearing silly goofy grins.

'You made a reservation?' Melissa whispered to Joss as they smiled their way through the restaurant. She felt like royalty, and wondered whether she shouldn't give a wave or two.

'Well, it's what you do when you have a date. I didn't want to turn up tonight and not be able to get a table. It is date night after all.'

They were seated and had assured Stig the table was perfect before being left alone to peruse the menu.

'How long has it been since you last reserved a table here?' she asked as she opened the menu but didn't even glance at it.

'Here? Uh…never.'

'You've never reserved a table before tonight?'

'No.'

'Then *that's* how everyone knows.' She closed her eyes and shook her head. So much for a quiet get-to-know-you evening. With everyone watching them it was going to be nigh on impossible to relax.

Joss shook his head slowly, clearly astounded. 'The news must have spread faster than a bushfire on a forty-two-degree day with a strong headwind.'

'Mystery solved.' Though she was still a little surprised at the *amount* of attention they were receiving.

'I didn't think when I made the reservation that it would receive such a reaction.' He looked around at the other patrons and saw they were all watching himself and Melissa quite closely. 'I feel like I really am living in a fishbowl.'

'Well, we did presume it would happen. People were bound to take an interest,' she pointed out. 'After all, you are quite the eligible bachelor, and they've never really seen you out on a date. It's big news. I wouldn't be surprised if we make the front page of the *Didja Gazette*.'

'I knew we'd be news, but I had hoped that for tonight we could…' He glanced around him again and smiled politely at all the other patrons who were watching them. 'Could have had a little privacy.'

'True, but…' Melissa put her menu down and looked at Joss. 'As that's not the case, we should simply forget everyone else and enjoy ourselves.'

Joss nodded. 'Agreed. We're out on our first official date, which is a big enough deal in itself, and we're going to enjoy ourselves.' He wanted very much to lean across the table and kiss her, to thank her for being so understanding in this town of eccentrics he'd chosen to live in, but he could still feel half the restaurant watching them so decided against it.

Their date continued, and after Stig had personally come to take their order, they chatted about their day.

'Excuse me.' Joss and Melissa looked up to find Bub standing beside their table. 'I'd like to say how wonderful it is to see you finally out with a beautiful woman, Joss.' She looked pointedly at Melissa. 'You're like a breath of sunshine to this town, darl, and I really hope everything works out for you.' Once that was said, she left.

Halfway through their entreés, Mr and Mrs Bloffwith came over and passed on their congratulations as well. Areva, the clinic receptionist, who was out on a date of her own, gave them the thumbs-up sign from across the room. Stig grinned widely at them both each time he brought them another course or refilled their wine glasses.

'We're thinking of booking the church for Valentine's Day,' said Veronica, the secretary out at the mine, when she came over to their table as they started on their desserts.

'Oh? What for?' Joss asked, totally perplexed.

Veronica laughed. 'For your wedding, of course.'

Melissa and Joss stared at each other in shock as Veronica headed off.

'Time to go?' Joss asked, feeling his breathing start to constrict.

'Time to go,' Melissa agreed. 'Desserts are seriously overrated.'

'Agreed.' He took Melissa's hand in his and headed towards the door, but not before calling over his shoulder, 'Thank you for a terrific meal, Stig. I'll settle up the account tomorrow.'

'Ahh…Dr Joss. This one is on the house, mate—after all, you've provided excellent dinner theatre for all my patrons tonight.'

'Thanks. So glad we could oblige,' Joss remarked as he held the door for Melissa. 'Goodnight, all.'

'Night,' everyone chorused, and as they exited Melissa couldn't help but let go of the giggle which had been bubbling up all night long.

She looked around, noting there were fewer people out and about now.

'I'd just like to say, Dr Lawson, that you definitely know how to show a girl a memorable first date.'

Joss grinned. 'I do, don't I?' He gave her hand a little squeeze. 'Talk about life imitating a sitcom.'

'Oh, I don't know that it was. The setting was very romantic, the food was divine and the company was first class.'

Joss was pleased with her words. When he'd realised the whole town was watching them, he'd been interested to see how she would handle the attention—and she'd done a mighty fine job. She hadn't thrown a tantrum, hadn't demanded he take her home as he'd half expected. Then again, he had to keep reminding himself that Melissa wasn't like other women—and particularly wasn't like Christina.

He looked at her and she smiled up at him. He couldn't resist the allure of her mouth any longer and leaned down to brush a light kiss across her lips. 'Thank you.'

'For?'

'For being you.'

'Oh, well, I'm good at that. I've had plenty of practice.'

He smiled at her words. 'Seriously, Lis, I don't think

you realise just how much you've helped me.' Joss shook his head. 'I never thought I'd go out on a date. I never thought I'd be able to let go of my past, take a step forward and actually try dating again.' He stopped walking for a moment, pulling her into his arms. 'Just having you here, listening to me, taking an interest in me, it really has helped.'

'I'm glad.' His words were heartfelt, and she appreciated how difficult it must have been for him to say them, but at the back of her mind Melissa wondered whether she hadn't just slipped into her people-pleasing role in order to help Joss get over his past. Had she? Had she put him before herself? It was what she'd done with Renulf. It was what she'd done all her life. She didn't want to start another possible relationship being the one who always made the compromises.

She was certain now, as she looked up into his eyes in the dim evening light, that she loved him. She loved Joss, and it was a deeper, more abiding love than she'd felt before, but surely that meant she should be extra-cautious? She'd given her heart before and had it broken. Could she risk it again? Sure, he was grateful for the help she'd given him—but how did he *feel* about her? Did he feel more than gratitude? Did he simply see her as someone who would be working here in the clinic and helping him out with his problems?

Joss tightened his arms around her and she smiled up at him, pushing her thoughts aside. 'I'm glad you came to Didja,' he remarked, and he started to lower his head.

The kiss wasn't as dynamic as the one they'd shared in the ute, it wasn't as hot or as heavy, and although it was still delightful she couldn't help but think he was holding a lot of himself back.

Someone outside the pub wolf-whistled at them and they quickly broke apart.

'Get her to agree to the kissing booth!' a bloke called.

'Rack off, Bluey,' Joss remarked, then looked down at Melissa. 'Sorry about that.' He shook his head.

'Am I going to be bugged about a kissing booth for the rest of my life?'

He chuckled. 'Probably—but I promise that if you ever decide to hold a kissing booth I shall be the one buying up every single kiss.'

She sighed and tightened her arm around him. 'My hero.' As they continued on past the pub Melissa looked in and saw Dex standing at the bar, talking to yet another pretty blonde.

'He's at it again.' Joss rolled his eyes.

'He's definitely quite the charmer—or so I've been told.'

'I'm looking forward to the day when some woman waltzes into town and knocks him for six.'

Melissa laughed and nodded. 'I think I'd like to be around for that show as well.' They continued down the street, Joss's arm still close around her.

'Poor Dex. He was like a bear with a sore head when he first discovered he was adopted.'

'What do you mean? First discovered? You mean he was angry when I initially tried to make contact?'

'Yes. Until that time Dex had no idea he was adopted. He has two younger siblings—siblings he thought were his real brother and sister.'

Melissa's eyes widened in total shock. 'I don't believe it! His parents never told him?' Her tone was one of utter incredulity.

'No. It was a really difficult time for him, but he got through it.'

'No wonder he didn't want to see me back then. And that's why he's been so reticent since.' She shook her head slowly. Why hadn't someone told her earlier? 'I had no idea.'

'He needs time to process everything. That's all. It's what we guys do.'

'Go into your caves? Hide yourselves away?'

'Something like that.'

'Is that in the hope that the problem might simply go away, or so you can figure out a solution to it?'

'Both—but mostly the latter.'

'And there's no telling how long these cave-dwelling activities can go on for?'

Joss shrugged. 'Depends on the man, depends on the problem, and depends on whether or not he has cable TV in the cave.'

She chuckled and shook her head. 'Men!' They were standing outside her apartment now and he pulled her into his arms, drawing her close. Melissa's arms went around his neck.

'We're an interesting species,' he confirmed.

'I can think of a few other adjectives,' she said, and he laughed.

'I'm sure you can, but right now I don't want you to think.' And he lowered his head, capturing her lips with such delicacy that all thought fled to be replaced by delighted tingles.

Two days later, with the town still gossiping about the dating doctors, Melissa found it difficult to focus on her clinic. She had a full schedule, and yet she kept falling behind as patient after patient grinned like a Cheshire cat and asked her all sorts of personal questions about her relationship with Joss.

She was never more glad when she was able to sneak into the kitchen for fifteen minutes to eat a bite of lunch. Joss soon walked in and sat down next to her.

'How's your morning been?'

'Exhausting,' she said.

'We're one hot topic.'

'You're not wrong. Hey, do you know where Dex is? I expected to see him around this morning.' She wanted to know what he thought about herself and Joss.

'He's gone out to the mine to do occupational health and safety checks. He volunteered, actually, even though I was rostered on. I think he wanted me to stay here and face the music.' Joss laughed.

'You know, Joss, I've been thinking that maybe we should take a few steps back for a while.'

'Why?'

Melissa shrugged. She'd been thinking about it since the other night, and was still uncertain of exactly how to explain to him what she was feeling. Joss was more than happy to hold her, to kiss her, to be seen in public with her—but she wanted more. She'd been in a relationship where only certain aspects had been satisfied and she didn't want to enter into another one.

If Joss was only attracted to her on a physical level, if he only needed her for his clinic, then she wasn't interested. She loved him, and it pained her to say what she was about to, but she'd made a promise to herself never to settle for anything but absolute perfection in a relationship, and at the moment she simply wasn't getting that.

'Why?' She sighed heavily. 'Good question. I guess I'm feeling a little disconcerted, a little disjointed. You know, things haven't really worked out the way I planned when I initially made the decision to come to

Didja. I had no idea that Dex didn't know he was adopted, and it makes me realise that he needs a lot more space then he's getting. Me being here is a constant reminder of that, and it can't be easy for him to deal with.'

Joss eased back in his chair, nodding slowly. 'You're thinking about leaving?'

Melissa closed her eyes for a moment, trying to say the words she needed to say but not wanting to hurt him at the same time. It was then she realised that if she didn't say what was on her heart she'd risk hurting herself a lot more. Looking at him again, she swallowed. 'There's a great attraction between us, Joss. Has been from the first moment we saw each other. We've both tried to fight it and it didn't work; it only became stronger. I'm glad I was able to help you move through your pain about Christina, and I can't thank you enough for trusting me with such intimate knowledge…'

'But…?' He folded his arms over his chest.

'But I don't know if I've sorted through my own past. I've told you I was in a relationship where things didn't quite gel. I've put myself second in every relationship I've had, and now I'm doing it again with both you and Dex. I don't know if I'm strong enough to survive another rejection.'

'So you're rejecting me first?'

'I'm not rejecting you. I'm trying to protect myself.'

'What are you saying? You want to leave?'

'Can you give me a reason why I should stay?' Her eyes were imploring. She knew he was attracted to her, she knew he liked talking to her, but what she was looking for was a stronger commitment. She loved him, and she needed to be loved in return. Was it too soon? Would he be able to give her what she needed?

'You're contracted until the end of the year.'

'Anything else?'

'What about Dex? He does need you, Melissa. More than you know. You're the only one who can help him through what he's going through. You're the only one who really understands.' There was a veiled hint of urgency in his tone. He'd just stepped forward into the light. He'd finally been able to leave the past where it needed to be and move into the future…a future he wanted with her. She was amazing. She was sexy. She was intelligent. He was sure he was on the way to falling in love with her. Never had he met a woman so incredible, so determined and so gutsy. She'd put up with him in all states of confusion, and he was grateful she hadn't let him push her away.

'I don't need to be in Didja to help Dex.'

'You have a gift for getting people to open up. To talk out their problems. You're so great with the patients. This community needs you.'

'They need a female doctor. That doesn't necessarily mean they need *me*.' She shrugged.

Joss stood from his chair, almost knocking it to the ground with utter frustration. He raked a hand through his hair, his agitation increasing. 'What do you want from me? The town needs you.'

'And?' Her tone was urgent.

'And Dex needs you.'

'And?' Melissa's tone was almost pleading.

'And I—' He stopped. Could he do this? Could he confess to her how he really felt?

'And what, Joss? *What?*' Hope was surging wildly through her. Could it be that he felt more for her than she'd realised? 'What?' she pleaded again.

Joss swallowed. 'I—'

'Joss! Joss!' Areva came running into the kitchen. 'There's been a bad accident at the mine. They've just called it through.'

Joss frowned. 'Dex's out there. Isn't he there? Can't he handle it?'

'That's just it. You don't understand. Dex *is* the emergency.'

'What?' Both Melissa and Joss spoke in unison.

Joss looked over at Melissa and saw the blood drain from her face.

'Is he all right? What happened?' She was starting to shake, to hyperventilate, and Joss immediately pushed her head between her knees.

'Breathe. Relax.' His voice was quiet and reassuring. Melissa focused on it, needing his soothing, sultry tones to calm her. He looked to Areva. 'What's the information?'

'Veronica called through to say there had been an accident in the workshop. Dex left his ute at the mine workshop because the guys there said they'd do an oil change for him, and when Dex was finished he went back to collect it. That's when the accident happened. He got hurt because of some tyre thing exploding.' Areva's words were disjointed as she stumbled over what Veronica had reported.

'Right. Areva, I need you to let Bub know what's happened, so she can organise the operating theatre and call in whatever staff she needs. Also, if you wouldn't mind cancelling the rest of our clinics, that would be great.'

'Oh. Right. Sure.' Areva headed off and Joss turned his full attention to Melissa, who was slowly sitting up.

'How are you feeling?'

'OK. A little dizzy, but OK.'

He had one hand on her arm, the other around her shoulders as he looked intently at her.

'You have a little more colour. Just breathe deeply.'

'We need to go and get Dex.' Urgency and panic laced her voice within her tone.

'And we will. But I need to know that you'll be all right to handle whatever we find. I'm sure Dex isn't too badly hurt, but even if he is we'll help him. We're his friends as well as his family. Trust me, Lis. Dex is just like another brother to me, and if there's one thing I do and do well it's look after my own.' He stood, holding out a hand to help her to her feet. 'Are you with me?'

Melissa took one last deep breath in and let it slowly out. The dizziness had settled. The panic was under control. Her brother—her only living relative—needed her now more than ever. With Joss, she would help Dex. They would be there for him. The two of them. Strong enough to pull him through whatever faced him. They would do this, and they were going to do it together. She placed her hand in his and slowly rose to her feet.

'I'm ready.'

He'd watched as she'd mentally pulled herself together, marvelling at how incredible this woman was. She'd faced so many hardships in her life, and it was her strength which continued to get her through. He honestly felt her pain because he'd meant what he'd said—Dex *was* like another sibling to him—but what they needed most right now was to keep level-headed if they were going to be able to get Dex through.

His eyes were alight with pride. 'You're a strong woman, Melissa Clarkson. I love that about you.' He gave her hand a little squeeze. 'Let's get to work.'

They both packed medical bags, Joss making sure

the emergency kit was fully stocked. As they hadn't yet received a more detailed report on specific injuries they were flying blind. They had saline and plasma, IV lines, morphine, bandages, neck braces and much more.

'Do you want to go and quickly change?' he asked as he packed everything into his ute. 'Your clothes will get dirty at the mine.'

She looked down at her navy trousers and red knit top. She didn't care. They were just clothes. Getting to Dex was more important than what she was wearing. 'I'm fine. Why don't we have an ambulance?'

'What use is an ambulance when I have the ute? The suspension is better than any ambulance, because as a general rule ambulances aren't four-wheel drive. I have a firm mattress in the tray, blankets and rope—all perfect for transferring patients short distances.' He looked across at her and then shook his head. 'We do need one. I've applied for funding, but…unless the town gets bigger…'

'Which it will. We have so many pregnant women at the moment.' She climbed into the ute and looked across at him as they put on their seat-belts. Putting a hand on his shoulder, she nodded warmly. 'You'll get your ambulance, Joss. You're an amazing man who has provided an incredibly high level of medical care for this community. You give and you give and you keep on giving. What a big heart you have, Josiah Lawson.' She smiled at him and caressed his cheek. 'I love that about you.'

It was probably the nicest thing anyone had ever said to him, and sincerity was there in her eyes. She was quite a woman.

'Dex…' he murmured, and she dropped her hand back to her side.

'Let's go help our brother.'

* * *

When they arrived at the mine site they were met at the gate by Jeff.

'Follow me. I'll take you to the workshop. Switch your UHF to six.' He walked ahead of them and climbed into his own ute. He drove down a large gravel road, leading the way further down into the enormous open cut mine. Even though Melissa was concerned for Dex, even though she was running through possible scenarios in her mind, she still couldn't help being overwhelmed at the sheer size of everything.

The enormous dump trucks that made trips up and down the slopes all day long, hauling their loads, were like something from Giant Land. The wheels themselves were as tall as a house, the drivers needing to climb a ladder just to get into them.

'You there?' Jeff's voice came over the UHF radio and Joss quickly lifted the handset and answered.

'Go ahead.' He replaced the handset and they both listened.

'Dex is still in the workshop. We have two other men involved. They were fixing dual wheels, removing the outside one, when the energy in the inner tyre was violently released. One man is dead, the other critically injured. Dex was there, too. He was thrown back quite fiercely. I've been down to see the area and I have informed head office in Perth.'

Melissa grabbed the handset and tried to talk into it, but nothing happened.

'Press the button,' Joss instructed.

'Oh.' She did so. 'What about Dex? When you saw him, was he OK?'

'He was up. He confirmed Milko's death. He was treating Vitchy when I left.'

'He's really OK?' Melissa couldn't believe the

relief which coursed through her, and she sagged back against the seat.

'I don't know. He looked it. He has a few cuts and stuff. Here we are. Now, wait until I give the all-clear for you to get out of the car. OK?' Jeff's tone was stern. There had already been one fatality today, and he wasn't taking any chances on anything else going wrong.

Jeff walked around, checking everything out, and Melissa thought her impatience was going to burst through the roof. Dex was inside the workshop. They were parked outside the workshop. So near, yet so far.

'Relax.' Joss put a hand on her knee. 'I need you focused, remember? Deep breaths.'

'Deep breaths. Right.' She closed her eyes for a moment and concentrated. 'Right. Focused.'

'That's it.' Joss watched her, unable to believe how incredibly beautiful she was. Did she have any idea? He felt her pain and he wanted to help in any way he could. He wanted to be there for her, to support her, to let her know she *wasn't* all alone in this world.

He loved her. He still couldn't believe it himself, but it was the truth—and it was a truth he wanted to shout to the world. Finally he'd been able to shrug off his past, to step into the future, and it was a future he wanted to spend with her. He loved her and he didn't care who knew it! Being able to be here for her, to support her in a time of crisis, had helped him to realise the most powerful truth in the world—he loved her with all his heart.

For now, though, they needed to put their personal relationship aside and focus on this emergency. There would be time enough for declarations and plans later on.

Jeff knocked on the ute's window and both of them

nearly jumped out of their skins. 'Ready,' Jeff called, and with a calm eagerness Joss and Melissa exited the cabin, collected their medical kits from the back and followed Jeff inside.

She hadn't been at all sure what to expect, but the sight of one of the enormous trucks startled her for a second. The 'workshop', as Jeff had called it, was more like an aeroplane hangar—it had to be to fit the dump trucks inside. It was just so enormous, and seeing one of the trucks up close, as opposed to driving around in the quarry, was quite overwhelming.

'Around here,' Jeff directed, and they carefully walked around the truck to the other side. The scene that met them there was one of total chaos. The explosion of the tyre had been so violent that the windows had shattered, tools and equipment had been blasted off shelves and debris littered the entire section.

Dex was half-sitting, half-reclining in the mess. He was lying next to a man she presumed was Vitchy, as the supine worker had a bandage around his arm and a pressure pad to his eye. Melissa rushed over to Dex, putting her medical kit down beside him.

'Took your time,' he muttered.

'Well, you were a little difficult to find,' Joss responded, coming to the other side of Vitchy. 'What's the diagnosis?'

'Fractured right arm, fractured tibia, vision impaired.' Dex stopped, his breathing heavy and laboured. 'Uh…' He closed his eyes to think, and Melissa immediately put her hand to his wrist, checking his pulse. His eyes snapped open at her touch. 'I'm fine. You need to deal with Vitchy. Milko's gone. He was too close to the tyre. It exploded. Shrapnel ripped through him.'

Melissa kept her thoughts focused. 'Dex, your pulse

is weak. Did you hit your head? Get thrown back?' She was reaching for her stethoscope as she asked the questions.

'I'm fine.'

'Answer her,' Joss ordered as he performed his own observations on Vitchy.

'You always were bossy in an emergency.' Dex tried to make light of the situation, but as he forced a laugh he groaned in pain.

'Where does it hurt?'

'I'm still mad at you,' he murmured, looking up at Melissa. 'My life was mine before you came into it. You…ruptured it.'

'Understood,' she said, acknowledging what he was saying. She couldn't pretend his words didn't hurt her, but at least he was saying them out loud. At least he was really communicating with her for the first time. 'Now, tell me, where does it hurt?'

'Hurts to breathe. Lots of lower abdominal pain.'

She listened to his chest. 'You may have a small puncture to your lung.' She then listened to his abdomen, moving the instrument around, listening carefully. 'I can't tell. I'll need to ultrasound the area.'

'Well, at least I'm not pregnant, right?'

Melissa continued to check him. 'Not this time.'

'So I'll be fine. I'm just winded—and I think I might have eaten something bad at lunchtime. Wazza made cheese soufflé, and maybe the cheese part wasn't— *owww!*' He slapped at Melissa's hand as she gently palpated his abdomen. 'That hurts, Lis.'

'Sorry.'

Joss looked at Melissa and met her gaze. Instinctively they both knew things weren't right with Dex, and the sooner they got him back to the hospital the better. Joss called Jeff over. 'Get another ute set up to take Vitchy to the hospital. We'll need help loading the patients into the vehicles. Make sure the coroner knows about Milko, and arrange—'

'I've just been informed that it's all been taken care of.' Jeff glanced across to where his deceased friend still lay, covered with a tarp. His jaw clenched, but he was a professional and he needed to behave as such.

Joss made a mental note to speak to the mine psychologist as Milko's friends and family would need counselling over this incident.

'Right. You'll find the items you need to set up the other ute in the tray of mine. There's a—'

'I know the drill.' Jeff turned and left the large workshop.

When Melissa checked Dex's blood pressure, it was to find it rather low. She set up a saline drip and gave him an injection of morphine.

'How is he?' Joss asked as they stood to one side, where Dex couldn't hear them.

'Not good. I think he has an internal bleed. The lung seems to be holding, but, Joss…' There was pain, panic and a penetrating urgency in her voice. 'We need to get him back to the hospital, *stat*.'

'Agreed. Vitchy will require surgery, but for now, thanks to Dex, he's stable.'

'How did he manage to care for Vitchy when he himself is so badly injured?'

'Adrenaline. We'll get him sorted out.' He placed a comforting arm around her shoulders, drawing her closer. The desire to protect her was now totally overwhelming. 'I promise you.'

Melissa looked up at him and saw the truth of his statement in his eyes. 'I believe you.'

And at that moment he realised she did. Not only did she believe him, he saw that she believed *in* him. She trusted him. He was struck with an incredible insight that if his world ever came crumbling down in a pile of rubble again, if she was the woman by his side she'd never desert him.

By the time Dex was back at the clinic his blood pressure was dropping quite rapidly, despite replacement fluids via an intravenous line.

'I can't wait for an ultrasound. I need to go in now, find the source of the bleed and get it clamped, *stat.*' Joss's tone was brisk.

Bub had everything organised, except for an anaesthetist. 'Dex usually does anaesthetics,' she pointed out to Joss.

'I'll do it,' Melissa volunteered. 'I've done it plenty of times.'

'You'll be all right?' Joss checked.

'I will. We need to focus and save his life. Now, do we need to cross type and match?'

Joss shook his head. 'No. Dex's blood type is the same as yours. Lis, there's something very special you can do for your brother, because we don't keep blood in stock. I've got him on plasma, but getting some replacement blood into him will give him that extra boost he needs.'

She held out her arm to Bub and tapped at her vein. 'Let's get this blood flowing. We've got my brother's life to save.'

Dex's surgery was long and meticulous. It was the first real opportunity Melissa had had to watch Joss operate, and she marvelled at how natural and brilliant he was at the task. He should be doing surgery full-time. He should be head of a surgical department. He should be lecturing, teaching others. Yet being here with him, in the Outback, caring for this community, she knew he was in exactly the right place at the right time.

The surgery progressed, and the nurses proved themselves to be well trained.

'Ahh. Finally—there it is. Offensive little artery,' he muttered, before clamping it off and continuing with the rest of the operation.

When it was time for her to reverse the anaesthetic, Dex's blood pressure was steadily increasing back into the normal range. She'd been able to give a unit of blood, which had really helped. Still, she would give him as much blood as he needed. He was her brother and she loved him.

'He's got a long recovery ahead of him,' Joss commented as they wheeled Dex to the ward.

When Bub had her star patient all settled, Joss and Melissa stood at the end of his bed, watching him sleep.

'We'll be there for him. We'll get him through.'

Her words carried such determination and love that Joss was once again struck by her inner strength. He put his arm around Melissa's shoulders and she instantly snuggled into him, placing one hand on his chest and sighing. He realised this was more than just comforting her. This was him *being there* for her.

It was an important moment, and Melissa wondered whether Joss's feelings for her were far deeper than he was letting on. Could she hope? Should she stay? Would leaving Didja be the right or the wrong thing to do?

They stayed for quite some time, both of them content to simply be with each other, watching the man who was dear to both of them. Then Melissa gave another few units of blood whilst Joss went to check on Vitchy. When he was satisfied with Vitchy's condition he returned to Dex's bedside, watching him, Melissa still sitting there holding her brother's hand. Finally Bub kicked them out of the ward, telling them they were in her way as she went about looking after her patients.

'When are you planning to operate on Vitchy?' Melissa asked as they walked through the quiet clinic to their apartments.

'I'll review him tomorrow and go from there. Rushing into surgery too early will simply cause further complications. Besides, most of his injuries are orthopaedic, so once he's stable we'll need to transfer him to Perth.'

When they arrived at her apartment door Joss pulled her close, simply holding her. After a while, Melissa spoke softly.

'Before I came to Didja I don't think I really had a true sense of who I am, deep down inside. I think I never really gathered a sense of who I am because I'd always lose myself in every relationship. I was a daughter caring for elderly parents. Then I was caring for Eva. Then I attached myself to a man who had an abundance of family and a loving heart. But it still wasn't me. That was why I *had* to search Dex out.'

'A journey of self-discovery?' Joss had come to the conclusion that if she really wanted to leave Didja, if she needed some space, then he'd give it to her. He wouldn't like it, but he didn't want to pressure her into loving him.

'If you like.'

'And have you discovered anything?' He tried not to hold his breath. He tried not to wonder at what she might say.

'Quite a few things, actually.'

'Such as?'

'I love it here in Didja. I love the people, and you're right—they *are* like a family.'

'And you have Dex.'

'I hope so.'

'You do. Especially after today. He needs you, Lis.'

What about you? She wanted to ask the question, to really find out just how Joss felt about her, but she yawned as the events of the day, both physical and emotional, started to catch up with her.

'You're tired,' he murmured. 'You need to sleep.'

'Is that your way of telling me I look haggard?' She smiled up at him.

'It's my way of forcing myself to leave you to sleep.' He kissed the tip of her nose. 'Goodnight, my Lis. Sleep sweet.'

For the next few days Melissa visited Dex regularly, taking breaks between her patients to go and sit with him. He'd recovered well from surgery and was improving at a dramatic rate. On Thursday Joss came with her after clinic had finished, and she was glad to have him beside her. He'd proved himself time and time again to be interested in her, to be interested in how she was coping with Dex, and Melissa's love for him grew.

'I always heal quickly, too,' she told Dex. 'Something else we have in common.'

'Is there anything I can say to make either of you go away?' Dex asked.

'Nope.'

'So we have stubbornness in common as well.'

She smiled. 'Yes.' Melissa paused, then took a deep breath. 'Dex, if there's anything you want to know about our birth mother—about why she had you adopted, things like that—then all you need to do is ask.' She placed her hand over her heart. 'I had no idea you didn't know you were adopted. My parents told me from the get-go, but then again I was almost three years old when they adopted me.'

'What? I thought you were a baby?' Dex was stunned.

'No. I don't remember those first few years of my life, but from what our birth mother, Eva, told me, there were times when she could barely afford to feed us.'

Joss shook his head sadly. 'Must have been tough for her.'

'It was.'

'Is she the one who wanted you to hunt me down?'

'I'm not *hunting you down*, Dex. When you say it like that you make it sound so merciless. I simply want to get to know you.'

'Why? I think that's a fair question. *Why?*'

'Because I don't have anyone else. My adoptive parents were both very ill and died four years ago. Eva died not too long ago. I have no one else, Dex. No aunts, uncles, siblings, long-lost cousins. You…you are the only blood relative I have, and I need you.'

Dex stared at her from his hospital bed. 'You have no one?'

'No.'

'You have Joss.' He pointed to where the two of them sat side by side.

'He's not my brother.'

'And just as well,' Joss replied with a grin, taking Melissa's hand in his own.

He'd thought a lot over the last few days, and whilst she hadn't said anything else about wanting to leave Didja, he wanted to show her just how important she was to him. Not because of the clinic or the community but because of *him*.

'Actually.' Joss cleared his throat, deciding to take the bull by the horns and step way out of his comfort zone. It was important. Melissa was important. 'That's something I've been meaning to talk to you about. You see, I find myself with a bit of a dilemma.'

'What's that?' Dex asked.

'I need to ask you a question, Dex, and I'm not really sure what your answer's going to be.'

At his words, Melissa felt as though her heart had stopped beating and she looked up at him. He sounded so serious. She looked from one man to the other and back again.

Joss cleared his throat again, and looked at his friend. 'As you are Melissa's brother, and her only living relative, I feel it's only fitting that I ask your permission to marry her.'

'What?' Brother and sister spoke in unison, and behind them Bub dropped a dressing tray she was carrying towards the hospital bed.

Joss rubbed his chin with his free hand. 'Not really the reaction I'd been expecting.'

'You want to…to…?' Melissa couldn't finish the words and she simply stared up at him, her heart overflowing with love.

Joss looked intently into her eyes. 'To marry you? Yes. More than anything. First, though…' he tore his gaze away from Melissa's to look at Dex '…I need Dex's permission.'

'This really is serious.' Dex was astounded. 'I thought you were just joining the real world again. You know…dating and stuff. I didn't realise it was *love*.'

'And now that you realise it?'

Joss hadn't denied it. He hadn't denied that he loved her. Melissa was so glad she was sitting down, because otherwise she knew she'd have crumpled in a heap on the floor. Joss loved her! Could this really be happening? Was she about to awake from the best dream ever? She hoped not.

Dex looked to Melissa and then back to his friend. 'Take her. Marry her. Make her happy.' He pointed a finger at his friend in warning. 'But just remember I have a pygmy blow-gun in my apartment and I'm not afraid to use it!'

Joss nodded, trying not to smile. 'In that case, you have my word that I will do my utmost to make her very happy.'

He turned to face Melissa, lowering himself to one knee. Holding both her hands, his tone clear and filled with conviction, as he started to speak.

'Melissa Clarkson, I love you. You've touched me deeply and helped me to let go of my past and start looking towards my future…the future I want to share with you. You wanted a definite reason to stay in Didja and I'm giving you one. I'm not trying to shackle you to me or to the clinic. I want you here because I love you with all of my heart. I need you by my side, to help me to continue to grow and so that I can also help you. We'll be equals—a complete loving partnership.'

The love was reflected in his eyes, in a look of pure sincerity, and she knew he meant everything he was saying. 'I need you, Lis, and I promise you won't be alone. Not any more. I want you to marry me and to fill our house with a loving family—which is what we both not only want but need in our lives. There's no one else I want to be the mother of my children except you, my lovely Lis.' He squeezed her hands and brushed a quick kiss across her lips. 'Please…' he implored. 'Will you do me the honour of becoming my wife?'

Melissa couldn't believe it. She couldn't believe this was happening. The man of her dreams was not only declaring his love for her, but was asking her to be with him for ever. He was also waiting for an answer.

'Joss.' She swallowed over her nervousness, projecting her voice, strong and true. 'I love you. I love you for so many different reasons. For accepting me. For supporting me. For saving my brother's life.' Tears started to gather in her eyes, but they were tears of pure happiness. 'But most of all I love you for who you are and for needing me in your life. You're an amazing man and I adore you.' She reached out and caressed his cheek, her eyes filled with love. 'I would be delighted to be your wife.'

Dex cheered, and Bub joined in, the two of them making so much noise it was almost as if they were in the pub!

Joss stood and swept Melissa up into his arms, planting a firm but sure kiss to her lips. 'You've made me so happy,' he said softly near her ear.

'The feeling is one hundred percent mutual.'

'No more talk of leaving Didja?'

'Why would I want to leave when everything I need in my life is right here?' Melissa kissed him again with all the passion and desire in her heart, and without a hint of doubt. He was the man for her, the most perfect man for her, and finally she felt as though she truly belonged.

0110/03a

MEDICAL™ 2-in-1

MEDICAL™

Single titles coming next month

ONE TINY MIRACLE...
by Carol Marinelli

Since losing his wife and unborn child, 'home' is just a word to doctor Ben. But disarming – and visibly pregnant – nurse Celeste captures Ben's heart and gives this damaged doctor a reason to smile again. Then Celeste's tiny miracle makes a premature arrival – is there a future for Ben right there by their sides?

MIDWIFE IN A MILLION
by Fiona McArthur

Ten years ago Kate abruptly called off her engagement to paramedic Rory, her childhood sweetheart. Now Rory's come home to finally ask her *why* she turned him down. When an Outback medical emergency forces them together, Kate and Rory must confront their past if they are to finally make a future – together...

On sale 5th February 2010

Bestselling author Melanie Milburne writes for

MEDICAL™

The Doctor's Rebel Knight

Her rebel with a heart of gold...

Dr Frances Nin has come to Pelican Bay in search of tranquillity...but motorbike-riding local rebel Sergeant Jacob Hawke gets her pulse-rate spiking! One glimpse of the heat in Jacob's icy blue eyes and Fran's fragile heart starts to bloom...

On sale 1st January 2010

Available at WHSmith, Tesco, ASDA, Eason and all good bookshops.
For full Mills & Boon range including eBooks visit
www.millsandboon.co.uk

Praise for Melanie Milburne

Her love scenes, no matter what genre, are never boring and I can't stop reading them!
—*Romantic Times BOOK Reviews*

I have come to love Ms Milburne's writing
—*Romantic Times BOOK Reviews*

millsandboon.co.uk Community

Join Us!

The Community is the perfect place to meet and chat to kindred spirits who love books and reading as much as you do, but it's also the place to:

- Get the inside scoop from authors about their latest books
- Learn how to write a romance book with advice from our editors
- Help us to continue publishing the best in women's fiction
- Share your thoughts on the books we publish
- Befriend other users

Forums: Interact with each other as well as authors, editors and a whole host of other users worldwide.

Blogs: Every registered community member has their own blog to tell the world what they're up to and what's on their mind.

Book Challenge: We're aiming to read 5,000 books and have joined forces with The Reading Agency in our inaugural Book Challenge.

Profile Page: Showcase yourself and keep a record of your recent community activity.

Social Networking: We've added buttons at the end of every post to share via digg, Facebook, Google, Yahoo, technorati and de.licio.us.

www.millsandboon.co.uk

2 FREE BOOKS
AND A SURPRISE GIFT

We would like to take this opportunity to thank you for reading this Mills & Boon® book by offering you the chance to take TWO more specially selected books from the Medical™ series absolutely FREE! We're also making this offer to introduce you to the benefits of the Mills & Boon® Book Club™—

- **FREE home delivery**
- **FREE gifts and competitions**
- **FREE monthly Newsletter**
- **Exclusive Mills & Boon Book Club offers**
- **Books available before they're in the shops**

Accepting these FREE books and gift places you under no obligation to buy, you may cancel at any time, even after receiving your free books. Simply complete your details below and return the entire page to the address below. You don't even need a stamp!

YES Please send me 2 free Medical books and a surprise gift. I understand that unless you hear from me, I will receive 5 superb new stories every month including two 2-in-1 books priced at £4.99 each and a single book priced at £3.19, postage and packing free. I am under no obligation to purchase any books and may cancel my subscription at any time. The free books and gift will be mine to keep in any case.

Ms/Mrs/Miss/Mr _____ Initials _____

_____

Surname _____

Address _____

_____

_____ Postcode _____

Send this whole page to: Mills & Boon Book Club, Free Book Offer, FREEPOST NAT 10298, Richmond, TW9 1BR.